FORTUNE

and

GLASS

by

JOHN MUTTER

EXPLORING UNCHARTED CREATIVITY
LEFT FIELD PUBLISHING
EST 2024
LITTLETON . COLORADO

Copyright

First published in the United States of America, October 2026 by

Left Field Publishing.

ISBN: 9781966883074

Also available:

eBook: 9781966883081

Audiobook: 9781966883159

Library of Congress Control Number: 2026903920

Book Cover by Kristen Gilligan

Dedication

To departed members of my family—especially my grandfather and my parents—who in various ways kindled my interests in history, language, reading, politics, family roots, and more. I wish I could share this with them.

AUTHOR'S NOTE

This book was inspired by the story of Fritz Kolbe, a career, midlevel employee of the German Foreign Ministry during World War II. Kolbe was an anti-Nazi and found a striking way to fight fascism: by giving some 1,800 top secret documents and reports to the U.S. Embassy in Switzerland, where his handler was Allen Dulles, who later became director of the CIA. The most detailed, insightful account of Kolbe's life is *Fritz Kolbe: Un Espion au Coeur du IIIieme Reich* by Lucas Delattre, published in France in 2003. The work was translated into English by George A. Holoch, Jr., and published in 2005 by Atlantic Monthly Press as *A Spy at the Heart of the Third Reich: The Extraordinary Story of Fritz Kolbe, America's Most Important Spy in World War II.*

Map

Rügen
Berlin
GERMANY
and
SWITZERLAND
1933
Basel
Bern
Copenhagen
Hamburg
Bremen
Berlin
Amsterdam
Essen
Leipzig
Elbe
Rhine
Bonn
GERMANY
LUXEMBOURG
Frankfurt
am Main
Stuttgart
Danube
Munich
LIECHTEN
STEIN
Vaduz
Salzburg
AUSTR
Zurich
SWITZERLAND

"Glück und Glas, wie leicht bricht das."

"Fortune and glass: how easily they break."

— German saying

From "Fortuna vitrea est: tum cum splendet frangitur"

"Fortune is like glass—when it shines, it breaks."

— Publilius Syrus, First Century B.C.

PROLOGUE

I put an arm around her and felt her shudder as I put the barrel of the pistol to her head.

She gazed at me, her eyes wide open, more in wonder than in fear.

"Really?" she asked.

I thought of all the times she and I made love, our arms and legs entwined, our faces touching, our eyes so close together they were blurs of color, completely visible but unfathomable at the same time, focused and separated, together and apart. We were as close as people could physically be.

And now, I held her in the same way. I kissed her. I wanted yet again to try to bridge the last things that divided us to make us one. I wanted to ask forgiveness, to let her know I loved her perhaps more than anything or anyone, that I would never let her down, that we would always be together one way or another. I would remember and honor her always. She would live forever in my soul.

I squeezed her even more tightly. I wanted to wait, wait, wait. But I couldn't keep waiting.

I started shaking, then calmed myself. I breathed in deeply, almost shut my eyes, and I pulled the trigger.

Part I

1932, 1933, 1943

Chapter One

November 1943

What is to be done?

Finally, after a decade, I could answer this question and devote myself fully to the battle. But first I had to get back to Berlin. Safely.

From beneath the locomotive, steam shot out and billowed into the sky. The engine hissed and growled ever louder, like a caged animal wanting to be free. The train sounded as impatient as I felt.

Why was the train delayed?

I leaned out the open window of the wagon-lit. All the train doors were shut. The few passengers in this station that technically was a piece of Germany had come through Swiss customs, then shown their tickets, visas, and passports to the train personnel. Since the station was in Switzerland, this was the one place on this trip there wouldn't be delays because of destroyed tracks and damaged stations.

We should be moving.

With Sara safely in neutral Switzerland, I was done with the nerve-wracking task of smuggling someone out of the country who couldn't stay quiet or always say the right thing, even when her status was so dangerous. Still, I began to worry that what I had done to sneak her across the border might have been discovered. My life might come to a painful end just when all that had made it difficult and dangerous was so close to being settled. Sara would no longer live with me so I would no longer feel guilty about my wife and children, who had been with my in-laws in the quiet countryside since the bombings started. And with Sara gone, I would be able to concentrate on my secret work and not be distracted by someone whose love was as beautiful, destructive, and powerful as a summer thunderstorm.

Let's go!

On the surface, this station was sleepy, a building constructed of lightly colored brick, with a solid little tower, a pleasantly domed waiting room, and curved glass roofs high over the platforms, with touches of comfort and elegance that the small but confident city of Basel wished to extend to international visitors in the late 1800s. Meanwhile, life-changing dramas played out in the faded customs hall, with its maze of worn metal tables and uncomfortable chairs that had been installed when this place became part of the Greater German Reich, and no longer a pleasant gateway to Switzerland. For Jews and other enemies of the Nazis, entry into this neutral country meant sanctuary and survival. But permission denied led to a return to the Reich, arrest, deportation, and likely death.

On the platform, several dark figures wearing greatcoats paced back and forth. The guards gazed ahead, their bodies and expressions stiff. They might be sleepwalking. They might be alert to everything.

It would be smart for the Gestapo to wait to seize a suspect at Weil am Rhein, the first station in Germany, where German customs had been moved at the insistence of the Swiss—one of the few direct provocations they had made to the Nazis. Another provocation: the Swiss had forced the Reichsbahn to stop flying the swastika flag from the station tower, a spot that could be seen easily across the city.

Then again, it would be even smarter to postpone an arrest for days and see who the suspect was working with. But such an approach would take patience and finesse, qualities that were rare among fervent Nazis. They were slowly recognizing that the war, once marked by easy, breathtaking victories, had become the kind of grinding, bloody conflict that Germany had never won and could never win. For years, the Führer had gambled and triumphed each time, but now many powerful countries were united against him.

These days, people suspected of treason were quickly hustled to Berlin, to the lower floors of the infamous Gestapo building on Prinz-Albrecht-Strasse, where they were stripped, flogged, made to stay awake indefinitely, starved, abused in other unimaginable ways—until a nasty, painful end. Their families wouldn't know what truly happened to them, and in an extra act of sadism, were forced to pay "the cost to the state" for their loved ones' captivity and execution.

I could hope for a trial, which, of course, would be a travesty. Still, I liked the idea of having a moment in a semi-public place to say what I believed and what I wanted to accomplish, no matter if they cut me off—before they cut my head off. But I might not be judged worthy of the guillotine. I could handle the quick shot to the head, but I grew nauseous imagining being garroted or hung from a meat hook, forms of execution, I had heard, for people deemed by the Führer to have personally betrayed him.

There was a commotion on the platform. In the dim light, I saw only vague forms. Several men in long coats hurried toward the train with at least one person who wasn't dressed like the others.

Was it happening now? Were they coming for me?

The group disappeared from view, and in a moment all but the one not dressed in a uniform returned to the station building.

The person had to be a civilian, since they hadn't entered my car, immediately behind the locomotive. This car was reserved for high-ranking Party members and military officers, government functionaries, and anyone on official business, the last two of which applied to me.

A late passenger, obviously someone special, since holding the train for anyone, even a government official like me, was unusual. Passengers had to pass through checkpoints that involved questioning, inspection of documents, and stamping, all of which were to be completed well before the train left. And these days only a handful of people crossed the border between Switzerland and Germany. The flow of refugees had nearly stopped because now one state didn't want its enemies to depart and the other didn't want to accept them.

For a second, something nagged at me. But then a trainman's whistle sounded. With a lurch, the locomotive's wheels started to turn. *Yes.*

After a slight jerk, the car I was in started moving forward. Then there was another jerk as the car behind us began moving, too.

At first, we barely crept forward. If I were walking on the platform, I could have outpaced the train.

Did it usually take this long to leave the station?

But in a moment, the train began to move faster.

Finally.

I shut the window and sat down again.

In the gathering darkness, as we left the station shed, the platform lights dimly illuminated the space just below them. The lamps showed something we missed at home because of the draconian blackouts. Snow had begun falling, and drifting down into the cones of brightness. Snowflakes that were invisible in the night sky above glowed as though they had burst into flame. One little sparkling star followed another, tumbling and dancing, magically lit—until they hit the ground and were extinguished.

Now I began to feel as I had on other trips when I was returning from Bern. I loved remembering that for a few hours, surrounded by foreign friends, the debilitating effect of the Nazis lifted. I felt myself coming alive again, speaking my mind. Life could be charming and enjoyable, not just about plotting and planning, trying to do seemingly impossible things, and hoping I didn't get caught.

This time I had travelled just to Basel, and our train south had been delayed so much that I had only enough time before catching the train back to Berlin to accompany Sara through the station and through customs and tell her I was glad she was finally safe. I hadn't volunteered to be a courier to Bern on this trip because I knew that traveling with Sara would be enough of a challenge. As always, around her my ability to think rationally floated away.

Another benefit of Sara being gone: I wouldn't be reminded regularly that in many ways, I felt more engaged with an old lover than I did with my wife.

The closer we had come to Basel, the more uncharacteristically quiet Sara became. Perhaps she was nervous about dealing with the Swiss, whose government had made clear it didn't want to accept more than a handful of Jews, no matter what the situation in the Reich. "The lifeboat is full," one official had said. Perhaps she was thinking about living outside the country of her birth for the first time and never returning. She was definitely miserable about leaving her grandmother, her *Bubbe*, safely hidden, but her life ebbing away. Likely she wouldn't see the end of winter.

I asked Sara to let me know when she was reunited with her family. A postcard depicting Lake Geneva or the Matterhorn with an innocuous, anonymous note in her handwriting would suffice. If she and her family wanted to travel farther away, I offered to create travel documents and visas for her and her family, get train tickets, put in a word with the right Swiss officials—whatever they needed.

She had an odd response.

"Why do all this?" she asked. "So I don't have reason to hate every last German?"

"As always," I said. "I want to help you. Because it's you. And also it's a way to fight back, to do something."

"In the meantime, you work for the Foreign Minister."

"Where I do what I can."

"Those papers you gave me were great," she said. "But what else do you do? Hide pencils?" She laughed. "Misspell words in memos?"

I longed to tell my secret to her and the other people who underestimated me. They included some superiors and colleagues at the Foreign Office, or Ministry, the officious block warden in my neighborhood, and, especially, my lifelong friend Hans, who worked as hard for the Nazis as I did against them. I had become used to revealing only what needed to be revealed and knowing that my work was more important than people's misjudgments about me. Still, telling Sara would be so satisfying. And because she was leaving Germany, this was a good time.

"All right," I said. "I'll tell you everything. Finally."

I paused, and she gazed at me in a serious, inquiring way. "What?" she whispered.

"Sara, I do much more to fight them."

"What?" she said.

I closed my eyes. *Still not right.*

"Sometimes I mix up the files that are supposed to go in alphabetical order," I said. "Other times I put what's supposed to go in one diplomatic pouch into another."

Her brows furrowed.

"But seriously," I continued. "The key thing is I'm helping save the life of a beautiful, wonderful woman, a woman I love."

"Ha! Who?" She laughed, then hugged me. "Thank you, my dearest Rudi. You do so much for me. You even let me tease you to no end!"

"It's a pleasure," I said. "It's all a pleasure."

As the train reached full speed, I shut my eyes. At work, on the street, during the bombings, and at the house, I was always with others. To be alone, especially in a public place, was a luxury.

I had begun to doze off when I heard a knock at the door. In my half-asleep state I didn't open my eyes.

This was not a passenger, since he had knocked. Any other official would have his pick of empty compartments in this car. Someone was looking for me.

Most people with privileges like mine eagerly took advantage of them, but usually I pulled rank only to help others. Tonight, however, after I had shown my diplomatic passport, my ministry identification, and my visa, I told the conductor and the porter that I did not wish to be disturbed. *For any reason.*

It might be the pair of Gestapo agents I had spoken with, who had respected my position and not gone through my personal belongings. Maybe they had been alerted by a Swiss Nazi sympathizer who spotted Sara and figured out her connection to me? I shouldn't have hugged her, I realized now. We lingered too long.

I kept my eyes closed, which is what an innocent person might do. In addition, it postponed, at least for a few moments, something that might be disastrous.

The door opened, and I felt cool air drift in from the hallway. Someone was standing there, looking at me but not saying anything—a kind of exercise of power. But I kept my eyes closed, which was my own exercise of power: only a superior could be so disdainful as not to open his eyes.

Slowly, my worst fears subsided. Gestapo agents wouldn't waste time. It was probably the conductor or porter. Or the person who had boarded the train late?

All right. Enough.

I opened my eyes.

Um Gottes willen.

Surely I was dreaming.

Sara?

Chapter Two

October 1932

A mid-level official at the Foreign Ministry, I sometimes represented the department at parties and receptions that didn't interest the bosses. At one event, I wound up in a group that included Sara Traum. I was struck immediately by her liveliness, her dark rich hair, bright light eyes, her olive skin, her easy laugh, her confidence, her sharp comments. I joked and bantered easily with people who enjoyed it, too, but with Sara the connection stirred me more than anything I'd felt in a relationship before. It quickly led into the most delicious flirting—simultaneously roundabout and direct. Neither of us, it seemed, wanted to stop; we began seeing each other almost every day. I was surprised by how quickly I was accepted by her family. They might all be afraid of Sara's reaction if they rejected me. Or maybe her parents just liked me. Either way, as a result, I wound up one evening at an elaborate dinner at the Traums unlike anything my family or friends put on.

"The hysterical hatred and paranoia sweeping the country are phenomena we usually observe only in clinically disturbed patients," Dr. Viktor Traum said. "Not an entire nation."

Dr. Traum's baritone voice was as tantalizing as the aroma of the butternut squash soup that had just been served on the long, elegantly set table in the Traums' Berlin villa. Family and guests leaned forward to hear clearly—and perhaps take in the luscious steam that rose from the bowls.

"Unfortunately, such people turn to simple, destructive solutions for complex problems," Dr. Traum continued. "In one case, a patient burned down his apartment building to drive out another tenant he didn't like."

"I'd set fire to my own house if a certain National Socialist was in it," someone down the table said. "That would be worth the sacrifice!"

"An understandable impulse," Dr. Traum said calmly.

After a moment, another person asked, "What can we do about *that man*?"

"It will take a lot of time and hard work to break out of this national psychosis," Dr. Traum continued. "On the face of it, that's a good reason to be afraid."

Several people murmured in agreement.

"But—" Dr. Traum paused. Everyone leaned toward his end of the table. "But I have faith in the ultimate intelligence and goodness of people." He paused again. "Even Germans."

When the laughter died down, he continued: "Despite what's happened since we lost the war, Germany is a nation of laws and learning and remains the most civilized, modern country in the world. Eventually, people will realize that our problems have nothing to do with supposed racial impurity or the supposed decline of tradition or supposed laws of class struggle."

Unlike many of my countrymen, I was naturally optimistic, but like many of my countrymen, I was also a realist, more than most because I knew too much about what was happening in the government. Still, that night I went along with the crowd, joining in the quick round of applause for Dr. Traum.

Besides, there were plenty of reasons to be reassured. For one, Dr. Traum's life work was understanding people—he was a psychoanalyst with a legendary practice who taught at Charité, Berlin's renowned medical school, and he lectured internationally.

In addition, Dr. Traum's low, rich voice made everything he said sound convincing, reinforced by his gentle, gray eyes—the color of soft clouds floating by in a bright summer sky. If Dr. Traum now gazed at me while patting his soft brown beard with the tips of his fingers and suggested that I cluck like a chicken or discuss a sexual dream involving my mother or tell secrets from the Foreign Ministry, I might do so.

Perhaps I was reassured, too, because for now, it seemed none of the political parties—National Socialists or Communists or Social Democrats or Catholics or monarchists, all of which loathed one another and most of which hated the Republic—could dominate the others. Political gridlock kept the extremist parties in check. And in the meantime, so what if the right-wing "Cabinet of Barons," too clever for their own good, ruled Germany ineffectually by decree?

Perhaps the rich food—several appetizers served on shiny china with silver utensils, which was followed by roast lamb and fall potatoes and eggplant, a presentation rivaling a state dinner—also dulled my ability to think critically. Certainly the excellent red wine improved my view of the world.

Most important I was in love with Dr. Traum's daughter. It was the kind of love that made me want to embrace everyone and everything that, like her, sparkled with charm and light and warmth, even if sometimes she confused and dismayed me. It was also the kind of love that made me pause before disagreeing with her father about anything.

Happily, this crowd kept me on my toes. I had quickly learned that at the Traums' house, no moment of agreement or satisfaction or smug self-delusion lasted long. Family and friends were often merciless about what they considered flawed or wishful thinking. At the same time, they were respectful, like members of a debating society, an effect emphasized by the maids, each wearing identical black dresses and smocks over white blouses, who stood attentively at the sides of the room as though judging a competition.

"But Daddy, millions can't find work and don't have enough to eat," Sara said, her sparkling hazel eyes gazing into the distance, her voice as calm and mesmerizing as her father's. "The National Socialists are the largest party in the Reichstag, and the Communists aren't far behind. Other countries can't help us because they're broke, too. The people at this table are doing well, but not the masses out there." She gestured toward the windows. "Why shouldn't we despair?"

Sara spoke with the air of someone who had seen this all before—even though she was barely 20 and had grown up in the Golden Age of the Republic. I was a decade older than she and had been through the Great War, the collapse of the monarchy, the imposition of the Treaty of Versailles, and the hyperinflation of 1923, but in our conversations about what was happening in our beloved country, she turned out to be the prescient one.

"Viktor, you analyze individuals well, but maybe not whole countries," said Simon Klein, Frau Traum's brother, who wore the finest clothes in the room and had built the family business, Klein, into the largest department store in Berlin—an amusing distinction considering that the family's name meant "small."

Trim with short, thick curly hair, Simon loved to talk about work. When we met, he immediately complimented me on my jacket, asked where I had bought it, how much I had paid, what I liked about the shop, how helpful the staff had been, whether I'd looked at other jackets either at that shop or another, and particularly when exactly I decided to make the purchase. Perhaps because he patted me on the shoulder and seemed to approve of everything I said, I eagerly answered questions that might have struck me as rude or excessive coming from someone else.

"Too many Germans feel they didn't really lose the war, but they had to give up territory, colonies, an army, billions in reparations, and worst of all, their self-respect," Simon said. "With the economy in ruins now, they're so desperate that a majority of them would welcome dictatorship, whether it's communist or fascist."

"Very similar things," Dr. Traum said.

"That's how powerful mass hopelessness is."

Dr. Traum nodded several times and murmured, "Yes. Mass

hopelessness is powerful."

Eagerly, Herr Klein continued. "If only you could get 65 million people on the couch at once to talk about their fears and unhappiness." But then he stopped and shook his head, adding, "And then 65 million times you would repeat what they say in a sympathetic tone!"

Everyone laughed except for Dr. Traum, who smiled but this time didn't repeat what his brother-in-law had said.

Sol, Sara's brother, spoke up. "What we need to do is emigrate as soon as possible." He laughed in a way that sounded like a taunt. "France or England aren't far enough. We should go to the Americas. Or Antarctica. I trust penguins more than most humans."

Tall, thin, with lips that were usually pursed and eyes that stared rather than looked, in some ways Sol himself resembled a penguin. He walked stiffly and talked in a hurry and had no time for fools, a category that for him included just about everyone. He acted too busy to speak much with me, for which I felt both insulted and thankful.

"I love Berlin, my beautiful Berlin," Frau Traum said. "Despite what some people say, our roots here run deep. But Sol may be right. We're hated by so many people in so many ways."

I was fond of Frau Traum, beginning with the fact that she had given birth to Sara. In her respectful tone, her polite queries, her simple dress and coiffure, she gave no sign that her family was among the wealthiest in Germany. And of all Sara's relatives, she showed the most interest in me.

"I wish I could share your optimism, Dr. Traum," said Herr Ullstein, a regular Traum dinner guest, a resident of the Villa Colony Grunewald, and a prominent member of society.

Earlier that evening over cocktails, I met Herr Ullstein for the first time and discovered he was part of the family that was the biggest publisher in the country. My family had read the *Morgenpost* and the *Berliner Illustrirte Zeitung* for as long as I could remember. To Sara, by contrast, Herr Ullstein was a friendly neighbor.

"How is Baron von Neurath?" he asked when he found out I worked at the Foreign Ministry. "If anyone survives wherever the country's going, Konstantin will. He can march and wave a torch as well as any National Socialist. And if the Reich becomes a Soviet workers' paradise, it could just as easily be Comrade von Neurath! Although it'd be smart to drop the 'von.' "

At that, he burst out in laughter.

A portly man, Herr Ullstein wore a dapper light green tweed jacket and dark brown corduroy pants, one of the considerable number of people in the capital who loved all things English, except for the English themselves—because of Versailles and because of joining the French in the Great War and because the English tended not to recognize Germans as cousins and equals.

"The Baron is excellent," I said, which was possibly accurate. Several weeks earlier, for the first time in months, I had seen the Minister at the end of a long corridor when I took papers to my boss for a meeting he was attending on the Baron's floor. The Minister had been scowling, and I knew enough about him to take the scowl as a sign of general well-being.

"Germans love science and logic and learning, but more than any people, they want life to be predictable," Herr Ullstein said, his voice booming down the table. "They want daily life to unfold with precision as it did before the war. Whoever can provide that wins power."

"Important distinction," another man at the table said. This was Herr Vogelsang, one of the leaders of the Institute for Sexual Science who, to my disappointment, never spoke about anything directly related to his work. He wore only black—even his shirt was black, and every button on it was closed, right up to his chin, although he did not wear a tie. "Whoever convinces people that they *can* do all they want wins power. That's what's so scary." He put down his wine goblet and said slowly, "Many people say the Nazis will restore order and keep us from going Red. Others say the Communists will create a more just society even though Soviet Russia is a disaster. 'How bad could it be?' they say." He shook his head. "If either party comes to power, this country could become a hell on earth. In a few years, most of us could be scattered across the globe—or dead."

The long, uncomfortable silence that followed was broken by Dr. Traum, who patted his beard and gazed benevolently around the table.

"Life and death forces always struggle against one another—in each person, in society in general," he said. "The death drive seems to be strongest now, but like all things, it won't last." For the first time in my presence, he raised his voice, as though he were speaking to a congregation or at a political rally. "We must do everything to nurture the life force while embracing and neutralizing the death force."

The room was silent a moment. Then someone began clapping, and others joined in.

"Herr Doktor should run for Chancellor," a man at the far end of the table called out. He was Herr Vetter, who was an executive at the UFA movie company and had arrived at the dinner straight from Babelsberg, late and in such a rush that apparently he had forgotten to take off his beret. Then again, perhaps he never took it off. "If you can sway us, you might sway the *Volk*, too."

"Dr. Traum's candidacy is doomed," said Herr Vogelsang. "He's decent and sincere."

"No matter!" Herr Ullstein, said, standing, lifting his wine glass and proposing a toast to Dr. Traum. "May you be right, but stay far from the right." Laughing, everyone else at the table rose, holding up their glasses.

I clicked glasses with Dr. Traum, who sat at the head of the table next to me. Then I turned and clicked glasses with Herr Ullstein and started to sit back down. A guest on the other side of the table, Max Weiss, clicked several glasses around him, then looked toward me and lifted his glass.

A few years younger than I, he had a thin face, pale skin, and large glasses. He and Sara's brother, Sol, had been friends since they could barely walk. The Weisses were as important in banking as the Kleins in retailing, and the families had long hoped Max and Sara might make a match and formally connect the families, Sara had told me. Although she had called this a ridiculous idea, I saw how Max looked at Sara.

I obliged his request to clink glasses. To reach across the wide table, I extended my arm and glass toward him, leaning precariously forward. Just before our glasses would have touched, however, he pulled back and turned to the side, as if he were losing balance, too. I paused, unable to tell through his thick, murky lenses if he were looking at me or had forgotten me. I began to sit down in my chair, but then he turned toward me again, pushing his glass at mine, smirking as though it were my fault that we hadn't toasted. I leaned forward again, pushing my glass vigorously toward his.

Crystal exploded. Patches of the white tablecloth turned red. The room went silent.

Wincing, Max held up what was left of his glass—its base and stem.

My glass was intact.

"Max, Max," Mrs. Traum called as she jumped up and went to him. "Are you all right?"

"Is that my blood?" he said slowly, looking down at the red liquid.

Had I pushed too hard? Did he annoy me that much?

Max set the stem on the table, then turned his hand slowly around. "No cuts," he said in a normal voice, wiping his hand with the large cloth napkin. "I'll survive." Then, glancing at me, he smirked once more and said in a low voice, "As long as no one tries to do me in again!"

For a moment, I wished I had hit his glass harder. "I'm so sorry," I said.

Sara and several others also stood and gathered around us. "It wasn't your fault," Sara said to me.

"It wasn't *my* fault," Max said, reminding me that he was studying law at the university.

Dr. Traum watched quietly, then asked, "Why didn't both glasses shatter?"

As if seeing it for the first time, I gazed at my glass, a thin, elegant creation that glowed in the flames of the candles on the table. By contrast,

Max's glass, which until a minute ago had been identical to mine, lay in pieces on the tablecloth—pieces that glittered like stars in the night sky.

At our end of the table, several maids swooped in, removing the settings, folding up our section of the tablecloth with all the broken glass in it, mopping and drying the tabletop, then putting down a new section of tablecloth. In a few minutes, all traces of broken glass and the red stain were gone.

"I might have been too enthusiastic," I whispered to Sara.

"Max doesn't exactly move gracefully—on the tennis court, walking down the street, making toasts!" She whispered back.

I smiled, not liking the image of the two of them playing tennis or walking down the street or being anywhere together by themselves.

We all sat and the conversation resumed. After a while, without any signal I saw, several of the maids began clearing the table and another asked each of us what kind of after-dinner drink we wanted. Sara rose again and came to the head of the table where her father sat. *What was this?* Sometimes I thought I knew her better than anyone on earth. Other times, I had no idea what she was thinking.

"Daddy," she said, arms outstretched, leaning toward him, seemingly about to hug him. He looked up and smiled. But at the last second, she turned to the side.

"I'm taking Rudi away," she said. "To a concert in the Mitte!"

I began to ask what concert she meant when he nodded and told us warmly, "Have fun." As Sara walked by me, she smiled, a smile that only I could see.

Chapter Three

November 1943

Her eyebrows rose. Sara half-smiled.

I stared at her.

What was worse? That a plan involving so much time and money and many favors called in was ruined? Or that the roller coaster ride of living with her and loving her would begin again?

"It wasn't hard to find you," she said. "No one else would have the nerve to close the compartment curtains. There's hardly anyone else on this train, but most of them are in one car, sitting stiffly—loyal and patriotic lambs." She laughed as she added: "For the Führer and final victory!"

Did she have to joke like this on a train teeming with secret police and soldiers?

"Not happy to see me?"

Sighing, I asked, "What happened? I saw the Swiss let you in."

"They did."

"The Germans came after you?"

She shook her head.

"You *decided* to come back?" I asked with some exasperation.

"Sometimes you're so slow." She laughed. "I pled a family emergency. Plans changed! Luckily I talked to a different officer. And thanks to you, I had enough cash to buy a ticket. Also I had impeccable papers. I do feel bad about the Swiss visa. Can someone else use it?"

I motioned to the bench across from me. "Sit down, please."

"I thought you'd never ask." She smoothed her dress under her as she settled in.

Chosen especially for this trip, the dress and jacket of worsted wool was something my grandmother in the countryside might wear. They kept their own rigid shapes, unchanged by the person wearing them. Likewise, Sara's shoes were especially utilitarian in these utilitarian times. I wanted her to look inconspicuous, but for me, this outfit, which disguised her beautiful body, stood out as much as if she wore a Wehrmacht uniform or a wedding dress.

She leaned forward and put a hand on my knee, saying, "Please don't be angry."

Her hand on my knee stilled me.

I waited, then said, "You're wonderful, like no one else I know. You're also impossible, like no one else."

She tilted her head down a little so she was looking up at me. Unfortunately, she knew how disarming I found this pose.

"You've never done anything simply or logically," I said. "Why did I think you'd be different now?"

"I can't leave Oma," she said. "I can't leave the only place I've ever lived, even if I'm not welcome anymore. And I want to find Max—at least find out what happened to him." She looked at me even more intently for a moment, then turned away. "I know what you're going to say about all this."

"Yes?"

"You'll say you did so much for me, but you can't do so again any time soon, if ever."

I nodded. "All the horrible things will only get worse."

Her lower lip trembled.

"I don't know, Rudi. I can't just run away." She paused. "Also." She paused again. "I can't leave you."

"Oh," I said, patting the part of the bench next to me.

She nearly jumped across the space between the benches. I put my arms around her and squeezed hard.

"Sara, Sara, Sara," I said.

"My dear Rudi," she whispered.

I kissed the top of her head and stroked her hair.

"I'm sorry," she said. "But I'm not sorry."

"Ha. It complicates all kinds of things. I have to think it through."

"Don't overthink it. No matter how much planning you do, in life things just happen."

"You proved that today!"

"I had no idea what it would feel like when I got to the point where I couldn't return. I should have thought *that* through."

"Now you have fewer choices than ever," I said. "Until recently, at least Jews with special work permits—or with friends in high places—could avoid deportation. But now even they aren't being spared. You have to disappear completely."

She bowed her head. "I want to be with Oma, but the people hiding her don't have much room and are risking everything as it is."

"Okay," I said finally. "Come back and stay with me again."

"Thank you. It'll be nice, Rudi."

"As nice as anything can be these days."

"You know what I mean. It was nice these last few months."

I nodded.

"We've had some wonderful times. And we'll continue to have some wonderful times."

"Especially if we don't get bombed or caught by the Gestapo."

"We'll make the best of it. The way we always do. We can make it better—make it wonderful. Like now."

"This is wonderful?"

"Oh yes." She made a sound like a purr. "It always feels wonderful when you hold me like this."

The skies cleared, and by the light of the moon, I saw hills that rolled far into the distance. Scattered in the forest were fields surrounding farms that looked like shadowy boxes. The blackout was thorough even here: the farmers were likely as afraid of the police as everyone else. Besides their homes, they wanted to save their dairy barns and pig houses and granaries from British and American bombers.

They wanted to save them even though none of the buildings were as full as in the past. Across the country, there was less and less food to be had. Forced laborers from the occupied countries turned out to be less enthusiastic than the farmers they replaced—the farmers drafted into the Wehrmacht who burned farms and villages in the East and wanted to keep the Red Army from doing the same to their own farms and villages.

"You can stay with me," I said. "But now you can't go out of the house. Ever."

"But Oma," she said. "I want to see her, take care of her."

"It's too dangerous. Besides, she doesn't remember you—or much of anything."

"When I visit her, I can wear a disguise so no one recognizes me. A big hat. A billowing scarf. Crazy big glasses."

"No, no, no," I cried. "The Gestapo is smarter than you think and they're going after every last Jew in Berlin. They're even sending out Jews to look for other Jews."

"Why would any of us help them?"

"To save themselves and their families." I paused. "Of course, eventually those people will be transported to the East, too."

"They won't stop until we're all working as slaves. Or worse."

I nodded.

"How long do I have to stay submerged like a U-Boat?"

"Until it's all over."

"That could take years." She smiled faintly. "A thousand years."

"A few years at the most."

She closed her eyes and slumped back.

"You're insisting on something," she said. "I have to insist on something, too."

"Yes?"

"Instead of hiding in fear and jumping at shadows, I'm going to do my best to treasure every day," she said. "Some way or another."

"So long as you do it quietly and discreetly," I said. "*And don't go out!*"

"If they do find me," she continued. "You have to promise to do everything you can to kill me."

"Kill you?"

"Yes. I don't want to have them kill me."

Then came a single, loud knock at the door.

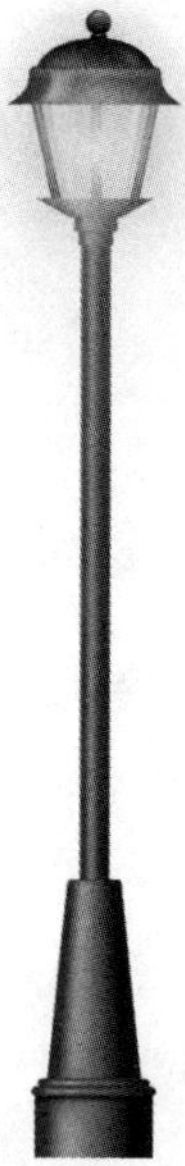

Chapter Four

October 1932

"That was depressing," Sara said as we left the dining room. "I had to get out of there."

"A concert?" I asked.

"We'll make our own music."

"Sure," I said, happy about this comment, even though I regretted that I was going to miss smoking a delicious cigar with Dr. Traum and some of the men in his study. But then I remembered that Max would likely be there.

Taking my hand, she said, "I want to show you something."

As we climbed the steps to the second floor, I sang a version of a Dietrich song that Sara loved:

Männer umschwirr'n Dich,
Wie Motten um das Licht.
Und wenn sie verbrennen,
Ja dafür kannst Du nichts.

"But you're the only man floating around me, and I won't burn you!" she cried. "At least I hope not."

I made my fingers flutter over my head, as though I were a moth bursting into flames.

She laughed, then pulled me by the hand through the library, where floor-to-ceiling bookshelves covered the walls. There were so many books that some lay flat along the tops of upright books, and piles of them on the floor blocked some lower shelves. Many of the books were in German, but some were in French, English, and Italian. I wanted to linger, but not now.

In another room, paintings and prints and watercolors covered the walls. The works, some large, some the size of a postcard, nearly touched one another. A few were illuminated by little lamps from above.

Some of the works depicted shadows on buildings or part of a garden or dishes on a table. There were also pictures of triangles and circles and strings of dots and what looked like mere drips of paint on the canvas. Several paintings were a single color—all blue or all red.

Okay.

Sara gestured toward a wall covered with works featuring people. Even though they were in a range of styles, obviously by different artists, they shared an odd quality: none of them flattered their subjects. Did that woman look so unformed in real life? Did that man really have red skin and features edged in bold black? And a series of nude women were gaunt and blue-white, as if they were painted in morgues.

Holding her hands behind her back and gazing at the floor, Sara began to speak but didn't say anything. I knew her well enough to ask, "Do tell."

She smiled and gazed at the wall. "I'm up there, too."

I looked at each picture, and at first none made me think of her. Then I noticed a painting of a figure with a few blotches of black representing her hair, and below the hair, an upturned crescent that was beguiling and familiar.

I gestured toward the painting. Sara nodded.

"The artist caught your smile perfectly," I said.

Underneath the face two black lines reached out from either side of a box-like torso. Near the top of the box were two small dots; at the bottom was a small blotch of black. "Below the neck, I bet you look better than the painting."

She laughed and leaned back. Whether she meant to or not, her arching body made her breasts, which were larger and more attractive than two dots of ink, become even more prominent.

I faced her and put my hands on both sides of her waist at the tops of her hips. I had touched her before—her face, her shoulders, her hands, her arms—but not her torso. My voice became a whisper: "I would need to make a thorough inspection because I'm so dedicated to facts and objectivity."

We both became still. Then something like a gentle electric shock passed from my hands to her hips and back.

"Did you feel something?" she said.

"Yes," I whispered.

It struck again. *"Wow!"*

"Otherworldly."

I locked into her eyes, which the artist also hadn't captured fully. When the tip of my nose touched the tip of her nose, her eyes became a tapestry of colors, like sunrise in a forest. Waves of brown and green were laced with specks of brilliant gold and red, shifting and glowing, never the same from moment to moment, right in front of me and yet elusive.

The artist hadn't completely captured her lips either. They were long and thin, a brownish pink. When she puckered them, they nearly disappeared. And yet they created the most radiant smiles and felt so good when I touched them with my lips.

Her thick, rich hair that fell past her shoulders looked black from afar, but, when I held it against my face, I saw it was dark brown with traces of red and orange. She enjoyed her hair almost as much as I did, sometimes wrapping strands of it around her fingers and holding it across her mouth and nose like a mask, especially when she said something that made me or others wonder at her boldness.

I kept holding her waist, and through her thin cotton dress I felt the hardness of her hip bones. She shifted back and forth, which made it seem as though I were massaging her ever so slightly. I started to speak, but I wasn't sure how to say what I was thinking and feeling: that I was deliriously happy, that I loved touching yet another part of her body, that I wanted to touch more of her, that I wanted her to touch me, that I needed to wrap myself together with her, create our own world and block out all that was around us.

"Let's go to the garden," she whispered, kissing me on the cheek.

Downstairs we put on our coats and went through the solarium to the garden.

In the twilight, a few soft lamps illuminated walkways that ran along the sides of the rectangular space. Several benches on the edges faced the center fountain. A pergola with wisteria growing up it swept over the two long sides of the garden. In the warm months, Sara told me, the fountain gurgled like a forest stream and something was always in bloom—roses, lilies, tulips, irises, hyacinths—creating a cascade of aromas and colors and shapes. And during the day, blackbirds offered delightful little riffs, doves cooed, warblers sang. Occasionally a woodpecker attacked a tree, sounding like a stubborn carpenter.

Beyond thick pines and walls, the S-Bahn and regional trains ran regularly and many of them stopped at the small Grunewald station just through the woods. Only a few blocks in the other direction was Kurfürstendamm, the boulevard that led grandly into the heart of the city.

Tonight all was quiet. We strolled around the garden, my right arm around her shoulder, her left arm around my waist.

"Do you know how wonderful you look in that dress?" My lips nearly touched her ear. "Do you know how wonderful it is to feel you in that dress?"

Underneath her wide-open coat, the dress swept down, folding in ways I didn't understand to outline her body in ways that I understood very well.

"I wore it for you," she said.

She squeezed me.

I sensed something and stood still. "A storm's coming," I said. "It may be too late to escape it."

Groaning, she let go of me and waved toward the house. "I've heard enough about the impending catastrophe."

I gestured toward the sky. "The clouds are dark with rain. Maybe even snow. Don't you feel the gusts?"

"Oh, you mean a real storm!" She laughed and hugged me again. "Let's dance in it!"

I turned and, reaching under her coat, put my right hand on her hip and clasped her right hand with my left. "Let's go!" I called.

I began to circle, and she moved with me. Waltzing down one of the walkways, we turned repeatedly. Around us, the pillars and pergola and trees became a blur. But as we gazed into each other's eyes and held each other tightly, she stayed in focus.

We spun and spun and spun until we lost balance and stumbled into each other.

Taking my hand, she said, "I want to show you a special place." She led me to the far end of the garden, where two benches faced a statue that I couldn't make out clearly in the dim light. It was a human form, arms lifted up, hands open, reaching to the sky. Was it celebrating? Was it surrendering? Was it crying out soundlessly in pain?

She slipped between the benches toward the curtain of pines that hid the wall around the property.

I hesitated, not seeing anywhere to go. She tugged on my hand, saying, "Come on. Right through here."

She let go of my hand, hunched down, turned, and disappeared through a gap in the branches that couldn't be seen until we stood next to it.

I followed, going into a tiny space with barely any clearance. Sara sat down cross-legged.

"Welcome," she said, stretching her arms out, palms up. "You're my first visitor. Ever."

I sat on pine needles that were as comfortable as a thick mattress. The tangy, calming aroma of the trees enveloped us.

"You can see the garden and the house, but no one can see you, right?"

"Smart man."

I stretched my arms out, and she leaned into me, nestling her head against my shoulder.

"What a beautiful place," I said. "And perfect for hiding."

"It's more a place I can be alone. Although I really like having company now."

I nodded, thinking, *let's stay here forever.*

At that, she lifted her head and kissed me on the lips.

I kissed her back, but instead of pulling apart after a moment as we usually did—we had never been alone like this—we kept kissing, letting our lips and tongues explore each other.

At the same time, slowly, gently, we lay down on the bed of pine needles. I grasped her head, stroking her hair. Her fingers traced lines across my temples and forehead.

For the first time, we ran our hands all over one another's bodies. She seemed to know exactly where to touch me to make me sigh in pleasure, and everywhere I rubbed her felt familiar and lovely.

I spread my coat on the ground, and then, wanting to, needing to, we quickly pulled most of our clothes off.

Her hands reached around me and slid up and down my back, squeezing, almost hurting. She murmured, whispered, clenched, shuddered.

At the end, she called my name loudly, then repeated it, her voice quieter but drawing the syllables out longer with each whisper. Who knew that my name could sound so lovely?

Then she stopped.

A breeze whistled through the pines. A bird called somewhere above us. The wheels of a train far away sounded *click-clack* on the tracks.

It felt like the beginning of time and the end of time.

My mind calmed. My body relaxed. My heart was full. All was right with the world.

"Darling, that was nicer than I ever thought it would be," she said. "What everyone says is right: you can't understand how good sex is until you do it."

"It wasn't good before?"

"Before?" She laughed. "This was my first time, silly."

"What?"

"Isn't that why you took your time?"

"I was enjoying the anticipation," I said, then added, "You're okay, right?"

"What do you think?" She laughed.

In a serious voice, I said, "This was a first for me, too."

"Your first? But you're 30!"

"*A* first," I said. "A special first. Because our souls touched."

"Yes!"

"We were both virgins—in different ways."

I squeezed her, and she squeezed me back, saying, "Thank you, Rudi. I'm so glad I started with the right person."

"*Started?* You're already thinking of moving on?"

She called out, as if to someone beyond the trees, "Next!"

I kissed her on the lips, enjoying the momentary silence. When I stopped kissing, she whispered, "Rudi, I want *you* next. Again and again."

"You remember my name."

"You're jealous about something that *might* happen?" she asked. "I could be jealous about things you *have* done. But jealousy is a useless emotion."

"I'm glad you're my latest." I laughed. "Because I have very strong feelings for you."

"I like you, too."

"I want to be with you for a long time," I said.

"Please." I heard something rare in her voice. She was pleading. "Not so serious."

"Okay." I laughed. "I'll be serious about not being serious."

"Thank you."

I held her tightly, noticing her breathing, happy that she kept hugging me, wanting to stay like this into the night, through tomorrow—and on and on.

Then I pulled back and looked at her, saying slowly, "Actually, I don't care if I sound serious. Whatever happens with us, I'll always be there for you. Because I love you."

"Sometimes if you hold things too tight, you break them," she said. "It's like a bird in the wild: you have to be able to let them go and trust they'll return. Someday. Somehow."

I stood up and said, "I hold you, and I release you."

Chapter Five

November 1943

As the compartment door opened after the quick knock, Sara sat with her hands clasped in her lap, looking like a dutiful German Frau. To me, however, she looked as natural as if she stood on her head.

It was the conductor again, and when he saw Sara, his face froze.

Would it all end just as I'd figured out what to do?

I spoke as if I were stating the obvious: "My wife."

He glanced back and forth at us.

"A late arrival," I added.

"You didn't mention her."

Part of me wanted to talk with him pleasantly, almost as equals, as we had when I boarded the train. But I was a Foreign Ministry official in the special car, and we were in Germany, where rank had always been ridiculously important and now, under the current regime, mattered even more. Despite all the talk about brotherhood and equality, this hierarchal attitude flowed appropriately from the top down, and all Germans were regularly reminded in newsreels and official portraits and on postage stamps of how a pose could express this.

I raised my head so my chin jutted out. I looked resolutely into the distance, the way someone might if he were dreaming of racial purity, of *Lebensraum*, of revenge for the Great War, of finally being accepted into the Vienna Academy of Fine Arts.

"Didn't you see me looking out the windows for her?" I said, my voice rising.

"I suppose—Yes."

"Everything satisfactory?" I barked.

After a pause, he replied, "Yes."

Then I turned so my back was to him.

After he left, I said, "I thought my days of lying for you were over."

"Thank you and I'm sorry," she said. "By the way, you do the Nazi really well. Maybe too well."

I tilted my head up, peered into the distance once more, intoning, "Comes in handy."

"Stop!"

I started to apologize in my normal tone of voice, but there was a knock again, and the door opened.

I turned, ready to stare down the conductor once more. But this time it was the Gestapo agent who had come around the train when we were waiting to leave Basel.

I couldn't blame the conductor for telling him about Sara. In his position, what else could he do?

But what was I to do?

Entering the compartment without hesitation, the Gestapo man acted as though he and I had never spoken. Looking at Sara, he commanded, "Papers."

Sara opened her bag and handed over, one by one, a passport, identity card, ration card, and residency papers.

He looked at them more carefully than he had looked at my documents. Then he glanced at me.

"You're traveling together?"

"We're married," I said. Sara took my hand and squeezed it with a minimum of movement but enough for the man to notice.

"Marriage certificate?"

I sighed. "We lost it quite recently—along with everything else we weren't wearing or carrying with us."

I avoided saying words like "direct hit" or "firestorm" since Gestapo agents might consider the use of such phrases defeatism, a crime the regime was cracking down on as the Wehrmacht continued a slow, steady retreat on the Eastern Front, all the while waiting for the release of the promised secret weapons that would change the course of the war.

"But at least we still have each other," Sara said, gazing up at me in a way that used to make my brain stop functioning.

"Purpose of your trip to Basel?"

"I was meeting Swiss relatives," Sara said.

"To be less of a strain on state resources," I interjected.

"But there was an emergency," she continued. "My cousin tried calling us, but we had already left Berlin." She bit her lip, and her eyes were suddenly damp.

I was ready to assume the pose I had taken with the conductor and mention my role at the Foreign Ministry—and how I'd always relied on the support of representatives of the Secret State Police. But now I watched Sara with a mix of curiosity and deep wariness.

"My uncle—" she said, her voice breaking. She seemed to collect herself, then went on. "At the station, my cousin told me that her father—my dear uncle—had died suddenly. And then I was so confused by the station. We were in Basel, a Swiss city, but I had to go through customs because, they said, the train was in Germany."

"Yes, a special arrangement," I said, hoping to stop her.

"Did I understand the station right?" She turned to the Gestapo agent. "It's a German station in Switzerland?"

He seemed to ponder something—whether to arrest us now?—then said hesitantly, "Yes, you understood correctly."

"I thought so!" Her gaze was full of deference and a bit of flirtation. I might as well not have been there.

This agent of death suddenly began to sound like a tourist guide, saying that the arrangement began in the 1850s, when the Swiss Confederation and the old Baden monarchy in southern Germany reached an agreement on extending German train lines into Basel. The Swiss already had their own station, but this one was separate, popularly called the Basel Baden Station. For many years, he continued, Germany had full control of the station, and even had customs offices there, since all the trains went north into Germany. But in 1940, the Swiss forced the Reich to move its offices to Germany proper, although the Reichsbahn still operated in the station.

"So in the beginning, the war wasn't one victory after another?" Sara laughed. "As early as 1940, the Reich lost some territory!"

Here we go!

"Nowhere near as much as now," she continued. "But still."

The agent stared at her.

Quickly, I said, "We'll solve the Basel station problem soon enough."

The agent glanced at me.

"When we unite with our German brethren across the border."

"But of course," he said.

I knew from his accent that he was from the northern plains like me. "And then we'll teach them how to speak proper German!"

His laugh was not exactly hearty, but I was relieved.

After the door closed, I said, "That was quite a performance."

"Thank you. You, too, my dear."

"Thanks, but a couple of times I worried this trip would end in Prinz-Albrecht-Strasse."

"Good to keep them off balance," she said.

"I want to avoid being off balance while hanging by a noose or meat hook wire."

Soon people were standing in the hallways in the coach cars. The car for government officials filled slowly. The new arrivals, who wore uniforms or dark suits, strode grimly and full of purpose. Eventually we had company in the compartment: a man wearing a gleaming Party pin who sat by the door. Within moments, he had opened a briefcase and begun shuffling paper, hurriedly writing, using his pen as though he were stabbing the documents.

"I'm glad we're going back to the house now," Sara whispered. "Even if it's not the way I remember it."

"Like most of Germany, it's a sad, pale imitation of what it was. But at least, unlike most of Germany, it won't try to kill you."

Halfway to Berlin, light appeared in the east and the sky slowly became a dull gray. It was one of the shortest days of the year, and the sun seemed barely to push above the horizon.

In the late morning, we stopped in Frankfurt, which so far had been spared the kind of terror and mass murder that Allied bombers had unleashed on other cities, including Hamburg. That city's downtown, with no military targets, had been destroyed in July. But soon this downtown might look like a moonscape, too.

I wondered about Allied bombing planners. Why didn't they focus on war targets: the military factories and concentration camps and the Führer's lair in East Prussia?

Near the main station, we traveled slowly through an industrial area. Several times we halted, and soon we were next to a freight train parked on a side track. At first, I barely noticed the other train. Then I nearly jumped.

"Someone's in that boxcar," I said.

Sara and the Party man looked outside, too.

"There," I said, pointing to a tiny open square on one of the boxcars, probably for ventilation. "A hand moved."

I saw a similar square on another boxcar. In the shadows, a pair of eyes seemed to be looking out.

"There again!"

"What?" Sara said, leaning toward the window, as if being slightly closer would make us understand what we were looking at.

The boxcar doors were closed, and now I saw several soldiers with rifles standing at either end of the train.

"People are in that train?" she said.

The man put down the sheets he had been reading.

"Enemies of the Reich, assuredly," he said.

"Who?" Sara asked.

I put a hand on hers, in part to warn her, in part to keep mine from making a fist.

"POWs? Saboteurs? Jews?" he said. "Does it matter?"

The man's eyes were unusually close together above a small nose. And his chin fell away too soon below his mouth. He reminded me of Reichsführer Himmler, who, for someone who held such a powerful position, didn't look at all like the Aryan ideal he touted.

"Packed into boxcars?" Sara said. "In the winter? Where are they going?" Then her voice trembled. "One of them's a child!"

The man sighed.

I squeezed Sara's hand harder.

She closed her mouth.

"It's a disgrace," he said.

I studied him carefully. I knew that the highest reaches of this government included people who were not as they seemed, who despised and worked against the evil that controlled the country.

"Yes," I said, wary, as always, of exposing my true feelings about politics, about justice, about life.

"An affront." The man shook his head.

I began to nod, but then, in a kind of shout, he burst out: "Transports should be done only at night!"

With a brusque flip, the man straightened out his documents, then sat back and began reading again.

Sara squeezed my hand as tightly as I had hers just a moment ago. She wiped tears from her cheeks.

The closer we got to Berlin, the more often the train slowed down and sometimes stopped. On the outskirts of the capital, crews worked on tracks next to ours, laying down new rails, their sledgehammers clanging furiously as the sun hovered just above the horizon and the sky began to darken. Twisted, misshapen rails were scattered nearby. There were other signs of a major bombing: wrecks of trucks and boxcars smoldered; several railway sheds had collapsed; craters were being filled in on a side road.

From the buildings bordering the rail line, clouds of smoke billowed toward us. It wasn't the appealing aroma of a wood fire. Instead, all kinds of things burned: metal, glass, rubber, food, and flesh.

As we inched toward the Anhalter Station, the smoke grew thicker and flames flickered in some buildings. Many streets were blocked by mounds of rubble. The city looked like something out of hell.

Our traveling companion set down his papers, which he had read and marked all afternoon. He stared at the scene, his lips closed tightly, his eyes unblinking. Then he said, "Criminals. Bastards."

"Oh, yes," I said, with some enthusiasm.

"The British," he nearly spat. "The Americans."

I thought of Sara's determination not to cower for the rest of the war.

"I imagine the British haven't forgotten the Blitz," I said.

He swung his head around and glanced at me.

"We haven't bombed the Americans' cities," I continued. "But we did declare war on them. Unnecessarily, I might add."

I glanced at Sara, whose eyebrows rose just enough for me to see.

The man turned and looked out the window at the dismal scene, and murmured, "Last night was the biggest raid on Berlin ever."

"I thought Reichsmarschall Göring promised to protect us from that kind of thing."

The man stared at me suspiciously.

Sara smiled, a smile that warmed me like nothing else I could imagine.

CHAPTER SIX

October 1932

At the end of the night, I wandered slowly through the Villa Colony Grunewald on my way home. The walk through the magical surroundings soothed my nagging worries and helped me savor my happiness.

Enjoying what could be enjoyed was what needed to be done.

Most of the residents of this development, only a few kilometers west of the Brandenburg Gate and the Reichstag, were among the country's most successful and prominent businessmen, bankers, politicians, artists, actors, and architects. They included writers like Lion Feuchtwanger and Vicki Baum, critics like Walter Benjamin, scientists like Max Planck, book and newspaper publishers like Samuel Fischer and the Ullstein brothers. Isadora Duncan had founded her dance school here. An inspiration for my own career, the early Weimar Republic foreign minister Walther Rathenau had lived—and been assassinated—in the Colony.

"Your neighborhood is as unreal as it is beautiful," I had said to Sara during one of our walks in the Colony.

"No, it's the rest of the city that's unreal," she had responded. "So many identical, unimaginative buildings."

Ironically for what appeared to be so whimsical, the Villa Colony Grunewald existed because of imperial calculation and central planning: after creating the German Empire with the crowning of Prussian King

Wilhelm I as Kaiser in the Palace of Versailles at the end of the Franco-Prussian War, Otto von Bismarck wanted to make the Kurfürstendamm rival the Avenue des Champs-Élysées. The Iron Chancellor had the Kurfürstendamm widened and supported businessmen who built the Colony at the far end of the boulevard, in part of the Grunewald woods, Berlin's version of the Bois de Bologne.

How we hated but wanted to be like the French!

The developers drained the swampy land, created several lakes, and laid out curving streets, many of which were named after German vineyards. They sold plots of land where families built villas. There were strict limitations at first: the villas couldn't take up more than ten percent of the plot; they couldn't be more than two stories high; they had to be country cottage style.

Overnight, the Colony became a symbol of the best parts of modern Germany, where creativity and brilliance and achievement found their reward, where a bucolic place could thrive in the midst of one of the continent's largest cities, where a range of people worked and lived and loved without the kind of discord that threatened to rip the rest of the country apart. The Colony was a center of power and wealth and business and the arts.

And many residents were Jewish.

"It's all out of proportion to the population," I had said to Sara once.

"How can we help it that we're so smart and talented?" She had laughed, but I knew that others wouldn't find such a comment amusing.

I walked along Erbacherstrasse and Trabenerstrasse, then stopped on the edge of the *Halensee*, Lake Halen. All was quiet. Light from apartment buildings on the far shore reflected in the water, making structures that in daytime were so solid shimmer like mirages.

Soon I passed Luna Park, the biggest amusement park in Europe, which was barely hanging on in this era of poverty. Who had extra marks to spend on the kind of frivolity that I'd adored as a child? Its rides and slides dark, Luna Park looked vaguely sinister.

I took the pedestrian walk under and over the various train and S-Bahn tracks that marked the northern edge of the Villa Colony. From the walkway, I looked down on a lone freight train, its cargo and destination a mystery. I didn't see the train's beginning or end, just one car after the other slowly rolling by, wheels clanking rhythmically, an unchangeable force that headed east.

Entering Charlottenburg, my old neighborhood, I came to the *Lietzensee*, Lake Lietzen, another of Berlin's many hundreds of parks and waterways that provided oases of nature across the great city. Although it looked manmade, it was natural, unlike the lakes in the Villa Colony.

I saw the bench where my grandparents had sat while I played; the water cascades that had fascinated me since I was a child; the boathouse where I had rented rowboats and first come to love being on the water.

Something moved near a streetlight in the distance. Birds? It took a moment to realize that I saw flakes of snow drifting down, floating so slowly they seemed suspended in midair.

The snow fell faster, and a white film began to coat the pavement, then buildings and fences and trees. The snow dampened all sound, which was like the absence of color or gravity or air: I noticed those elements only when they were gone. In the void, in the silence, my head felt empty, as if the snow blanketed all thinking and memory, too.

I couldn't remember Berlin ever so still as it was at that moment. There were no footsteps, no barking, no engines or motors running.

Likewise there were no taunting chants, no street battles, no trucks with loudspeakers screaming.

And the woman I loved loved me back.

It was like heaven on earth.

I stopped and stared straight up, where one after another, snowflakes suddenly appeared out of the darkness. They were huge and sparkled for a second, blotting out everything else in the night sky, then landing on my eyes and nose and lips. The cold stung, but in a moment, the warmth of my skin melted them. Soon my face was a messy mix of cold and warm and wet and raw. It all hurt, and yet was so alive and beautiful.

Chapter Seven

November 1943

All had changed in the three days we had been away. Sidewalks were gone or covered with debris. Paths wound around the wreckage of busses and streetcars. Many buildings were destroyed, but a few were only partly damaged, leaving bizarre scenes. In a living room several stories up, portraits hung undisturbed on the wall above a sofa, and a bookcase full of books was perfectly aligned. The place looked cozy and homey except that the exterior wall no longer existed.

The people we saw showed the kind of fortitude that made me believe that terrorizing civilians from the skies stiffened resistance rather than broke it. Berliners cleaned up and went about their business after the raids. And for all their criminal faults, the Nazis organized relief well. Then again, Germans couldn't help but neaten up, even when it involved cleaning roads of debris, making sidewalks passable, helping people whose homes had been damaged. Perhaps in their bones and in their blood, Germans really did share a kind of tribal unity and equality that the regime attributed to our ancestors. Too bad that such characteristics could be twisted in such murderous ways.

The S-Bahn wasn't running so we walked several kilometers in the slowly dying light. At one intersection, a policeman directed traffic, which consisted mainly of somewhat battered sedans with little swastika flags flying above the headlights and official trucks.

Another policeman blocked traffic and pedestrians from going down a street where there was a tangle of wires—some of which sent out sprays of sparks. "*Vorsicht!*" he called. "Careful!"

Sara, who was carrying the smaller of the two suitcases that she had so carefully packed for a new life abroad, began to lose her balance by the policeman just as she stepped off a pile of rubble. As fast as a bolt of lightning, the man grabbed her arm and steadied her.

She thanked him.

"We can't do enough for our fine German women," he responded.

When we were out of earshot, I laughed and said, "What would he think if he knew the truth about this fine German woman?"

"That I'm just a fine woman?"

"Very fine."

At the next intersection, I let Sara go ahead, following a little path through the debris. An official car—the usual black model with broken-cross pennants on the front—paused next to me. Several officials in uniforms sat in the back seat. Something made me look closer, and I recognized the man next to the window, nearest to us.

Hans was my friend since childhood, someone who shocked me not only by going along with the Nazis, but by joining the Gestapo. He was also Sara's lover for a short while, which, of course, made everything even more complicated than it already was.

Hans glanced at me as I whispered to Sara, "Keep moving! Keep looking down at the ground."

Hans's stern face started to melt—his version of a smile these days. He raised a hand, much like the kind of casual salute the Führer would give. I stared blankly at Hans as if I had no idea it was him. Then he glanced in Sara's direction. I followed his gaze and held my breath: she wore a hat, and her long, full coat hid the shape of her body. Even I barely recognized her from behind.

Hans watched as Sara stepped high over a beam that crossed the path, lifting the suitcase to clear the rubble. Then he turned back toward me, his eyes opening wide for a moment, as grim as he had been when I first saw him.

I hoped he hadn't recognized either of us, but I feared the worst.

The car moved forward, followed closely by other cars and trucks. If he made the driver stop, many other vehicles would be blocked. *Gott sei Dank* for the debris choking the roads.

When I caught up with Sara, I exclaimed, "Did you see Hans?"

"Where?"

"In the car."

"I should have waved."

"No!"

"I'm not afraid of him."

"You should be."

In the Tiergarten, trees were smashed. Craters broke up the walkways. The old site of the *Siegesallee*—the Avenue of Victory—was one of the few places that hadn't been disturbed, only because it had already been destroyed. The statues of Prussian princes, kings, and emperors had been tasteless, of course, since Wilhelm II had conceived them. But years ago, they had been moved to make way for the center of the new city of Germania, another tasteless German leader's dream. Put on hold because of the war, the world capital was supposed to have a triumphal arch so big that the Arc de Triomphe could fit under it. The *Volkshalle*—the People's Hall—would be a dome a thousand feet high, almost as tall as the Empire State Building.

If Germania had been built, it would now be a monumental pile of rubble.

At the Zoo, smoke rose from the wrecked buildings. At first, I thought this might have been a chance for the animals to rush out of their pens into freedom. But soon we saw bodies scattered among the destroyed halls and cages. A few colorful feathers were scattered by the sidewalk.

I pointed to the huge concrete block with antiaircraft batteries on top. "So much for the protection of the flak tower."

"They should have taken in the animals," Sara said. "They're the only innocents in this horrid place."

Chapter Eight

October 1932

I had gotten to know many of Sara's family and friends well, but she hadn't even met my family or friends. I began introductions with an intermediate step: taking her to see where my family and friends had once lived.

If I could mix her into my world the way I had become a part of her world, surviving the darkness would be all the easier.

Like so much of Berlin excluding the Villa Colony, the five- and six-story buildings in my old neighborhood had modest apartments. No one was rich and no one was poor. Ground-floor shops sold most anything a person needed—food and drink, clothing, shoes, jewelry, tobacco, and newspapers. My favorite shop was full of books, and I was happy to see it was still in business. The proprietor, Herr Rosenwald, had been, for me, a combination of teacher, librarian, and wise friend.

When I was growing up, Charlottenburg bustled. People belonged to clubs dedicated to anything from chess or sport, to collecting coins and stamps, to learning foreign languages, to train travel, to amateur engineering. Some went to church or political meetings or union events. They followed soccer religiously, read newspapers and magazines from front to back, went to the cinema—that new magical mode of entertainment. They gardened around their beloved huts in the *Schrebergärten*—allotment gardens—and took long walks that always included the park at the *Lietzensee*, Lake Lietzen.

I knew most of the shop owners and people who lived on our block, and everyone in our building. It felt like a large family. The problems of the times were occasionally overwhelming—during the war and at the height of the great inflation—but life went on, with respect and dignity.

Like so many in Berlin, our apartment had the basics and none of the elegance of the Traums' villa only a kilometer or two away. But for my parents, it was a palace compared to their parents' homes in the countryside, where plumbing and heating consisted of outhouses, chamber pots, and wood- or coal-burning fireplaces and stoves.

My father had risen from leather worker to owner of a small leatherworking studio and was both proud of living in this comfortable neighborhood and slightly ill at ease about it. Despite his rise in the world, he felt deep solidarity with working people. Sometimes, he feared I might become as spoiled as some of the other children in Charlottenburg. Always, he told me, I should be an independent thinker. "Don't go along with the crowd unless the crowd is right, which will happen when pigs have wings."

The last time I'd been to the apartment building, I had helped my mother move to her sister's after my father died. Since then, many of the nameplates at the door had changed and now some had several family names to identify tenants, not just one. And some shops were shuttered. With the economic collapse, so much had changed.

"I can't show you the apartment," I said to Sara as we stepped closer to the building. "So I'll just tell you about it. Which is actually much better than seeing it, because how it was is gone forever."

"Your memories of it are more real than it ever was," she said. "So tell me about it now before your memories fade and it's all lost."

"That sounds horrible," I said.

"All the more reason to enjoy this moment. And the next moment. And the moment after that."

I put my arms around Sara, embracing her very real, reassuring body, and started to kiss her. Just as our lips touched, someone behind me shouted, "Rudi!"

It was Hans, my lifelong friend who had grown up in this building, too, in an apartment with the same layout as ours and with furnishings confusingly identical to my parents'. "Wrong apartment," Hans had commented once as I called out to my mother for tea—while we played in his bedroom.

"What're you doing here?" Hans and I asked each other at the same time.

He had just visited his parents, he said, and was heading back to his own place in Pankow. I told him about my mother's move and introduced Sara as a friend, as I held her around her waist.

"Friends of Rudi," he said, gazing at Sara. "Different kinds of friends, but maybe we can complete the circle and become friends, too."

"Isn't a triangle the more accurate shape?" she said.

Hans laughed. "Rudi might not want us to be friends. I can tell you all kinds of things about him."

Over their laughter, I said, "There's not that much to tell."

"Of course, he would say that," Hans said. Then he looked at Sara in a way I'd seen him do before with some women. Without explanation or a smile, he stared at her eyes, not blinking or glancing away. Many women found this overwhelming or rude or silly, although a surprising amount enjoyed it.

This forwardness usually amused me—but not now. I pulled Sara closer, wanting to shield her from the stare, and also from things that wouldn't be so apparent. Hans didn't know about Sara's background, and I had no idea what he would think. When we were children, politics didn't matter the way they did now; he had always seemed tolerant, but many people's views had changed dramatically in the past few years.

Of all people, however, Sara didn't need shielding. She stared back at him, just as directly.

"What's to know?" She paused. "About Rudi?"

"Where to begin?"

It struck me that Hans fit a type that many people in these difficult times found inspiring. Thick blond hair swept across his broad forehead in a boyish wave, its golden sheen contrasting with his ruddy skin. His wide lips and large gleaming white teeth looked as healthy as the rest of his face. His pale, pale blue eyes had always been so hard to fathom. Distant? Judging? Cold? And yet they glowed brilliantly, perhaps friendly after all. Tall and with an athlete's body, he smiled and laughed often—his entire being exuded strength and confidence.

By contrast, Sara didn't look obviously Jewish, but with her thick dark hair and light olive skin, and her independent, challenging manner, no one would mistake her for an innocent Nordic farm girl. Sara was part of that broad swath of the population that didn't fit the Aryan ideal, a group that, oddly enough, included the leaders of the movement that idealized blond hair and blue eyes.

"Nothing could change my feelings for Rudi," she said.

"Don't speak so soon!" Hans laughed. "Let's see. What is the best story?" He glanced at me as if seeking my advice, but I stayed quiet.

After a moment, he said triumphantly, "Ah! Okay. So sometimes he was such a goody two shoes. Like when he confessed that our little gang had stolen magazines from one incredibly mean shopkeeper. But at the same time, he did do the punishment for us—helping the old bat in the store for a few weeks."

"Rudi is loyal and has a big heart."

"Nothing else big, though."

She gazed at him a moment, then said, "He may have one flaw: when he was younger, he wasn't smart picking friends."

Hearing their laughter, a stranger might have thought that they were the pair who had grown up together in this neighborhood.

We went to the *Kneipe* down the street, where, as Hans said to Sara, "We learned more about life than we did at school."

A poster celebrating the national team that went to the Summer Olympics in Los Angeles was the only new object in the place since I'd been here last. A pane in a window near the front door was covered with tape. One of the light fixtures didn't work. The walls and ceiling needed a coat of paint, and the heavy wooden tables and chairs would have benefited from refinishing. Like much of Germany, the *Kneipe* was solid but worn.

Hans and I recognized a few of the older men at the *Stammtisch*—the regulars' table—and asked after friends and relatives. Sara acted as comfortably as she did at the villa. Soon the three of us sat at a table in a corner.

"So Herr Foreign Ministry," Hans said. "What's your take on the big elections? Ours are on November 6. And two days later is the one in America."

"No question that Roosevelt will replace Hoover in the White House," I said. "Here, it's a strange situation. The Nazis want to win a majority, stop a Communist putsch, and stage their own putsch while the Communists want to stage a putsch, but they're fighting the Social Democrats, who you'd think would be their allies more than the Nazis. The conservatives and monarchists are happy with their pathetic cabinet of barons." Shaking my head, I added, "Whatever happens, more than half of the Reichstag will continue to want to overthrow the Republic."

"Foreigners must think we're crazy," Hans said.

"Natives, too," Sara said, then quickly focused on Hans. "Who's your favorite in the elections?"

Hans seemed to like the question, one that I would never have asked, saying, "This vote is going to be difficult."

"It shouldn't be," she said sharply.

"I've spent a lot of time considering it." He smiled at her as if she should be delighted with him.

"The only parties worth voting for are the Communists and Social Democrats," she said.

"That's the only choice?" He kept on smiling.

"You can't be interested in the Catholic or farmers' or monarchist parties. You aren't thinking of voting Nazi, are you?" Her voice rose.

"There's one candidate I really like. He inspires people, has vision, and can take the country in a new direction."

"You can't mean—"

"Many people are afraid of him, but that's normal when you have a plan to remake a country that's falling apart."

Her voice wavered as she said, "Please don't vote for him."

"I could never vote for him."

"Good."

He shrugged amiably. "I can't vote for him because I'm not eligible to vote."

"You aren't registered with the police?"

Continuing to smile, he said, "I'm not registered in the right location."

"You just moved?"

"No."

"But this is the most important election ever." She looked as though she might hit him or burst into tears—or both. "You can't not vote!"

Hans just kept smiling.

Chapter Nine

November 1943

We neared the house as the sun touched the horizon, making the air feel even cooler. Years earlier, we'd have found a café and sipped *Glühwein* and rubbed each other's hands. Instead, now, I wanted to get home before all became dark. Clear skies like today's made it easier for the bombers to find their way.

Along the Kurfürstendamm, into the Halensee neighborhood, there were new piles of rubble, new holes scooped out of once-solid blocks of apartment buildings. Acrid smoke wafted over us.

"I knew Berlin would look like hell soon enough," I said. "But now that it's happening, it's so painful."

In the Colony, more houses were damaged than the day we had left. Here and there, trees were shattered or had fallen. Craters made it impossible to drive on some sections of the streets—and would remain until the repair crews were finished in busier neighborhoods. So far, it seemed no villa had taken a direct hit. And because there was so much land between houses, there was less rubble and debris than in central Berlin.

"For the second time in my life, I thought I'd never see this house again," she said as we neared what I still thought of as her street.

"You still may not ever see it," I said. "It might be destroyed."

"One can only hope..."

Earlier in the year, there had been some damage to the villa, which was why it became available to me. After the Traum family fled the country in 1939, Herr von Thünen, one of von Ribbentrop's aides in the Foreign Ministry, had taken over the villa, paying a nominal sum at "auction." He and his family enjoyed the villa for several years, but thanks to a few stray British bombs, the von Thünens decided to move to the relative safety of the suburbs. The villa was added to the list of emergency housing for lower-level but important Ministry employees—in other words, the ones who, like me, did most of the work. That was around the time my apartment had been destroyed and after I'd moved my family to the country. And around the time Sara came back into my life.

Parts of the bedrooms on the second floor were open to the sky, but the kitchen and servants' wing was fine. Sara and I had created a few livable rooms using wartime furniture—worn, damaged, mismatched. In the dining room, for example, the mahogany, oval-shaped table that could seat 25 people in matching chairs—the centerpiece of the elegant room—had been replaced by a rectangular table about the size of a large desk and several chairs of different styles and heights, one of which was missing an arm.

Still, I was better off than many Berliners. A colleague we called *Herr Unglück*—Mister Bad Luck—lost his apartment early in the war during what were then rare Royal Air Force raids. We were relieved that he and his family survived, and we eagerly donated clothing and personal items to replace some of what they had lost. When his second apartment burned in another raid, we rejoiced that he and his family were unscathed again and we sympathized with his unusual misfortune but donated a bit less. By the third time he and his family had to move, we kept our distance.

There was no new damage at the villa. Everything was as we'd left it three days before, when Sara had slowly walked around the house in a kind of farewell to a place that, as she had said about my childhood apartment, was more real as a memory.

Sara didn't want to wait until daylight to see the state of the garden, so we made our way outside. Blackout rules were so strict that car and truck headlights were covered in black tape except for tiny slits; people wore phosphorescent badges so other pedestrians wouldn't run into them; and curbs were painted white to be more visible in the nighttime. So I aimed the flashlight directly at the ground and turned it on only for a moment to see what was in front of me, then turned it off, moved a few paces, then turned on the light again, all the while making sure that Sara could see by this light, too.

A while ago, the winter garden had lost most of its windows and was now more of a wintery garden, exposed to the elements, without furniture, the floors damp and icy, littered with rubble. At the far end of the garden, in the time we had been away, a bomb had smashed more of the lattice work and dug another deep hole in the flower bed.

"It's worse than ever," she said.

"And you *chose* to come back."

I couldn't see her face in the dark, but I felt she was pouting as she said, "I did."

"You barely had a taste of Switzerland," I continued. "It's so peaceful and safe. I did everything I could to make it happen."

"Maybe too much."

In this garden, we'd had premonitions of what was to come.

More than ten years earlier, Sara had lain on her back on one of the benches with her head in my lap, looking up at me, one hand twirling a lock of her hair.

"My parents have mentioned that you're not Jewish," she had said.

"They don't approve of me?"

She shook her head. "They don't approve of how suddenly everyone's so aware of such things."

"Just what the fascists want."

She smiled at me. "Not long ago, a lot of us didn't even know we were Jewish. And if we did, we didn't care."

With a smile back, I said, "Are your parents at least happy that an Aryan adores their Jewess?"

"They're concerned because they think everything's going to get uglier, which will affect everyone, even you and me."

"Ha," I said. "It'd be easier to change my eyes from brown to blue than my feelings for you."

"Don't change," she said. "And let's hope nothing else changes."

Chapter Ten

October 1932

Hans stopped smiling, and his voice softened. "Before you have a stroke, let me explain." As if he were speaking to a foreigner who barely knew German, he said slowly, "I want to vote—"

"For whom?" Sara nearly screamed.

"For Roosevelt."

"What?"

"Roosevelt will turn America around, which will help us. I wish he could be Chancellor, too—he could get us out of this mess."

"God! I was beginning to think—"

I felt as relieved as Sara sounded. "Hans likes to keep you guessing," I said. "Which reminds me of someone." I glanced at Sara.

"What about the election here?" she asked Hans. "You didn't answer."

Hans shrugged. "I can live with all of them."

With the same tone of surprise, I asked, "Even the Communists?" and Sara asked, "Even the Nazis?" Then I added, "Even the Nazis?" and Sara added, "Even the Communists?"

He smiled at us. "Either party would get people back to work. The factories would be roaring again. Look at Russia!"

"The German Reds would shoot or starve half the population," I said.

"The Nazis would do the same thing," Sara said. "With some overlap."

"No need for you to worry," Hans said to me. "You'll fit in well in either the workers' paradise or the fascist Fatherland. You're hardworking. You love exercise. You're the epitome of the new man."

"Who will the new man vote for?" Sara asked.

I laughed. "I don't put a lot of faith in political parties, but the least objectionable to me are the Social Democrats. At least they support the Republic. I wish I could cast a vote against the Communists and the Nazis."

"Yes, but the more I think about it," Hans said, "the more I think you'll do just fine under the Nazis."

"Aren't you afraid of the Nazis?" Sara asked Hans.

"They want to rebuild Germany," he said. "Restore our place in the world."

"Then why not bring back the monarchy?" she said. "Wilhelm II is about 50 kilometers over the border in the Netherlands. From what I hear, he would be delighted to become Kaiser again."

"From what I hear, he's an idiot," I said.

"Why aren't the Nazis satisfied that Hindenburg is President?" Sara said. "He's conservative."

"Hindenburg's not conservative enough," Hans said. "Worse, he's only technically alive. He's not the energetic leader we need."

"We need an energetic leader?"

"You'd rather drift?"

"Better than speeding off in the wrong direction."

"Tell that to the hungry and unemployed."

They stared at each other. Abruptly, I said, "It's tragic that democracy came to Germany only after we lost a war, gave up so much territory, had to pay impossible reparations, and had the currency and economy collapse."

It was as if neither of them heard me.

"How does it help the hungry and unemployed to blame Jews and Bolsheviks and foreigners for everything that's wrong?" Sara said, looking at Hans.

"If they aren't to blame for everything that's wrong, then it might be our own fault," I said.

Sara laughed at this.

Hans said, "Foreigners did give us Versailles, seized the colonies, dismantled the military."

"France and Britain did that. But Jews and Communists, too?" She shook her head. "Also, the Nazis say Germany needs to expand into the East. What will they do with all the people who live there already?"

Hans sighed. "I wouldn't take that rhetoric seriously."

"Even the name National Socialist makes no sense," Sara went on. "Nationalism has to do with a single country and a strict social hierarchy. Sometimes it's even feudal. And, of course, it's usually based on ethnicity. Whereas socialism is international and egalitarian. 'From each according to his abilities. To each according to his needs.' "

Hans waved his hand in the air, as if sweeping away her words. "Germans are different," he said. "We value tradition, honor, and duty—and we believe everyone in the community should follow the same rules and share a common destiny. We *are* national *and* socialist."

"To create a kind of tribal, primitive Eden—something that never existed—the National Socialists will destroy everything that makes Germany great," she said. "And why do they call Hitler 'the Führer?' I don't want to be led by someone who screams about hate and revenge and death and destruction."

"You have to get past his shrillness."

"Look into his eyes," she said, looking into Hans's eyes. "They're dark and empty."

He peered back, saying, "I'd rather look into your eyes."

"They are the most beautiful eyes," I said, reaching for Sara's hand.

She smiled and said pleasantly, "National Socialists should all be neutered. If anyone could find what needs to be neutered."

"Wow, how do you know about any of that?" Hans said.

"Doesn't the overcompensation make it obvious?" she said.

"What a hilarious reason for a political party," I said.

"Rudi, you should set up your own party," Hans said. "But I doubt it would gain power. You would require everyone to run marathons and row and hike. Members would be thoughtful, eccentric, but they'd spend so much time asking and talking about 'what is to be done' that they'd get nothing done."

They both laughed, and I said, "Sadly, Germans worship authority and the military. If they were fit and healthy, they'd be more independent. Germany needs the *Wandervögel* movement more than ever."

"Ha, the wandering birds," Hans said. "The *Wandervögel* were great when we were teenagers. At that age, who didn't like wandering around like birds, singing and hiking through the countryside, and sleeping under the stars without a care in the world?"

He paused, his large blues eyes unblinking. "Weird that we were part of it as the war was raging. If the fighting had continued much longer, we'd have gone from forest paradise right to the bloody trenches. Most of us were lucky enough to outgrow *Wandervögel* in less brutal ways."

This last comment had the strangest effect on me. As if Hans were *encouraging* me, I began to speak about how everything had felt fresh and alive and hopeful in those days. So many of us *Wandervögel* were away from our parents for the first time and heard new ideas and met others who wanted to throw off society's expectations and rules. We discussed new ideas endlessly, always wanting to be good and just and help others and make the world a better place. We loved one another completely and in so many ways. Despite the worship of things German that must have resonated with the Nazis, I still believed. Little since then had been as wonderful.

I said that if all Germans lived according to the best *Wandervögel* principles—peace, harmony, wholesomeness, equality—the country would have no problems.

"Skipping through the forest like Goldilocks would end the economic crisis?" Hans said.

"The *Wandervögel* live on," I said. "In me and in many others."

Hans turned to Sara. "Does it live on in you?"

"The *Wandervögel* were before my time. And my idea of a country trek is a walk through the Tiergarten," she said.

I laughed. "There's much more to the *Wandervögel* than hiking. There's nothing like the *Wandervögel* spirit. But if the Reds or Nazis take over, I don't think the movement will last long. It's not doctrinaire enough. Besides, the Nazis have the Hitler Youth and the Communists will import the Young Pioneers from Russia."

"One of the many things I like about Rudi is that most Germans prefer complicated, abstract systems to explain human existence," Sara said, turning to Hans. "He believes in things that are concrete and good and straightforward."

Hans smiled and put an arm around my shoulder. "If only we were all as virtuous as you, my dear friend. But sadly, virtue will get you only so far. And few people are fully virtuous."

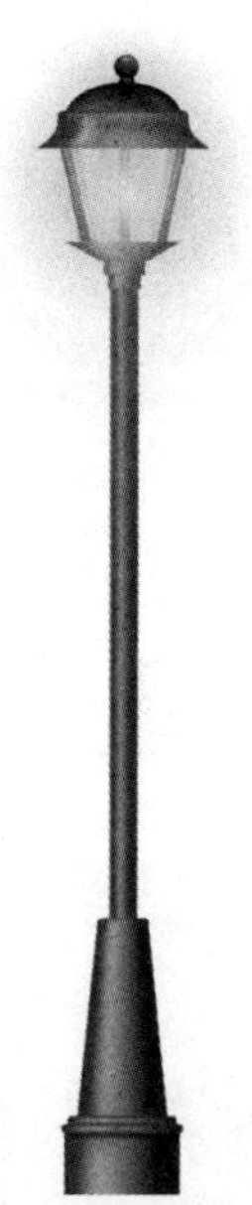

Chapter Eleven

November 1943

As we stepped inside the villa, sirens began to sound. "Air raid!" Sara exclaimed, sounding strangely cheerful.

Usually, the Royal Air Force didn't appear overhead until two or three in the morning. Then, the flak guns started pounding, and Berliners stumbled down to basements and shelters. If we were lucky, the planes dropped their bombs quickly, and we climbed back upstairs for a little more sleep.

"Basement," I yelled.

"I want to see the show!"

I protested, but she was already heading up the stairs to the roof. "Coming?" she asked.

As I did so often with her, I paused to consider her outlandish proposal, then followed.

Boom boom boom.

In the south, 88mm flak guns began to fire into the sky before we saw any airplanes.

Boom boom boom.

"A thunderous welcome for the British," I murmured. "So much for the famously pleasant Berlin air."

Boom boom boom.

Beams of light reached high into the darkness, slowly moving across the night sky one way, stopping momentarily, then crossing back.

Tracer bullets arced overhead like shooting stars.

The first airplanes, small groups of little silver specks against the blackness, appeared.

"There they are!" Sara cried. "Lovely!"

"They're going to cause an unlovely amount of death and destruction," I said.

"On just the right people."

"The ones who really deserve it are in deep bunkers or far from Berlin."

"Most Germans have supported them, so they deserve whatever's coming—or falling."

"But some people who'll be hurt tonight will be friends, neighbors, colleagues. A lot of them loathe the Nazis."

"But no Jews will be among them."

"Maybe one."

She laughed, yelling, "When the bombs fall, we get such clarity about life and death. It's all random. Beautiful randomness."

She hugged me as she gazed at the sky.

The whirring of the planes grew louder. South and west of the city, more 88mm guns pounded in staccato rhythms. Tracers continued to shoot upwards, and flak explosions filled the sky. A bright green flare descended from the front of the Royal Air Force swarm.

"The Christmas tree lights!" I said. "The Mosquitos are marking the target area."

"Looks like Zehlendorf. Right down the street."

Red flares drifted from the sky around the original flare.

"Merry Christmas," I said.

"I don't celebrate that."

The sound of the sirens changed to the screaming that meant the attack was upon us.

Now the spotlights focused on individual planes, which seemed oblivious—they stayed in formation, without changing speed or course to avoid the lights.

"Avro Lancasters," I said, recognizing both their outline and sound. "They're bigger and more dangerous than the planes they sent at the beginning of the war."

"That's not what State Radio says."

"Shocking." I scoffed.

The flares slowly drifted downward.

"Glad we're not in the square they've marked out," I said.

Then, what looked like little cylinders began to drift down from the closest planes. They were like rungs of a ladder that had no sides, the lines curving and separating as they descended, steadily falling but not as fast as one would think thousands of pounds of explosives ought to. They might have been toy batons, a gift of the people of England to the people of Berlin.

I put an arm around Sara, who put her arms around me. Even though this felt like a distant show, we both knew what was coming next. It was the kind of force and power that led complete strangers, huddled in bunkers, to hug or shout or weep or laugh hysterically.

The first bomb to land flashed brightly. A moment later, the sound of the blast hit us. Then came a new flash and roar as another bomb hit. More flashes and roars followed, one after the other, faster and faster.

Then the flashes became a continuous blaze, and the roar was like a huge grinding machine. It shook the ground and building and pounded through our bodies.

Red and yellow flames shone from the area where the bombs were landing. The thundering flak guns seemed to be shooting even faster and more ferociously up into the sky. The spotlights stayed trained on individual planes.

We watched in silence. Soon, most of the planes had swept beyond us, and the last bombs, the ones that were nearest to us, had exploded.

ǂǂǂǂǂǂǂǂǂ

"That's it for now," I said.

"No more?" Sara said, sounding disappointed.

"You must be the only person in Berlin saying that."

"I love what Berlin was. What it's become should be flattened."

"And you chose to return to this?"

The guns stopped firing. The drone of the planes faded. Only a few searchlights scanned the quiet sky. I imagined that the boys and older men in the batteries were falling to the ground, exhausted.

The horizon glowed red and orange; smoke wafted over us.

"Time to head back down," I said.

"The night is young."

I took a step away from her but stopped. I couldn't leave her here alone.

Then I heard the faint droning of engines laboring high in the sky. Again, the sound came from the south and west, far from us, becoming louder. Again, sirens began to wail. Searchlights arced back and forth. Flak shells rose and exploded across the sky. Silvery bombers approached high, high above us in diamond-shaped formations. The first Royal Air Force marking flare appeared and began to drift down toward us. Then the corner markers appeared.

Sara and I clutched each other again. We were thrilled and scared and enraptured all at once.

The white batons began falling once more, and we heard a steady rumble in the distance and felt tremors through our feet. The same areas flashed with light, and the roaring came closer. Soon it would end and we could go to bed and try to sleep.

But then I noticed more batons, maybe from straggling planes, that were coming down outside the square that had been marked and much closer to us than the thousands before them. Their slow, lazy fall made them seem even more ominous than if they had barreled down toward us.

I squeezed Sara hard and yelled, "We have to get down!"

She screamed. A scream of fear? A scream of enjoyment? Both?

I pulled on her, yelling, "Get down!"

She screamed again and clutched me, but she remained standing, looking fearlessly upwards.

The bombs landed closer and closer. The building shook. Gusts of wind swept over us.

Then all was quiet, and for a second, I relaxed. It was over. We could go back downstairs. We had survived.

But then, out of the silence, came a thunderous roar and a string of explosions that pounded into us with more sound and force than anything I had ever felt in a bombing raid. We rocked and held on to each other as though we were on a ship deck that a huge wave was crashing over.

The building shook so hard I thought it would collapse.

We had to run, I thought.

Move.

A flash of light blinded us. A *whoosh* of air and a roar lifted us up from the rooftop.

Chapter Twelve

January 30, 1933

The winter sky stretched fragile and blue over Berlin. There were no clouds, only a hint of whiteness at the far edges of the azure expanse.

The bitter cold permeated everything that Monday morning. The capital's lakes and rivers were solid gray-white ice, every molecule locked into place. Like skeletons, leafless trees reached futilely toward the heavens. Shrubs and parks were covered with frost. Coal smoke and steam were the sole signs of life around buildings whose doors and windows were tightly closed. Even the pale sun seemed subdued.

On this dead day, death came to power.

My footsteps echoed on the cold, hard surfaces as I walked to the S-Bahn station. I should have felt forlorn in this seemingly lifeless place, but I was thinking once more about Sara, whom I had seen the night before and whom I would see after work. Evenings we met at our favorite café, where we talked, drank, and flirted with each other and with others. Then we went to my place. I didn't care that she laughed each night at the worn, late-Biedermeier furniture I had bought for a song from a colleague who had been posted to Japan. Here, we had privacy. As usual, she left in the early morning, before the city awoke. During the night, we shared the loveliest moments: in the dark, under the covers.

She asked me many questions, more than anyone ever had. They were probing, sweet, curious, challenging:

"If your father came back to life, what's the first thing you would say to him?"

"What's the best dream you've ever had?"

"If you could change an event in history, what would it be?"

"What piece of music most melts your soul?"

Remembering Sara, remembering being with Sara, made me feel as if it were a sunny, bright day. I skipped along the sidewalk. I felt so warm and light and carefree that for a second, I thought I might just lift off from the ground like a large, happy balloon.

In the middle of the morning, I heard about the event I had thought, despite everything, would never happen. I was beginning to sort through the latest batch of cables and letters from our offices around the world addressed to my boss, the chief of the department that oversaw the day-to-day management of embassies and consulates. I could track the rotation of the globe by the timing of these cables. In the morning, there were piles of them from the Americas, which had been busy while we slept but had since shut down. Then more came from Australia and eastern Asia, and in the late morning, Europe and Africa came alive as the Pacific drifted off. In the afternoon, Central Europe wound down, and the Americas awoke, and the cycle began again.

Frau Riegler appeared in my doorway, saying, "Hindenburg did what he promised he'd never do."

Even though her background was so different from mine, Frau Riegler felt like an older sister. Her grandfather had been an ambassador in the imperial era and she had studied at Ludwig-Maximilians-Universität in Munich, yet she had few of the airs of men with similar backgrounds. With blonde bobbed hair, she wore dresses that fell precipitously from her narrow shoulders, down her thin body. A few northerners in the office called her "the Italian" because she was from Bavaria and loved spending holidays in Venice. Often, I had to concentrate when she spoke: her voice was soft and her southern vowels sometimes took their time developing, like bubbles stretching, slowly filling, then drifting away. Today, I understood her perfectly.

"Hitler's in the cabinet?" I asked.

"Worse than that."

I paused, delaying confirmation of the news for a few seconds. "He's Chancellor?"

She nodded. "The Barons are joining the Brown Shirts in a German National People's Party-National Socialist coalition. They're being sworn in now."

"Someone must have gotten to Hindenburg's son since the old man's senile."

Frau Riegler shrugged. "There's a Vice-Chancellor again: von Papen."

"With portfolio?"

"The unofficial portfolio is to serve as a check on his new boss."

All I could say was, "Ha."

Frau Riegler continued, "There are just two other Nazis in the cabinet, which at first glance seems reasonable."

"But?"

"Frick is Minister of the Interior. Göring is Minister of the Interior for Prussia."

"The Communists would've taken the police spots, too," I said. "On the other hand, the Social Democrats would be happy to be in charge of postal affairs and transport."

After a pause, I asked who was Foreign Minister.

"Baron von Neurath continues in the post," Frau Riegler said.

"The only bit of good news, I suppose," I said.

"But how long can this cabinet last?" Frau Riegler said. "Despite their many faults, the barons aren't gangsters."

As the news spread, a small group formed in the hall. Strikingly, my boss, the head of the department, Herr Doktor Müller, who rarely left his office suite, joined us, saying, "Surprising! Not long ago, the President called the new Chancellor 'the Austrian corporal.' "

"The pressure must have been extraordinary," Frau Riegler said. "The military, industrialists, monarchists, so afraid of the Communists that they embraced the National Socialists."

"Of course, they believe they can control the Führer," said Herr Vater, a tall man who, in my presence, had never spoken about anything but work. As a result, except for his slight Frankfurt accent and the fact that he dressed impeccably and spent an inordinate amount of time washing his hands, I knew little about him. "After all, the people who put him in charge have the army, corporations, and much of the aristocracy on their side," he continued. "Maybe the new chancellor will find it's a lot easier to criticize from the outside than manage a country."

"You're sounding like von Papen." I laughed. "Or Hindenburg. If he's still capable of speech."

"Here's to hoping he can't do much," said Herr Forst. "Among his plans are destroying the Jews, colonizing the East, and waging a war that will make the last one look like a skirmish."

Herr Forst, who had worked in the Ministry since before the Great War, held a hand over his brows, as though shielding himself from the sun's glare, even in our dim offices.

"He's an odd combination of revolutionary and reactionary," Herr Forst went on. "He says he wants to go back to traditional times, but he also wants continual upheaval and to smash everyone and everything in his way. Who cares about peace and the social order?"

"People are desperate," someone said.

"Desperate for him?" Herr Forst replied. "Haven't they heard him speak or read his book? His program is very simple—and brutal."

I must have known before that Herr Forst was Jewish, but until recently it hadn't registered beyond the significance, say, that someone was red-haired or left-handed or a birdwatcher.

In the quiet that followed Herr Forst's comment, Herr Doktor Müller said, "He's a mesmerizing speaker who makes some people feel good. I can't say the same for his writing."

"He did make a compromise today," I said. "Last summer he refused to be part of a coalition government. It was all or nothing then."

"That's because the November elections were his first big setback," Frau Riegler said. "Who would imagine the Nazis would lose votes and the Communists get more, just enough to scare everyone? What an irony. Because an increasing number of Germans want a Red government, we get a black one."

After a pause, Herr Forst spoke up. "What does this change mean for *our* world?" This sounded more like a statement than a question.

We all gazed at Herr Doktor Müller, who stood with his shoulders back, chest out, arms at his sides. The high ceilings made him appear smaller than he was. Yet his words were firm. "The Foreign Ministry is a branch of the state," he said in a stiff voice. "As always, regardless of the composition of the government, we will do our best work. We serve the Reich and German history and tradition. Perhaps we even serve a higher entity, one we haven't discerned or needed yet."

We nodded and quickly moved towards our desks, the most tangible way of showing that we were taking his advice.

Frau Riegler stopped at my doorway.

"He's probably in the Chancellery already," she whispered. "Which he'll never leave voluntarily."

"What can we do about it?"

"I'm afraid we'll have years to try to figure that out."

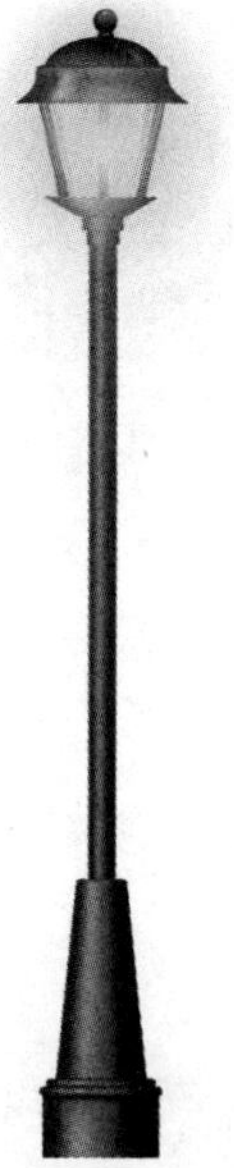

CHAPTER THIRTEEN

November 1943

Sara and I drifted, suspended in the air. There was no light and no oxygen, no up, no down. Nothingness.

Then a wall of debris hit us. We fell, which seemed to take hours.

I screamed but couldn't hear myself in the roar.

We smashed onto a hard surface with a thud. The smell of singed hair and skin overwhelmed my senses.

I tried to open my eyes, but I couldn't. Or maybe they were open and I couldn't see.

I tried to get up but my body didn't move.

I stopped trying to do anything.

In the darkness, I remembered other times Sara and I had floated together. Years before, when we made love, often we couldn't tell where one of us ended and where the other began. Inside her, I felt she was inside me. I kissed her ear, and simultaneously I felt she was kissing my ear. She stroked me, and it felt that it might be me doing it. When energy exploded throughout her, I felt it throughout me, too. All walls dissolved. We were completely connected.

Whispering, I had tried to describe the sensations I felt. I told her that the world had become perfect. She had smiled back at me, holding my head, humming and moaning, her body rippling beneath and around and through me, her eyes continuing to open and close at random.

Sometimes she had watched me steadily with a clinical focus, her thin lips smiling inward. Sometimes she closed her eyes for a while, then opened them wide for a moment, then closed them again. Sometimes she giggled.

IIIIIIIIII

I moved my neck slightly. Had I broken anything? Had I lost any limbs?

I couldn't move my hands to check myself.

I blinked several times, then suddenly I could see.

In the darkness, flames gave everything an orange-red tinge.

IIIIIIIIII

"I want you again," she would say, sliding the back of her hand down the side of my face, looking somewhere close to me but not directly at me, smiling to herself, maybe at me, too.

All was wonderful. Her words, her gaze, they made me forget everything.

I learned quickly that if I wanted to have sex with her, I had to wait for those moments.

Thank God for Fromms Act condoms, the miracle product of the '20s. I made sure to carry several at all times.

It could happen anywhere, sometimes late at night, in quiet parks and alleyways. Once we snuck into an office building whose service door was ajar and found a luxurious office with a long leather couch. A few times in cafés or restaurants, we went into the bathroom together, locking the door.

In bed, it was almost a shock when afterwards, as we held each other silently, she said she needed to pull her arm from under my body.

I had forgotten that it was her arm, not our arm.

After I moved and she was comfortable again, I lay gently next to her once more.

She shifted, and I opened my eyes. I loved the view of her shoulder and neck and chin so close I could see individual hairs on her ear lobes.

"What time is it?" she asked.

"Time to kiss you again."

IIIIIIIIII

Covered in dust, Sara was a pale ghost next to me. We stared at each other. I realized I must have looked as deathly as she did.

"Are you all right?" I asked. Actually I *tried* to ask this, but my mouth didn't make sounds.

Her mouth moved, too, but she didn't say anything either.

All I heard was a dull ringing as if from all around me.

Now I shouted. I knew I shouted. But I heard nothing.

She pointed at her ears.

I nodded and pointed at my ears, too.

IIIIIIIIII

Her observations about sex were as scary as they were exciting. "I'm a lucky girl for coming so easily," she said several times. "Most women don't."

"How do you know?" I asked.

I should have realized. One of the Traum family friends was a founder of the Institute of Sexual Science, and in dinner conversations with him, Sara had asked all kinds of questions and devoured his answers.

"Partly it must be anatomical," she said. "I'm so easily stimulated, as much as any male."

I nodded.

"Then again, it may be a question of attitude." She laughed.

I nodded once more.

"Can you imagine these poor women who can't or don't want to come? It's amazing what they're missing."

True, the women I had had sex with before Sara didn't enjoy it in the same sweaty, joyous, sloppy way she did. With them, it was almost perfunctory, an exercise, a kind of cheerful ritual, like a good night kiss. With them, sex was clinical; with Sara, it was an experience.

Finally, I was able to move an arm, which I used to grip her hand, and we stayed like this a while. Breathing seemed to take up most of my energy.

There were a few flashes behind her in the Villa Colony. More bombs? Yet another attack?

I was so very happy for months. Why wasn't she?

"Rudi, Rudi, Rudi," she said. "You dream of a nice house and garden, three or four charming children, me cooking and keeping the home. Kirche, Küche, Kinder. Church, kitchen, children. Well, maybe not the church part."

"Temple, kitchen, children?"

"Never."

"You know I don't care about that horrible stereotype."

"Still, you want something simple and sweet. Something that's not possible."

"I like what we've had, which is different from what you're talking about."

"It won't last."

"It won't last if you keep saying it won't."

She stared at me, and for a second, I wondered if she had not heard me.

Spotlights still crisscrossed the sky, where mercifully no airplanes now flew, but all around us was the orange-red glow of fire.

As the ringing began to subside, I felt Sara's arms and torso, which were intact under the dust. I didn't see any blood on her head or body.

Then I checked myself. I ached, but nothing seemed broken.

I asked Sara how she felt.

"You were right," she said. "We should have gone downstairs."

I laughed as we slowly rose and began to go downstairs from the roof, one of the slowest walks of my life. My body navigated the steps and hall as though from memory. She was behind me. Neither of us spoke, and as soon as we got to the bed, we both undressed and lay down. Exhausted, we wrapped ourselves around each other and fell asleep immediately.

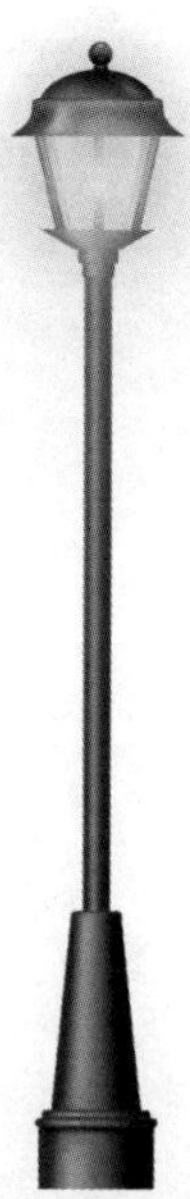

Chapter Fourteen

January 30, 1933

On this cold, dark evening, a crowd blocked the sidewalks outside the Foreign Ministry, cheerful and expectant. Many had brought their children. You might have thought New Year's fireworks would explode soon.

The explanation was simple: just as dogs loved to be walked several times a day, the National Socialists loved to march. They took to the streets for and against the smallest things. The Reichspost delivered the Führer's mail late? There was a protest march. The Party had beaten up and humiliated another defenseless old Jewish man? There was a celebratory march. Now, because they had achieved one of their greatest goals, tens of thousands of Nazis would stomp their boots in time to drums and sing militaristic tunes late into the night—a spectacle as ridiculous as it was terrifying.

Could this all be put back into the hell hole it came out of? How could it be contained?

I asked a policeman where the crowd was headed.

He said the National Socialists would march past the Chancellery.

"The new Chancellor will review them?"

"He greeted crowds earlier."

"Isn't Hindenburg living across the way while his residence is being renovated?"

"Genau." Exactly. He looked directly at me for the first time. "Maybe they'll wave at each other. After all, it's gotten very cozy between them."

"The corporal and the field marshal."

We both shrugged.

I wasn't meeting Sara until later, and I didn't need to be anywhere else for now, so I lingered. Here in the heart of the capital around the buildings where many of the most powerful people in the country worked, I might get a sense of how Germans were reacting to the news and of what would happen to our desperate country.

Maybe crowds would jeer the Führer and demand he go back to Austria. Communists could break up the parade and battle the Brown Shirts. Millions of other Berliners from a range of parties might begin a general strike. Or, instead of ranting, Hitler could speak of a newfound respect for democracy, which after all had given him this reward. Then again, maybe the sun would rise at midnight.

The crowd continued to grow. Some people wore National Socialist pins and arm bands and a few were in Party uniforms. Brown Shirts lined the edge of the street.

I walked slowly along Wilhelmstrasse to the Chancellery, which blended in with the other buildings in the Government Quarter, all neoclassic limestone blocks with rows and rows of identical windows. Did the architects believe that repetition inspired respect for authority and did they intend to create a sense of monotony and emptiness?

Every window in the Chancellery was lit up. Several times, figures appeared in a large open window. This caused a ripple of reactions in the crowd. "Is that him?" people called. "Is he there?" But then the figures stepped away from the window and out of view.

As the figures returned to the window, I was jostled by someone trying to slip by me, moving closer to the Chancellery. But then he stopped, blocked by the crowd.

"Hey!" I said. The man turned. At first, all I saw was a smile, which made me angrier.

"Rudi!" the man called to me.

It took a moment to realize that it was Hans.

"You're celebrating!"

I said, "I'm here—"

A roar from the crowd cut me off. People around us moved in unison toward the Chancellery.

"Yes, you're here!" Hans shouted. His grin—oh those bright white teeth—had always been confident and infectious. Now I saw another quality. Jubilation?

I tried again, "I'm here to be—" But someone moved between us, and another roar burst forth from the crowd.

"I'm here to be a witness," I said quietly, knowing no one could hear me. "Hoping this idiocy will end."

Over many heads, I saw several men in the large window, gazing out over the sea of delirious people. A figure I'd never seen in person before stood out.

It's you, I thought.

In what might have been a show of respect for his new position, instead of the Brown Shirt uniform that looked like a traditional Bavarian outfit with Lederhosen—kitsch to us northern Germans—he wore a suit. The drab outfit emphasized that if you took away the blunt, unnatural moustache, his shrieking speeches, and his icy stare, there was little distinctive about him. At rest, he was nobody. But sadly, he was rarely at rest.

This is your opportunity, I thought. *Be magnanimous in victory and bring the country together.*

As though he heard my thoughts, he glanced in my direction. His eyes flat, his face expressionless, he looked like a waiter who had just realized that his prize apron had been stolen.

Give me a sign that you will do better than many of us fear. Give us hope.

He turned to the others around him, one of whom was easily recognizable: Göring said something to Hitler, then laughed. Hitler nodded but did not laugh. Tall and round, Göring could have overwhelmed the new Chancellor, but he kept smiling in his strangely girlish way, hovering as though he weren't sure where to stand or what to do, maybe hug and kiss the crazy little man who was making all his dreams of glory and power come true?

But Hitler knew what to do. He stepped to the edge of the window. Göring and the others moved back.

Show me, please.

There was a long pause. Then the new Chancellor came to attention and, grim-faced, saluted the crowd.

In an instant, the people around me roared and raised their arms like Hitler: high and up in front of them, elbows locked, hands forming a flat plane, as if en masse they were about to slam their hands down and swat thousands of flies.

The roar turned into a chant.

Like any German, I was familiar with the simple phrase. On newsreels and on the radio, I had heard it bellowed by National Socialists. But I had never been in the middle of a group that was chanting it.

"Heil Hitler! Heil Hitler! Heil Hitler!"

I lost my balance as people pushed forward behind me. Standing up straight again, I looked for Hans. Near where he'd last been was a man who might be Hans. I couldn't tell for sure because his back was to me as he faced the Führer. The man was as tall as Hans and stood in his confident way. Like Hans and most men here, he wore a fedora.

This man, who I hoped was not Hans, was saluting, too.

"Heil Hitler! Heil Hitler! Heil Hitler!"

Anyone else receiving such adulation might have nodded or smiled or motioned for the crowd to stop. But this man continued to stare. Did he expect more than hysterical pandemonium?

This is wrong. You want blind obedience.

He stared again at the area where I stood.

Not all of us are sheep.

The chants came in waves, one after the other, the noise ringing in my ears.

You aren't Germany, I thought. *You can't have this beautiful country.*

I didn't want to stand out, so without raising my arm, I began to chant in the same rhythm and cadence as the others, in a whisper and with a twist.

"Höll' Hitler! Höll' Hitler! Höll' Hitler!"

With a snap, the new Chancellor lowered his arm and stepped back from the window. He turned and said a few words to several of the men around him, including Göring. Once more he looked out on the crowd, seeming to focus on the area where I stood. It made no sense, but I felt that somehow he sensed my determination to fight him.

Hell Hitler! Hell Hitler! Hell Hitler!

As the people around me continued to surge toward the Chancellery, I stood still, which made it feel as though I was moving backward. As soon as most of the crowd had passed by me, I made my way to the street.

Then I heard a rumbling from far down Wilhelmstrasse. For a moment, I thought a train was passing under the street. But this was not the usual noise made by the U2 line.

I saw flames before I saw the marchers. High above them, thousands of torches burned brightly in the darkness.

There were flags, too. The long narrow red banners had a white circle in the center containing a thin, black broken cross. Once again, I wondered why the eagle and iron cross and Reich flag weren't good enough.

The roar from the marching Brown Shirts slowly separated into distinct sounds. A band played, deep male voices sang—more enthusiastic than harmonious—and boots thumped rhythmically on the pavement.

The marchers sang:

> "*Die Fahne hoch!* The flag on high!...

Clear the streets for the brown battalions,
Clear the streets for the stormtrooper!
Millions are looking upon the swastika full of hope,
The day of freedom and bread dawns!
Millions are looking upon the swastika full of hope,
The day of freedom and bread dawns!"

Some in the crowd sang the Horst Wessel Song, too, almost as loudly as they had chanted minutes earlier.

Then the band broke into the national anthem, which stirred me, as it always did, even in this place, even with these people.

Hundreds of Brown Shirts went by. Then hundreds more. And hundreds after them, thousands altogether. The crowd continued to chant and salute and wave.

Usually Nazi marchers tried to win over bystanders, almost frantically, but not tonight. After a decade of few victories and pointless battles in the streets with Communists, today they had achieved a dream that seemed impossible as recently as six months ago. They would head the government. They seemed aware of their new power: their faces were aggressive, orgasmic.

Germany awake. Germany move forward.

By the flickering light of the torches, I observed the people around me. They stood on tiptoe, their faces bright and eager, almost innocent, so different from the usual stern Prussian visage one saw every day in Berlin. For the younger ones, who had missed everyone's cheerful confidence in a quick, easy victory at the beginning of the Great War, this was likely the first occasion they saw such full, open enthusiasm in public by anyone for anything.

As the marchers continued to stream by, for a moment the bands went quiet. A wind kicked up and the flames of thousands of torches burned even brighter, creating a sea of fire that undulated along Wilhelmstrasse. The flames reflected orange-red on the walls of the Chancellery and the

Kaiserhof and the other stately buildings farther down the way. Everything seemed aglow, as though a fiery carnage were beginning to devour the heart of the capital.

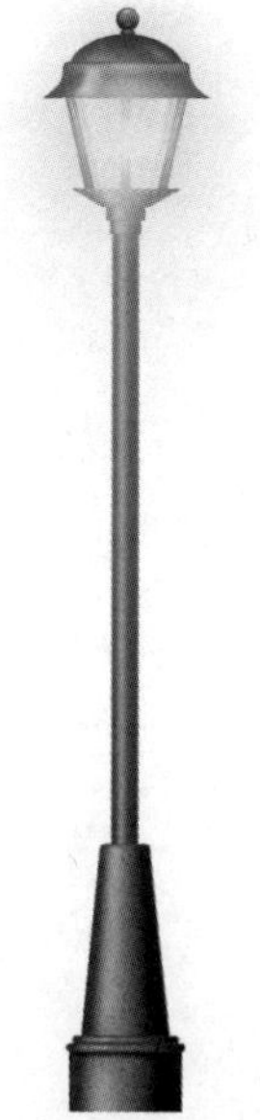

Chapter Fifteen

January 30, 1933

Away from the Government Quarter, it felt like any other late January weekday evening. A group leaving a movie theater split up hurriedly, more affected by the bitter cold than a change of government. Streetcars sped by, metal wheels singing on curves, motors whirring as they accelerated. A taxi or two passed. Still, I walked at least ten minutes before the singing and chanting and clomp of boots on cobblestones stopped echoing in my mind.

Couldn't "normal" life continue and somehow overwhelm the craziness?

I went to the Oasis Café, which was Sara and my favorite spot along the Kurfürstendamm, a boulevard catering to pleasures of all kinds—movie palaces, cabarets, coffee houses, clubs, strip bars, brothels, game parlors. In the café, people were jammed around the impossibly small round tables. A few shared their wrought-iron chairs. The usual jazz trio played at the far end of the room, but I couldn't hear a note. Maybe the crowd was trying to drown out the marchers elsewhere in the city. Maybe they didn't want to acknowledge that someone they despised—and who despised them—had become Chancellor.

Although everything had changed, nothing had changed. Some of the clientele dressed as members of the opposite sex or of no particular gender. Many had no legal sources of income. Most were younger people who spent their days asleep and their nights awake, worked in cabaret, theater, and film, and loved literature, art, and dance. If they were political at all, they tended to be Communist but not official comrades since the Party didn't value irony and coyness and flirtation. Everyone here, especially those who were foreigners or Jewish, was abhorred by the new government. I loved the openness and acceptance we all had for one another, including for me, a Foreign Ministry staffer, although who knew how long that would last.

"Monsieur Baumann!" Maurice, who owned the café with his wife, greeted me at the door. This French pair had created an ambience that reminded me of my favorite cafés in Paris, combining the best of France and Germany. I didn't know what I liked more: the variety of beer, wine, and liqueurs, or the Jugendstil dark wood paneling, or the huge mirrors, or the efficient, knowledgeable waiters who were masters of Berliner humor.

"Glad to see you're busy tonight!" I said.

"This is an anti-celebration. Unfortunately, that means your usual table is occupied."

"I can live with that kind of change."

I ordered Sara's favorite wine, a Riesling, a grape she loved almost as much as I loved her.

She liked to hold a glass of it by the stem with her thumb and forefinger and twirl it slightly, admiring the golden liquid that glowed in even the faintest light. "It's sweet or dry, depending on the weather, the soil, the vineyard, the part of the vineyard, the row in that part of the vineyard," she would say. "It throbs—with life and pleasure."

Leaning forward so our foreheads nearly touched, we would drink from our glasses. Then we would sit back and watch each other as the liquid slowly went down our throats, into our chests, warming and tingling as it spread.

When Sara arrived tonight, I imagined we would drink an extra glass or two and revel all the more in each other and our own little world. Maybe now I would be able to get a posting abroad and she would be happy to travel away from this country with me. For sure, we would go to my place later. After what had happened today, more than ever, we needed to share our love.

I spotted Sara before she saw me. I waved and watched her make her way to me across the room, dipping down, sliding around tables and people, cutting through the crowd like a dancer. I was smiling. I was beaming.

I forgot about the new government. I forgot about the scene in Wilhelmstrasse.

"Sara," I said happily.

Silently she sat down.

Gesturing toward the bottle on the table, I said, "Our Riesling!"

She didn't look at the bottle. She didn't look at me.

I asked what was wrong.

Taking a deep breath, she said, "This is the worst day of my life."

"You're not alone." Uttering phrases she had used about politics, I continued, "We can't let them ruin everything. We have to savor each moment of life. We have to love everyone like there's no tomorrow." I reached out for her hand.

With the detachment of a scientist studying a slide through a microscope, she looked at my hand, then my face, then my hand again and didn't reach for it.

"There was a fire at the new store," she whispered. "The work was almost done, and it was as beautiful as I'd dreamed."

"Oh no!"

"A pipe had to be re-welded—"

"I'm so sorry." I grabbed her hand.

"Our first new store since the crash. Gone in a moment." Her eyes welled up. "I don't know if we'll start over there. I don't know if we can start over at all."

"You put your heart and soul into it."

"And it happened the same day as—" Her hand waved toward the distance.

"Yes," I said solemnly.

She shook her head. "I almost didn't come this evening. I didn't want to disturb you."

"*Disturb me?*"

"Germans are happy that a decision has finally been made," she said. "I know it's not what you want, but at least things are settled. And you'll do well in the new world."

"You know how I feel!"

"Adapting will be easier than you think. But I *can't* adapt. They won't let me."

"They won't last."

"Only *real* Germans have the luxury of being able to feel that way."

"I won't let it happen!"

She watched at me with curiosity. "You won't let it happen?" Her voice was so soft I could barely hear. Then she giggled, but turned away from me as if sharing her amazement with someone else.

"It's not a joke," I said.

"What can you do to stop the gangsters? You're just one person."

"I'm serious," I said. "And I love you more than ever. I'll do everything I can to protect you."

"Germans can be so sentimental and sweet sometimes, but you're that way with me all the time." She sighed. "I wish we'd met in another era, another place."

I shook my head, but she looked beyond me in surprise and fear and concern.

It was Sol, Sara's brother. I had never seen him dress other than in the most impeccable manner, but now his tie was partly undone and the knot had shifted to the side. His shirttails weren't fully tucked into his pants.

"You have to come home," he said, almost shouting, standing over the table. "Mother says."

"Why?"

"She's afraid for your safety. Because—"

"What happened, Sol?" I asked.

He gazed at me as though he'd noticed me for the first time. Then he looked back at Sara.

"Max and I—" He stopped.

Ugh, I thought. *Max Weiss again.*

"Is Max okay?" Sara asked, her voice quavering.

I stood and motioned for Sol to sit in my chair. Without looking at me, he slumped into the seat I held out for him.

"Thank you," Sara mouthed at me.

In a flat voice, Sol told us that he and Max had walked this cold, dark evening from the university to the Traums' villa because they didn't want to be on a bus or the subway with crowds of celebrating Nazis. They thought they'd be safest in the open. They didn't know that tens of thousands of them were marching around the capital.

Not far from the university, a mass of Brown Shirts turned onto a street that Sol and Max were about to cross. The pair had to stop and they noticed that instead of trying to control the marchers or even chasing them as they used to, the police cleared the roadways and kept back the crowds on the sidewalks. Some even talked like old friends with the marchers.

As had happened with me, Sol and Max were soon surrounded by fanatics. They stood out because they didn't join in and were anxious. Worse, they didn't look at all like stereotypical Aryans.

One of a trio of ruddy faced men who were either drunk on victory or beer or both shouted at them. "Boys, show some respect!" The three were a few years older, short, stocky, with muscles instead of necks.

Sol and Max looked at each other and said nothing.

"There's a new order," the man said. "Time to celebrate!" He gave the Hitler salute, as though to teach them. "You can do it, boys."

"Unless they don't want to," another of the trio said ominously.

"Jews wouldn't want to, would they?"

Sol and Max still said nothing.

"Look at them," one of them shouted. "They *are* Yids!"

Max spoke up, saying quietly, "We're on our way home." He gestured to the crowds. "We can't get by."

"Ignoring the parade?" Suddenly the three of them were laughing, a humorless laugh, which Sol said was scarier than anything they had said until then.

"Your presence here is an insult," one of them said.

Perhaps because Max had spoken, the three pushed and shoved him first. Soon they were punching, too, and after Max fell to the sidewalk and put his hands up in front of his face, they kicked. Most of the blows were inaccurate, probably because they had been drinking, but a few connected.

Sol looked at the people in the crowd that surrounded them, silently pleading for help. They looked like typical Berliners, men in suits and long coats, wearing fedoras, women with long dresses and coats, respectable compared to the trio who were abusing Max. But when he caught people's eyes, they always looked away. They didn't encourage the bullies, but they didn't try to stop them either. Sol wondered if this could wind up like a Brown Shirt-Communist street brawl. *Could he and Max be killed?*

Then a band came by and the first bars of the national anthem rang out. Everyone, even the three bullies, stood still.

"Deutschland, Deutschland über alles, über alles in der Welt," the people around them sang, their voices blending in a deep, powerful baritone. *Germany, Germany above everything. Above everything in the world.*

Max was doubled over on the ground, holding his stomach. Sol said he tried to pretend as though he, too, were stirred by the "Song of the Germans." Then he noticed the three thugs had turned to the street, away from him and Max. In the middle of the first stanza, Sol reached down to Max.

"Wenn, es stets zu Schutz und Trutze Brüderlich zusammenhält," the crowd sang. *For protection and defense, always taking a brotherly stand together.*

Sol grabbed Max around the shoulders and pulled him up. Once Max stood, Sol pushed him through the crowd, away from the Brown Shirts. "Let's go, brother," he whispered. "Faster."

They walked quickly for several blocks and hailed a taxi, which they took to the Traums' house.

With a sickly smile, Sol said, "Saved by the anthem!"

Sara had been slowly shaking her head. Now, she said to me, "I have to be with my family, my people."

"Your people?" I said.

She waved at Sol. "Everything's changed."

"That's what the Nazis want you to think."

She stood. I stood, too, and tried to take her hands, but she turned to help Sol up.

"I'll come along and make sure you get home all right," I said.

"No," she whispered.

I had a horrible realization. "Tomorrow," I said. "I want to see you."

She said nothing.

"Sara?" I said. "Wednesday, then?"

Sol said, "We'll let you know." His snarl had returned.

They headed toward the door, and he put his arm around her, as if to guide her away from me.

"I'm not going to let it happen," I said loudly. "I promise."

Her head started to turn, as though she wanted to look back and say something, but in that instant, they went out the doors, into the night.

I walked ever slower along the Kurfürstendamm until I stood at a traffic light. I barely registered the little light man's change to green, then back to red and again to green, as people moved around me.

"Hey, Gramps," someone called out behind me.

A familiar voice was next to my ear, "Just as the country gets moving again, you come to a complete stop."

"I've had a shock," I said matter of factly. "And I seem to have no say in the matter."

"Always so negative, Rudi." Hans patted me on the back. "You have two choices: go forward with the forces of history, or continue unending decline and misery."

"We aren't talking about the same things."

"From now on, we'll all be talking about the same things!" He leaned in close to me and continued, "Come! You need a drink!"

This *Kneipe*, a square room with only a few tables and chairs, made our old Charlottenburg neighborhood *Kneipe* look like a luxury restaurant.

The patrons were all men and had the empty, glazed, happy look of the people I'd seen watching the torchlight parade. They made so many toasts we might as well have been in a beer hall in Munich.

Hans ordered beers, which the bartender carefully drew from the tap.

"Not all Germans are happy," I said.

"If they aren't happy, they aren't real Germans!"

"Ha. I remember last time we met you hit it off with someone who's suddenly not considered a real German."

"You're still seeing her? Now's the time to reconsider it."

"I've been trying to tell you—"

"I bet she's hard to give up. She's beautiful, challenging, smart as a whip, all at once. And, yes, I was taken by her, too."

"You don't understand."

"I understand that you're going to miss her, but I also understand that she and her family should get out of Germany. This isn't their country or culture."

"We all came from somewhere else. Aryans are from India, remember."

"But that's prehistoric."

"And Jews have contributed so much to Germany."

"Some say they've taken a lot from Germany."

"Sara's father fought in the Great War."

Hans set his mug on the table, then put a hand on my arm. "Sara and her family will be fine," he said. "In a year, they'll be living happily in England. Or even America." He laughed. "They're going places, too, just different places from where we're going."

I shook my head and asked, "Do *you* adore the new Chancellor?"

"Adore?" He frowned. "It's enough that big changes are coming. It may get messy, but that happens when the world is transformed." He lifted his mug and said, "Enjoy the ride!"

I let him clink my glass, then drank from it.

"The Foreign Ministry will become very important, Rudi," he went on. "Don't be your obstinate self. The new Germany needs help."

"Are you talking about yourself?"

"Most Party members are hacks. They need people with brains."

"You think we qualify?"

We both laughed, and even though I didn't like making a joke that somehow accepted National Socialism, I did like feeling on the same wavelength with Hans for a moment. *My old friend couldn't go along blindly with them, could he?*

Chapter Sixteen

March 23, 1933

The National Socialists moved faster than we thought possible. The most accurate news was communicated through Berliner humor:

As an excuse for crushing the Communists, the National Socialists would stage an attempt on the Führer's life and blame it on the Reds. We prayed that a Stormtrooper would make the attempt, since the Brown Shirts' competency in most things meant that the shooter might accomplish by mistake what he was supposed to fake.

On February 27, less than a month after the new Chancellor took office, the Reichstag was destroyed by fire. When the top Nazis arrived on the scene they were baffled, but then realized it was a gift. Of course! Communists had set the fire to signal the beginning of a national uprising!

The Red witch hunt burned faster than the Reichstag even though everyone wondered how the accused—a crazed former Red from the Netherlands—could start such an inferno by himself. A possible explanation lay in the striking fact that Göring's office as President of Prussia had a tunnel to the Reichstag large enough for a group of men to carry many cans of gasoline...

Another question: if the fire was the sign for an uprising, why didn't the Communists then do anything to overthrow the government? Many people in the country now wished the Reds would seize power, even though this was what they had feared so recently. Only the Communists were strong enough to halt the Nazis.

To make sure the greatest symbol of democracy in Germany wouldn't burn down again, Hindenburg signed the National Socialists' Reichstag Fire Decree, a law suspending all guarantees of personal freedom, freedom of the press, freedom to organize and assemble, personal privacy, and protections against home searches and confiscation of personal property. The Reichstag's famous motto, which in huge letters over its main entrance read Dem deutschen Volke—to the German people—might now be restyled Gegen das deutsche Volk—against the German people.

The National Socialists promised the Reichstag Fire Decree would be used sparingly, but overnight camps were set up near Berlin and Munich and quickly filled with Communists and other political opponents.

On March 5, Germany's last free elections for many years took place, and despite all that had happened, the Communist Party won almost five million votes, down just a million from the November 1932 elections. At the same time, the Social Democrats won seven million votes, up slightly. The National Socialists took only 44 percent of the vote, not the majority they wanted.

Naturally, this led the National Socialists to demand passage of an Enabling Act, an amendment to the Weimar Constitution that would allow, in an emergency and with a two-thirds vote in the Reichstag, for the Chancellor to rule by decree for up to four years. If the National Socialists banned the Communists and made an alliance with rightists and Catholic Center Party, they would have enough votes to make this a law. After all, their minority status in the Reichstag was an emergency—for them.

As he said when the Reichstag Fire Decree was being considered, the Chancellor promised to use the Enabling Act's absolute powers sparingly. This led much of the population to start sorting through their books, magazines, letters, and other possessions as well as nervously try to remember what they'd said to whom about such dangerous subjects as the rights of citizens and the importance of legal procedures.

We repeated again and again to ourselves that the National Socialists couldn't last. They would collapse in a week. They would collapse in a month. They would collapse by summer. They would collapse by the end of the year.

They would collapse because:

They couldn't run a country, and the economy would become even worse. Then the army and big industrialists and the nationalists would step in or workers and the unemployed would rise up against the new government.

They promised to ignore the Versailles Treaty so the Allied Powers would invade.

They were flouting German law and ideals, which would lead good people across the country to stand together and demand an end to the new government.

So I wished.

"Have you heard the latest?" Frau Riegler stood in my office doorway, glancing up and down the hallway.

I didn't like hearing this question—these days the news was never good. Still, I was grateful that Frau Riegler was so well-informed, which made me more informed than the average citizen. It was less than two months after what the National Socialists called the *Machtergreifung*, the seizure of power, an indication of how they felt about the Republic and democracy. Newspapers were disappearing or parroting National Socialist newspapers, making it ever harder to differentiate unbelievable rumors from the unbelievable truth.

"The Enabling Act has passed," Frau Riegler said.

I shook my head slowly.

We spoke in hushed voices. In the past two months, several people had moved into offices on our floor. The first things I noticed about them were the Party pins in their suitcoat lapels and an air of innocent eagerness.

They spoke excitedly about everything from our new leadership to serving only "real" German food in the canteen to organizing a variety of National Socialist groups in the Ministry. In a matter of days, their demeanor changed. Their jaws clenched and eyes narrowed when they realized that many of us didn't share all their views.

There were other changes: several Jewish staff members left the Ministry and a few colleagues began wearing Party pins. For the staff, *Gleichschaltung*—coordination or alignment, the Party's term for making everything in its image—was a sometimes subtle, sometimes blunt process, marked by many unhappy surprises.

"The Catholics sided with the National Socialists to give them the two-thirds vote," Frau Riegler said. "They believed the Chancellor's promise that rights will be respected even while Brown Shirts in the aisles threatened them during the vote, even though the Communist deputies have been arrested or gone underground."

"Odd that the Enabling Act's official name is the Law to Remedy the Distress of the People and the Reich," I said. "This law increases my distress."

"All credit to the Social Democrats," she continued. "They were the only ones who voted no. Otto Wels is a true German hero. 'You can take our freedom and our lives, but not our honor,' he said. His last speech in the Reichstag, I'm sure. And he's probably right about his freedom and life."

"Now Hindenburg will stop the insanity?"

"He's signing the bill this afternoon," Frau Riegler said. "In time for a new wave of roundups."

"I thought he'd see through the Chancellor's show of obedience in Potsdam," I said. "A public bow and handshake is enough to convince him that National Socialism is part of German tradition?"

We were silent a moment.

"The tragedy of this law is that now most Germans will consider the National Socialists legitimate," I said finally. "No matter what they do."

That evening, I sipped tea in the kitchen of my mother's apartment in my aunt and uncle's house. My mother had moved there after my father died, an arrangement that satisfied my mother and my aunt. The two had each other's company, and my mother's contribution to the rent was manageable for her and a bonus to her sister.

Mom sat in her favorite spot, at the kitchen table, wearing a dress that was similar to what she wore when I was growing up—something like a smock, a few bits of lace around the sleeves and neck, navy blue. She might have been a nurse or nun—certainly someone who had missed the fashion revolution of the '20s.

Almost immediately, my mother asked, "This new enabling law will stop anarchy and Communism, they say?"

Usually visiting my mother was like a less glamorous version of an evening at the Oasis Café. Every piece of furniture, every book and memento, every item that hung on the walls was familiar from the apartment I grew up in. I had a sense of being at home, although not fully at home, since the place was smaller and the old objects were in different spots. Sooner or later, however, I was reminded of the most disturbing change. Why wasn't my father coming through the front door and sitting in his favorite chair? Why couldn't I tell him a joke I'd heard today that I knew he'd appreciate?

My father often said that if rightists succeeded in destroying the Republic, they wouldn't bring back the monarchy, which for all its faults, had been stable and slowly evolving toward a constitutional democracy. Just one measure of progress: the Kaiser had made Jews full citizens. Instead, my father said, the rightists would set up a reactionary, militaristic state that would make the monarchy seem like the Paris Commune. I had laughed, telling him that once again, he was too gloomy, too German.

He waved at me saying, "Better a realist than a dreamer."

"Why not both?"

I was not used to speaking about such things with my mother and wished that she would interrupt me to tell me in detail about a new recipe she had tried or something else from her day-to-day life.

"The Enabling Act allows the Führer to do anything," I said. "He claims he'll be restrained, but he's been brutal so far."

"Friedrich explained everything so well." She sighed. "But now the Führer sounds so convincing. And he makes so many people happy."

"The National Socialists won't stop until they crush everyone who doesn't agree with them—all the other political parties, the churches, the working class. It's so hard to fight back against state violence."

"Your father believed in basic things like working hard, being thrifty, everyone treating everyone else decently and fairly." She nodded at me. "The way you are."

I laughed. "It's made me a revolutionary. Who'd have thought?"

"In some ways, I'm glad your father isn't alive," she said. "His heart would be broken."

"He's not the only one."

There was a knock at the door. A few months earlier, a knock would make me curious and eager to see who was there. Tonight, I frowned.

At least there was no pounding. No one demanded that the door be opened.

"Ah, Inge checks in on me every evening," my mother said.

I opened the door and saw my aunt along with one of my cousins from the country and a woman I didn't know.

"Rudi!" Tante Inge cried. "How is my favorite nephew?"

I smiled and kissed her on both cheeks. "Lovely to see you, Tante." I held the door open and let her and the others in.

I greeted my cousin Lotte, who introduced me to her friend Magda. I shook Magda's hand.

Lotte and Magda were from western Pomerania, where my parents had grown up. In the summers, as a child, I had loved visiting our relatives on the farm. I woke at dawn and ran and swam and explored. I also did many, many chores. Milking the cows, cleaning the stables, tilling the fields, digging up potatoes or picking vegetables. Simple and logical, the work satisfied me more than the chores I did at home. In the evenings, I collapsed into bed, sleeping deeply, feeling better rested than I ever had in my life. I also liked visiting during the winter holidays when we worked in the barn while it was still dark outside, went skating on the frozen lakes, and sat by the kitchen stove that burned day and night.

I didn't have the same warm feeling when my country relatives visited us in Berlin. They gawked at things like the fixtures in the bathroom and the gas oven in the kitchen. They stared at streetcars and wanted to ride in the front of the U-Bahn and S-Bahn to see the tracks as the train sped forward. Giggling with fear, they hesitated getting on elevators and escalators. At the movie theaters—their favorite novelty in Berlin—they laughed like hyenas.

My mother invited the three of them to have coffee with us. My mother sat with Tante Inge. Lotte and Magda sat on either side of me.

As the older women talked with each other, Lotte asked me about Berlin, which she was visiting for the first time as an adult. I tried to answer as best I could. Yes, the Museum Island perhaps had more art per square meter than any place in the world. Yes, Haus Vaterland on Potsdamer Platz was the shopping and entertainment and restaurant center of Berlin. It was also a technological wonder; via conveyors and dumb waiters, its central kitchen supplied each of the many restaurants.

I told them they should go to Haus Vaterland to see a movie or a show, shop, then eat. Each restaurant featured a different cuisine from around the country and around the world.

"Is there a Pomeranian restaurant?" Lotte asked. "That would make me feel at home."

"You should try food you've never had before," I said.

"Like what?" Lotte frowned. As ever, this young woman who sometimes had bossed me around on the farm was unsure of herself in the capital. She even looked provincial—from her unfashionably long hair to her sturdy shoes that needed a polishing. Her skin was rosier than so many Berliners', yet she gazed around timidly and her mouth never quite shut, which made her appear both naïve and suspicious. Worst of all, she had a stubby nose.

By contrast, Magda smiled at me and said, "What would you recommend?"

"Go for the most exotic—the Japanese or Indian restaurant."

"Wow," Lotte said. "Can German stomachs handle that?"

"What are those foods like?" Magda asked.

I told her that the Japanese liked to wrap raw fish in rice and sheets of seaweed, dip them in soy sauce and in a kind of mustard-like substance, and eat them with sticks of wood.

"Raw?" Lotte said with surprise.

"Raw," I answered.

Like Lotte, Magda had flush skin from being outdoors in the country, but unlike Lotte, she smiled and laughed easily, her dark blue eyes focusing on me.

I said that Indians liked rice, too, and cooked all kinds of vegetables, lamb, and fish—but no beef—all swimming in sauces with the most delectable spices like curry, most of which were unfamiliar to Germans. "Sometimes they burn like hell," I said. "But other times they're heavenly."

Magda laughed, saying, "Anything heavenly is worth a try."

"The Chinese also love rice," I continued. "They cook everything in tiny pieces in huge pots, and use many spices. Their food's delicious."

"Would you come along and show us what to order and how to eat it?" Magda smiled yet again at me.

Lotte nodded.

"And will you show us other interesting places in Berlin?" Magda said.

"This weekend?" I asked.

"Yes!" said Magda excitedly.

Before I answered, I thought a moment, realizing that in a matter of minutes talking with them, I had forgotten about what had happened earlier that day. It was as though a breeze had wafted through a long-closed, stuffy room.

Then I found out Magda lived on Rügen, a place that was nothing if not a spot for refreshing one's soul.

"What a beautiful island," I exclaimed. "I've been there and loved it."

She beamed at me. "It's more heavenly than any food."

I laughed. "Steady breezes off the Baltic, haunting pine groves, lagoons you have to circle way around if you want to go in a direct line, so close to the mainland but a land apart."

Magda nodded. "Remember, Berlin isn't the center of the world." Surely this was true, but also insulting. I couldn't help but smile at her.

When Lotte and Magda asked for department store recommendations, I didn't mention Klein, whose steep prices and international flair likely would make girls from the German countryside uncomfortable. Besides, Klein reminded me of Sara, whom I didn't want to remember at that moment. But, of course, then I remembered her, and remembered a comment Sara had made—of everyone in the family, her late grandfather would have been best suited to deal with what was happening to the country. "Despite all he built, he never believed it would last forever," she said. "He loved the saying, 'Fortune and glass, so easily broken.' "

I had the urge to tell Lotte and Magda about Sara's grandfather, to let them know about another very important side of Berlin.

Schmuel had died before I met the Traums, but Sara's grandmother, whom she called *Bubbe*, the person Sara seemed to care about more than anyone else, was often at dinner, lighting up when her husband was mentioned, adding to a story or disagreeing with a detail, in a thick

Yiddish accent using some words I didn't know. After I mentioned having trouble following her, Sara said, "It took her a long time to learn Polish. And now she should learn German, too?"

I heard the stories of Schmuel, who in several decades went from running his father's small clothing shop in Lublin catering to poor Jews to becoming one of the most brilliant and wealthy retailers in Germany. He also went from being nominally Jewish to becoming a Lutheran and changing his name officially to Otto, which no one in his family used.

The Klein flagship store on Leipziger Platz in the center of Berlin instantly became one of the world-class department stores in the capital, a rival of Wertheim and Kaufhaus and Hermann Tietz. The building was five stories tall, with more marble than many temples in Greece and Italy and a central atrium that rose to the top of the building. Besides clothing, Klein offered food, glassware, jewelry, even books. The store had a restaurant and tea room on the top floor, with views overlooking the heart of the capital, which quickly became a popular place for locals to have lunch and afternoon tea. There were elevators and the first escalator in Berlin. Swarms of employees were at the ready to offer help to every customer, no matter what their appearance. Soon Klein opened branches elsewhere in Berlin.

Schmuel's genius came in recognizing that in modern imperial Germany, which in just a few decades had become one of the most industrialized and wealthy nations of the world, a vital middle class had developed that included business people of all kinds, civil servants, artists and entertainers, and others. These people had much more money than their parents' generation and wanted to live more comfortably. With his commercial palace, Schmuel Klein, also known as Otto Klein, met those desires, and he and his family became fabulously wealthy.

Under the new regime, this kind of story already sounded dangerous. So instead of relating any of it, I told Lotte and Magda there was much I wanted to show them in Berlin and made plans to meet them on Sunday.

Chapter Seventeen

March 25, 1933

I walked along the Villa Colony Grunewald's quiet streets, past lakes and mansions partly hidden by walls, hedges, and trees, and stopped at the *Bismarckallee Brücke*, the Bismarck Boulevard Bridge, where the *Hubertussee*, Lake Hubertus, and the *Herthasee*, Lake Hertha, met. On either side of the span, the long, narrow lakes wended their ways into the distance, wide streams that barely moved. Tall trees bent over the banks, where lawns from the villas swept down to the waterside. The lakes were almost hidden—secret, quiet jewels in the great city.

From the distance, the bridge looked utilitarian, spanning the lakes and connecting both sides of the Bismarckallee. Even its name was utilitarian—*Bismarckallee Brücke*—implying that the bridge was merely a continuation of the road that honored the man responsible for building the Colony. But the bridge was a marvel, apparent only up close. Along the walkways on both sides of the span were four obelisks carved out of sandstone; four huge urns also carved out of sandstone and filled with flowers in warm weather; wrought-iron railings and gridwork; and most striking, four large sphinxes, one at each end of the two walkways on either side of the bridge.

The sphinxes had the torsos and heads of strong, young women with powerful lioness bodies. Each sat in regal pose, paws confidently resting in front of them, their long hair sweeping back from their faces and down the napes of their necks. They wore necklaces with brooches from which robes swept down, not covering their breasts. Seemingly oblivious to their near nudity, each sphinx gazed forward boldly at all who approached the bridge. Perhaps they would demand people answer a riddle before crossing. Then again, these stone sphinxes looked as coy as the Mona Lisa.

Each sphinx was slightly different from the others, and I preferred the one that gazed toward the south on the eastern side of the *Bismarckallee*. This sphinx had a Greek face updated for Central Europe in the late 19th Century: confident and intelligent and not threatening. When I saw this sphinx for the first time, I thought she resembled Sara.

Sara had neither agreed nor disagreed. "She's so, well, rigid," she had said.

"That happens when you're made out of stone."

"She's a *Gründerzeit* ideal—such a Kaiser-era cliché—a preview of today's racism. If she had color, her eyes would be blue and her hair blonde."

"But she isn't blue-eyed and blonde-haired. More important, you're a kind of a sphinx—quite mystifying at times!"

"Ha. I'm open and direct."

"In some ways. But in many ways not."

"Now *you're* talking in riddles!"

In the solarium at the Traums' villa, palms arced gracefully overhead, bamboo shoots grew like a miniature forest in planters, and birds of paradise beckoned. I settled on one of the wrought-iron chairs close to Sara, who sat cross-legged on a chaise longue.

We had seen each other only a few times since the end of January and the moments were like this—not at the Oasis, not at my place, but during the day at the Traums' with her family nearby. Sometimes I despaired, but I kept hoping we would return to the way we had been.

Outside, the sky was gray and the air on the other side of the panes of glass was cool. Sometimes during these late March days, the sun shone bright and warm gusts swept through seemingly from nowhere, reminding us that spring was coming, and, in nature at least, soon the world would be a most welcoming, enjoyable place. But this was not one of those days.

Rocking gently from side to side, her back to the windows, Sara cradled her cat, a black-and-white tuxedo, who hung loosely in her arms. She had named him Willi, after Kaiser Wilhelm II, because of several characteristics he had that were similar to those of our former majesty. For one, Willi's handlebar black "moustache" turned upward on both sides of his mouth like that of the last Hohenzollern ruler. Willi also had piercing but flat eyes that made him seem distant, regal, and condescending, also like his namesake. The little cat was impetuous and vain at times, and he, too, was not an intellectual giant. The resemblances ended there—the victims of little Willi's bellicose adventures were merely a handful of birds and rats in the shrubbery. He didn't help destroy a powerful, promising country that slowly, steadily had been becoming a modern democracy.

When I first met Sara, Willi was a large, legendary tomcat who had been a part of her life for as long as she could remember. Since winter had arrived, however, he had inexplicably lost weight and now had the physique of the average cat, looking healthier than I'd ever seen him.

As I sat down on the closest chair to her, I hesitated from doing what would have come so easily before, clutching her the way she clutched Willi. Or better yet, she could clutch me and I could imitate him—as she petted me, I could lie back and close my eyes in pleasure.

I could survive anything with her.

"Hi," I said.

Without looking at me, she said, "Willi is dying."

"Oh, Sara!"

"We heard from the vet.. His kidneys are failing. That's why he's lost weight."

"I'm so sorry," I said.

A moment before, Willi had looked like a sultan in a harem, enjoying the sensuous petting of a mistress. Now he seemed doomed and pathetic.

"We're giving him medicine and water injections every few days, but they just delay the inevitable," she said.

"Can't anything else be done?" I said softly. "I don't believe in giving up."

"You're very persistent."

"I miss you," I whispered.

"Please, Rudi," she said, then leaned back, away from me. "I want things to be light and easy."

With a little wonder and surprise, I said, "I should pretend nothing unusual is happening?" I gestured toward the windows. "Out there or between us?"

She looked at me for the first time since I'd come into the solarium and, holding Willi with one hand, she reached out to me with her free hand and said, "That was a lovely time."

As our fingers entwined, my heart pounded happily, and it felt as if rays of sunshine washed over me.

"Sara," I said. "We can rise above it all and be whatever we want."

"But everything's changed."

"My feelings will never change."

"Feelings *do* change—and sometimes mercilessly."

"I can't do anything about my feelings."

She regarded me with a mix of what looked like pity and fear. "Rudi, you're wonderful and such a German at the same time."

"I wish you would stop saying that kind of thing."

She looked down at Willi and said, "What's happening to him is like what's happening to all of us. It's getting worse and worse, and there's no way to stop it."

"He'll always be there for you. In your heart. In your memories. He'll live forever."

She glanced up at me, her eyes glassy with moisture.

I moved from the chair down to the floor and put my arms around her. Continuing to hold Willi, she leaned into me, her head resting on my shoulders. "Rudi," she whispered. "What am I going to do?"

"He loves you, and he'll always love you. Even when he's gone."

She whimpered a few words that I couldn't make out.

"You couldn't end this kind of love even if you wanted to," I said. "It's like air or water—it's all around you, now and forever."

"Be a dear and turn on that light, please," she said a few minutes later. She nodded toward the lamp on the table next to her, which was closer to her than to me.

I looked at her questioningly.

"It's the Sabbath," she said.

As I flicked on the switch at the base of the lamp, I said, "Oh, Saturday. Jewish Sabbath."

She nodded, saying that Orthodox Jews weren't allowed to use mechanical devices on the Sabbath. They couldn't ride in a car or train or bus. They couldn't turn on a radio. They couldn't turn on lights. "Taking a full break from the day-to-day world is a way of respecting God."

"Since when did you know anything about Orthodoxy?" I asked.

"I have to follow my own path, Rudi." She reached for my hand again, and I grasped it tightly. "I learned so much with you. About having a real relationship. About how lovely sex is." Giggling, she added, "That I can have orgasms over and over again."

I couldn't even think.

"I have so much to thank you for."

As I tried to take in her words, the door to the main part of the house opened behind us, and footsteps sounded on the stone floor. I sat back, expecting to see one of Sara's parents. But it was Max Weiss.

"Sorry to interrupt," he said, not sounding apologetic.

He sat on a chair on the other side of Sara and said to her, "You don't look very well, my darling."

She shook her head, saying, "It's Willi."

"What happened?" He glanced at me. "Has he been declared unreliable? Un-German?"

"His kidneys are failing," she said. "He's going to die."

"Won't we all," Max said softly. He knelt by Sara and rubbed the top of Willi's head. When Sara or I did such a thing, Willi's eyes closed and he relaxed even more. But after Max touched him, Willi slowly sat up, shook himself, then tumbled out of Sara's arms.

"Apparently he's had enough cuddling for now," Sara said.

I rubbed my fingers together, and Willi trotted over to me.

"So nice of you to come today," Sara said, holding Max's hand for a moment.

He glanced at me. "These days we have to stick together."

The door Max had come through opened again. It was Sara's brother, Sol, who called out, "There you are! And Rudi's here."

"Very sad news about Willi," I said. I hadn't seen Sol since the night of the *Machtergreifung* or Max well before that. They acted towards me as they always had.

Sol tilted his head to the side as I spoke, as if he couldn't hear me, or didn't want to hear me.

"Darling, do you need a drink?" Max said.

"God, yes," Sara said.

"Okay," Max said, "In this new era of Enabling Acts and proclamations, I decree drinks all around. Wine. Beer. An aperitif."

"I will happily follow this command," I said.

He smiled at this, which made him seem less irritating.

"Drinking's okay on the Sabbath?" I asked.

The three of them laughed loudly. "More than okay," Max said.

"Live a little," Sol said.

"And forget a lot," Max said.

When the maid came out, we stopped talking.

In the silence, we all watched her, and it seemed to take her a long time to set down the silver tray, pick up a glass and napkin from the tray one at a time, and then set those down on the tables around us. Would we all have been as mute as recently as last December or January?

"Care for anything else?" she asked softly.

Sol said no and thanked her. She gave a hint of a curtsy and left.

As the door to the solarium shut, we gestured toward each other with our glasses and then sipped from them. I avoided looking at Max, not wanting to remind him of our last toast.

"The staff look at us differently at the stores, too, as though a wall has gone up," Sol said. "Then again, we look at them differently."

"I bet some of them report on us." Max nodded at me. "Some of them even work for the new rulers."

"I work in the civil service," I said. "For the country. Not for the government."

"How long will that distinction last?"

"It's time for another exodus," Sol said. "We're used to them."

We all laughed, and I said, "It's relatively easy to emigrate."

"So long as we leave everything we own behind."

"We should take Rudi with us!" Sara said. "Why should he go through this hell, too?"

"It's not as much of a hell for him," Sol said.

"I want to stay and fight the thugs."

"And yet you help them," Max said.

I ignored this comment, saying, "I want to keep Germany's many good traditions, reform the bad aspects, and make this country the best nation on earth."

"There are good German traditions?" Max laughed.

"Of course," I said sharply.

"Good German, please explain." He laughed again.

Considering the audience, I didn't know why but I listed in some detail German thinkers and authors and composers and artists; German accomplishments in science and technology; the German love of nature.

"None of that matters," Sol said. "Such is our fate." Reminding me of his father, he added, "The National Socialists have a powerful death wish for themselves, even more than they have for Jews. These people will not die peacefully of old age in their beds."

"Believing that death and destruction are heroic is one of the German tragedies," I said.

"Aren't Jews one of the German tragedies, according to the Minister of Public Enlightenment and Propaganda?"

"Not a tragedy, but an *Unglück*," Sol said. *Misfortune, disaster.*

"What are the other German tragedies?" Max said.

I mentioned a subservience to authority, a love of rules and order, a glorification of the military, a yearning for predictability, and a need for systems to explain everything in the universe. "Mixed together and carried to an extreme, they're dangerous," I said.

"Ah, Rudi," Sara said. "What are you going to do?"

"I'll find something to do to destroy the government."

"Lead a one-man revolt?" Max said.

They all laughed.

I said firmly, "I will do something. Someday. I promise."

"Maybe you could get close to the Führer and—" Sol drew a finger across his throat.

"I don't know, Rudi," Sara said. "We should adopt you. You can be an honorary Jew and join the exodus."

Sol and Max began laughing. "I can't think of a worse time and place to become a Jew," Max said. "If it was ever a good time to become a Jew."

"Talk about a tragedy," Sol said.

Afterwards, I went to the Zoo station near the western end of the Tiergarten, where, if anything, there seemed to be more women and more men dressed as women milling about than there had been during what the new regime called the decadent Republic. Most of them were impossibly thin and even in the dark, their skin seemed to shine in a sickly but beguiling white.

"Sweetie," said one creature as she swept over to me, an arm gesturing as though she were a doorman waving me into a palace of delights. She wore impractically high heels and a long dress that glittered slightly. "Come to Lily."

I laughed.

"I'm entertaining you already?" she asked, hands on her hips. By the curves of her body in the gloomy streetlight, I could tell she was a woman for sure.

"You are." I looked at her body again. "But aren't you cold?"

She emphasized each word of her response: "I'm hot, baby, so very hot."

I laughed again, and she said, "And I'll warm you up fast, sweetie. I can do it all—from vanilla to crazy. Bells and whistles. Chains and whips. Whatever you desire."

I shrugged.

She said, "Why are you here, honey?"

"I thought there would be fewer of you since the change in government."

"The only change here is all the Party people who come around now, some are very high up. You'd think that would be good for business, but they don't like to pay." She mumbled, "For the greater glory…"

"They're treating you the way they treat the country."

She laughed.

"Do you want something warm to drink?" I asked.

"That's one way to put it."

It took a moment to understand.

"I'm offering coffee or tea," I said.

"Something to take into the alley or woods with us?"

"No, just come with me to a café. I know a good one nearby."

"I'm not doing it in a café."

I laughed.

"Baby, I *can* make you happy," she said. "Give me a chance."

"Here's your chance. In the café, hold my hand and tell me you love me and love me forever and that everything will be all right."

Slowly, she nodded and said, "That's not part of my normal repertoire, *Schatz*, but I can make it happen."

Chapter Eighteen

Spring and Summer 1933

Snow drops began poking up from the ground—the tiny, delicate white blossoms were the first sign that the cold of winter would soon end, that the sun, instead of flitting across the southern end of the sky, would climb higher above us each day, shining longer on places that had been in shadow for months.

It was decreed that police could ban any publication deemed a threat to public order. Brown Shirts officially became auxiliary policemen. Homosexuality and pornography were declared illegal.

Soon afterwards, crocuses began to unfold, sometimes knocking aside the last bits of snow; their tiny, brave blossoms surviving late winter storms and occasional freezing nights.

The hastily constructed concentration camp at Dachau received its first prisoners. The death penalty was applied retroactively for a range of crimes committed after January 30.

Forsythia appeared, its yellow the first bright color to light up the gray landscape. The ice on the rivers and lakes disappeared. Water flowed again, and the winds traced diamond-shaped patterns across the slick surfaces.

It was decreed that the legislatures of all German states be dissolved and replaced with delegates based on the last national election—with a plurality of National Socialists—and that all state governments be given the same extraordinary powers granted the Chancellor by the Enabling Act. In addition, the Berlin City Commissioner for Health decreed that

Jewish doctors could no longer work in the capital's charity services, and a one-day boycott of Jewish-owned shops was held, during which Brown Shirts stood outside targeted buildings holding large anti-Jewish signs.

Weeping willows came alive in glorious yellow-green, their delicate leaves trailing down from the heights to the ground.

It was decreed that the central government would appoint a governor to lead each state and that Jews and "politically unreliable" people such as Communists and homosexuals could no longer be part of the civil service. They were also fired from government and teaching jobs, although President Hindenburg forced the Führer to make an exception for Jewish veterans of the Great War and their relatives.

Daffodils sprouted in parks and gardens across the capital, their blossoms creating a sea of green and yellow on fields and hills.

It was decreed that Jews could no longer be admitted to the bar.

Tulips blossomed in brilliant colors.

It was decreed that a census would be taken to identify all Jews and other non-Aryans and that Adolf Hitler's upcoming birthday, April 20, would be a national holiday.

The soil in parks and gardens softened, and the grass lost its gray-brown hue, slowly taking on a green tinge that deepened every day. Trees were suddenly covered by thousands of little light green buds that quickly became leaves of a delicate, evanescent green.

It was decreed that the number of Jews in public schools and universities could at most constitute one and a half percent of all students. Also, the Geheime Staatspolizei, or Secret State Police, better known by its abbreviation, Gestapo, was created.

Hydrangeas bloomed.

It was decreed that all trade unions would be folded into the official National Socialist workers' organization, the German Labor Front.

Peonies blossomed, their luscious, full blooms carrying the most enchanting aroma.

It was decreed that a new unified national church would be formed. The National Socialist German Students' League burned "un-German books" in bonfires at universities across Germany. As part of the *Aktion*, 40,000 people in Opernplatz in Berlin heard Dr. Joseph Goebbels denounce most of the country's best writers and works as corrupt, rotten, threatening the reborn Germany.

Roses began to bloom, a sea of crimson, ranging from the palest pink and yellow and white to deep, blood reds.

It was decreed that the Horst Wessel Song, the Brown Shirts tune, would join the Deutschlandlied—"the Song of the Germans"—as the national anthem.

More roses bloomed, adding to the bright colors in the landscape.

It was decreed that a marriage loan be given to all German newlyweds so long as the wife did not have a job. The loan principal was reduced by 25 percent for each child born to the couple. Also, it was decreed that Jews were banned from youth, welfare, and gymnastic organizations and could not use athletic facilities.

Summer arrived and daylilies blossomed, their orange flowers opening for a single glorious day, then dropping, one after the other, for several weeks. Houses and apartment buildings seemed to come alive. Windows and doors opened and curtains drifted back and forth in the breeze. Chairs and tables appeared again on balconies and in gardens. Flowers filled window boxes.

It was decreed that all government employees had to give the Hitler salute and use "Heil Hitler!" as a greeting and closing in letters, and that all Germans with mental illnesses, handicaps, and disorders be sterilized. Also, in early summer it was decreed that all parties but the National Socialists be disbanded, even the parties that had allied with the National Socialists in the seizure of power. All offices and property of those parties were taken by the National Socialists. Members of the few parties that remained at this point, following the dismantling of the Communist Party and the Social Democratic Party, were advised to join the National Socialists or refrain from politics. At the same time, it was decreed that the citizenship of naturalized Jews and other "unreliable" immigrants be revoked.

Rhododendrons blossomed pink and purple and exuberantly.

It was decreed that the black-red-and-gold flag of the Weimar Republic would be replaced by the black-red-and-white flag of the monarchy. In addition, the National Socialist Party flag featuring a swastika in a white circle on a field of red became an official flag of the Reich.

That spring I was especially glad that the sun rose earlier and earlier and set later and later in the day. The pleasant weather made my runs easier. My body warmed up faster, and I didn't have to watch my footing on frozen ground.

I ran. Then I ran some more. After that, I ran again.

The sports center where I once trained was now operated by the National Socialist sports group. Young athletes wearing identical paramilitary uniforms regularly exercised together, chanting and singing tunes that were already too familiar. Somehow I knew the words to the Horst Wessel Song by heart, even though I had never tried to learn them.

Instead of running at the track, covering the same ground lap after lap after lap, I began to run in the parks, along roads, taking new paths each time, seeing things I had never seen before. I liked to take the S-Bahn out to the country and then run back to my apartment in the city.

One Sunday I traveled by train and bus to the royal park in Potsdam, then headed back, running along the Havel and several lakes to the Grunewald forest. I saw the Prussian kings' abodes and palaces, which were modest compared to the buildings their cousins had in France and England and had amusingly personal twists. Frederick the Great designed Sans Souci as a place to live simply. Frederick Wilhelm II built Lustschloss on the *Pfaueninsel*—the Peacock Island—as a summer place for him and his mistress, on the western side of the island so he could keep tabs on her when he was at his official residence, *Marmorpalais*—the Marble Palace.

The Grunewald forest was the best part of this route. It was wild and large even though the far end was where the Kurfürstendamm began, leading into the heart of Berlin. In the woods, I didn't have to pay much attention to the route I was taking. And here, all was fresh and pure—just earth and grass and trees and walkways. There were no government or Party offices festooned in banners with swastikas or the familiar ugly slogans. There were no Stars of David or threatening messages painted on the windows of stores. No Brown Shirts or S.S. strutted on the sidewalks. No radios were tuned loudly to state stations. No Party newspapers with blaring headlines were displayed at kiosks, and there were no *Litfass* columns with Party posters plastered all over them. Here I could pretend that nothing had changed.

That summer, Magda and I did all the things Sara and I had talked about doing in the warm weather. They were as lovely as I had imagined, just odd to do them without Sara. I had been so happy when Magda moved in with my aunt and mother. She found Berlin most attractive and wanted to live here. Oh, and get to know a certain gentleman better.

We went rowing on the Grossen Wannsee, where she held a parasol and I wore a straw boater hat for shade. While I manned the oars, in the center of the boat, facing backwards, she sat in the stern facing me. I loved it. Besides being able to watch her, I didn't need to keep looking over my shoulder. Instead, she could tell me what was ahead—and give me directions.

At the center of the lake, I maneuvered so we stayed away from the other rowboats and sailboats. Then I slipped the oars into the boat, and we drifted for a while.

The sun warmed us. At the same time, cool air from the fresh water swept upwards toward us. Our conversation rolled along like the current that slowly carried us to the southwest. We commented on the water, the boats and people we saw, and the brilliant blue sky. I told her about how my father had taught me to row. We talked about what we would do the next day. We discussed where we would go to dinner once we were back on shore. I rowed against the current upstream to the far end of the lake where the River Havel entered, and then let us drift again. If the sun didn't go down, we might have remained on the lake for days, separated from the Reich for a small, delightful eternity.

I liked her amusing observations about life and about me. "The whole time you row, you go backwards," she said.

"I see so clearly where I've come from."

"But what about the future? You have no idea where you're going."

"Maybe I don't want to see ahead. On the other hand, maybe I'm confident about the future and sure there will be much happiness." With that, I learned forward and kissed her.

We also went for long walks in the Tiergarten and the Grunewald forest. We discovered fields and woods we didn't know existed. Under the trees, we ate lunch. Some Sundays we made an *Ausflug*, an outing, outside the city wandering for hours, then catching a train or S-Bahn back to Berlin.

We dined on terraces at restaurants and cafés as the sun went down, listening to the sounds of the city that grew more distinct the darker the sky became: cars, trucks, streetcars, a crying baby, a whistle blowing. Sometimes we sat in silence taking this all in and I would reach across the table, enjoying the feel of her hand all the more as twilight made everything slowly fade.

I had seen Sara only once that summer. As Magda and I were leaving the Oasis Café, Sara had come in, holding Hans's arm. I must have looked like one of my country bumpkin relatives: mouth open, staring. Sara had been laughing, looking up at Hans, and she stopped smiling when she saw me.

Hans had gazed back and forth at Magda and me, and later told me that if I had a sister, she would have been Magda because we looked that much alike and because we seemed so comfortable together.

I don't know what I thought. In the past months, I had been in shock about so many things. This was maybe the most difficult.

"What's the matter?" Magda had asked as we walked away from the Oasis. "You look like someone punched you in the gut."

I had wanted to explain. But what to say other than something that would offend her: *I saw the love of my life with my best friend.*

Magda was reasonable and understanding. What a welcome relief during a horrible time. I didn't want things with her to fall apart, too.

"Something I ate?" I had said, hugging her. "I'm having trouble digesting things."

PART II
1938, 1941

Chapter Nineteen

November 9, 1938

Thud…thud…thud.

The sounds came in quick succession. Not in the hallway or next door. Maybe from the street.

Thud…thud…thud. Again.

It was late in the evening, when many people were already asleep. Despite all that had happened in the country, most Berliners continued to be civil and wouldn't cause a ruckus like this.

Thud…thud…thud.

Magda sat up in her lounge chair, where she had been skimming through a magazine, one of her favorite activities when the children were asleep. Tonight she had done this in her usual way, turning the pages slowly. As she finished a page, she moved it up and over to the left, then let it loose so the sheet of paper floated in the air a moment before falling into place and revealing the next pair of pages. Shutting the magazine, she whispered, "What is that?"

I folded the Swiss newspaper I had been reading and put it under a book on the coffee table.

So many things large and small had changed in the five years we'd been out of the country—stationed at the embassy in Ankara, happily at a remove from what was happening in the Fatherland—and now, back in Berlin, we were adapting. Even though Turkey wasn't far, when we visited home, we usually went to the country to see her family. The farms had the same magic and quiet I'd always loved. By contrast, the changes in Berlin grated, from the obvious national Nazi horrors, right down to the undiplomatic Joachim von Ribbentrop being Foreign Minister, to the addition of a runic S.S. key on new Ministry typewriters.

Maybe a Nazi work battalion was starting a night project on our street. Maybe a Brown Shirt band was warming up nearby by drumming on pieces of wood because their real drums had been sacrificed to national rearmament.

There was a *thud* louder than any before it. Right after that came a crash—and a scream. From inside the building.

I went to the front door of our apartment, opening it slowly. Neighbors also peered from behind their doors. Several of us went to the central staircase and looked down over the railing. We saw other tenants on the floor below peering downward over their railings.

From far below came more crashes and the sound of glass shattering. Again, someone screamed.

"What on earth?" someone a floor above said.

"Call the police!" another person said.

Herr Bestler lived next to our apartment and had spoken several times with me since our arrival, about the weather and about stamp collecting—he specialized in stamps issued by countries that no longer existed, with the Russian and Ottoman Empires among his favorites. He said, "I tried calling the police just now, but all circuits are busy, according to the operator." He shook his head. "Bizarre at this time of night."

"We must do something!" Frau Zimmer cried. A small, fearless woman in her 60s, she had introduced herself to us the day we moved in, asked many questions, and from that moment on had looked after us—and especially the children—as though we were her own family.

I took her hand, the way I did when she told me about her son who worked in the Saarland, near the French and Belgian borders, where the growing tensions made everyone fear a French invasion. "Stay, Frau

Zimmer," I said. "I'll see about it."

She squeezed my hand back.

From our apartment door, Magda said sternly, "Be careful, Rudi! Be careful!"

As I began to go downstairs, two men appeared from the floor above. We descended together, taking each step as though a mine might explode.

On the floor below, the sounds of crashing and smashing were louder, and again there was a scream. Another man from this floor joined us.

When we came into the lobby, we saw that the main door of one of the ground-floor apartments was gone—lying in pieces by the doorway. As if guarding the debris, several boys in Hitler Youth outfits that hung loosely over their young bodies stood uneasily at attention. Without the uniforms, they would have looked like any awkward kid on the block.

Through the doorway, we saw smashed glass and china, broken furniture.

"The Wellenbachs," the man next to me whispered. I remembered a couple in their early 30s who had a daughter the same age as my own. The two had played together several times in the weeks since we had moved in.

Although the boys held a couple of pieces of lumber, I went over to them and said loudly, "What's going on here?"

Their expressions were both haughty and fearful. The tallest of the group swallowed as he said, "Official action. Go back to your—."

"Who's in charge here?" I yelled.

The boy paused, as if considering something, then pointed silently into the apartment, where, at that instant, something else crashed to the floor.

I walked into the apartment, telling the other men who had come downstairs to keep the boys in check.

No one was in the living room, where tables and shelves and cupboards had been upended. Lamps, books, paintings, and photographs were strewn around the floor. Shards of glass and porcelain ground under my feet.

In the next room, something large, maybe a bureau or table, crashed. A figure in uniform, his back to me, reached high on a bookcase and began to pull it away from the wall.

I looked into the other rooms and found one of the Wellenbach children—a teenaged daughter—cowering in a corner. She opened her mouth as though to scream but then recognized me. I stepped over to her and said quietly, "I'm from upstairs, remember? I'm not with them."

She nodded.

"What's your name?" I asked.

"Miriam," she said.

"Miriam, where are your parents? Is anyone else in your family here?"

"They went out with my sister." She paused. "They were supposed to be back by now."

"Where'd they go?"

"I promised not to say."

I nodded and told her to go upstairs to our apartment.

Gesturing to the other rooms, she said, "He told me not to leave."

"Miriam, I'm telling you it's okay to leave. Go upstairs now."

She nodded but didn't move. I waved for her to go. Still, she didn't move. Now I frowned deeply and waved a second time. She darted out of the room.

I made sure the boys outside didn't stop her, then followed the sound of destruction into a bedroom where the man in uniform continued to topple furniture. I said loudly, "What's going on here?"

The man stood up straight and turned to face me. He wore a Brown Shirt uniform that emphasized his muscular body. He had a strange moustache, larger than the Führer's, closer to Himmler's, and just as unnatural as theirs. Didn't the Nazis know how to shave? Couldn't they afford barbers?

"What's going on?" I repeated, louder.

"Official business," he said coolly, looking me up and down. I saw he was gripping a long piece of pipe.

"What kind of official business?"

"Who are you?" This sounded more like a statement than a question.

"I'm with the Foreign Ministry."

He might have assumed that I was a fellow member of the movement and that I deserved respect because I was a state official. Then again, he might have known that many people in the ministries were holdovers from the old era and not enthusiastic Nazis.

"The residents of this apartment are Jews," he said, as if that explained everything.

"Why are you doing this?" I asked.

"They're the eternal enemy of Germans, our *Unglück*."

"We're notifying the police."

He laughed. "We are the police."

"You've done enough damage."

He stared at me grimly, and his fist tightened around the pipe. I took a step backward. But then he looked around and laughed again. "Perhaps you're right," he said. "We have done enough damage."

With that, he stepped over an upturned nightstand and came in my direction. I tensed, ready to absorb a blow. But again he laughed, which made me let down my guard. As he swept past, his free arm swiped me. It was somewhere between a punch and a solid pat on the shoulder and made me lose my balance and fall toward the wall. I got up and followed him out of the apartment.

"We're done here," he said to the boys, ignoring me, ignoring the men who had come down with me and who stood in front of the stairs, blocking it from the goons.

Chapter Twenty

December 4, 1941

It was a cool, brisk night, and I was near where I wanted to be. But the last few blocks were proving difficult.

Berliners fastidiously followed the strict wartime blackout rules, partly because the rules were carefully enforced but also because each of us benefited if the occasional British bombers couldn't see the outline of Berlin from thousands of meters above.

Earlier, as I'd walked along the streets, I had been able to see the shapes of buildings and parked trucks and telephone poles in the darkness. But when I turned into the alley that wound between several factories, I stepped into utter blackness.

From the darkness, I would spread enlightenment.

I had planned to come early, but when two people approached from the other direction, I ducked into an alcove of an apartment building. The pair stopped at a nearby door. I listened as a young man tried to convince a young woman to spend the night with him. He did most of the talking, speaking quickly, changing tones, one moment his voice full of confidence, almost casual, as if her answer didn't matter. A minute later, he became insistent, and when that didn't work, he sounded desperate. I couldn't make out what she was whispering, and I wanted to yell for her to decide one way or the other, even if just to go upstairs and keep negotiating.

If you love each other, you should embrace each other in all possible ways.

"I love you so much," he said to her, as if picking up on my sentiments. "I want to be with you all the time. I never want to let you go." After a silence that might have come from a long kiss, they slipped inside the building.

So I was late.

In the blackness, I bumped into someone. I quietly apologized. A familiar voice mumbled his own apology. I remembered the last words he had spoken the evening before, "To save all, we must risk all."

"Herr Zimmermann?" I whispered.

"Herr Baumann." His voice was soft and congested, as though he hadn't expected to speak and needed to clear his throat. *"Guten Abend."*

"Guten Abend."

No matter what the circumstances, we Germans couldn't ignore social niceties.

"All here?"

"You're the last," he said.

The longer I couldn't see, the more I heard. Someone shifted his weight from one leg to another. Another person took a deep breath. Although I knew all of them, I was glad I couldn't make them out—if I couldn't see anyone, no one else could see me. Besides hiding Berlin from the bombers, the blackout hid us from the police.

We were in a commercial area of the Wedding district, just north of Charlottenburg, where my family and I lived. Most of us still thought of Wedding as "Red" Wedding despite the Nazi effort to eradicate all traces of Communist influence. One example of the limits of that effort was this printing plant, where Nazi pamphlets and books and the Berlin and regional editions of the Nazi rags *Der Stürmer*, *Der Angriff*, and *Völkische Beobachter* were printed. A pink strain lingered among the printers, whose skills made them indispensable. I wondered how many "special" jobs like ours were done on the presses.

I heard a slight bang.

"My friend is ready," Herr Zimmermann said.

I nodded and remembered that no one could see this gesture.

I was ready to take the material and leave this place. All of us together, about to be in possession of deeply incriminating materials, was so risky. Even during the day, a gathering of this size was dangerous. In the middle of the night, we might as well be waving British or Soviet flags.

Was I safer working alone?

In a different era, I wouldn't have spent so much time with this group. Then again, in a different era, the group wouldn't even have formed, since our personal interests and points of view were so different.

We regularly sat together at a table in a secluded corner of our favorite *Kneipe*. We felt it would be good to have some kind of activity that explained our gatherings, so we always had a game of chess going. To our surprise, we were drawn into what had been intended as a pretext. We debated and tested opening gambits and strategies and focused on how to attack a seemingly impervious opponent, chipping away, waiting him out, wearing him down, all so we could win in the end, even if most of our pieces had been wiped off the board. We pondered a difficult question: was a suicidal assault worth it?

My favorite of the group was Herr Zimmermann, a metal worker who frequently quoted Goethe, Schiller, Heine, and other great German writers even though now it was seditious to quote Heine. Often Herr Zimmermann uttered pessimistic pronouncements: "Sleep is good, death is better, but, of course, the best thing would be to have never been born at all."

"Against stupidity the very gods themselves contend in vain."

"I have never seen an ass who talked like a human being, but I have met many human beings who talked like asses." A few of us brayed at this.

My favorite words that Herr Zimmermann uttered: "He who has done his best for his own time has lived for all times."

A door slowly opened. In the dark, still night, the metallic creaking sounded like a freight train rolling through.

Beyond the open door was a faint glow of light far inside the building, blocked partly by large hulking machinery. A man in the shadows whose name I didn't know and didn't want to know gave small bundles to Herr Zimmermann, who handed one to each of us. I whispered my thanks. He said nothing in response. As I put the papers into my briefcase and made sure several copies of yesterday's *Völkische Beobachter* were on top, the door closed, much more quietly than when it opened. A bolt slid into place.

Herr Zimmermann intoned, "Education leads to political change."

Without speaking, we left in different directions, and I was happy when the sounds of their footsteps faded.

In the weeks and months before, I had thought again and again about this moment. Until now, the most I'd been able to do against the regime was supply blank documents to several people I trusted who were able to use them to help Jews and others leave the country. Of course, that saved lives, but I wanted to do more, and taking to the streets, even in this shadowy way, seemed a big step.

Chapter Twenty-One

November 9, 1938

Miriam huddled on the sofa in our apartment, wrapped in a blanket and sipping tea. Her eyes were red and watery, and she kept glancing at the front door, as though someone might burst in. At least, she had stopped shaking.

Magda, Frau Zimmer, and I stayed in the foyer, whispering among ourselves.

I told them the men had gone.

"Animals," Magda said. "They're awful."

"Where's the rest of her family?"

"Her parents are at a friend's house," Frau Zimmer whispered to me. "They should be safe. The friends aren't Jewish."

"Pardon?" I said.

"Several people I've talked with on the phone say Jewish homes are being attacked across the city," she explained. "Stores and businesses and synagogues, too."

I shook my head.

Frau Zimmer had tried calling the Wellenbachs but hadn't gotten through, so I decided to go tell them to wait to return and reassure them that Miriam was safe. And, I wanted to see if Frau Zimmer had misunderstood. *Could what she described really be happening?*

The smoke outside was acrid from burned metal and glass and other things that weren't meant to be set aflame.

Down the street and around the corner, several Brown Shirts stood in front of a shoe store that now resembled the Wellenbach apartment. The windows were gone, shelving and counters were in heaps on the floor, and papers, boxes, and shoes were scattered on the sidewalk.

I went over to two city policemen, who stood apart from the Brown Shirts. "What happened?" I asked. "Who did this?"

The pair looked at the Brown Shirts, then back at me. The older of the two, who had a beefy build but whose voice had a gentle, reasonable quality, said, "These are Jewish businesses."

"*They* did it?" I asked, without looking at or pointing at the other men in uniform.

"Not exactly," the younger officer said. He was more my age, a trim man with eager eyes. "They ordered other Brown Shirts to do it. Some were in civilian clothes. They did their business in a hurry."

"Why is this group staying?"

"To be sure no one cleans up."

A particularly strong gust of smoke wafted down the street. "What's burning?" I asked.

"Synagogues."

"They're on fire?" I said, astounded. "In the city?"

"The fire department is present."

"How are they putting out so many blazes at the same time?"

"They aren't. They're just making sure the fires don't spread." He paused. "The synagogues next to German buildings haven't been torched. They're just trashed, like these shops."

I didn't speak. I couldn't speak.

I wondered about Sara and the Traum family and the Klein stores.

Along the way to the address Frau Zimmer had given me, I came across several more wrecked shops. There were Brown Shirts on guard as well as many civilians, who stood around in small groups even though it was after midnight on a weekday.

"What happened here?" I asked one group, pointing to another destroyed storefront.

"It was Mandelbaum's bakery," one man said.

"The family's Jewish," another man added.

Ever the German, I noticed several loaves of bread trampled on the sidewalk and thought, *What a waste.*

Herr Wellenbach pulled on his chin as though the goatee he didn't have needed constant readjustment. Frau Wellenbach folded her hands as if in prayer.

I told them their older daughter was with us and could stay for as long as necessary. I told them they should be prepared for a shock when they returned to their apartment.

Frau Wellenbach asked if Miriam had been physically hurt. I said the men ignored her.

"Good for that at least," Herr Wellenbach said.

"Did they take the china and glassware?" Frau Wellenbach asked.

"No."

"Thank God. They're precious."

"Instead of taking them, they smashed them all."

She gasped and seemed more disturbed by the fate of her china and glassware than by anything else I had said.

As I was putting my overcoat on by the front door, Herr Wellenbach stood with Herr Schmidt and me. "The most ironic thing about all this is that we had finally decided to emigrate," he said. "In fact, that's why we were here." He glanced at Herr Schmidt. "Now we'll move as fast as possible!"

"A smart decision," I said.

"But there's so much paperwork," he said. "You'd think they want us to stay."

"It's another kind of torture," I said. "But mainly it's to get as much of your wealth as possible."

"To fund the upcoming war," Herr Schmidt said in a saddened voice.

"Wasn't it enough to take Austria and the Sudetenland?" Herr Wellenbach asked, looking at me.

I said, "In a word, no."

"I'm ashamed to be German," Herr Schmidt said.

Chapter Twenty-Two

December 4, 1941

We had hoped for a night like this—the sky was cloudless, and the moon, a sliver in the southern sky, gave us enough light to make out the shapes of buildings and the edges of sidewalks and read large signs, but it was still dark enough to allow us to hide in shadows.

Several times, I had to slow down. Who wouldn't wonder about a man nearly running down a dark street at three in the morning?

Finally, I was doing something tangible against the regime.

In my neighborhood, I left two leaflets on the shelf above the mailboxes in the first apartment building. At the café next door, where fresh rolls and other baked goods cooled in the doorway, I put a leaflet in each of the bags. I stuffed a leaflet under the doors of a bookstore, a shoe repair shop, a butcher, and a dry cleaner. I had practiced my movements at home: as though I were leaning over to pick something up, I dropped the leaflets in one quick, sweeping motion. And I walked purposefully, as though I was the owner of the buildings I entered or the shops I walked up to.

I didn't leave more than a handful of leaflets in any one spot. I assumed that many people would recoil after reading the first lines. They would either destroy the leaflet or obediently turn it over to the police, as the population had been instructed to do many times *under the most severe penalties*.

An engine sounded somewhere behind me. It was louder than a car. A police wagon? A Gestapo patrol van? I slowed slightly and squeezed the briefcase shut with one hand, anticipating a screech of brakes and shouts for me to stop.

But the vehicle kept moving, in a low gear that made the engine sound desperate to go faster. I glanced over as casually as I could and saw a dark van with a name and other information on the side—but not the word "Polizei." Like all vehicles at night, it moved slowly because of the blackout. The headlights were almost entirely covered by dark tape, except for a slit, its size precisely mandated by authorities, and they cast two meager cones of brightness into the gloom, barely worth the effort.

I paused until the van went by. Then I put sheets under the doorways of several stores and left a few in the lobby of an apartment building.

A door opened nearby. Again I stopped, listening and peering ahead into the darkness. I faintly heard a lock turn, and then there was silence again. I waited, but when I heard nothing, I began moving again, distributing more leaflets.

I crossed a street, then heard footsteps behind me. The person was walking slowly.

A policeman on the beat?

I stopped.

The sound of the footsteps stopped.

Should I set down the briefcase, which had nothing to identify me, and run?

If he caught up with me, I could say I had been out late with friends. Yet why did I appear cold sober?

I could say I had attended to a family emergency. After all, my mother was often sick.

Of course, I could tell him I was with the Foreign Ministry and had been working late. There was no end of things to do in wartime.

I breathed deeply. I was ready. I turned around, nearly losing my balance on a broken part of the sidewalk. My briefcase fell.

The man wore a long coat. *This was worse than I imagined. Gestapo?*

I heard a very soft clattering, as if someone were tapping fingernails on metal.

Was it some kind of weapon?

A small, dark animal with very short legs was walking next to the man. It was a dachshund, almost invisible in the darkness. Now I saw the leash, too, just barely.

"Ach," I said quickly, kneeling and picking up my briefcase. "I was trying not to fall in this infernal dark."

"Of course, my *Schatz* couldn't wait until dawn." The other man laughed.

"One good thing about all this," I said. "I've never seen so many stars in Berlin."

After a pause, he sighed. "A silver lining."

The dog ran along, its leash tugging the man.

As he stepped away, I said, "*Guten Abend.*"

"*Guten Abend,*" he called back to me.

Once I couldn't hear him, I went into several apartment building lobbies and left more leaflets. I began to feel more optimistic. Among the many dozens or hundreds of sheets I'd distributed, a few would be picked up by curious people. It would take only a minute or two to read, maybe in a quiet, private place. Then, for the first time in years, they might have a flash of insight and look at the world differently from the way they had been forced to since 1933.

If a handful of people could suddenly think clearly again, then maybe they could mention their doubts and criticisms to others and slowly more people could stand up for what they knew was right.

Chapter Twenty-Three

November 10, 1938

Near dawn, I left the apartment where Herr and Frau Wellenbach were staying. The crowds and Brown Shirts were gone, but broken glass and smashed wood and trashed food and goods remained in front of the Jewish shops. The cleaning would likely be ordered later in the day, since, like all Germans, even Nazis believed in neatness and tidiness in public places. Yet no cleaning could scrub away the great stain of this *Aktion*, which was more violent and public than any of the brutal things the Nazis had done so far. For a moment, I bowed my head to the people whose stores and homes and temples had been attacked.

Forgive us if you can. Someday.

I promise to do more, to do something.

At the office, I heard the official version of what had happened. Outraged by the death in Paris of Ernst vom Rath, a German diplomat shot by Herschel Grynszpan, a Polish Jew, citizens across the Reich had spontaneously reacted by striking at the heart of the Jewish conspiracy. This meant Jewish homes and businesses.

"Spontaneously, as the reports emphasized, they all went out at the same time in the middle of the night, knowing exactly which houses and apartments had Jewish residents," Frau Riegler said.

"That's quite a feat," I responded.

We spoke in whispers in my office with the door closed.

"Lists were spontaneously handed out."

"After spontaneous orders were given."

"They've arrested a lot of people, mostly men," Frau Riegler said. "They're being put in the detention camps, which keep growing."

"Spontaneously."

I learned that Grynszpan, only 17 years old, had been born in Germany and was protesting the treatment of his family, who were among many thousands of Polish Jews in Germany that Germany had decided to send back to Poland. Beginning in late October, they had been rounded up by the S.S. and taken to the border. But Poland had passed a law in March disowning citizens who had lived abroad continuously for more than five years—mostly these were Polish Jews in Germany. As a result, many of these Polish citizens, not wanted by Germany or Poland, had been herded, with only a few belongings and no money, food, or shelter, into a kind of no-man's-land in a few villages on the border. Poland had begrudgingly accepted several thousand of the expelled Jews, but a majority remained.

The official German press said that on November 7, Grynszpan, wanting to strike at Germany, had shot the highest-ranking German diplomat he could find at the Paris Embassy. In a horrible twist, Ministry gossip said that vom Rath was being investigated by the Gestapo because of critical comments about anti-Jewish policy.

Just before he was to give his annual November 9 talk in Munich celebrating the failed "Beer Hall Putsch" of 1923, the Führer learned that vom Rath had died of his wounds. The Führer decided not to speak. In his place, Goebbels discussed vom Rath's death, saying that the Führer had decided that "demonstrations should not be prepared or organized by the party, but insofar as they erupt spontaneously, they are not to be hampered."

Immediately calls went out to Gestapo, Brown Shirts, and S.S. units around the country, so quickly that many members barely had time to change into civilian clothes for the *Aktion*. Police and fire units were also notified that they were not to interfere except to protect "German lives and property."

Some people thought that what had happened during the night would have happened sooner or later, but it happened this way for a sickeningly personal and petty reason.

For years, Dr. Goebbels, the Minister of Public Enlightenment and Propaganda, had been taking advantage of his position as head of the sprawling Babelsberg film studio, behaving like a Weimar-era movie mogul with a casting couch and harem of young actresses. Frau Goebbels knew of his behavior and overlooked it, until her husband lost his heart to a Czech actress and made it clear to his wife, in front of others, that he didn't care what she thought.

Frau Goebbels, a favorite of the Führer and at times his unofficial First Lady, appealed to the person for whom her husband felt the most affection. Soon, the Führer, who was proper in his personal life but usually tolerated his lieutenants' crass appetites, told Dr. Goebbels to give up his girlfriends and devote himself to his National Socialist wife and children. Of course, Dr. Goebbels agreed.

Although he did not blame or resent the Führer for the order, the lack of this outlet apparently crushed the last flickers of humanity and empathy in him. The main focus of his fury was an old target: Jews.

In the aftermath of the *Aktion*, the top National Socialists, perhaps caught off-guard by Dr. Goebbels's new viciousness, began trying to outdo each other in punishing Jews. Göring was pleased with himself even more than usual because of his idea of having the victims of the carnage pay for damages. A fine of a billion Reichsmarks was being levied collectively on the Jewish community. The state was also seizing all insurance money that would have been paid to Jewish business and home owners because of the damage.

"It's the turning point, all around," Frau Riegler said. "The violence shows they don't care what the world thinks."

"The only possible advantage is that so many people here are repulsed. Maybe, finally, the regime has gone too far," I said.

"Don't count on it. Goebbels and the rest will learn to be less open. And if the people still object, there'll be more roundups, more trials, more executions. War's coming. And war against the Jews."

Chapter Twenty-Four

December 4, 1941

In one lobby, I was pulling several leaflets out of my briefcase when the main door leading to the stairs opened. I froze. There had been no sound from the other side.

I saw a figure wearing a long coat and clutching something in both arms. A baby?

I swept the leaflets into my briefcase as if that was what I had planned to do. Then I looked up at the person's face.

I was surprised again.

He looked older and thinner. His coat was worn and had lost its shape; it might still be the one he had worn when I saw him regularly.

"Max?"

"Rudi," he said. His unblinking stare was familiar.

Was I risking everything to help him?

"You stayed in Germany?" I said. "They're starting to round up people and ship them East."

"Do you think I don't know?" He used the tone I so disliked. "I wanted to escape, of course. But not everyone close to me did. So I couldn't leave."

"Your family?" I hoped he hadn't stayed for Sara—if she was even still here.

He smirked as if he knew exactly what I feared.

"Family, sure," he said. "We all debated emigrating for years, but when it became worse than anyone ever imagined, it was too late."

"You live here?" I asked.

He nodded and looked at my briefcase. "Why are you here?"

I remembered that generally he was in a more dangerous position than I and said, "I was just leaving."

"So soon?"

But as I turned, I asked, "You didn't follow Sara?" and wished immediately that I hadn't mentioned her.

"Ha!" He shook his head. "What *are* you doing here?"

I don't know why, but I revealed myself to him, of all people. I pulled a leaflet from the briefcase and held it out.

Grabbing it, he read quickly, then asked, "Why are you doing this?"

This mystified me. "Because," I said. "I want to do something."

"You believe this will change anything?"

"I hope people will start thinking again and start fighting the regime."

"Isn't it a bit late for that?" He glared. "Are *you* still working for them?"

I wanted to respond, but I felt as flustered and defensive as I had when I'd last seen him.

"I'm going," I said.

"Me, too."

He lowered the bag in his arms, and I saw a yellow six-pointed star patch sewn onto his coat.

"You shouldn't go out with that, with the curfew," I said.

"I'm going to the Jewish Home down the street," he said. "They need food."

He pulled the bag up again so that the star was covered.

I offered to accompany him.

"I can handle it," he said. Then he surprised me again, saying, "But thank you."

He was gone before I could say anything more.

Lingering in the doorway, I read for the first time this night what we had written:

Dear Reader:

Thinking freely should be a simple, basic matter, but in our times, it's dangerous. It's so dangerous that one can die because of it. Who would have thought that such a thing would come to pass?

In our new world, black is white and white is black. Up is down and down is up. Consider various ways of looking at what is happening:

We are fulfilling our destiny by expanding in all directions. Or so we hear. Could it be more accurate to say we're at war on multiple fronts against multiple enemies in a conflict we cannot win?

They say the government represents the will of the Führer who represents the will of the German people. Could it be more accurate to say the government tells us all what to do and think and ignores the will of the people?

Dear reader, please think about these questions and please think freely. Thinking freely is the first step toward the respectful, sane national life that we once knew and again will. Our country, our future, our civilization all depend on it.

From,

Friends

Note: For your own safety and well-being, if you don't agree with these views, we advise you to take this to the nearest police station. If you do agree, do the same, but know that many think as you do.

When I came home, Magda hugged me at the door, clearly relieved. "You're okay. You're okay." Then she kissed me several times. "You shouldn't make me so worried."

I smiled and kissed her back. "It was fine, but all quite useless, I'm afraid. I'm thinking of giving this up. Odds are high that one of the group might be an agent provocateur or an informant. Or the type who would say the wrong thing at the wrong time and be overheard. Or someone being interrogated about something else could tell everything about what we were doing."

"Isn't there something else you can do?"

"I can keep giving blank passport and visa forms to the few people I trust," I said. "But the forgers have to be really good, and it's so hard to get out of the country now even with proper documents."

I shrugged and quoted Goethe: "Thinking is easy, acting is difficult."

"Kill that man?"

"I wish it were possible," I said. "I want to communicate with people who matter—Germans and our 'enemies.' But the war's sealed us in."

"You'll figure something out. And when you do, seize the opportunity."

I shrugged. "Maybe I should just go into internal exile. It's very popular. We can create a lovely cocoon together. With the children."

She seemed a bit surprised. Maybe I did want a conventional life. Maybe more than Magda did. When we married, I was surprised by the happiness I felt as we stood in front of the pastor—me in a suit, she in a long dress, its brilliant white contrasting with her lightly tanned face and her golden hair.

She and I fit well together in so many ways. She was slightly shorter than I and tucked nicely into my arm. Her gait was the same as mine so that even when we walked together, we could keep holding on to one another. Like me but unlike many Berliners, she went to bed early and rose early. She even preferred to sleep on the right side of the bed, and I was used to the left. I enjoyed holding her in bed; she enjoyed being held. She was as sweet and tender and thoughtful making love with me as she was sitting outdoors at a café on the Ku'damm.

"Can we just pretend none of this is happening?" I asked.

"Ha. Maybe you could do that for a few minutes." She paused. "But not much longer than that!"

Chapter Twenty-Five

November 1938

Right after *Kristallnacht*, I saw a ghost.

Late in the evening, as I left the Foreign Ministry to go to Potsdamer Platz to catch the S-Bahn home, an older man stepped from the side of the building.

He seemed to be coming toward me.

In the near darkness, I could see a beard and thin face. His coat hung loosely.

He called my name, and I recognized his voice. Unlike his appearance, in five years, his voice still had a lush, confiding, intimate tone.

"Herr Baumann!" he said, raising his hat and putting out a hand, adding unnecessarily, "Dr. Viktor Traum."

I took his hand, saying, "Dr. Traum. Of course."

Later, he told me that after learning I was back in Berlin after my posting in Turkey, he had stood outside the building several days in the late afternoon and early evening. He wasn't sure that my office was in the main Ministry building or how late I would stay or whether I was even present. But he was patient, and he had a lot of free time.

When Dr. Traum spoke, it reminded me of the evenings he sat at the head of his elaborate dining room table and led fascinating discussions of culture and politics and all that was good and beautiful in life. As he had in those days, when I spoke, he gazed at me, never interrupting, waiting until after I finished before he said anything, even though he had to have been under deep stress.

Was he so enlightened that he could rise above such things or, even after five years of nastiness and vitriol, was he in denial?

He had sought me out not for the reasons I expected. He didn't ask for help getting out of the country or dealing with the regime. What he wanted was something I never would have guessed. He wanted to ask questions and hear my responses, as though the ailing, crazed country were a patient, and I represented it. At first, I was reticent. Why should I share dangerous, deeply personal considerations with him? And why did he care what I thought?

But he persisted, and suddenly, it seemed, all the conflicts I had about what a person could do and should do that I had rarely discussed with anyone poured out. I spoke on and on, to the point where I kept thinking I was boring him. I said this to Dr. Traum, but he brushed my suggestion aside, saying "Please, continue. This is fascinating."

I had never experienced psychoanalysis, but I imagined that this happened with all of Dr. Traum's patients.

It started simply. The day after he approached me, we met at what had once been the Oasis Café. Now called the Heimat Café—the Homeland Café—the place was German-owned, and though an obligatory portrait of the Führer hung in a place of honor, the spirit of the Oasis lingered. Few customers wore Party pins or armbands. The radio was always off, sparing us state broadcasting. Like many other foreigners, Maurice and Marie had shown their opinion of the new Germany by leaving the country. Still, the former Oasis remained an oasis.

Dr. Traum and I sat in a far corner from the bar and spoke quietly.

"The mobs ruined one of the stores," Dr. Traum said. "But the main store is fine, so we're in better shape than most people." He paused.

"Most Jews."

Dr. Traum was remarkably calm. He must have been born this way, and his profession only strengthened this quality. Emotions and thoughts, whether his own or others', were something to observe and analyze. On his deathbed, he would likely forget to say goodbye because he was too busy watching how others behaved even as he monitored the sensation of dying.

"The irony about the destroyed store is that we're in the process of being Aryanized." After uttering one of the many ugly words that had entered the nation's vocabulary after January 1933, he smiled faintly. "So, they wound up trashing their own property."

I shook my head.

He sipped slowly from a large cup of coffee, saying, "Worse, this brew is weak."

"Blame unofficial, unacknowledged rationing."

"Yet another affront."

"No one came and trashed the house?" I asked.

"Luckily, no." He smiled. "So my personal enterprise was overlooked. The couch and chair remain intact."

Unable to teach or practice publicly, Dr. Traum used a room in the villa to meet patients, most of whom were Jewish, although a few "Aryans" continued to see him, too, despite the ban on Jews practicing medicine on non-Jews. These people were friends, he was prepared to say, who were stopping by for a chat, which wasn't that far from the truth, even if they lay on a couch facing away from him for exactly 50 minutes.

The Jews and the non-Jews talked about very different things, he said. The non-Jews, regardless of profession, grumbled about working long hours, having to contribute sizable parts of their paychecks to hazy National Socialist charities, earning barely enough for expenses, coping with food shortages, and wondering what to do about a criminal regime.

Most Jewish patients had, of course, deep existential concerns. They also had no money, so Dr. Traum didn't charge them. "I need the routine, and they need the therapy," he said. "By definition, all healthy Jews have gone abroad."

"Why haven't you left, too?" I asked.

He smiled sadly. "Of course, we should all leave, but the older generation doesn't want to start all over again, and many of them are too frail to travel. Sweetly, the younger ones don't want to leave behind their *bubbes* and *zaydes*."

The family was also waiting for the sale of the business to be completed, to a long-time employee who was not Jewish and whom the family trusted. Herr Kurz had been at the store at least since the Great War and would do anything, he said, to make things easier for the Klein family in this "difficult" situation. But some of the family had noted that he seemed quite comfortable around the government representatives overseeing the "Aryanization."

"Funny about the Aryans—" Dr. Traum paused as he said this word. "They're excellent administrators. Give them good ideas and they can put them into effect. But on their own, they aren't very creative."

He stopped and gazed at me, as though he had forgotten that he was speaking with someone whom he had just called uncreative.

"Go on," I said, waving my hand.

Herr Kurz would make regular payments over ten years, with the last in late 1948. "God knows where any of us will be then," Dr. Traum said. "The price is ridiculous, but at least we're getting something. They could have just seized the company like so many others."

"Having a brand that tens of thousands of Berliners know has protected you somewhat," I said.

"They're working on destroying that brand," he said. The Nazi "part owners" had decided to rename Klein the General Retailing Company.

I laughed out loud.

"There's nothing so criminal as a lack of imagination," Dr. Traum said.

I laughed again but feared he didn't recognize fully the dangers of his situation. "They are criminals in much worse ways. You should leave as soon as possible," I said. "Tonight, even."

"Do you want us to go away?" He stared at me, those gray eyes seeming to sparkle and look through me. "Or do you want Sara to go away?"

I waved at him, then around us in the café. I didn't like being reminded of Sara. "I'm concerned about everyone," I said. "As for Sara, she was long ago. I'm married now."

"You mentioned that."

"I have children, too."

"The idea of family scared Sara."

The idea of family with me *scared Sara?*

"Nothing personal." His voice trailed off in a quiet, suggestive way. "She has never liked feeling constrained. Especially constrained by others' love for her. I know that as much as anyone."

I looked at him blankly.

"What's the matter?" he asked softly. "You're suddenly as white as a sheet."

Chapter Twenty-Six

December 1941

I burned the leaflets I hadn't distributed, slept for an hour, and then went to work. Later that morning, a tall, trim man about my age whom I had never seen before appeared in my office doorway and brusquely told me to follow him. His language was precise, and he looked comfortable doing whatever he was doing, but also perhaps bored, as if this matter meant little to him. He was exactly the sort of confident, intelligent, well-trained person I had long feared would come for me.

Had one of my compatriots been arrested? Had I been seen and identified?

I had always wondered what I would do at this moment. I had considered the speculation a waste of my time and energy, but now I realized it had been good preparation. I was surprised at how clearly I could think.

It was only the one man, and it was happening in the office, not at home in the middle of the night. So at least it wouldn't be messy. Magda and the children wouldn't witness it.

I wanted to call her, but that was impossible with the man standing here. Besides, Magda was taking the children to school, then checking shops again to see if anything new had come in. I knew she wasn't at home. "One second," I said and quickly wrote a sentence on a sheet of paper that was on top of the desk.

"Now," the man said and took a step forward.

"Yes, yes," I answered as I put down my pen.

Taken for questioning? was the message.

Saying nothing, the man walked to the side and a step ahead of me. This was odd. I had expected several men would accompany me and maybe hold my arms. At least one of them would walk behind me.

At the first corner in the hallway, I imagined running in the other direction. As we went up the main staircase, I thought of running down. And, once more, when we came to a crossroads in the hallways, I considered bolting. I was well-conditioned and I could get away from him quickly. But each time running crossed my mind, I remembered that this man obviously knew who I was, which made Magda and the children vulnerable. Besides, I had nowhere to hide that I could be sure of. And so it was better to follow this man who arrogantly but accurately assumed I wouldn't flee.

We climbed stairs, which also struck me as odd—most interrogations took place in the basements of special buildings. We should be going outside to a van or police car. Then again, I might be cashiered in style—I might be dressed down by one of the deputy ministers or even by von Ribbentrop himself.

We went along a corridor where many of the highest functionaries in the Ministry had offices, one floor below the Foreign Minister's lavish suite of rooms.

The man stopped abruptly and took several steps into the office of someone I had worked with in the consulate in Turkey. In a period when so many colleagues became exceedingly concerned with ideological purity, Martin Becker was refreshing. He worked hard, rarely talked politics, and seemed to have no personal life. We didn't become exactly friendly, and yet I liked him, or at least I liked working with him. He had moved up through the ranks quickly, in large part because, besides his hard work, he had joined the Party.

"I've brought him," my escort said to a secretary whose table was the main piece of furniture in the outer office. The woman thanked him, and without acknowledging me, he left.

The woman stood and motioned for me to come to the inner office.

Inside, Herr Becker sat behind stacks of folders and binders at a desk with trestles that looked as though they could support a house. A round man, he had a full head of hair that wasn't severely cropped in Nazi style. He repeated many jokes, the best of Berliner humor, sparing no group or person, even our "leaders."

One recent joke I particularly liked, "A man says to his friend, 'After the war, I'm going to tour Germany by bicycle.' The friend responds, 'And what will you do after lunch?' "

Still, if one of the "reliable" members of the Ministry appeared, Herr Becker's right arm would jump up and he would give the greeting I abhorred.

As he looked up from the desk, for a second he seemed baffled, as though not sure of who I was or why I was there. Then he smiled, and said, "Herr Baumann! Sit down. Sit down."

For him, this was effusive friendliness and made me fear he was being sarcastic before lowering the boom. While I loved his rebellious sense of humor, I didn't want to be the subject of his jokes. Was he stretching this out for his own entertainment?

"Can't stay out of trouble, can you?" He shook his head.

Again, I was glad to have considered what I would do at a moment like this. I smiled and said, "You know me."

"Indeed, I do."

He opened a folder and tapped a piece of paper I couldn't see. He paused, maybe reading it, then looked up and asked, "Why, my friend? Why?"

CHAPTER TWENTY-SEVEN

November 11, 1938

I asked Dr. Traum directly about Sara and immediately regretted it.

Wasn't it easier to stay oblivious?

"You know her," he answered. "Just when you think you understand her and all is settled, she darts away, figuratively and literally."

I nodded.

"That is to say, she quietly goes out."

I became intensely aware of the noise in the café, the clouds through the windows, my heart pounding.

I breathed in deeply several times to calm myself. I asked after Sol and Max, but I regretted asking a question.

"With the expulsion of all Jewish students and professors, Sol and Max are studying informally with many brilliant teachers," Dr. Traum continued. "With no bureaucracy and a sudden realization of what's most important in life, they're learning more than they ever would at university."

I started to ask Dr. Traum if he also taught informally. Instead, I said, "Is she going out with Max?"

Couldn't I silence myself?

He smiled. "She goes out to her grandmother's as her full-time aide. At least she has a soft spot for *someone*."

He laughed, and I was very happy to laugh with him.

Nothing personal, indeed.

"Maybe life isn't perfect, but things have worked out well for you," Dr. Traum said.

I shook my head. "Sara said that more than once."

"Was she right?"

"Neither of you are right," I snapped.

"You sound angry, and anger is dangerous unless properly and constructively channeled." Then he stared at me, his face expressionless.

"Yes, I have a family I love. My career has gone well. I'm relatively comfortable. So I can survive, and the idea of internal exile is appealing. I can live in a bubble and come out when this hell ends, which will happen sooner than people think."

I wondered what had happened to my unofficial therapist, the wonderful listener who seemed to relish every thought and feeling I uttered.

When he began talking again, his voice and tone changed completely. It was as though he were speaking to someone at the next table. And oddly he began to talk about his military service during the Great War.

In his sector in France near the front, he said, casualties were especially high, and because of his coolness under fire, excellent judgment, the ability to lead—and the death of many superiors—he was promoted several times within months. Senior officers also noticed his organizational skills and that he read and wrote excellent German. He soon became aide-de-camp for the divisional command, a promotion out of the trenches that increased his life expectancy many times over.

Conditions were still primitive, but compared to soldiers in the trenches, he lived like the Kaiser. And he learned much more about army plans and positions than the average soldier and civilian, he continued. It was information that would have been of great value to the French and British—and the Americans, too, after they joined the Allies.

"What are you saying?" I said, interrupting him. "You thought of giving information to the enemy?"

"I realized how valuable the information was," he said. "I was a patriot, even though that sounds naïve now. And even if I wanted to do anything, I was deep behind German lines. My point is that I realized the value of what I knew." He paused. "You must see sensitive materials at the Ministry."

I laughed. "Important matters like a diplomat who took off for a week with his mistress or the entertainment budget of an embassy that went out of whack after the arrival of a boozehound. I know less than the average idiot reading *Der Stürmer.*"

He smiled. "But you've mentioned interesting things, such as the situation in Soviet Russia."

"Ha," I said. "With the purges, the revolution is devouring itself, destroying the state administration, the armaments industry, and the officer corps. Under Stalin, the country has lost its ideals."

"You see? You know more than most people," he said. "Maybe it doesn't seem that way to you, but as this country moves toward war, what you see and hear will be very valuable."

"Perhaps."

"You're near the center of power," he continued.

"But I won't join the Party, which limits my career."

"Maybe you should join the Party."

I started. "Wow. I—I can't imagine."

"If it means you have even more access and opportunity."

"I'm good at my job, which is very helpful." I paused. "But it is true that I'm helping the Nazis."

"Yes, but that's a small price to pay for the kind of access you have—or could have. Wait and when the time is right, take advantage of that gift."

"Most people would consider that treason."

"We're all taught to obey authority," he said. "But obedience can be abused in terrible ways. And this government knows how to do that!"

"I'll take this as another opportunity to urge you to leave."

He whispered, "A group in Zürich is working to get the entire family out.

They're well connected. We just have to convince the older generation. As I've mentioned, Sara's grandmother is quite frail and loves her home. Her late husband communicates with her, she says. He tells her he wants her to stay with him in Berlin."

"Really?"

"He doesn't want her to go east."

"Switzerland is south."

He shrugged, then said sharply, "Rudi, when you're presented with opportunities you can't imagine now, I hope you'll have the courage to take them, the courage to risk everything."

I considered what he said, then stared back at him. "You're right. Someday I may need to risk everything."

He nodded, then put his hand out. We shook on this—my second promise to a member of the Traum family.

Chapter Twenty-Eight

December 1941

Like so many of us, Herr Becker looked tired. His hair had gone gray at the temples. I had seen him only sporadically over the last several years, yet I felt as comfortable as I had when we had worked together daily.

"It was a matter of principle," I said.

He shook his head. "Such a waste."

"I'm proud of my actions."

"You would be."

I relaxed a little. The thing was in the open, and we could move on to the ugly matter of what happened now. Interrogations? Torture? Garroting? Meat hooks?

"You couldn't just go along like the rest of us?" He sounded more disappointed than angry or shocked.

I nodded, not understanding why he didn't get to the point, which was so unlike him.

"It's caused a lot of problems for me," he said.

"For you?" I was confused. *How did my anti-Nazi leaflets affect him?*

He slapped the paper and closed the file. "Most of the people they tried to foist on me are fools or lazy, or both." He waved a hand toward the hallway. "But I need someone who works hard. Someone with a brain. Someone who doesn't think his job is spouting the usual drivel." He lowered his voice. "I need you."

"Huh?" I had no idea what he was talking about.

"Despite everything, I have faith in your work and your analytical and critical abilities. And you come highly recommended, which just confirms what I remember about you."

"Recommended by whom?"

"By Frau Riegler. And just about everyone you've ever worked for."

I nodded.

"And Herr Thiele."

Hans!

He didn't seem to notice my momentary shock. He went on, "As the Foreign Ministry military liaison, I need an assistant who can shift through reams of papers every day, recognizing the important ones, prioritizing them, making sure I see what I should see."

I nodded again.

"But you still haven't joined the damned Party."

I prepared to recite the reasons I usually gave: *I didn't want to do something just because it was popular. Wasn't Party membership supposed to be an honor? If someone like me were a member, where was the distinction? The Party required disciplined believers, not people with questions.*

"I don't understand it," he said. "What would it matter if you signed a piece of paper?"

"Many people say that, but for me it matters."

He tapped his fingers on the table, and I wondered if he might yet bring up the leaflets or something else dangerous. I tried to compose myself and not do anything further to irritate him.

"I admit my own membership means very little," he went on. "It just helps a lot if you want to get ahead."

I shrugged, and he said, "You're incorrigible."

We looked at each other silently. Then he laughed a kind of jolly laugh you didn't hear much those days in Berlin and said, "When can you start?"

"Right now."

“That’s perfect. Let’s celebrate.”

In a moment, he filled two glasses with schnaps and we clinked glasses, quickly, casually, then talked about the job.

If this promotion had occurred a few days earlier, I might have celebrated in the Heimat Café with my friends. Likely we would have talked about distributing leaflets again and planned to distribute more of them. But I had worried about mixing with them and now I had all the more reason to avoid them.

I might also have celebrated by going out with Magda except that a dinner in a restaurant would involve choosing from the few items available and spending much of the meal remembering what it was like to peruse a real menu.

Magda acknowledged that our household budget would increase, which would seem to help her in the constant battle to find some fresh, healthy food for our children. But she mentioned what everyone noticed but was afraid to speak about publicly. Already the flood of cheese and butter and ham and beef and wine from France and the Low Countries after we had “absorbed” them had been exhausted. And now that manufacturing was dedicated solely to the war, farmers across the Reich, who had labor shortages, were beginning to refuse to accept cash, no matter what the amount, for their produce. After all, what was the use of money if there wasn’t much of anything to buy with it?

“This is getting ridiculous,” Magda said. “The army’s almost in Moscow and Leningrad and sweeping across northern Africa. We control the continent. And we have a barter economy?”

“Imagine if we were losing.”

“When will this war be over?”

“It’s going to get worse now that the Führer has declared war on the United States, which wasn’t necessary. After all, the Americans declared war only on Japan. Now we’re fighting the U.S., Britain, and the Soviet Union. We’ll lose, but at least the war will end, even if takes a few years.”

How quickly things had changed. The war seemed easy when it began in 1939. Even I couldn't help but smile when nine months later I read the headline: "France surrenders!" For one brief moment, all the shame and pain from the Great War dissipated. The elation of average Germans was overwhelming. Now they were convinced that the Führer's wild risks always paid off.

Then, after conquering most of Europe, came the most audacious move yet: the invasion of the Soviet Union. Surely, I thought, going against Stalin without first dealing with Britain would lead to disaster—a two-front war. And the Soviet lands were so vast. How could Germany take control of another continent?

But in the first weeks, millions of Red Army soldiers were surrounded and taken prisoner. Entire armies disappeared, as the Wehrmacht drove deep into the Ukraine and White Russia. It seemed like yet another lightning campaign that made each vanquished army, even the vaunted French Army, look inept.

This year, however, the war changed into a grueling affair, with one of the coldest winters halting all offensives, and for the first time, resulting in some retreats. Perhaps because of this, there was a new viciousness in the war. In the East, this included regular executions of Communist Party functionaries, villages torched at random, and Jews of all ages—entire families, entire communities—shot en masse.

Germans learned of the anti-Jewish *Aktionen* in bits and pieces—in strangely worded reports, in letters and even pictures from soldiers at the front, in comments from men home on leave. The Nazis argued that in a war of this scale, self-preservation dictated that all enemies be dealt with in the most severe manner. After all, they said, civilization hung in the balance. It was a final, necessary reckoning with the forces that wanted to destroy us and our way of life.

Thus, we had to engage in total destruction—of them and, in other ways, of ourselves.

Chapter Twenty-Nine

November 1938

Judging from where Hans had asked me to meet him and what he was drinking, his tastes had risen along with his role in the New Germany. We were in the Hotel Adlon, the bastion of imperial elegance in the center of the capital, a hotel built just after the turn of the century with the help of Kaiser Wilhelm II. It was a marvel in many ways. Behind the Adlon's stately façade was a sophisticated, modern facility, with features that were revolutionary when it was built. It had its own power plant and hot-and-cold running water. There was a grand restaurant, an elegant café, a library, ballrooms, a lush interior garden, and the famous lobby.

Lorenz Adlon, founder of this temple to modernity, remained devoted to the monarchy, not making the transition to a republic as well as his own hotel did. Adlon believed so much in the Kaiser that, even after Wilhelm II's abdication and flight to Holland, Adlon continued to respect the rule that only the emperor could travel through the middle arch of the nearby Brandenburg Gate. In 1918, Adlon was hit by a car while crossing in front of the middle arch. He survived, yet stubbornly refused to learn his lesson and, three years later, he was hit again in the same location and died.

We all respect the past in different ways.

Today, half the men at the tables in the Adlon's Palm Court were in uniform—the black of the S.S. stood out. Members of the foreign press and diplomats and likely a few spies lived here, so it didn't feel quite as much like a Nazi canteen as the Kaiserhof, several blocks down Wilhelmstrasse, a place nicknamed the Hitler Hotel.

The chill in Berlin was most obvious here in the heart of the city. In Pariser Platz, named in honor of Prussia's occupation of the French capital at the end of the Napoleonic Wars, long, narrow red banners with swastikas in the center hung from the lampposts. The doors of the French and U.S. embassies were tightly closed and all curtains drawn.

The Nazis had been unusually restrained about the Brandenburg Gate, perhaps because they had already destroyed the other major symbol of the country, the Reichstag, and perhaps because the Gate had been remade several times in ways they approved of.

The Gate's history reflected the struggle between progress and reaction that had raged for at least a century and a half in Germany. Friedrich Wilhelm II, King of Prussia, built the arch in the late 18th century as a monument to peace, and it was originally called the Peace Gate. In the early days, atop the gate, peace goddess Eirene held laurels and an olive branch and stood in the front of a chariot. Ironically, a foreigner began the reactionary changeover: Napoleon Bonaparte led the first victory parade through the Gate in 1806 after prevailing over Friedrich Wilhelm III at Jena-Auerstedt. Then, he took the quadriga from the top of the Gate to Paris. After Napoleon's fall and the occupation of Paris, the quadriga was brought back to Berlin, to be restored with a military bent. The goddess Eirene was transformed into Victoria, and now she had a Prussian eagle and Iron Cross on her lance along with a wreath of oak leaves.

Instead of a Pilsner from the tap as in the old days, Hans sipped something I rarely saw in Germany: a Scotch malt whiskey. He smiled as he explained that he had been introduced to this drink by one of his bosses, and that the hotel kept it in stock for them.

"Shouldn't you have a German drink?" I said. "Beer? Schnaps? A fine Rhine wine? Even *Bärenfang* honey liqueur?"

He seemed not to hear me, saying, "Cheers, my friend. To the Reich!" We clinked glasses lightly, almost as an afterthought.

"To the German wine I'm drinking," I added. "And friendship."

We clinked glasses again.

It was taking a while to get used to his appearance. When I saw him in the lobby for the first time in five years, I saw him less than I saw his S.S. uniform, its rich black cotton tracing his muscular body, right down to his high, brightly polished black boots. The insignia included a Totenkopf—a skull and crossbones, known as a 'death's head'—centered on the cap, pairs of silver runic S's, a broad leather belt and shoulder strap, silver braid, and silver oak leaves. Knowing that many elements of the uniform, even the death's head, had roots in Prussian and European history, didn't allay my unease.

His skin was pale. I imagined he spent most of his days in windowless rooms whose uses I didn't want to know about. His hair was severely cut on the sides, perhaps done by the same alleged barbers used by the highest-ranking Nazis. He pressed his lips together and showed a coldness and seriousness I hadn't seen in him before. And yet, from time to time, he grinned in his old cheerful, disarming way and slapped my back as though we were still comrades in school.

"Don't worry. It's still me," he said. "These threads scare most people. Which has its advantages."

"You've done well."

He shrugged, yet it seemed he inhaled deeply, making his chest expand and his insignia stand out.

"What do you do there?"

"Rudi, what a question."

"I hope it's not too nasty."

He watched me without answering.

He didn't understand why I held the same job I had when I left for Turkey five years earlier.

"There's so much more you could do, Rudi! A man of your talent and energy. Germany needs you."

"Germany has me."

"Is someone blocking you? The old guard? The Junkers? I can do something about that."

I shook my head.

"Are you slacking off? I can't imagine that."

I told him what others considered to be a problem, and he was astounded. "I can sign you up immediately."

I demurred, saying, "I wouldn't make a good Party member."

"Rudi, you don't have to do anything." He laughed. "You know how to do the salute and say, 'Heil,' so no problem."

"I like to work alone. You know that."

"You'll be welcomed, and once you join, a new world will open up."

"I could say the wrong thing so easily," I insisted.

"Crazy Rudi," he said, shaking his head again. "You and you alone have created such a hurdle."

I nodded.

"I'll work on you." He laughed. "It's time for some personal *Gleichschaltung.*"

"But the attacks on culture and science…" I said. "The attacks on the Jews."

"It is somewhat over the top."

"Somewhat over the top?"

He waved dismissively. "It'll sort itself out. Jews are smart and have resources. They'll take care of their own." He paused. "Then again, they *better* take care of their own. No one else will!"

I shook my head. "I can't believe you talk like that."

"You think I'm bad? Then you should hear what I hear." He laughed. "Rudi, the economy is improving. Unemployment is gone. People are proud to be German again. The stupid, endless political debates have stopped. Everyone is putting all their energy into moving forward."

I waved to the side. "Most of the new jobs involve marching back and forth all day or building armaments. And pride based on hate is nothing to be proud of."

"Germany needs to be strong."

"There are many ways for a country to be strong," I said.

He paused, then said softly, "You may be right that it's better you're not in the Party."

I shrugged.

As if reciting and looking beyond me, he listed more of what he called Nazi accomplishments, including overturning the Treaty of Versailles, reclaiming Saarland, taking over Austria and the Sudetenland, and more.

"The new regime also wants to take over countries without Germans or countries with only a few Germans like Poland and Russia," I said. "What will we do with them?"

"We need *Lebensraum*."

"We have enough here, I think." I paused. "I hope you don't believe all of what they spew."

"Keep your voice down, Rudi. People might misunderstand your views."

Glumly, I said, "What you mean is they might understand my views all too well."

He smacked the table with his hand. "Don't believe all you hear." He paused. "Not everything is as black and white as our uniforms."

We laughed, and for one brief, lovely moment, I felt a reassuring, calming human connection with Hans, this representative of the new order. Perhaps the sea of coldness and barbarity wouldn't completely overwhelm us.

Then we jumped to a favorite topic.

"Have you seen Sara?" I asked.

"Ha. You know the answer to that," he said. "She left both of us behind long ago. Or did she? Have *you* seen Sara?"

"I've heard she's still in Berlin."

"She is."

"You know? For sure?"

"No." He gazed at me, his eyes unfocused. "But I sense her. I always have." Neither of us spoke, then he shook himself and said, "That's only appropriate, right? She has all kinds of wild powers."

And we laughed again.

PART III

1943, 1944

Chapter Thirty

July 1943

In the Masurian Lake District of East Prussia, the far reaches of traditional Germany, the sun poured down over the gentle pines, spruce, and birches, and here and there beams of light reached the dark forest floor, creating spots of brightness that flashed like lightning as the train passed by. The mass of trees was broken occasionally by marshes and peat bogs and small lakes that gleamed a rich black. The lake water was remarkably still, as though undisturbed for eons.

The rail line passed a few tiny villages with no farmland. The soil was shallow and acidic, much less fertile than the plains to the south. The gingerbread brick buildings from the imperial era looked recently deserted. They were clean and well-maintained, but I saw no people or animals. Other than station names, there were no signs, and no flags flew. You might have thought it was decades, even a century, earlier. Humanity had intruded only slightly in this land.

I wanted to step off the train and hike through this placid countryside in *Wandervögel* style, singing, stopping to observe birds, collecting mushrooms, stripping down for a lake swim. As I had years earlier, I would immerse myself in a majestic setting that emphasized how small and inconsequential people's place in the world ultimately was. Oceans, mountains, skies, forests, plains, rivers all had existed long before humans arrived and they would last much longer than us.

A bank of clouds high above the forest transfixed me. The thick, round puffs seemed to hang motionless, a cliff of whiteness that reached far into the sky. Like an older person's face, the clouds had many lines and crevasses, as though they had been slowly worn over the years. As I watched, the wall of cloud moved, and the surfaces that had appeared as unchanging as granite began to change form.

More clouds unfurled and disappeared and came together, one after the other. But in a moment, the train braked—once, twice, then a third time, and slowed to a crawl. My reverie ended. Now the view featured guard towers, fences topped with barbed wire, mine fields, military vehicles, and many armed men in uniform. All of this reminded me of what I wanted to forget.

So close to the center of evil. What could I do to fight it?

With a lurch that made me reach for the armrests, we came to a stop, and guards came through the train, checking the papers of the few of us on board. Although the men wore familiar uniforms and acted as sternly as military and police forces did in Berlin, here they seemed all the more overwhelming.

Several others and I transferred to cars that moved to a second checkpoint that was not as formidable as the first. After a few kilometers we stopped at a place where four or five trains were parked on sidings. It was obvious, however, that they weren't trains like the one I had taken here. Each had four or five cars, with large windows; the ones with open shutters showed lavishly decorated dining, lounging, and conference rooms. The trains were covered by netting with pine branches woven in. Steps led up to the doors, and awnings covered the entrances.

After we got out of the cars, an S.S. captain sought me out. First, he gave me a uniform that I had to put on immediately in a nearby hut. The plain field gray outfit was similar to what the average soldier in the Wehrmacht wore. It was mandatory attire in this encampment of the man who was now officially commander-in-chief of all German military forces.

After I changed, the S.S. captain had a soldier take away my luggage, then escorted me to a blockhouse that was full of people talking on radios and phones, or typing, or reading files and memos. Herr Strauss, who worked as an aide to Herr Becker, greeted me with a more enthusiastic Hitler salute than he ever gave in the Ministry building in Berlin. I handed him the courier bag and asked when I was to see Herr Becker.

"Too busy to say just now," he said.

"Should I wait here?" In the entryway, there were several chairs occupied by officers who sat at attention silently.

"Better to get settled," Herr Strauss said. "We'll let you know."

The captain who had escorted me from the train led me outside and along a pathway covered with netting.

"Whose trains are those?" I asked, knowing that at least one was the Foreign Minister's. Of course, Göring, Himmler, and the rest each had to have personal trains. I imagined the Reichsmarschall's was the largest and most luxurious.

The captain said nothing.

The building he took me to was a depressing block that, like the other buildings I'd seen so far here, had a flat roof with bushes, tall grass, and little trees growing on top of it. Beyond the far side of the building was a small lake.

The captain showed me the room I was to stay in and gave an overview of the rules. I couldn't wander through the camp without authorization. Meals were served at precise times. I had to wait until I was called for.

I asked if I could meet briefly with Herr Becker, if only to be sure he knew I was here.

He didn't answer this question either.

I unpacked what little I had brought, aware that within a few hundred meters were the Führer, his top aides, the chiefs of the armed forces, several ministry heads, many hundreds of other top officials, a thousand guards and support staff. In Berlin, all the civilians and elegant buildings made it easier to miss the presence of the people who ruled the country. By contrast, this camp's barbed wire fences and guard posts surrounding concrete bunkers, with military vehicles and armored trains emphasized that this was the center of power in Germany.

I thought of the man on the balcony ten years earlier, the newly appointed Chancellor, taking in the adulation. Even then, he probably impatiently looked forward to being in a place like this, waging the kind of war for which this camp had been created.

Chapter Thirty-One

July 1943

No call came, and I had dinner at a canteen among men, many in S.S. uniforms, who spoke little and ate quickly. In contrast to most military sites I'd visited, the canteen workers—the cooks, the people ladling dinner, the dishwashers—were Wehrmacht soldiers, not Red Army prisoners or Polish or French laborers.

I had been sitting for most of the day and needed to move. After dinner, I asked where there might be a training facility, but the officer in charge of the canteen said brusquely, "No one here has time for that." I restrained myself from saying that so far, I had done little but wait.

The next morning, just after sunrise, everyone seemed to be asleep. I had heard many times that the Führer usually stayed up late, sometimes until dawn, working or delivering monologues on all sorts of subjects to aides and guests. *This was my chance. I needed to remain fit so that I'd be ready for an opportunity.*

I put on shorts and an athletic shirt and track shoes. I stretched and did calisthenics in my room, then went outside to a spot where there were no buildings, just a path by a lake. I started slowly, letting my body warm up. I kept my eyes on the path, trying to ignore what was around me. In fact, I wished I could close my eyes as I ran. Occasionally I looked at the water, which was still and placid, like the lakes I'd seen from the train the day before. This one looked as if it were absorbing light instead of reflecting it. I couldn't tell if it were shallow or deep, clear or full of muck. It was as warm and revealing as the eye of a shark.

On the third time around, at the part of the lake farthest from the building where I was staying, a group of S.S. men appeared on the path. They were gazing in all directions and saw me immediately. Almost in unison they aimed their rifles at me, yelling, "Halt!"

In my haste to stop, I nearly fell. My hands rose high over my head.

None of these soldiers had been there on my last lap.

A German shepherd on a leash slowly ambled out from behind the knot of soldiers. It was coming in my direction, clearly interested in me, pulling its leash.

Perhaps it was part of the canine corps. Or a bomb-sniffing dog. Except that it didn't seemed disciplined. Its mouth was open and it gazed at me as if it wanted to play, not inspect.

In a moment, the person holding the leash came into view. It was a figure I recognized instantly.

I didn't move. My hands were still raised high above my head. The dog kept approaching; his owner's head bent down, focused on the dog.

Panting, sweating, I stated who I was and my position with Herr Becker.

The Führer's head jerked up and looked at me for the first time, with an intensity that mixed a hint of curiosity with cold alertness. His eyes were like the lake's surface.

Could this be the opportunity I had wanted for so long?

He wore a peaked military cap that had the shape of the formal caps he wore in public but without the insignia. Likewise, his soldier's tunic and pants had no markings. His boots were regulation issue. His generic uniform was like the one I had been forced to wear the day before. In this superficial way, we were equals.

I tried not to stare as I stood silently with my arms raised.

The Führer made a movement I didn't discern. All at once, the guards lowered their rifles and stood in circular formation around the Führer, looking into the woods, across the lake, but no longer at me.

He let the dog pull him over to me.

"You work for Herr Becker?" he said.

"Yes, my Führer!"

I wondered at how easily I sounded like an enthusiastic Nazi.

He nodded slightly. "Becker's indispensable."

I said nothing.

"We've met before?" he asked.

"Only at a distance," I said, slowly lowering my hands, my heart pounding as much from the run as from this conversation.

For a second, I wondered if he would remember the night he had been named Chancellor and stood in a window before an adoring crowd—except for me—and shout, "Seize this man!"

I held his gaze. I had no idea of what else to do.

Then the dog licked my hand, and both of us looked down.

"Blondi likes you," he said.

As she licked my hands again, he smiled, which softened his face. This was very strange. I had no concept of a friendly Führer.

"She's discerning," he continued. "She doesn't like most of the crowd around me, particularly the generals. Can't say I blame her."

I let Blondi lick until she stopped. Then I knelt and petted her, and she half stood, putting her forward legs around me, in a sweet embrace. I hugged her and rubbed the back of her neck.

"That's the spot she loves best," he said approvingly.

"How old is she?" I kept looking at Blondi.

"Still a pup. One year."

"She's beautiful," I said, patting her more.

"Yes, yes."

I stood, taking my hand away from the dog. Blondi stared up at me longingly. *Did she have any idea about her owner?*

"I'm very sorry to disturb your walk," I said.

"You look healthy and fit," he said.

"I don't run as much as I used to," I said. "Nowadays there are other priorities."

"Indeed." After a pause, he added, "But health and fitness will always be an important part of the German ideal."

I nodded.

Blondi turned away from me and pulled gently at the leash. Her owner took a step, then stopped. I waited expectantly. Then he glanced at me again and said, "Resume running!"

If we were on the street in a normal town, I imagined he would have lifted a modest homburg and tipped it at me. But he vaguely pointed with his index finger at his military cap, then turned and headed back in the direction he had come, encouraged by Blondi. The guards swiveled back and forth, watching the path and the distant woods at the same time.

I ran only far enough to get out of sight of Blondi and her retinue. Then I stopped, leaned over, and put my hands on my knees, panting as though I had run a marathon.

Remembering where I was, I stood up abruptly, as if snapping to attention even though no one else was in view.

I tried to absorb what had happened. But all I could do was take in what was around me, an unlikely setting for such a meeting.

The dense pines were quiet. No breeze or wind blew through the boughs. The forest seemed to have taken a deep, wary breath.

The sun was beginning to show through the tops of the trees, hinting at the heat to come. In the distance, in the area I hadn't been allowed to go, a truck or car engine started—a sound that seemed to reverberate through the place.

I closed my eyes, wishing that when I opened them again, I would be back in Berlin. Or Rügen.

How had I managed to speak so causally with this person?

Amazing that someone who hated most people was capable of loving a dog.

My heart had calmed down somewhat. My breathing was almost normal. I opened my eyes.

Then I wished I had been able to carry a pistol or knife.

Later that morning, I was summoned to the Army staff train, then directed to a cramped office where Herr Becker sat at a small desk covered with files, books, and bound reports. Finally, we were meeting.

Normally, when I and others on his staff came in, he kept reading or writing and, barely looking up, gave crisp orders or demanded reports. My hair might be dyed orange or I might be wearing an eye patch, and he wouldn't notice.

Today, he stopped his reading and gazed at me.

"Baumann," he said, making this sound almost like a question.

I couldn't remember the last time he'd used my name.

"Sir?" I said.

"Do you have dress clothes?"

Confused, I paused. "A few things have survived."

"Do you have them with you?"

"Of course not."

He turned to the papers in front of him, which made me relax slightly. "Let's see what we can round up," he said.

Again, I said, "Sir?"

"Oh," he said, without looking at me again. "Haven't you heard? We're dining with the Führer tonight."

Chapter Thirty-Two

July 1943

"Happy birthday, Fräulein Meyer!"

The chorus resounded, "Happy birthday! Happy birthday!"

Fräulein Meyer beamed, and I felt happy for her, as I might toward a niece who was beginning to make her way into the adult world. She seemed not yet fully grown. Her bobbed blonde hair framed a round, cheerful face that showed a range of endearing emotions all at once—surprise, appreciation, wonderment. Her body was slim, like a boy's. She had a soft, appealing Bavarian accent that I imagined felt familiar to our Austrian Führer and helped her understand his every word, at least better than most Germans. Her voice chirped a bit, making me think of a fledgling bird, almost grown, still with some fuzz as her feathers grew, eager to learn how to do everything right, eager to leave the nest, and yet still needing her mother to bring worms.

Were we celebrating her 18th *birthday?*

I had heard she was a star in the secretarial pool, one of several who traveled wherever the Führer went. He dictated memos and reports to them night and day, reworking the texts again and again. They were devoted—not so much to the principles of National Socialism as to the boss himself, who was as kind to them as he was to Blondi. This little birthday party was an example.

The Führer encouraged Fräulein Meyer to enjoy a slice of cake even though he declined to eat any. He asked what had been the favorite birthday gift she had ever received. For a moment, her eyes opened wide, stunned. But then she breathed deeply and said, almost as if reciting, "Being with the people I care about, my friends, and most of all my Führer. This has been the perfect birthday gift!" The Führer smiled and said he hoped she would be able to celebrate her next birthday with her family, too.

Then the Führer said, "Happy birthday!" again, but without a smile. And this time he didn't look at the birthday girl, but instead lowered his head, as though he were reading a report under the table.

She knew him well, it seemed. She stood, saying, "Thank you all, and thank you, my Führer." She took a few steps, walking almost backwards, enough so as not to turn her back on him, as though he were an Eastern demigod whose subjects always had to face him. "I don't want to interrupt anymore," she said quietly.

Perhaps in appreciation of her understanding that the sentimental moment should end, he looked at her again and said, "I'm so happy to celebrate with you, dear Fräulein Meyer."

After the secretaries left, the Führer said, "So nice to mark a ritual that might easily be overlooked under the present circumstances." His voice was soft and flat. You might have thought he was dictating a memo concerning the production of paper clips. Or that he wanted to conserve energy. Still, he spoke without stopping. Of course, if he paused, he wouldn't have to worry about being interrupted. People at the table didn't speak unless he asked them a question.

"They're refreshingly young and innocent," he went on. "And yet they, too, have the steely determination that's needed to wage this struggle to its necessary conclusion."

In the dim lights that hummed and flickered occasionally, with skin tinged gray-yellow, the Führer looked older than someone whose 50th birthday had been celebrated in such elaborate, enthusiastic style only three years earlier. Of course, now he was indoors most of the time, exercised little, and waged war on many fronts without the wild successes of the early years. Although his voice and his occasional stare had the power familiar from the radio and newsreels, when he was quiet, I might have thought he was someone's elderly father who was visiting, perhaps for the last time.

The Führer ate food from small bowls that appeared to consist of green and gray mashed material, probably vegetables. At least I hoped they were vegetables. The rest of us were served a salad, braised beef, onions, carrots, and potatoes, all of which were a treat in the war economy. Yet they lacked spices and sauces, and I was reminded that the meal had been prepared in a military kitchen.

There was, however, one striking thing to eat—striking because of the extent of food rationing. The bread was served with real butter, which several people I knew would die for.

What would I die for?

As I ate real butter for the first time in months, I thought how simple it would be to train a small pistol on the Führer from my chair across the large round table. I might not even need to take the weapon out of my jacket pocket. Or, when I had entered the room and stood briefly in front of him, I could have fired several shots into his chest before anyone could stop me. The target would be so close. I imagined dark spots suddenly appearing on his field-gray jacket. Perhaps he would stare at me again, as he had in Berlin the night he became Chancellor. Perhaps he would utter a few last words, "I should have had you seized then." Maybe he would look at me in a new light and say, "You've shown determination and perseverance, like a good German."

But guards were always around him and silently watched us all. If I drew a weapon, they would shoot me, likely before I could do what I wanted to do. Besides, I had been searched several times over the last few days as I got closer and closer to the center of *Wolfsschanze*. No one could have brought a pistol this far undetected.

As we ate the somewhat overcooked beef, I wondered if it would be possible to bring a knife into this building. I could put it inside my jacket, create a little pocket for it, and there would be no bulge like the one made by a pistol.

The men who had patted me down a half hour earlier might have missed it.

But a knife would be more difficult to use. I would have to be very close to the Führer or find a way to lunge at him. I would likely have only one chance, maybe two, to strike him. And unless I hit a vital organ, I would cause only superficial wounds. And I wasn't sure of the best place to stab him. His throat? His stomach? His heart seemed most promising, but how would I pierce the bones that partly covered it? Did he even have a heart?

I looked at the knife and fork I was using to cut the meat, wondering how effective either would be if a person tried to attack raw human flesh with them. The fork could puncture skin, but it would do nothing lethal. Was the knife sharp enough to kill? Perhaps. If enough force were used. If the person wielding it believed fully in the justice of his action and knew how many lives would be saved and how much destruction would be avoided.

But again I noticed the guards who stood around the room, barely moving, not reacting to the conversation. At the moment anything threatening began to happen, they would spring to life, do their jobs, and defend the person they had sworn to protect. I had seen their vigilance already that morning.

Some of them would cover him. Others would charge and crush the attacker. Or simply shoot him.

Even if the Führer died, he had many followers just as vicious and ambitious, some at his side here at *Wolfsschanze*, ready to take his place and continue his policies.

No matter what, I would die either immediately or after being tortured for as long as they could keep me alive. And likely the Führer would have a bruise or scratches. Would that be worth leaving Magda and the children forever?

Still, as I stuck my fork into the beef on my plate, I noticed, probably for the first time in my life, just how the prongs punctured the piece. It was also likely the first time I considered it as flesh, rather than food. In the same way, I noticed how the sharp edge of the knife cut into the meat. I suddenly realized Herr Becker had noticed that I was gazing at my plate with unusual intensity.

So I whispered to him, "Utterly delicious. I can't remember the last time I had such a good cut."

Herr Becker smiled, and I was happy that he might chalk up my rapturous reaction to a rube's first visit to what would seem like a banquet to most Germans.

The Führer launched into another denunciation of Germany's "many enemies." This time, it was the Slavic hordes, personified by the Red Army.

"Their subhuman soldiers have no higher purpose and never will, even in a thousand years," he said. "Their only advantage is numerical; they can throw waves of these beings at us. But sheer numbers are not enough. Our soldiers show their superiority in so many ways. They use their higher intelligence to exploit the many weaknesses of the enemy. They obey orders, continuing when others would give up. They are determined to win. All those qualities will bring us victory."

He paused, but no one spoke. I assumed if he were really finished, he would give some kind of sign that they all understood.

He began nodding and then went on, "Those qualities are shared by all Germans. Fräulein Meyer, for example. Her work is excellent. She is devoted. She is diligent. At the same time, she represents what we fight to protect. She is kind. She is trusting. She is deferential. She is nurturing. She is wise. She is all that we love about German women."

A slight smile formed even though his eyes continued to stare at nothing in particular. "It's important to step back for a moment from the demands of our heroic work and remember why we do what we do."

He looked up and peered across the table. In a second, our eyes locked. I felt as though a flash of lightning were striking me.

He stared, expressionless. *Was I supposed to say something?*

Several of the people whom I had met only since arriving here in the Führer's dining room an hour or two ago turned and stared at me, too. The silence seemed to suck away what little air was left in the room.

"Herr—?" he said. "Herr—?"

I felt as though I were in school again, about to be quizzed by my teacher. But this was a different kind of master, with much more power than my childhood teachers.

At first, I nodded.

"Herr—?" he repeated.

Then I understood.

"Baumann!" I exclaimed.

"Yes, yes! Herr Baumann." He said this as though it were a revelation, thankfully a happy revelation. "Such a solid, strong family name. Farmer. Builder. Honest, constructive professions. Both of which the Reich needs."

I nodded so deeply it might have been a bow.

"Herr Baumann is a dog lover," the Führer said. "And dogs love him." He pointed his right hand vaguely in my direction. "I've seen this for myself."

I nodded.

"Blondi approved of him," he explained. "In fact, she embraced him. Quite literally."

"Happily I was able to return Blondi's embrace," I said. Everyone else at the table seemed surprised, and Herr Becker looked at me with wide eyes, as though he wanted to order me again to be quiet.

"Who can resist the charms of Blondi?" I continued.

The Führer smiled, saying, "Blondi couldn't resist your charms."

I resisted the desire to try to charm him and said with some gravity, "You've raised a fine dog."

The Führer was nodding. "She knew you're a German patriot."

Was a dog the key to my undermining its owner?

I bowed my head forward slightly.

He smiled again, saying, "I should use her to sniff out traitors."

He glanced around the table. Everyone looked the way I felt—guilty on all counts. And yet I couldn't imagine that others had thoughts like mine.

"I should create a special loyalty corps, led by Blondi." He snorted, as close to laughter as I had seen in him. Then he added, "Herr Baumann, could you assist?"

"But, of course, my Führer!"

He smiled at me, and everyone laughed as much as I, perhaps because we were all relieved he wasn't going to speculate in his often unforgiving way about our dedication. I might have laughed most.

He returned to what I'd quickly learned were some of his favorite topics:

Germans settling in the eastern territories, especially Poland and Ukraine, creating huge farms using native peasants who were good for little but basic manual labor.

The "momentary setbacks" of earlier this year, which he discussed without using the word "Stalingrad," the biggest disaster of the war.

Imminent brilliant attacks that would help the Wehrmacht take the offensive against the Red Army.

The continued development of superior military hardware, particularly tanks, planes, missiles, and secret weapons.

The history of Russia, which featured the Jewish-Bolshevik conspiracy that did away with the Tsar.

The underestimation by the world of the fatal flaw of the United States—the mixing of races, which had ruined the advantages of having so many German, English, and other Northern European immigrants.

The litany of hatred and distortion made me wish all the more that I could end his life before this meal ended.

"Well done, Baumann." Herr Becker sounded congratulatory and in awe, but also a bit jealous.

By the light of a sliver of the moon, we were walking to the buildings where visitors stayed.

"It was entirely accidental," I said.

"The beginning, yes. But after that, you said and did the right things."

"I didn't think. I said what came to me."

"Lucky for you that pleased the Führer." Now he laughed. "You don't know how difficult it is when he's unhappy."

"I've heard stories."

He sighed. "Don't let your success tonight go to your head."

"Never!"

"With him, it can last as long as a flash of moonlight on a cloudy night." He gestured upwards. Here, the camouflage netting was particularly thick and I couldn't see the moon.

"You see! Gone already." His arm descended from the sky. "It's good you're leaving tomorrow. That way your star will keep shining."

I laughed. "My star would prefer being with the stars up there, far, far from here. But such is fate."

"For all of us."

Chapter Thirty-Three

July 1943

Back in Berlin from the *Wolfsschanze*, I went directly to the office.

Magda and the children were on Rügen, so I knew the apartment would be empty and sadly quiet when I got home. I missed them, but this arrangement was best. In the country, they avoided bombings. On her family's farm, she and the children had more food than in the city. The children avoided being evacuated under the government programs that were as much about indoctrination as safety.

Magda had initially said, "We stay with you, husband and father!"

I had laughed. "Sweet sentiment, my dear, but you'll all be so much safer on Rügen."

"And you?" she said, rubbing my arm.

"If it gets worse—if I'm afraid for my life—I'll join you."

"Ahh," she said, then smiled. "Much better. You mustn't forget this promise."

I took several files I had brought back from *Wolfsschanze* to Frau Riegler. After I said hello, I started to tell her which were the most important and what they dealt with. But then I noticed she wasn't looking at the files or responding to what I said. Instead, she was looking at me, as though she hadn't seen me in years or I'd grown a third eye.

I stopped mid-sentence and said, "What?"

She smiled in a way I had rarely seen her smile, the kind of easy, jovial smile that few people seemed capable of anymore. "You've made some impressive new friends, Herr Baumann," she said. "Who knew that one way to the Führer's so-called heart is through his dog?"

Now I smiled. "Blondi is adorable."

"And dinner with the Führer, Herr Baumann."

"It wasn't exactly a table for two. More like a group audience where food was served."

"Yet you made an impression."

"Only because of Blondi."

With that, I picked up one of the folders and began to speak about work again.

Frau Riegler lifted a finger, a sign for me to be quiet. "First, an order of business," she said.

"Blondi backlash?"

"Au contraire." Her voice lowered and sounded almost grim. "You've expressed an interest in acting as a courier abroad."

"I have."

"Herr Baumann, as we've discussed, your refusal to join the Party has been a tremendous stumbling block."

"I still haven't joined—"

"I did add you on the list of people to be considered for courier runs."

"Yes."

"I thought it might take months or a year, but suddenly you've been approved."

I was sincerely surprised and whispered, "Thank you!"

She smiled and said, "No. Thank Blondi."

"Who would imagine that meeting Hitler's dog would lead to this?"

"She must be special and recognized that you're special."

I was still at my desk when sirens sounded. The Royal Air Force liked to send a few fighters and bombers in the middle of the night to wake everyone and force them to move to shelters. But this was early for such a maneuver, so I moved with a little more speed than usual to the Foreign Ministry shelter, one of the best shelters in the capital. We were in part of the basement of the Hotel Adlon, which had utility areas that were almost as luxurious as the famed lobby and rooms above. Not open to the public, our space was quieter and less crowded than most shelters.

In the early evening, even fewer people were in the shelter than usual. We chatted as casually as we did during our occasional drills, but at the same time we listened carefully to the sounds above, especially as the flak guns started firing.

We all paused a moment as the noise of the anti-aircraft guns grew, which had to mean there were many targets in the sky, not just the teaser sorties. Soon there were noises we weren't accustomed to—deep, distant rumbles accompanied by slight tremors in the ground. Mercifully, the explosions weren't close by, and after 20 minutes or so, quiet returned, and the all-clear sirens sounded.

Above ground, I saw that nothing had changed in the Government Quarter. I decided to go home. The bombing had been relatively brief, so the electricity and water lines were probably undamaged. The apartment would be too silent, of course, but at least I would sleep in a familiar bed again.

The trams were running, and the other passengers and I kept glancing around, looking for damage. The bombs must have fallen far away, I thought.

But after I got out at my stop, I smelled burned wood and metal, and on our block, I saw a red glow.

I stared a moment before comprehending what I saw.

Where there had been several buildings, now there was nothing. Only smoke and flames rose from rubble. My building had been in the center of the group.

Several fire trucks were parked in the street, and crews trained hoses on the debris. Groups were shoveling the roadway clear. An ambulance crew tended to several injured people. Other civilians stood in groups talking among themselves.

Where were our beds, the tables, the chairs, our belongings? I saw the empty space where they had been. I looked below, where flames shot up from a pile of glowing rubble. I had never realized how disturbing it was to look at and take in something that didn't exist.

Had sections of the apartment landed somewhere intact?

The other apartments were gone, too. Had people from the building been in the shelter below? *Had the shelter provided protection? Were they still hiding there?* Yet I knew that even if a shelter were intact, a fire could use up all of the oxygen.

I glanced at the people around me.

Where were my friends and neighbors?

Someone next to me asked if the people in the building had survived. I said I didn't know, at which point another man nearby said the obvious, "It was a direct hit." He shook his head. "No one made it, I heard."

I thought of Frau Zimmer, the Bestler family, and our other neighbors. Likely they had dutifully gone down to the air raid shelter. Fortunately, the Müllers were spending most of their time these days at their country place. And the Wellenbachs were long gone, either safe in England or America, or transported to the East.

We were remarkably lucky, of course. Magda and the children were on Rügen, and I had been at work. What had been destroyed—furniture, clothing, the little supplies of daily life—could be replaced easily, once the war was over. There were pictures I couldn't replace, books I'd kept, but most of our important papers and documents as well as family keepsakes were on Rügen—once the Royal Air Force began bombing Germany regularly, I had prepared for a disaster like this.

No one would know for sure who had survived and who hadn't, unless they saw or heard from the survivors.

The people who were missing in the rubble would never be found in recognizable form. And because hospitals were overwhelmed, no one would make the effort to identify remains. Survivors would be recognized only when they called in or appeared for work.

I thought again of Magda and the children on Rügen. The farm was at the end of a long dirt road beyond thick woods and fields. The closest neighbors were at a distance on their own isolated farmsteads. The area was as untouched as only a few parts of the Reich were, a place where one could easily disappear.

Now, I saw in the distance, high above the horizon, a sliver of moon, the same moon I had seen in the *Wolfsschanze*. It was in the north, in the direction of Rügen, not bright enough to help the flak gunners or dissuade the Royal Air Force, but perhaps a kind of beacon for me, lighting a path north.

When I first visited Rügen with Magda, I was reminded of why this island in the Baltic Sea drew so many tourists from the rest of Germany. We walked and walked around its lagoons, its bays, and the peninsulas so narrow and low they felt they might disappear at high tide, then along the sandy beaches, up and down steep bluffs and chalk cliffs. Even though it was Germany's largest island, it was not very big, with just a few villages, farms, and isolated inns, but because it stretched and folded back on itself again and again, it seemed much larger than it was, with treasures that revealed themselves only slowly. You couldn't go directly from one point to another on Rügen; if you didn't swim or row the route, it might take 15 kilometers to travel from one beach to another just a few hundred meters across a bay. Likewise, it wasn't easy to get from the mainland to Rügen, even though it was just off the northern German coast. There were few ferries and no bridges.

On maps, Rügen appeared like a dragon or pterodactyl, drawn in on itself. Perhaps it was about to unfold its wings and fly off, skimming the waves out over the Baltic Sea or traveling south, into the heart of the country.

Rügen's air was as striking as the terrain. The salty breezes blew in off the waves and cleared my mind, soothed my nerves, gave me energy. This was the secret to my dear Magda's calmness, I thought. If only all Germans could live in such a place.

Magda's father and mother did most of the labor, tending the fields, chickens, pigs, and cows. They were nearly self-sufficient, and since the war had started, had even less contact with the world than in more peaceful times.

I imagined they would happily accept help, particularly from a healthy middle-aged man who enjoyed physical labor and who was a quick learner.

It would be easy to hide when others stopped by. And the war wouldn't last longer than a few more growing seasons.

For so long, I wanted to do something to alter the course of this war and this regime. I distributed anti-Nazi leaflets to people I didn't know. I gave blank passports and visas to people persecuted by the regime. I had helped Jewish friends find shelter and aid. None of this had been as effective as I'd wanted. And now that, at least officially, all Jews had been transported out of the city and the Gestapo had cracked down even more ferociously on dissent, there was less I could do in my day-to-day life to help others. Somehow I had been approved for a courier run, but it could take months or years actually to go, and it might not be to neutral countries. I might never be able to make contact with the British.

I knew one thing: if I disappeared, I would no longer be helping the regime through the work I did at the Foreign Ministry.

I might have been the luckiest person in the Reich. I could go on an internal exile of a most profound, healthy kind. I could be with my wife and children again, away from all that was brutal and depressing. I would have the time to be a good husband and father as well as a good son-in-law. I could do manual labor that would reinvigorate me. I could read again and perhaps write. When the war ended, I would be ready to help rebuild the country in a new, peaceful, democratic way.

I turned from the ruins of my old apartment building and walked away.

Chapter Thirty-Four

July 1943

Because of the bombing, many people were out in the middle of the night in my neighborhood. I kept the brim on my hat down and walked on the empty parts of streets, close to buildings, in the darkest shadows I could find.

I went to the Kurfürstendamm, heading to the city center, past darkened hulks of buildings that a decade earlier had been brightly-lit centers of pleasure and entertainment—cabarets, cafés, restaurants, movie theaters, bordellos. They were closed now to help the country achieve *Endsieg*—final victory. Along here all was quiet. There weren't fires, emergency crews, or dazed people staring at the ruins of the buildings where they had lived for decades.

I went by the Zoo and the huge flak tower, which, despite triumphant press from the regime about their cannons' abilities to knock bombers out of the sky, hadn't done much to help my block.

By the light of the moon, I came to the heart of the Tiergarten. In several large fields, I noticed dark shapes, some stretched out on the ground, some hunched on benches. They were here for any of a variety of reasons. Maybe their apartments were gone, too, and they couldn't find shelter, or because they were lovers needing the privacy of darkness, or because they didn't want to be found. I avoided them—after all, if they were being hunted, I might get caught, too, or one of them might recognize me.

I moved even farther into the park, where paths narrowed and wound through darker woods. The path I was on came to a familiar pond, where a side trail led to a dead-end circle with benches surrounded by trees—one of the most secluded parts of the Tiergarten.

I hadn't been here in years, but I remembered it well. A decade earlier, Sara and I had stopped a few times while strolling across the city. In the fall, it would have been mid-afternoon, with the sun slowly setting, its nearly horizontal rays shining through the bare trees, the air cool. There were few people in the park, and we could hug and kiss without anyone walking by and frowning.

Tonight, which was just as quiet, I sat on a bench we had shared several times, putting my briefcase at one end. Then I turned, raised my legs onto the bench, and lay down, using the briefcase as a pillow. I pulled my coat tightly around me and looked up at the many stars that shown through a break in the dark canopy of leaves. One of the few advantages of city blackouts was that the night sky glowed brightly now, no longer washed out by streetlights and vehicles and signs. I thought I would fall asleep quickly because I had one of the worst shocks a person could have, but my mind was as lit up as the city had been a decade ago.

I could do something millions of people could only dream of. I could escape this war and this fascist regime by silently stepping away. Because my apartment building had been destroyed, all would assume I hadn't survived.

My life would be healthy. I would do manual labor of the most direct, satisfying kind. I would help take care of the children and teach them everything from academic subjects to how to treat people and view the world in ways they weren't learning in school. I would spend more time with Magda and make her feel less anxious about the war, and she would no longer worry I might die in a bombing raid. *Could she ever have imagined a raid might be my deliverance?*

I would need to convince Magda's parents that my stay with them would be beneficial for everyone and that I would act in a way that wouldn't put them at risk. Her mother would accept my presence. But her father was of typical Prussian stock and believed that one did his duty in all facets of life—to his family, to the Lutheran church, to his community, and to the state. He might not ask directly, but he would wonder why I wasn't still at my job, and if I had left my position at the Ministry, why wasn't I serving in the armed forces?

I might need to work hard on Magda's parents, who, from the beginning, didn't seem to know what to make of me. I wasn't a native of Pomerania—my father had moved to the loud, disconnected city. I wasn't a relative or friend. They had no business with me, except that their daughter had married me.

On my first visit, I had talked about the joy of nature, especially on my treks with the *Wandervögel*. This, I learned quickly, was not a positive thing. "I'm sure it's pleasant to wander around the countryside and take in nature at one's leisure, but I'm with nature every day—in the stables, in the fields, in the woods," Magda's father had said not long after I met him for the first time. "All my walks have a purpose. I'm going somewhere to do something. I don't have the luxury of *wandering*."

Her parents had gazed at me as though they were listening to an insurance man explaining the fine points of an annuity plan. Whether I spoke of the delays in the trip to get to their farm from Berlin—bombing runs by the Royal Air Force sometimes wreaked havoc on the Reichsbahn's schedules—or whether I spoke of my gratitude for the food they sent, they watched, expressionless and alert, as though waiting for a catch that would confirm their suspicions that something was not right with me.

Magda's father's pale blue eyes were framed by wrinkled bronzed skin and strands of gray hair. He was a tall man with strict posture who literally looked down at me. Beneath hair that swept back from her face, Magda's mother's hazel eyes glowed brown and green and red: a range of emotions seemed to flare in them, but I couldn't detect what they were.

"They're like that with strangers," Magda had said.

"But I'm their son-in-law."

"As I said, they're like that with strangers."

I had frowned, and she burst out laughing.

"How long will it take to be accepted?"

"A few decades."

"How did you avoid being like them?"

She had shrugged and said, "I've got my secrets!"

Her parents were as dour as ever when I arrived with Magda and the children to drop them off for the duration of the war. I worried that they saw their daughter and grandchildren merely as three mouths to feed. I thanked them for making sure they would be safe, and I gave them money to help feed and clothe and house Magda and the children. I knew that giving them livestock or grain would make a better impression than currency, but I had no choice.

Over time, her parents had warmed ever so slightly. Although he had a farm that was as demanding and productive as the other farms on the island, Magda's father also worked at the nearby chapel. It was a labor of love. He donated back the modest pay he received for doing "the Lord's work," which included giving sermons when the rotating pastors in this rural area were unable to attend Sunday services.

Like so many northern Germans in the countryside in the early 1930s, he was partial to the National Socialists, and he might even have voted for them a few times. But his opinion changed when the new government began to intrude in religious life and the organization of the church. "How can the state overrule the word of God?" he had asked.

This led to a terse, diplomatic discussion of how much things had changed in the past several years since the *Machtergreifung*, although neither of us referred to the shift in power openly.

"It's been head-spinning," he had said. "Hard to understand at times."

"Oh yes."

"And not always for the best." He had paused for a long couple of beats. "Not at all."

I had nodded and lowered my voice slightly. "You can imagine what it's like for me, in the middle of it. Not always easy. Not at all."

We had nodded together.

This had been enough. Because in this day and age, you had to speak carefully about treasonous subjects, even with your wife's father or your daughter's husband.

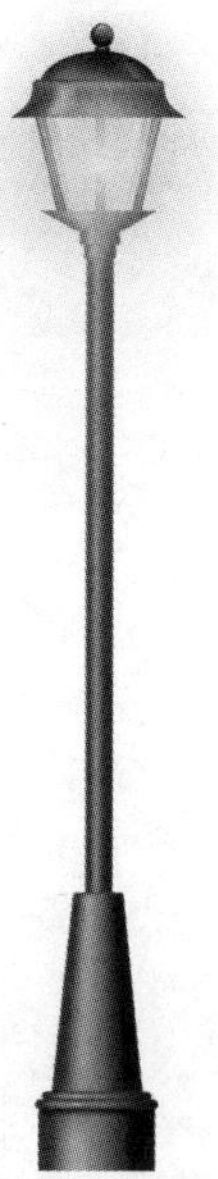

Chapter Thirty-Five

July 1943

As the sun glowed in the eastern sky, I woke after a few hours of fitful sleep. My body was stiff. The wooden bench was unrelentingly hard.

I wanted do stretches and work out the tightness in my body. The best thing would be to run. I would start moderately, letting my muscles warm up and then increase my pace. Once I got into a rhythm, I would slow for a few minutes, then speed up for a few minutes, and continue alternating. Finally, I would wind down, reveling in how, all at once, I felt tired and energetic and refreshed.

But my gym clothes and running shoes no longer existed.

Still, I was warming up in a different way, ever since I had seen the ruin of our apartment building. It was time to start a slow jog out of this city and into the country.

I stood, tucked in my shirt, and straightened my clothes. First, I had to go to the Stettiner Bahnhof, the station that served Stralsund—just across the water from the island of Rügen. I wanted to find out when trains were running since printed schedules tended to be more of a reminder of bygone reliability than an accurate rendering of the current reality.

If I had to wait long, I would stay away from places where people might recognize me. I would say as little as possible. In order to become a new person, for a day or two I needed to be no one.

More people than usual were walking since fewer trams and busses were running. As ever, the military had priority over everything, including transportation and general repairs—some of the bombs might have hit depots or wrecked train tracks.

I left the Tiergarten, meandering through the embassy district, then past the Charité, where Dr. Traum had once practiced, toward the station. I saw another building that had suffered the same fate as my apartment building, a white wispy trail of gray smoke rose from the rubble, twisting slightly in the sky as breezes shifted. Several men in uniform stood on the sidewalk, which had been cleared, talking and observing the scene.

At the far end of the block, in front of a building that was next to the destroyed one, a group of people were sorting through boxes and bags on the sidewalk.

At least they could salvage some things.

Luckily my family was better off. Instead of resulting in us huddling around a few half-ruined possessions, the destruction of our apartment would lead to a rebirth of our lives.

At the Stettiner Bahnhof, I doubted I would see anyone I knew, unlike the Anhalter Bahnhof, where I sometimes ran into diplomats and others traveling south and southwest.

At the ticket counter, I asked when the next train to Stralsund left. I was surprised when the older man behind the counter said it would leave this evening around eight o'clock.

"No more morning run?"

"Not according to the new plan."

I asked when the new schedule had been instituted, more curious than complaining.

He looked away from me, then said, "A few hours ago." It was almost a question.

I saw that no one else was on line or even near us.

"How bad is the damage?" I asked quietly. "Will the train really leave tonight?"

He lowered his voice, too. "I don't think the Tommies were targeting us. Just a few random drops, but they wrecked the switches just beyond the platforms."

I thanked him and bought a ticket, noticing that I had only about 30 Reichsmarks, less than what I wanted.

I considered going to the bank to withdraw more money, but, of course, this would be evidence that I was still alive. And I might run into people I knew. Besides, money wouldn't matter so much once I arrived on Rügen. In the countryside, bartered food and fuel was worth more than banknotes.

Now, I wondered where to spend the time before my evening departure. It would be best to hide, but the two places where I had any privacy were off limits. My apartment was destroyed, and I couldn't be in my office. A quiet café might be a pleasant place to stay for the day, although I would have to avoid my favorites. I could spend hours in a museum, too, although they tended to be closed these days, another casualty of the war.

I could go back to the Tiergarten, but in daylight, it wasn't as safe as it had been the previous night.

I could wander through the city, far from the center and far from my neighborhood. There I might burn off my nervous energy and find a secluded spot.

I walked. I walked. And then I walked more.

At times I tired, but whenever I sat down, I felt as I had the night before on the bench. My mind raced too much for me to rest.

As I walked, I noticed things I had passed by many times but hadn't really taken in. It was as if, instead of having a chance to begin living again, I'd been told I would die soon. It was like a final farewell.

Had the sky ever looked so blue? It seemed to vibrate, as though it were a living organism stretched over the capital, not a distant vacuum. I wanted to reach up and twirl it in my hand.

I realized now how much I loved the famous Berlin air, the sweet scent that suffused the city day and night, which I had taken for granted for so long. I wanted to breathe in this subtle, intriguing air as deeply as possible.

Through all the nastiness and horrors of the past decade, the air had remained unsullied, a reminder that some things in the world wouldn't change regardless of what the regime did.

Before today, when I imagined leaving Berlin, I thought of missing my friends and some colleagues. I realized that most of all I'd miss the sky and air.

Although I had intended to stay in the northern suburbs, far from places I knew, and where people knew me, late in the day I walked toward the Mitte. I felt drawn to the center of the city and to the Foreign Ministry offices. I wouldn't see my city for a few years, I knew, and I wanted to say goodbye, for now.

As I walked, I remembered things in my office—pictures of my parents, of Magda, and of the children; letters and postcards from them; souvenirs from our travels and my travels. A few pictures of my father, which were irreplaceable.

It was late, and I knew that most people wouldn't be there. Several were on trips. One was sick. My boss was in East Prussia at the *Wolfsschanze*. It would be so easy to slip inside, put what I wanted into my briefcase, and leave. *Who would notice?*

Tipping my hat forward to cover as much of my face as possible, I came down Wilhelmstrasse to the Foreign Ministry building, its monotonous, repetitive windows dark, filled with blackout curtains. As soon I saw the building, I realized I couldn't go inside. Just one person passing me in the hall could ruin my plan.

If I took my few personal items and treasured objects, it would become obvious that I hadn't died suddenly and unexpectedly.

It was enough, I realized now, to take one last look at the building where I had spent so much of my professional life.

I decided not to linger. Sentimentality in this era was a dangerous, sometimes deadly thing.

It was time to go to the train station.

"*Auf Wiedersehen*," I said softly.

"Hallo" echoed back.

Had the building spoken to me?

A breeze came down the street, and it sounded like my name.

"Rudi!"

Had one of my colleagues seen me?

I looked around, but all I saw was a woman with a large hat covering much of her face. She was several paces away, coming up to me.

I recognized the voice. She was saying my name just loud enough for me to hear but not loud enough for others to make out.

I hadn't seen her in years.

Sara Traum's summer jacket hung loosely. Her hazel eyes seemed to float in her bony face, looking toward me but not focused. It was as if she were blind and could tell generally where I was by the sound of my voice but couldn't lock in on me.

Except I hadn't said a word.

She came toward me, looking to the left, then right, saying rapidly, "I want to say hello and ask how you are, and I will, I promise, but first I have to say I'm so desperate, I have to say it right away. I have to say I need your help. *I really need your help.*"

She stopped, and it took a moment for me to grasp that this once-vibrant creature was here in front of me and how worn she looked, let alone what she was saying.

At the same time, I was comprehending another change as profound as seeing Sara for the first time in a decade: my dream of internal exile on Rügen, my dream of disappearing was destroyed.

"Sara," I said.

It wasn't much, but apparently it was enough for her. She continued talking fast, as though she had only seconds to speak. "They've rounded up and shipped away whole families, whole neighborhoods. When the transports started, sometimes friends wrote from camps, but that's stopped. Some of us have managed to evade them, but we're being hunted like animals now. Everyone's disappearing, and I fear that terrible things are happening. I *know* terrible things are happening."

I stared at her, wondering whether to confirm that it was worse than she could imagine.

I realized that if I hadn't seen her, I would be on my way to the Stettiner Bahnhof now.

She clutched at my jacket. I looked down at her bony hand holding my coat, whose material was rich and luxurious compared to the thin cloth of her worn clothes. She followed my gaze. Then we both looked up and at each other. At first, I thought I might cry. Then I saw that she might cry, too. In this momentary exchange, we shared so much—the knowledge of how awful things were, all that we had experienced together, and a recognition that we both still cared so much for one another. This bond was something I hadn't felt in a long time. It was the closest kind of connection any two people could have. These days, it was as shocking as it was wonderful, a reminder of what the Nazis and the war had taken from us.

Once more, we were together, but in a different way. My heart beat faster and happier.

She let go of my jacket. "I'm sorry," she said. "I'm so desperate. I feel they're getting closer and closer."

I took her hands in mine. “It’s okay,” I said. “I’ll do whatever I can.”

She had a blank expression for a moment, as if surprised by my response. Then, she laughed as if none of the horror around us was happening.

“Could you whisk me away from all this and make life the way it was before?” Her lips turned up slightly in a kind of smile.

“Ha,” I said, loving her smile, even if it looked like a grimace. “But first let’s move down the street a ways. It isn’t safe around here.”

Gently putting my arm around her, turning away from a few people going in the other direction, we walked several blocks and down a side street, to an alleyway whose entrance was partly blocked by a pile of debris. No one would be able to see us easily.

“Are you getting enough food?” I asked.

She gave a sickly smile and looked down at her body.

“Where are you staying?” I asked.

“It changes,” she said. “No one can keep me long. Sometimes I sleep in the open.”

“I know what you mean.” I laughed. I told her what had happened to my apartment building.

“What about your family?” She seemed even more confused. “Where are they?”

I explained, and she said, “If you have to be in Germany now, Rügen is a wonderful place to be.”

“Yes,” I said wistfully.

“Like them, I was safe in Switzerland for a while, but my *Bubbe*’s still here.”

“It was very loving of you to come back. And very dangerous.”

“Stupid even. But I had no choice. And now that I’ve lost my shelter, I want to go back to Switzerland.”

We were silent a moment. Then I said softly, “I made a promise to you.”

“I remember.” She paused. “That was very thoughtful of you, but it was a long time ago.”

"I meant it."

"But who knew how awful things would get?"

"I knew it would get much worse. That's why I made the promise."

"We can both forget it, Rudi. It's okay."

"I'll hide you," I said. "And I can feed you. And it may take a little while, but I can get you back across the border. With the right papers. And I'll take you there to make sure nothing goes wrong."

She said my name with what sounded like a mix of shock and gratitude.

Without thinking about it, without wondering if anyone was close by watching, I dropped my attaché case and put my arms around her.

I held her as if our connection could protect us from the rest of the world. I held her as if this moment mattered more than any sad or tragic moments in the past or to come. I held her as if nothing had ever changed between us. And I held her, because I wanted her to know that at least one person in the city cared about her and would help her.

I felt a kind of jolt, a shock between us. "Do you feel that?" I asked.

Her eyes opened wide. "Yes," she said.

Another spark jumped between us.

"And again!" she said.

"Like years ago!"

"Yes!"

I squeezed her harder and made up my mind.

Chapter Thirty-Six

July 1943

At work the next day, I attributed my absence the day before to the shock of having my home destroyed, then went to the proper government office and made a requisition for a new domicile in Berlin. Within hours, I had a new place. I inquired about its general features, and the woman nodded, saying that I would be happy with what they had found for me. It was an elegant freestanding home that had some recent bomb damage, she told me, but a key section, including the kitchen, was sound. It had just been vacated by a senior Gestapo man and his wife, who after a year in the place had found something farther from the center of the city. I took this to be a euphemism for farther from bombs and that the damage had been substantial.

Until a few years ago, Jews had likely lived in the home. High-ranking Party members and government functionaries had flocked to the luxurious houses or apartments vacated by their Jewish owners when they were told to report to the old synagogue in Levetzowstrasse and held until the next train to the East. Some were so eager they asked for notification in advance and waited outside the residences as their occupants were rounded up.

The house, the clerk continued, was spacious, with a large garden, and was located in one of the villa colonies.

I asked which villa colony.

"Grunewald." she answered. "You've done very well."

I asked for the address.

When she answered, I didn't say anything, but my expression must have betrayed something.

"Is that not acceptable?" she said, her brows furrowing.

"Quite acceptable," I said. "I know the house. Very well. From a while ago."

"Rather elegant, right?"

"It was," I said distractedly. "And maybe still is, in its own way."

Sara shook her head when I told her about my new residence, saying, "I don't know if I want to see it again."

"This is strange enough for me," I said. "I can't imagine how strange it is for you."

She shrugged. "I thought I'd never see it again."

"If I turn it down, I might not get another permanent place right away." I paused. "If this isn't fate, I don't know what is."

Sara and I walked slowly toward the house. Neither of us had been in the Villa Colony Grunewald in years, and even in normal circumstances, it would have been jarring to see these once-familiar streets and houses and landscapes again.

Years ago, I had been in a fog when I was here, concentrating on what Sara said or her gaze at me or the way her lips slipped into a smile. Of course, I'd admired the woods and lakes and beautiful houses, but in many ways, I was seeing the neighborhood for the first time.

There was less damage here than in much of the city, but it was more painful to see because this had been such a sylvan idyll.

Toppled trees lay across walks and gardens. A few large trunks still firmly rooted in the soil rose partway into the sky, with jagged edges where a crown of leaves and branches had been. Lawns and shrubs looked as though they hadn't been trimmed in years.

There were craters near the road and in the yards of some houses. Only the craters in the roadways were filled, usually with a mix of dirt and brick and stones from broken walls.

Worst were some of the villas.

"Oh, my," Sara whispered. "The Ullsteins' house!" What remained were a few blackened chimneys and the ash-covered foundations. "But luckily they're long gone. They were smart, had money, and made it across the Atlantic." She paused. "Can you imagine the poor people who fled to Austria or France and thought they were safe?"

On her street, there was no pattern to the destruction. Two houses in a row looked as they might have a decade ago—weathered, with uncut lawns and sprawling bushes, but intact. The next house was a pile of rubble. And the house beyond that was untouched, followed by several mostly destroyed structures.

We came to a curve. Just beyond it was the Traum family villa, or, more accurately, what had been the Traum family villa.

Sara took my hand, squeezing it tightly. "I hope it's gone, completely gone. I mean, it might as well be."

I squeezed back and told her we could turn around. She laughed and said, "No, I need a place to stay tonight!"

Like the neighboring lots, the drive and front lawn were in disarray, grass grew high, bushes were untamed, and branches and splintered linden tree trunks lay where they had fallen.

The tall, narrow windows either had glass crisscrossed with tape or were covered by wood and cardboard. Much of a wing of the house seemed to have disappeared, blocked off by tarps and wooden planks.

"Wow, it's still here," she said, as we stood at the beginning of the drive. "Sort of."

Now it struck me that moving into her family's old house was a ridiculous idea. Why hadn't I turned down the assignment at the housing office? I could still retract my acceptance. In fact, it would be easy to do.

I suggested again that we turn around, and once more she took my hand.

"Let's see how it's fared," she said. "Together."

We shared the most unlikely things now—not at all what I'd dreamt about a decade earlier, and yet just as I had years ago, I squeezed her hand and we moved forward.

Although the gravel on the drive was missing in places, it crunched in a familiar and beguiling way.

The old front door was gone, replaced by several planks with cross pieces that covered most of the entryway.

Sara let go of my hand and pushed on the door, which opened slowly, revealing a dark room. Years ago, it was a fancy foyer. Now it looked like a storage shed.

Near the door, the floor's finish had been ruined, probably by rainwater. Dust covered the few plain, broken pieces of furniture that survived and were pushed against the far wall. *Were they cowering from something?* A dank smell wafted over us.

"Oh my," I said.

"Is this the same house?" she said.

We walked through the intact part of the villa. As in the foyer, all the furniture and decorations that had made this place so special were gone. As Sara had said, some things had been taken by her family, but even after paying large bribes, they were allowed to take only a few objects.

Had the books I had pored over for many hours been burned, or more likely tossed out by ignorant party hacks?

Had the paintings that made me soar and that pleased and bothered me, sometimes at the same time, survived? Were they hanging in Carinhall, where Göring might find a few moments to salivate over them, at least long enough to figure out which storage site to send them to? Or had they been labeled degenerate art and hidden away so the masses wouldn't be tainted? Then again, maybe fools had dumped them in the trash.

As we went through the house, I said, "There's an echo without the carpets and furniture."

When we glanced at vacant walls where hundreds of paintings and etchings and drawings had hung, in a whisper, Sara said, "The art." In the study, in front of the empty shelves, she said, "The books." Then she listed several more things that were missing. "My mother's flowers." "The stained-glass windows."

"We can leave," I said yet again. "This is difficult to take in."

"We have to see it all," she answered. "What's no longer here wants to be remembered."

Upstairs, most of the rooms were empty, a few windows were nonexistent, and there were holes in the ceilings. The connection to what had been the master bedroom, a place I'd never seen, was boarded up; we could see a little daylight through the cracks.

We went down the stairs and toward the back of the house, to the kitchen and servants' quarters. Unlike the rest of the house, this area looked lived in. The kitchen had a table and chairs. The sink and ice box looked undamaged. At the far end, two battered armchairs that didn't match had a small table between them. The servants' bedrooms had beds, night tables, and chairs and were intact. I wondered why the place was on the list of available housing. Yet, I didn't care. In the ruins, in this servants' quarters, we could create a nest for ourselves.

"Home sweet home," I said. "At least for a little while."

She gazed a moment at me silently, then headed toward the solarium, the gateway to the garden. Almost all the panes of glass had vanished, and the iron framework was bent in several sections, perhaps melted by fire or smashed by exploding debris. It looked as though it might collapse at any moment. The chaise lounges and sitting chairs with their thick cushions were gone, and the palms that once made this place feel like an oasis remained only in memory. The damp floor was covered with glass shards and rubble. A path had been cleared to the door to the garden.

Just outside the solarium was a crater. In the pit, the earth was raw, with no leaves or debris covering it. The explosion had torn away part of the main walkway that led to the center of the garden.

All the other times I had been in this garden, I had felt I might as well be deep in the woods, like the dark forests of Teutonic myth—surrounded by beautiful flowers, pines, and firs that stirred in the breeze, and a fountain that gurgled like a stream in the mountains. Here, long ago, Sara and I revealed ourselves fully to each other, where I had felt a kind of wild love I hadn't known before.

At first, I didn't recognize the pile of broken concrete as the remains of the fountain. Much of the pergola that had run around the center of the garden was shattered and lay on the ground, too. The few flowers were crowded by tall grass and weeds. The once meticulously trimmed hedges grew wild. Damp leaves covered the benches.

After some silence, Sara spoke again about what was obvious in front of us. "The fountain. The pergola. The walkway. The trees. The flowers. The bushes." Then she stopped.

"One miracle," I said. "It looks like your hiding place has survived. The trees over there have been spared."

"Yes," she said.

Sara was sniffling.

I said her name and put my arms around her.

She slipped into my embrace as easily as she had years earlier. Her body shook, and she wiped tears from her face.

"It's so sad," she whispered. "Everything's destroyed."

"The garden's a wreck."

"More than that," she said. "Much more. The people who made everything here so wonderful are never coming back. Many aren't even alive."

"Yes," I said, hugging her tighter.

"It's all so hopeless."

For a moment, I felt as miserable as she. But then I remembered how Sara herself had spoken during other dark times long ago.

"We're still here," I said, my voice surprisingly firm and cheerful. "We will endure."

She made a kind of bleating sound, a combination laugh and cry of pain.

"We have to keep going."

"Why?" she asked.

"We have to be witnesses who make sure that everyone knows what happened. And they need to know your story. The Nazis wanted to destroy you, but you're still here, in the heart of their vile empire. You've defeated them. Your victory is as important as any military victory. It's enduring and human."

I couldn't tell if she thought I spoke brilliant words or that I was delusional beyond belief.

"This is victory?" she finally said.

The coal stove still worked, and the first night we used it to heat the few cans of food that had been left behind. The electricity was on, but some of the light fixtures were broken or missing bulbs. I was exhausted and decided to go to sleep. Sara followed me to the bedroom I had taken.

"Can we share the bed?" she asked.

I put my arms around her and squeezed. "Of course, my love."

"Oh my," she whispered, hugging me back.

"Who could have imagined?"

"We have to take what's given to us."

I blew out the candle, and in a moment we were entwined in the bed. I massaged her from her scalp to the soles of her feet, as though I needed to feel that it was her, that she was back again after so many years. She sighed happily as I kept rubbing. Soon I stopped massaging and took her into my arms. Our love-making was both so familiar and utterly different. A reunion. Solace after all both of us had been through. A lovely new connection. Something that could help us through the difficult days ahead.

I didn't fall asleep immediately. As Sara softly snored, nestling against my chest, I lay on my back, staring upwards. In the darkness of the blacked-out city, I couldn't see anything. Small noises I didn't notice in the daytime became overwhelmingly loud. A truck in low gear drove nearby. A person pushed or dragged a cart with metal wheels. Several times I heard a pop, perhaps electricity arcing in the air from a severed wire, sparks showering as though it were New Year's Eve, as dangerous as they were magical and beautiful.

I had no idea how long this would last, but unlike a decade ago, that didn't trouble me. The times were extraordinary. Magda would be furious, but I loved her, and I loved Sara, in different ways. One had to embrace whatever bit of joy and happiness that appeared in whatever form it took.

In the dark, I sighed and fell asleep.

Chapter Thirty-Seven

July 1943

In 1939, not long before the war started, a postcard had arrived in the mail at my apartment. Postmarked Zürich, the front depicted an idyllic scene of a farmhouse high in the Alps. The only living creatures were a few birds above the farm. In elegant script on the back were the words: "Greetings from Switzerland! We are settling in but we're missing Oma. The birds sing loudly here, much like those in the garden in the Grunewald villa. Visit soon!" It was unsigned.

I had read the message several times, flipping the card around to look at the Alpine scene between each reading.

I admired all the news Dr. Traum had crammed into this missive. Dr. and Frau Traum and Sara, and maybe Sol had been able to leave Germany, but Sara's elderly, sickly grandmother remained in Berlin. They were happy, especially Sara, who always wanted to be free to fly wherever and whenever she wanted.

The next communication from Dr. Traum had come several months later. This time it was a simple envelope. No return addressee, no stamp. The handwriting was unfamiliar. It had been slipped under the apartment door.

The brief letter began: "Dr. Traum says you can reach him here, using this name." That name was Valéry Oiseau and was followed by an address in Zürich.

The letter had also said that colleagues in the world of medicine and psychology had vouched for the doctor and his work, enabling him to settle in Zürich and teach and practice again.

The letter was signed "A Friend."

I had thought of Sara again. Oiseau was French for bird.

Over the next few years we wrote each other occasionally, sending postcards with brief messages that wouldn't attract the interest of the mail censors. He signed his cards, "Valéry." I signed mine, "Fritz."

Sometimes I commented on general things. After the invasion of Poland, I sent a card of a photograph of snow in the Tiergarten with the phrase, "So sunny now, but winter is coming!"

Most times, I tried to show that I was thinking of him or perhaps *them*. On the back of a picture of a lush garden, I wrote, "It takes time, but well-tended seeds eventually sprout into the most brilliant specimens. You should see what I'm growing."

"Dear Valéry," I wrote another time on a postcard depicting a beach scene on Rügen. "Fresh air and a cleansing breeze! Lovely change of scenery. Wishing you and yours all the best!"

Eventually I received a postcard from him depicting the Alpine skyline. He wrote: "Glad you had time to bask in the sun at the seashore. Here we're enjoying the many views from the distant mountains. Come climb the heights with me. Yours, Valéry."

Finally, in the spring of 1943, I sent Dr. Traum the kind of message I had hoped to be able to send for years.

"Dear Valéry," I wrote on a postcard with a picture of Gutenberg's printing press. "Official business may bring me to Bern in the near future.

If that works out, I hope we see each other again. Can't wait to catch up! Yours, F."

I received his reply in only five days:

"Dear Fritz. Wonderful news! If it happens, I will adjust my schedule to be fully at your disposal. Call on arrival. Yours, V."

So accommodating, I thought. I stared many times at the phone number that followed.

"Dear Valéry," I wrote in return. "Excellent. Hoping for my trip to work out and us to have a happy reunion and a productive few days. Will enjoy sightseeing in Bern. Yours, F."

One of Frau Riegler's duties was assigning couriers to relay top-secret documents back and forth to our embassies in Sweden and Switzerland, the closest neutral countries. For several years, I had volunteered regularly, emphasizing that I had personal business in Switzerland. No one in my family had seen my mother's elderly cousin and her husband, who lived in northern Switzerland since 1938. I wanted to check on them. I omitted saying the couple were Nazi enthusiasts, which made me happy not to have had any contact with them. I also said I missed hiking in the mountains near my relatives.

I had stressed my *Wandervögel* background since Frau Riegler had made it clear she had also been a *Wandervogel* and still admired the movement, which was another indication that we shared feelings about the current regime.

Early morning dew on a mountain meadow versus the burning of books, buildings, and people.

I had to jump a major hurdle to become a courier. Frau Riegler discovered the problem when I made my first request, which was why hadn't I become a member of the National Socialist German Workers Party.

My decision not to join had also limited my rise in the ranks, although my diligent work and the shortage of office staff had helped me climb farther than I would have otherwise. And because I would loathe myself if I became a member of a party whose ideas and Führer I loathed.

I had resisted the temptation to speak freely with Frau Riegler, answering the way I answered most people who asked me this question: since the *Machtergreifung*, joining the Party was obviously opportunistic. I didn't want to be one of the millions who applied for membership, since it was obvious that the Nazis would be in power for a long time. If everyone who applied was accepted, there would be nothing special about membership and it would dishonor the courage and conviction of those who became members before 1933. In addition, I feared I couldn't think in ways that meshed with the Party's approach. Not that I was against the Party, just leave that up to the people who knew best, I continued. Also, in general I preferred not to join groups. "I work best alone," I said. "I love Germany, and my record in the Ministry speaks for itself."

"You're very thoughtful, Herr Baumann," she had said. "These days it's unusual to hear considered arguments—about much of anything."

Frau Riegler had folded her arms and looked away from me. In a cold voice, she had said, "If you were a Party member, it would be so easy to help you. You're still on the list of staff to be considered for courier runs to the embassy in Bern. Several more approvals are necessary."

I had said, "Thank you, Frau Riegler," and sternly looked downward in deference. Saying, "It's only a first step, Herr Baumann," and she walked away.

When the assignment came, I was surprised in a way I hadn't expected.

I had to leave in two hours?

Luckily, for several years, I had made some preparation for a courier run, even though I had no idea when or if it would take place. As I sifted through the usual documents that came across my desk, I pulled out ones I imagined would intrigue analysts in London. Instead of destroying the copies, as I was supposed to, I set them aside in my office, secure in a folder I labeled, "Ministry Procedures." At the beginning of the folder were at least 20 memos and notices we had received in recent months about day-to-day department matters. For one, cleaning services were being cut back to monthly from weekly and we were asked to be even neater. Another stated that the eastern entrance to the building was temporarily closed because of "construction." *'Destruction' would have been the more accurate word.*

Below these were copies of memos and reports that dealt with much different subjects: details of troop strength in the East; outlines of manpower deficiencies and supply problems caused by the increased activity of Soviet partisans behind the lines; estimates of the fighting power and morale of Red Army forces; armament production figures; reports on bombing damage in the western regions of the Reich and its effect on the populace; some evaluations of the military strength of our allies Italy, Hungary, Romania, Bulgaria, and Slovakia; and much more. To keep the files up to date, I weeded them out as time passed and some of them became irrelevant.

I went to my office, locked the door, put some of what I thought were the best documents in several envelopes. Then I took most of my clothes off and taped the envelopes around my thighs.

I felt awkward and walked slowly and a bit stiffly to my train at the Anhalter Station. I had no choice and stayed dressed this way for the long journey through Germany, during the transfer in Basel and the ride to Bern, and then being picked up for a meeting with several Embassy staff. I didn't undress and take off the bundles until I was finally alone in my hotel, about 24 hours after I'd left my office in Berlin. In the summer heat and with my extra insulation, I sweat the whole time from Berlin south. I was already nervous, and because I became nervous about sweating so much, I sweat more. I worried the ink on the damp documents would run, and they would be unreadable.

On my first day in Bern, I felt like a creature from a cave who stepped out into sunlight for the first time.

Civilians drove passenger cars on the streets. Movie theaters were open. People sat leisurely outside at cafés and wore clothes that were clean, some even looked new. Streets and buildings and trees were whole. The only posters on walls were advertisements or public service announcements. The national flag was a familiar blood red, but the symbol at its center was a peaceful, unbroken cross. Perhaps the most stunning thing I'd noticed was the simplest. It was a sound I hadn't heard in Berlin in years—the *plunk* of a tennis ball being hit back and forth on a court.

Unlike in Berlin, there was no sign of the military. The whirring of an airplane didn't make anyone cringe. There were no signs for air raid shelters. No sirens sounded.

At the embassy, even though I was with colleagues and we talked about work in much the same way as in Berlin, this felt different, too. Windows were not covered with light-blocking material. Everyone was dressed presentably. Most amazing, there were a few pieces of chocolate on a tray to snack on.

I was dropped off at my hotel later in the afternoon after declining an invitation to dinner. I had spent all night and the morning on the train from Berlin, I emphasized, and hadn't really slept in a day and a half. Happily, my colleagues were more than sympathetic.

After I checked in, I undressed and peeled the damp envelopes off my legs, then set them out to dry. After I showered and dressed again, I left the hotel, walking up and down several remarkably peaceful streets. Streetlights were on. Lights shone in windows. There was enough light for me to see the way and not be wary of tripping over something or walking into a building.

After a few blocks, I went into the lobby of another hotel and found a public phone. I dialed a number that I had memorized long ago.

A person who was not Dr. Traum answered. I asked for Herr Oiseau and identified myself as his friend Fritz. The man told me that Herr Oiseau was not available. I said I was now in Bern and hoped to see him as soon as possible. The person said he knew that Herr Oiseau would be very happy to hear that I was nearby and would most likely be in Bern by the morning. "He is very eager to see you." We agreed that I would call this same number again in the morning.

Only later did I come up with a better system for carrying my treasures from Berlin. I put the important material in the bottom of my satchel. Usually, it consisted of many pages of reports and cables and memoranda. Some I'd copied by hand, but I also had carbon copies and even a few original documents. Many of them had *Geheime Reichssache*—Secret Reich Matter stamps on them.

Above this mass of paper, I put a piece of leather, which I had fashioned on my own and was nearly identical to the satchel's interior.

On top of the fake bottom, I put memoranda I had made up. Undated, unsigned, they concerned department housekeeping: an outline of how copies of cables should be routed in the office; suggestions for further savings in the canteen offerings, all aimed at the war effort; and so on.

On top of the memoranda I would never send to anyone, I set something that was the ultimate protection, something no one would disturb. The deluxe edition of *Mein Kampf*. The bookstore clerk had gazed at me as I discreetly measured various editions. "The centerpiece of my bookcase," I had said.

On top of all this, I added the sealed and stamped Foreign Office envelopes

I had been entrusted to deliver. I liked to think the fierce Nazi eagle in the blob of dried wax on the uppermost envelope would also deter inquisitive eyes.

Chapter Thirty-Eight

July 1943

Dr. Traum and I met for the first time in four years in the back of a café in the center of Bern. I arrived ten minutes early; he entered the door exactly on time. Again, on the walk to the café, I had seen unusual things: clean streets, intact sidewalks, undamaged buildings, and plump dogs being walked. Trees were full and green. Gardens blossomed. I saw rubble only once, at a construction site. I stared at the scene for a moment.

Even though I knew I didn't have to, I kept listening for ominous sounds in the distance: the buzz of planes, the whine of bombs falling, the roar of explosions.

The absence of noises I had come to expect was unsettling enough. But I was struck, too, by more things. In the café, there was an aroma I hadn't smelled in a long time, freshly brewed coffee. Not chicory "coffee," not acorn "coffee," not malt "coffee," not barley "coffee." But real coffee. The smell alone made me swoon. There were some rationing and food shortages in this island of neutrality, but somehow they had obtained coffee and chocolate.

As I waited at the café, I stayed alert, even though I had been careful to be sure no one from the embassy was following me. As I walked here, I doubled back several times. I even went into another café, then left via the rear door, where I waited a moment before making my way through one of the many alleyways in the Old City. I planned to see my official compatriots later this morning, when I was to return to the embassy for more meetings.

I worried, too, about being followed by members of the Swiss police, who suspected all German diplomats of nefarious deeds and who might inadvertently interfere with something that most of them privately would approve of. But, of course, I couldn't tell them anything about my most important mission because I knew they had to remain officially neutral. If they didn't maintain this posture, that would provoke the Nazi and fascist armies that encircled the Confederation.

I rose from my seat when Dr. Traum came in and for a moment we looked at each other silently.

Even though we saw each other infrequently, he was the person who had challenged me to find a way to use my position at the Foreign Ministry to fight the Nazis in a manner few others could. He helped me not go into internal exile, not give up and wait things out. From the time we met, he had said, I stood out because of what he called my grounded sense of right and wrong, my desire to do the right thing. Now I needed his help to do the right thing.

This was the second time we had met after a long period of not seeing each other. He looked as healthy as he had ten years before, not like the gaunt figure I remembered from four years ago. In fact, because of the walk here, his skin had a rosy glow. This time I was the one who had an older, loosely fitting suit, made several years earlier for me when, like so many of my countrymen, I had more flesh on my bones.

We shook hands vigorously. We were both grinning.

"I'm so very glad to see you," I said.

"I always knew we'd meet again."

We sat down. I thought I would dive into the reason for my trip to Bern, but in Dr. Traum's presence and after hearing his soothing voice, the urgency and near-panic I had felt for so long vanished. Despite needing to return to Berlin in just three days, I felt as if I had all the time in the world.

We asked about each other's families, and I told him about several mutual friends in Berlin. He had kept somewhat informed, but didn't know the latest news, including that a friend's brother was missing on the Eastern Front and that another friend had been arrested for "activities against the state."

He took this in quietly. His long, thin hands, like pianists' hands, rested patiently on the table, as though waiting for the right moment to strike keys and create beautiful sounds.

He asked about the general mood in Berlin and the state of the war. I stressed that many people hated the Nazis but supported the war because they were fighting for Germany, not the Führer. We couldn't surrender to the country's many enemies, they believed, even if the Führer had unnecessarily expanded the war beyond the justifiable retaking of former German lands. A reckoning with him would have to come later.

"Reckonings may come sooner," he said. Then he stared at me and asked, "Sara? How is she?"

Did he already know we were living together?

I regretted not remembering sooner his profession and how his silences in the past had compelled me to fill the void with things I might not have said otherwise.

"She's safe," I said. "With me. Which is as safe as anyone like her can be in Berlin."

"I know things got much worse since we left."

"Yes," I said. "No Jew is safe in Berlin. If they're caught, they're deported immediately, and these days that usually means one thing."

"The rumors are true then?" he said in an oddly serene tone. "We're being slaughtered?"

"Those they don't kill right away they work to death."

He shook his head and said, "I understand why she returned, but I wish deeply she hadn't."

"She went from a haven most people only dream of to the center of hell," I said.

After a silence, he said, "You look well. A little older. A little thinner. But in excellent shape."

"Despite everything, I keep a strict health regimen."

"Long ago you and Sara were in bars every night."

I tried to shrug nonchalantly. "The follies of youth and love."

"But that's when you and I got to know each other and started having deep discussions that are continuing in ways we never imagined."

"Do you remember a conversation from four years ago?" I asked.

"I do!"

"I can answer fully now," I said. "I'm risking everything. I'm pushing myself to the maximum."

"Really?" he said.

I told him about the documents I had brought. "And, of course, I can get many more."

"My friend," he said, gazing at me with a dreamy look I had rarely seen. "I've hoped for a long time that something like this would happen."

"I want to pass them to the British," I said. "A handful of documents, enough to whet their appetites. And I need your help. Do you know any British diplomats?"

"No, but some people I know may."

"I'm here for only three days. We have to move quickly."

He nodded. "In that case, I'll simply go to the embassy and explain the situation. I have no obvious connection to you so you won't get in trouble. The worst that can happen is they'll throw me out."

"I'll be forever indebted."

"It's the least I can do."

"Just as this is the least I can do."

I spent several hours at my own embassy in the morning, then left for lunch. Dr. Traum and I met in a corner of the main train station, sitting on a bench, several feet apart. No one else sat near us, and we had excellent views of the entrances.

We both arrived via circuitous routes, doubling back several times. I tried not to stare at every adult I saw, especially men in suits, but I hadn't seen anyone twice and no one was lingering behind me.

"I'm relieved to be here," I said. "I had so much trouble concentrating this morning."

"This is a momentous undertaking, my courageous friend."

Again, his voice calmed me.

In hushed tones, we discussed how he should approach the British Embassy, which likely was under surveillance by Reich and Swiss agents. He could wear a hat tilted forward, he said. I suggested he carry something distracting, say, a large bouquet of flowers. What would they remember—his face or the surprising flowers?

"I hope there's someone on staff who handles this kind of thing," he said.

I laughed. "There's only a handful of real diplomats in the German Embassy. The rest are spying on the Allies. And the British are spying on the Axis. And they're both spying on the Swiss."

On the bench between us I set a copy of the *Neue Berner Zeitung* in which I'd put the sample documents. I told him about each, told him how I wanted him to describe my general position, my motivation, my lack of desire for any compensation.

"And I will, of course, attest for your sterling character," he said.

"Don't start making things up now!"

In the late afternoon, I again met Dr. Traum, whom I now thought of sometimes as Valéry, this time in the deserted Rosengarten. We followed the pathways on the outer edges of the garden to the side farthest from the road, overlooking the city. The elevation was slightly higher here than the rest of the park, which gave us good views of the paths.

I remembered walking in parks in Berlin, especially the Tiergarten before the Nazis, before the war, and sometimes in the company of another member of the Traum family. In those days, the parks were like this one, with trees full of leaves with all branches in place. The walkways were smooth. Grass was neatly mowed. Birds chirped contentedly. No people who had lost their homes were sleeping on benches. No dogs searched desperately for food.

As we spoke, we gazed down over the oldest part of Bern. The churning, fast-flowing Aare River contrasted with the calm, elegant, medieval city. The Swiss weren't perfect, making it nearly impossible for Jews and others to come here. Still, the hills and nearby mountains, unlike the flat plains around Berlin, felt protective, trying with some success to shield the place from murder, militarism, and all manner of ill winds. The only obvious beasts in the area were contained in the bear pit near the river that honored the animal after which the city was named. The sunlight made the houses and towers and cathedral glow. Fresh air redolent of thick forests blew from the mountains nearby and the Alps in the south. Here we were reminded of what life should be like.

Dr. Traum told me that at the British Embassy, he had been let into the foyer immediately, to his relief and surprise. The young man at the entrance desk asked what Dr. Traum wanted. Dr. Traum said he had a matter of utmost international urgency to discuss. He was encouraged that the secretary or concierge took this in stride and said someone would speak with him shortly. He was asked to wait in the lobby, where he was distracted by the formal, heavy, dark *Mitteleuropäisch* furniture and decorations. It wasn't at all what he expected of a place that was in essence an outpost of Britain.

Then a man who called himself Mr. Jones appeared in the lobby through a far door.

Mr. Jones—Dr. Traum assumed that his name was a pseudonym—sat down in a chair next to him and tilted his head back ever so slightly as he gazed at Dr. Traum. Dr. Traum explained that a "high-level" official in the German government, an anti-Nazi, wanted to give information to the British to help end the war sooner and rid Germany of the National Socialist regime. This man had access to a range of the most sensitive documents and reports, and, Dr. Traum said, he had samples with him he was willing to show right away. More were available, and the official in question might be able to meet them in person to discuss the documents. Dr. Traum gave his own references and mentioned that he was a Jewish refugee from Germany who lived legally in Switzerland.

Several times, with both hands, Dr. Traum held up documents he had brought, hidden in the pages of the *Neue Berner Zeitung*. Mr. Jones puckered his lips slightly at the paper as though weighing whether or not to give in to his natural curiosity. After ten minutes or so, Mr. Jones abruptly rose from his chair and excused himself.

Again, there was a long wait, and Dr. Traum imagined that Mr. Jones was speaking with others who had names like Mr. Miller and Mr. Williams about the things he and I had assumed would make them very cautious. How could they trust someone who simply walked in off the street? How could they be certain this wasn't a plant by the Germans or even the Swiss? And if Dr. Traum and the official were what he said and were sincere, how could the British be certain the information was accurate and that the pair hadn't been unknowingly set up by the Germans?

When the door Mr. Jones had used opened again, a different man appeared. He was younger than Mr. Jones and didn't say a word at first, instead observing Dr. Traum as though trying to place his face or to memorize it. The man was dressed in the same kind of suit as Mr. Jones and had a thin moustache with hair that was slicked back severely. He stayed silent so long that Dr. Traum wondered if the man was looking for someone else. Finally, Dr. Traum said, "Yes?"

The man seemed to start. "Ah," he said, looking away, not introducing himself. In that moment, Dr. Traum knew what was coming next. "We're so sorry," the man said, "but at this time, we can't help you."

"Perhaps I was overeager," Dr. Traum said when he was telling me what had happened. "Or my English didn't convey what I wanted to convey."

"Your English is excellent," I said in English.

He laughed and said, "Now on to the Americans. I hope my English isn't too British for them."

I smiled. "If they give you the cold shoulder, we can try other Allies," I said. "The Canadians. The Australians."

"I can also see about finding someone with connections. But that takes time."

"I have only two days. Can you stay in Bern until I go back?"

"It's the least I can do," he answered.

Chapter Thirty-Nine

July 1943

I had never seen Dr. Traum so obviously happy. Had the people he met earlier that day, Americans who telegraphed every thought and emotion, proudly, confidently, innocently, impressed him so much that he began to shed some of his Prussian demeanor?

He whispered excitedly, "The Americans want to meet tonight!"

Finally! Contact.

He and I were in a different café, in the hours before dinner. And now he told me about his detailed instructions on how to approach the private home of one of the embassy officials, climbing stairs through a park that led to a rear entrance that couldn't be seen from the street. The trees and bushes were thick and the path was not well-lit, he continued, so we would need to make our way carefully. We were to knock on the door in a certain rhythm.

I felt as enthusiastic as he sounded. This is what I had imagined my connection with the Allies would involve: nighttime meetings, clandestine hideouts, secret passwords, and codes.

At first, Dr. Traum said that what happened at the U.S. Embassy was remarkably similar to his experience with the British. On his arrival, he explained in detail why he was there and what he was offering. After a few minutes, the man who had introduced himself as Mr. Turner and asked several questions, excused himself.

While Dr. Traum waited, he wondered why the staff, like the British, chose bland pseudonyms. Why not something creative? Even just Mr. Washington or Mr. Lincoln? Still, he understood. He said they must be fearful of a setup by Germans to plant a double spy with them. The longer he waited, the more he worried. To make a fair judgment, they should want to know more. Nearly 30 minutes passed before Mr. Turner reappeared.

Mr. Turner asked Dr. Traum to come along to another room, a kind of parlor, with several wing chairs and floor-to-ceiling shelves full of books that appeared to be bound documents or collections of magazines. In a moment, from another door, a second man joined them. He didn't introduce himself and sat back in the largest of the chairs, letting Mr. Turner ask questions.

Dr. Traum told them again what I wanted him to say. Mr. Turner regularly interrupted, several times asking Dr. Traum to repeat himself. Dr. Traum was not sure whether this was because, in his excitement, he might be making mistakes in English or because Mr. Turner was incredulous about the story and wanted to be sure he understood it completely or if he wanted to see whether he could keep details of a made-up story straight. Several times he noticed the quiet man seemed to raise his eyebrows slightly for a second or two when Dr. Traum mentioned original documents and Army reports. Few people could hide all reactions to important things they heard, and Dr. Traum was trained to recognize these little, deeply telling signs.

When Dr. Traum finished, Mr. Turner and the other man didn't say anything. Dr. Traum wondered if they were stunned by the treasure that was falling into their laps. Or was he going to get the same reaction he had gotten at the British Embassy? Then Mr. Turner asked Dr. Traum to see the sample documents he had brought along.

Dr. Traum pulled the slim folder out of the carefully folded newspaper and handed it to Mr. Turner. Taking the documents, Mr. Turner and the other man excused themselves.

Dr. Traum had to wait again, almost 30 minutes, but this wait was easier because the people he was waiting for were looking at the documents he had supplied. The quiet man's eyebrows would likely rise quite a few more times.

When the door opened again, the silent man appeared alone and introduced himself as Mr. Wallace. He asked Dr. Traum to come with him. Dr. Traum felt like raising his eyebrows in response.

They walked down a short, dark hallway, then stopped in front of a particularly large wooden door. Mr. Wallace knocked once, then opened it. In this office, a desk took up much of the space, and a man sat in a chair on the far side of the desk. The folder Dr. Traum had given Mr. Turner was open on the desk. The man at the desk had been staring at the top document, his hands clasped in front of him as though praying.

He was a large man, with what felt like a genuine smile and eyes that lit up when he saw Dr. Traum. This man acted differently from Mr. Turner or Mr. Wallace. He did not have their formal, reserved, studied manner. He asked questions, too, but took his time. The first thing he did after introducing himself as Mr. Clark was to ask Dr. Traum about the same things Mr. Turner and Mr. Wallace had asked about.

Dr. Traum went through the story in detail yet again. He was relieved to be speaking directly with someone who obviously had a high position in the embassy, likely in the intelligence services. Mr. Clark listened intently, and only when Dr. Traum finished did he ask a few more questions, including the most important one—could Dr. Traum and the man he represented meet late that night, around midnight at a different, discreet location?

During the next few hours, I sat in my room, trying to read several Swiss newspapers, whose unfettered reporting was as refreshing as the chance to keep lights on inside without covering the windows.

A few times, I tried to nap. But again and again, I thought about the meeting, which documents to show first, and what to say.

At about 11 at night, I met Dr. Traum in an alleyway near the Federal House. No pedestrians walked the streets, and only a few cars drove nearby. Late in the evening, on a weeknight, the Swiss capital felt like a village in the country. Even in blackouts, Berlin felt busier.

Following the directions Mr. Clark had given, we started the circuitous route to his elegant house on Herrengasse, in the heart of Old Town. At first, I felt safer because of the lack of people. But then I wondered if it would be easier for the Abwehr or the Gestapo or the Swiss police to follow us with no one around. They couldn't mix us up with anyone else, and we couldn't get lost in a crowd.

Dr. Traum and I had both gone over city maps carefully, since the Swiss, to confuse possible invaders, had taken most street signs down right after the war began. Several times I turned around and scanned the area behind us. Once or twice, we went in a loop to see if anyone was following us. But all seemed clear.

Without too much difficulty, we descended from the heights of the Old City to the river and soon came to the park at the base of the hill on which the Old City was built. All we heard was the swift-flowing Aare on the other side of the street, which washed against the shore and through several sluices, where the water churned steadily, sounding like surf at the beach. We found a discreet gate that seemed to open onto nothing but thick bushes. Still, following directions, we pushed our way onto a barely visible path, climbing steadily up toward the townhouses on Herrengasse.

This area was so dark I nearly bumped into the building. After feeling in front of me, I found the door. As I was about to gain the access I had wanted for so long, my heart began to pound. I knocked twice, paused, then knocked once, as we had been requested to do, but I wondered why he hadn't already responded to my heart's wild beating.

The door to the back of the house opened slowly. The light inside wasn't particularly bright, but after the darkness in the park, I had to shield my eyes. I couldn't make out who was standing in the doorway, saying cheerfully and in very good German, perhaps for the benefit of anyone who was listening, "Welcome, friends. Welcome!"

Now I could see part of the terrace we had walked through to get to the house. There were several tables and chairs we had somehow avoided as well as shrubbery on most sides. It looked secluded and was probably delightful on a sunny day. Tonight, however, the garden and the black masses of bushes and trees seemed like ideal places for people to hide and watch us. I said nothing until we were inside.

Once the door was shut, Dr. Traum introduced me to Mr. Wallace. As my eyes adjusted to the light, I saw we were in a kind of game room. A pool table was in the center. A chess board without pieces on it was on a shelf nearby.

"Delighted to meet you," I said, continuing in German. "It's taken a long time to get here."

"I can only imagine the hurdles." He spoke German almost perfectly.

"From darkness to the brightest light." I laughed, and was pleased that Mr. Wallace at least smiled.

"Mr. Clark is waiting for us upstairs."

"Excellent," I said.

The house had high ceilings, with a broad staircase, floor-to-ceiling bookcases with many leatherbound titles in German, high windows, all of which were covered by heavy curtains, and Biedermeier furniture that looked as though it had been here since it had been made in the previous century. Thick carpets covered the floor. All was as serene and imposing as some houses I remembered in Berlin before the war.

We entered a study full of the aroma of rich pipe tobacco, the kind that was no longer available in the Reich. Mr. Clark stood and came around the huge table, gazing at me with intense curiosity.

I tried to imagine his thoughts. *Was I a fraud? Was I well-meaning but over my head? Was I the catch of the century?*

He smiled and put out his hand, saying, "Thank you for coming. And thank you for coming under these special conditions." His German wasn't as good as Mr. Wallace's.

"It's the least I can do," I said. "Thank you for meeting with us."

"May we speak in English?" he asked in German.

"Of course," I said, breaking into the language of our northern European cousins. "And now I extend apologies in advance for my English."

"You speak well."

He asked us to sit, offered drinks, and gave me coffee as I requested. The questions began right away:

Are you a member of the Nazi Party?

Why are you not a member of the Nazi Party?

How were you able to travel to Switzerland?

How do you want to be compensated for the information you give us?

Why do you not want money or other forms of consideration?

What is your position in the Foreign Ministry?

What other departments, agencies, and government organizations do you and your section in the Foreign Ministry interact with?

Do you have any relatives outside Germany and German-controlled countries?

Is anyone else in Germany aware of your desire to supply information to us or any other allied authorities?

Who else have you approached to give information to?

Are you a member of the Nazi Party?

Why are you not a member of the Nazi Party?

How were you able to travel to Switzerland?

How do you want to be compensated for the information you give us?

Why do you not want money or other forms of consideration?

I understood that Mr. Clark needed to be sure I wasn't a plant sent by the Abwehr. The ploy had worked at least once, early in the war, when two British agents were seized on the Dutch-German border after they were lured there by a Nazi pretending to be a turncoat.

This was his quandary. How was it possible that a plain-looking, overly eager man who sometimes stuttered because he talked so fast worked in the German Foreign Ministry in Berlin and wanted to pass along copies of the many top secret documents that came across his desk—as many as he could, as many as the Allies would take? How could it be that these documents discussed in detail just about every conceivable aspect of Germany that an enemy would want to know? How could it be that this included information about German codes, about Allied codes the Germans had deciphered, about German spies and sources abroad, about how German diplomats and other sources viewed Germany's allies, as well as reports from the Eastern Front with details about troop movements, suspected Red Army strength, and more? How could it be that this man could occasionally be given the extra job of traveling to Switzerland as a courier?

I had learned quickly that some Americans, a people who professed to be individualists, believed that for Germans, no shades of gray were possible, as though none of us could be a conservative or a monarchist or a social democrat while loathing the Nazis. *Ha*, I wanted to say, *democracy is not a matter of an election every few years for candidates from two parties that aren't all that different from each other. And despite all the glowing words about life, liberty, and the pursuit of happiness, how could a country founded on genocide and slavery judge others?*

I might have been accepted sooner if I simply asked for gold. Still, while a check of my background was pending, I presented him with the rest of what I had brought from Berlin and discussed its significance. After several hours, he suggested it would be a good time to end since dawn would come soon, and we would lose the cover of night.

An hour or two later, in the breakfast room at the hotel, I felt so light that I might be floating above the quiet crowd that ate and sipped coffee. Despite having no sleep, I was happier than I'd been in a long time.

The meal of eggs, sausage, rolls, cheese, and a cup of real coffee felt like a reward for my efforts. On my way to the embassy, I walked down the Lauben on Kramgasse and enjoyed the sheer normalcy of functioning shops in every storefront, the civilian traffic, the leisurely pedestrians. Someday I hoped Berlin could be like this again.

I bought chocolate for Frau Riegler and other colleagues. I felt like buying more chocolate to hand to the clerk, to the people waiting to be helped, to passersby I saw on the way back to the hotel.

I bought a box of Cuban cigars for my boss, Herr Becker, and several other boxes to give away when a gesture of that sort would make it easier for me to get another courier run to Bern.

I had one last meeting with Dr. Traum. We walked through the Rosengarten, and I thanked him profusely for all his help. He deflected this, saying that he wanted to thank me for all I had done and for allowing him to help. And he offered to continue to help me in any way he could.

We went over how we would communicate, particularly about code phrases I had come up with for us to use. He repeated that he would watch for mail from me, which I would send via other couriers, all of whom regularly carried items for colleagues in the Ministry in the sealed diplomatic pouches that were beyond the reach of the Gestapo.

I asked if I could do anything for him in Berlin. Did he want me to deliver anything? Did he want me look after any friends or former colleagues? I paused. Did he have any messages for Sara and her grandmother?

At this last question, he said, "Please try to get Sara out. Her grandmother can't make the trip and doesn't even recognize Sara." He paused. "Sara will need help leaving."

"I can help her get out of the country," I said. "But wish me luck convincing her to do something like that!"

"I've had the same problem."

We both laughed.

"But if she changes her mind, I'll do anything to help," I said.

"Anything."

He nodded. I thanked him again and told him I had to pack and leave for the train station.

I realized I didn't know when I'd see him again, if ever. It made me feel as though I were leaving my father. As Dr. Traum kept nodding, not moving away, I imagined he felt like a father saying goodbye to a son, also wondering when we would meet again.

Without thinking about it, I embraced him. He seemed startled, but then hugged me back. When we let go, we left in opposite directions, without saying a word or looking at each other. Everything had gone far easier than I'd ever thought possible. *Was that good or bad?*

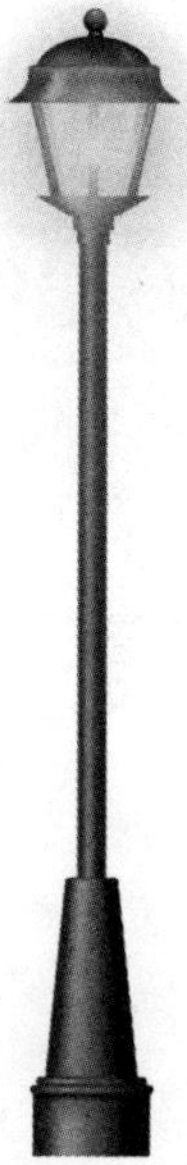

Chapter Forty

December 1943

Mr. Clark always said the right things, but none of the Americans, in their comfortable little mansion in Switzerland, where war and Nazism were distant, fully understood.

Only a week before, at the battered table in the corner of what had once been the dining room, where during meals, a gleaming cherry side table had held dishes and warming trays, I wrote quickly in small script. The paper in front of me was filling up from one edge to the other, as I copied every word and every bit of punctuation of the "Report on the Military and Diplomatic Situation in Hungary," which was stamped *Geheime Reichssache*, secret Reich matter.

As always when doing this sort of task, my stomach tightened and I hoped I wouldn't throw up. It was much easier to think about such a challenging, brazen thing than do it. Again and again, I wondered at how simple it would be to stop. I could put down my pen, burn what I had written, and return the report to the safe in my office at the Ministry.

But I would be in Switzerland again the next week, and I wanted to bring the usual trove of material to help my American friends.

I was almost done copying the report on Hungary when the phone rang. I was surprised. As the bombings got worse, we stopped counting on basic services we had taken for granted before: running water, electricity, the phone. Sometimes they disappeared, then reappeared at random, then disappeared again. Odd that now, after many nights of bombings, the phone functioned. I couldn't remember the last time it had rung.

I set aside my papers and answered, "Baumann."

The connection wasn't perfect, but I clearly heard the agitation in Frau Eberhard's voice. She was Herr Becker's secretary and said right away that he was meeting "in moments" with the Foreign Minister about several matters, including the situation in Hungary, and needed the report on Hungary. "You have it, and we need it."

I gazed down at the *Geheime Reichssache* document.

"I'm so sorry for the confusion," I said. "It's in the safe in my office."

She asked who could open the safe right away.

"I'm the only one who knows the combination," I said. "For security reasons."

"Please tell it to me."

"I'm so sorry."

"The Department Head needs it immediately," she said. "He's already late for his meeting."

"I'm on my way," I said. "And please convey my deepest apologies to Herr Becker."

Only after I hung up did I realize I was as agitated as Frau Eberhard sounded. I had begun sweating. My hands were shaking.

Despite the risk, it was so much easier to copy a document in peace outside the office, where no one could stumble in and see what I was doing. This had never been a problem.

I placed the report in my briefcase, put on my overcoat, and was half-walking, half-running to the bus stop before I realized I had forgotten gloves and a hat. Even though the cold hit my skin, I didn't have time to go back.

I was not a religious person and couldn't remember ever praying, but now that I finally was asking the Lord for something, it was a most unlikely thing. My plea was that busses would run with some semblance of regularity. Perhaps, I thought, focusing on just one request would increase the chances it would be granted. But if God wasn't listening or didn't exist, there was one objective reason for hope. The bus I'd ridden back from the government center earlier in the day had taken more time than it would have just six months ago or even last month, but I had arrived home.

Why hadn't my friends abroad given me a damned camera yet? I'd asked frequently enough.

With a camera that was easily concealable and simple to use, I could copy a document like this report in minutes in my office and not put myself at risk.

At the stop, a pair of women waited. I asked how long they had been there and if any busses had come by. My bus to the Mitte, the main bus on this route, hadn't appeared in the ten minutes they had been waiting, they said.

Several other women came to the stop and asked questions like mine. Again, it struck me that most of the people in the capital nowadays, staffing shops and offices and agencies, driving busses, cleaning the wreckage, were women. With only some exceptions, most men were at the front and children had been evacuated to the countryside. I felt like an oddity at times, and yet to continue to operate, the government needed functionaries like me.

I debated what to do. In normal times and in the right clothing and shoes, I would have enjoyed sprinting to the Ministry, which was five kilometers away. But rubble was everywhere, sometimes blocking sidewalks. In Berlin, across much of Germany and Europe, for that matter, there were no easy paths.

I missed the trams, whose tracks were easily wrecked in the bombings and often wound up resembling huge pieces of spaghetti.

I kept looking into the distance, waiting, trying not to think.

But the longer I waited, the more I thought about what might happen.

If everything had to end, I didn't want to be caught because of something so simple as a "mislaid" top secret document. I'd rather be caught coming back into the Reich *after* I had completed a mission or caught because counterintelligence discovered that my information had caused severe damage to the National Socialist regime.

When I worried about being caught, I wanted a trial to be able to confess— to confess my humanity and desire for freedom and justice and a peaceful world. Then, so long as they dispatched me quickly, I would be as satisfied as a condemned man could be.

I unbuttoned my overcoat and held my briefcase in front of me with both hands, crouching slightly, ready to begin running. But then a bus appeared, chugging slowly in our direction. *Please, please*, I thought. It wasn't the bus that ran on my usual line, but it went to the Mitte, perhaps only a kilometer or so from the Government Quarter.

I sat close to the front of the bus, gazing forward, elated that the way was clear, at least for the first block or two. But then, we had to edge slowly around a crater in the center of the road that had been only partly filled in. The bus tilted one way and then back as we crossed the side of the crater. After we leveled out, the bus sped up again.

We came across a truck that had burned and was on its side, partly blocking our lane on the Ku'damm. We slowly worked our way around the burned truck, then came up behind a line of vehicles that were idling. They may have just paused or they may have been there for hours. Crews were working; police stood nearby. I almost jumped off the bus, but as I rose and headed to the stairs, I saw that the trucks and busses blocking the way were beginning to move. I sat down again.

I saw more damage. The Kaiser Wilhelm Gedächtnis Church was mostly rubble. The KaDeWe store down the street seemed like a shell. Shops and cafés and offices that used to be full of people were dark, missing windows, and partially boarded up.

Near the southern edge of the Tiergarten was a sight that would have been mind-boggling just a few months earlier. On the sidewalk, in front of a three-story home that had no roof and from which smoke poured, several people sat in elegant chairs next to a few pieces of furniture that had boxes and bags on them. The middle-aged couple and an older woman, probably the mother of one of them, were in a little semicircle, with a coffee table in front of them, perhaps the way the seating had been arranged in the apartment they had vacated. The three looked almost bored, as if they were waiting for water to boil in the next room. I imagined one of them would step over to the bed and stretch out for a nap.

We came into the Mitte, close to the Government Quarter, where a section of the street was deep with water, presumably from a broken main. Several trucks and what looked like Party limos had water up over their hubcaps. The door of one was open, and it looked abandoned.

I leapt off the bus into a pile of slush, but I didn't care. Once I got to the sidewalk, I ran full speed, trying to avoid people and the many holes, craters, and debris in my way. Lunch hour had ended so office workers who had gone out trying to find food and supplies were now back at their desks.

I ran past the burned-out hulk of the Reichstag. It had gone from being a striking eyesore, the only ruined building in a healthy city, to yet another battered structure in a battered city. Why hadn't the National Socialists repaired it after burning it down a decade ago? Did they want to remind citizens of their excuse for imposing a dictatorship? Of course, they had no need for the building's original use, the meeting place of a democratically elected parliament.

I ran through the Brandenburg Gate. Other than a few pockmarks from flying debris and shrapnel, it looked as majestic as always. Still, I missed the quadriga on top. I hoped that someday this structure would again be called the Peace Gate and that the peace goddess Eirene would take her rightful place once more in the chariot, casting aside the usurper Victoria.

I passed the old French and U.S. Embassies, which now bore no trace of their pre-war uses. Then I came to the Hotel Adlon, which had been spared so far. Outside, several black Mercedes flying small swastika flags were tended by a doorman wearing one of the few uniforms in the city that didn't have swastikas on it.

I turned onto Wilhelmstrasse and ran by the former British Embassy. Here the sidewalks were crowded, and I had to slow my pace, weaving around the people in front of me, running only when space opened up. Few pedestrians seemed to notice me; a man I nearly hit merely stepped back and let me go by. People were hungry and everyone was tired from the nighttime bombings that repeatedly forced them from their beds. During a time when all kinds of unimaginable things took place, day in and day out, why would a man running on the sidewalk be noteworthy?

Soon, I arrived at the Foreign Ministry. After the guard nodded, I bounded up the stairs. This would be the most difficult part. If Herr Becker or Frau Eberhard came into my office before I could take the report from my briefcase, I didn't know what I would do. Open the safe and pretend it had vanished?

I looked up and down the hall when I came in. As I hoped, all was quiet. I walked in brisk strides towards my office, along one long corridor, then slowly came around the corner. In the distance, a man in uniform was walking away from me. I waited a few beats, and when he didn't turn around, I headed toward my door.

I was already thinking about how I would phrase what I needed to say when several people stepped out of an office across the hall from mine.

"Herr Baumann!" Frau Eberhard called out. She was with Frau Riegler, who looked at me without expression. "Thank God! We need the report!"

I glanced at the two of them, then said softly, "As I mentioned, the report is in my safe."

I walked into my office as the two followed me in.

No.

There was a shout in the hallway. The two women turned and stepped back.

"Where is it?"

This was the angry voice of my boss, Herr Becker.

He seemed to leap into the doorway, yelling, "Baumann!"

I glanced at my briefcase.

Would it end like this?

How deeply unfortunate and stupid.

I took off my coat and hung it up on the hanger, making sure it fell smoothly. Then I put the hanger on the coat rack. I sat down and placed my briefcase on the desk.

"The report!" Herr Becker yelled.

I turned my chair to face him and put my hands together, as though I were praying, as if I had all the time in the world.

"The report!" he repeated. "The meeting's already started!"

I kept looking at him.

"The safe!"

I smiled and said, "Exactly."

"What?"

"Protocols must be followed," I said. "I've sworn an oath about it."

He frowned and shook his head.

Without moving, I said, "I must ask you to leave."

He stared at me.

"Please." I gestured to the door. Then I leaned back in the chair and folded my arms over one another.

A vein began to pulse on his forehead.

I began to quote from applicable regulations, orders, and commands. To myself, I sounded like a member of the Gestapo.

The most secret documents had to be secured when not being used and could be handled only by those specifically entrusted with their care. Even others with the same security clearances couldn't be allowed access.

"The safe is full of top-secret material," I said.

After a pause, he yelled, "Whatever! Just do it now!" Then he stepped into the hallway, slamming the door shut behind him.

As soon as the latch clicked, I pulled the report from my briefcase and set it on the desk. Then I knelt by the safe, dialed the combination, opened the door, paused, then shut it, with slightly more force than usual. The resulting *thud* was very satisfying. I picked up the report then opened my office door. I held it out with both hands to Herr Becker. I bowed slightly, saying, "My deepest apologies for the delay."

Shaking his head, he grabbed the report and hurried down the hallway.

I slowly closed the door and sat down in my chair, leaning back and exhaling. Only now did I notice that my clothes were damp with sweat, my hair wet.

CHAPTER FORTY-ONE

December 1943

"It's a peculiar phenomenon," Hans said. "Berliners are politically solid and reliable. They've mastered National Socialist principles. But at the same time, they have a sentimental streak toward enemies of National Socialism. They've always pushed back against our efforts to restrict the influence of the Jews and now they try to stop us from ridding the last of them from the capital."

I noticed he sounded much like the Minister of Public Enlightenment and Propaganda in his phrasing and intonation. I was tempted to look down to see if he had a club foot as well. But considering his black S.S. uniform and the many other men in S.S. uniforms who filled the lobby of the Adlon Hotel, the usual spot for our infrequent meetings, I shouldn't have been surprised.

He laughed, something I couldn't imagine Dr. Goebbels doing.

"It's just the opposite in Vienna," he said. "Those people are outstanding antisemites, but they're political fools."

"Quite Austrian," I said. "The part about foolishness."

He nodded enthusiastically. "All in all, I'd rather deal with the Berlin problem."

I had a sense this was how he was with his colleagues, genial and amusing no matter how vile the topic of discussion.

But then, of course, his tone could change in a second. And it did again now. He stared at me, his partly shut eyes cold and glassy. You might have thought he was an ever-vigilant Gestapo officer and I was a person suspected of heinous crimes against the state.

"You're an example of that problem," he said slowly. "No, you're worse. You're a traitor both ways."

"Traitor?" I sounded as though I were squeaking.

He flicked a finger in my direction. "No need to deny what I'm saying. You've made it clear what you think about the movement."

I said nothing.

"And I know you're helping your Jewish friends."

"You've had Jewish friends," I said.

He laid his hand flat on the table. "That indiscretion was a long time ago."

"Your own Berlin problem." I paused. "Does anyone know?"

Again he stared at me, but this lasted just a moment. Then he laughed out loud, a laugh that sounded as though it came from deep inside. "Are you *threatening* me?"

"Of course not," I said. "As always, I'm just *curious*."

"My friend, if you tried to cause me problems, I could easily crush you." He paused. "But that won't happen because you aren't that stupid. I hope! Besides, I need you, Rudi. You don't know how refreshing it is to be with an old friend, someone who's different from the people I see every day, someone I can speak freely with—for the most part!"

After a pause, I said, "I find it refreshing to talk with you as well."

"Yes, when we talk, it's as though we're back in school. I feel as free and light as we were then."

"If only we could be like that all the time."

"Ha! But now we're adults in a mad rush to remake the world."

"And our personal worlds got crazy."

"Fräulein Traum," he said.

"So full of life."

"And so outrageous sometimes!"

"*Sometimes?*" We laughed. "She always challenged me, kept me on my toes," I went on. "I was never fully comfortable, and for some reason I liked that. Even miss it."

"Ha. She kept me on my toes, too. Unlike you, I don't miss it."

"She was nothing like what we were supposed to want. She was different, an inspiration. Even if one of us wound up a reactionary."

He smiled in a sickly way, then spoke. "My friend, you really know how to push things. You and her." He patted my wrist. "Maybe that's why I spare you."

I barely breathed.

Then he laughed. Loudly. Happily. Regretfully.

Despite what he did for the Reich, I felt I had to maintain contact with Hans. He was so powerful, and his friendship could be very helpful at some point. Still, it took some effort for me. The next time Hans and I got together was one of the most difficult meetings we had ever had, so much so that I didn't sip the whiskey reluctantly as I usually did. Tonight, I downed it almost as quickly as Hans did.

As I sat at his table, his voice icy, he said, "I'm not dense. I'm also not blind."

I nodded. I would never dispute either statement.

"And yet you think that."

I glanced around the room, wondering if some of the S.S. officers at other tables were waiting for a gesture from Hans to take me to the basement of Prinz-Albrecht-Strasse.

"Please don't underestimate me, Rudi," he said.

For some reason, I thought of admitting everything. In many ways, it would be a relief. My stomach wouldn't constantly be tied in knots. And I might enjoy telling Hans and others about the depth of my efforts to fight the criminal regime and enjoy watching them grasp the idea that I, someone they considered kooky, eccentric, inept, essentially harmless, had fooled them all.

"Where is she?" he asked.

I drank some more of my whiskey and then said, "She?"

He got colder the angrier he became. "I asked you not to underestimate me," he said slowly. After a pause, he added, "Sara."

I shook my head. "How would I know? She dumped me ten years ago!"

"Actually, I don't need you to confirm anything. I have an annoying ability to sense her presence. Whether I want to or not."

"If you sense her presence, why do you need my help?" I took yet another gulp of whiskey.

Without blinking, Hans looked directly into my eyes. His face was still, his mouth tightly shut. There wasn't a hint of friendliness or irony in his features. *Was he angrier at himself than at me?*

"I need your help in knowing exactly where she is. As well as others."

Others? Her family? He of all people knew that they were in Switzerland.

I wanted to change the subject. But, all I could think of involved my own treason.

Had he enjoyed the unexpectedly mild temperatures yesterday?

"Where would anyone hide?" I said. "I'm sure you can find them."

"They often stay overnight in cemeteries. Who'd have thought?" He paused. "But there's something more obvious."

I tilted my head as if I wanted to hear more. I wasn't sure, but I sensed the alcohol was making it a little easier to react in a way that might lessen his suspicions.

"They hide in traitors' homes," he said. "In their attics and basements. Their garages. Their garden huts. Their country homes."

"Wow. They could be anywhere." I tried to sound appreciative of the challenge this posed for Hans and his colleagues.

"Not anywhere!" he said. "Loyal, patriotic Germans don't harbor them. So that limits the possibilities."

I didn't believe it was possible, but his stare turned colder. Then he looked away, saying, "Sometimes you make me despair."

I opened my hands and said, "I work in the highest levels of government. I have nothing to hide."

He laughed. "All I care about is that you have *no one* to hide!"

Luckily I was able to laugh with him.

"If you're hiding anyone, I won't be able to protect you."

I nodded and was surprised that when I tried to swallow, my throat felt blocked.

"In fact, I can help you." He paused. "But only if you help me."

"Help you?" I asked. "How?"

"Rudi," he said warmly. "Tell me where some U-boats are."

I thought of the "submarines," the people who went underground. The first who popped into my mind was Max, who, like Hans and I, had fallen, for Sara.

"There's one possibility." Now I wondered if the alcohol was making me open up in ways I wouldn't without it.

"A Jew? Or other enemy of the state?"

"I don't think of him as an enemy of the state," I said. "More of a personal enemy."

"Yes?"

I remembered goblets of wine shattering years ago. "Sometimes they lean in, gesture as if to be the closest of friends, and more, and then all explodes, and they blame you."

"Are you speaking historically?" he asked. "A stab in the back?"

"I'm speaking more personally—" I didn't like saying what I was saying, but I knew this revelation would make him less suspicious of me and stop asking so many questions that I couldn't answer truthfully.

What if giving up one person could help save the lives of many more, thousands or hundreds of thousands more?

"You might have met him back in the day," I said.

Chapter Forty-Two

December 1943

Again, I met Hans for talk and drinks at the Adlon. And again, I felt on edge. He was increasingly suspicious, and there was more for him to be suspicious about.

I had to keep him from wondering about me for obvious reasons, but also because someday Hans might protect me in one way or another. *What would I sacrifice to protect myself? Had I told Hans about Max?* I hoped I hadn't mentioned any details that would lead Hans to Max. I barely remembered the building where I had run into Max five years ago. He had moved since then.

But I couldn't remember what came next that evening the last time Hans and I met. By the time I had mentioned Max, I was mispronouncing some words and losing my train of thought. Hans had been drinking more than I, as usual, but if anything, also as usual, he was the more collected of the two of us.

If I had said something about Max, would Hans have remembered? I didn't recall Hans responding or writing anything down. Then again, he didn't need to write down important things.

"These days you can't trust anyone," Hans said.

"But our friendship goes back decades," I said.

He laughed. "We can trust that old friendship. Let's honor it with a toast!"

I had reluctantly joined in each round. I knew that drink would make Hans happy, and possibly he would forget a few moments that I didn't want him to remember. I tried not to drink much, sipping while he tossed back glasses. His voice was slightly louder. The smile, showing his large, bright white teeth, grew wider.

Just when I thought he might not notice if I stopped drinking, he suddenly leaned forward in his chair and pointed at me, exclaiming, "Sara!"

I hoped I didn't look as startled as I felt, as though next he would strike me with his hand.

"Sara," he said again, in a more normal voice.

What could I say? That I was madly in love again?

"What about her?" I asked.

He repeated her name again, almost in a whisper. He glanced down at the tabletop silently for a moment, then at me again, his head turned to the side, looking more weary than angry. I expected he would finally take the step that made the most sense: demanding to search my house.

"She dumped you, too," he said.

"I thought you dumped her," I said. "For political reasons."

"I think she was attracted to me in part for political reasons," he said, laughing. "She thought she needed protection. But back then, there wasn't much danger. And she realized that pretty quickly. It was a lot of fun for a short while. And I couldn't keep seeing her if I wanted to continue in my career."

"I had political problems, too," I said.

"You suddenly realized she was Jewish?" He laughed.

"No, *she* suddenly realized she was Jewish."

His brows furrowed.

"The movement threw it in her face," I said. "After that, something fundamental changed between us."

We sipped our drinks. "Later, sounding very hurt, she asked why I had left her," I said.

His eyes opened wide. "She asked me the same thing."

"Bizarre that she would feel we had left her."

"She was nothing if not feelings," Hans said. "And sometimes they were contradictory."

"Such are feelings."

"And dreams."

I wasn't sure I wanted to know the answer, but I asked about his dreams.

"My dreams might have come true with someone like Sara. I'd have had a family life, but not like our parents'. It would've been more exciting and included cabarets and cafés, parties until all hours. After we started a family, none of that would change. We would add family picnics and bedtime stories and walks to school to the mix. Somehow, it would all work out." He smiled. "Great dreams, and great illusions."

"I've had them about her, too." I waited a moment. "Although I wound up going a different way."

"I should have, too. But no such luck. Sara was so beautiful. And brilliant. And beguiling." He stopped for a moment. "But in the end… brutal. And contrary. A pain in the ass." He paused. "A Jewess!"

"All undeniably true, even the part about her being Jewish. But did that really make a difference to you?"

He ignored me, saying, "Why couldn't I have been happy with a simple German girl? You know the type. Very well."

"Yes." I smiled. "I married one. We have a nice little family. Although maybe she's not as simple as she seems. I wish I could spend more time with them, but they're safer in the country. What about you?" I asked. "Don't you have someone?"

He nodded.

"Does she make you happy?"

He laughed. "We understand each other."

"That's always a good thing," I said.

"But we have no children. It's been disappointing to my superiors, who believe part of the job is to breed a master race, but dreams are for another time and place, my friend." Hans turned his glass back and forth on the tabletop. "Nightmares are more common."

He spoke in a calm, quiet voice, as though sharing things he had considered for a while but not spoken about with anyone until now.

"We're surviving because we're a community that would exist no matter who was in charge, war or no war," he said. "Germans are rallying to help other Germans. We care for the wounded, treat the sick, feed the hungry, find shelter for people who are homeless. It's inspiring."

"And it wouldn't be necessary if not for the National Socialist state."

He went on as if he hadn't heard me. "It's absurd for me. It's as if I'm in a house on fire that's going to collapse soon but instead of doing anything about that, I'm ordered to chase mice and destroy them with flamethrowers." He paused. "Do you know the resources we're putting into persecuting and killing them?" He shook his head. "And they helped so much in the Great War."

"You're sounding like me."

"Things have gotten that bad!"

"Some people resist in various ways, even though it isn't easy," I said.

He stared at me, and I wondered if he might finally admit that all he had believed in had been a waste and destroyed most of what had made the country great.

He kept staring, and I said nothing, watching him and occasionally lowering my gaze.

Finally, he spoke. "Careful, my friend."

I nodded.

"This is still Germany, the state we swore an oath to. Doing anything against it would be treason, of course."

"Of course."

Later at the door, far from the other drunks and the bar staff, he hugged me quickly, then pressed a finger in my chest so hard it hurt.

"If you remember one thing from this evening, it's that this conversation never took place," he scowled.

I nodded several times, and then he added, "That's to protect me as much as you!"

Before I could think of what to say, he laughed.

Then we each started off in different directions. After I'd taken a few steps and begun to relax, I heard him call my name. I turned, and he was facing me, his arm upraised, his hand in a fist, reminding me of Lenin or Thälmann in proletariat pose. "Remember," he shouted. "Not only did we not have this conversation, but I didn't give you this salute!" He laughed again, spun away, and was gone.

Chapter Forty-Three

December 1943

On my fourth trip to Bern, after spending a day at the embassy and dining with colleagues my usual routine in the Swiss capital I went to my hotel, then went out again, using the back entrance, when I knew that this small city would be at its most quiet.

Instead of my usual suit, I wore casual pants and a parka, inside of which I had tied a large office envelope. I pulled down the brim of my hat. I took another circuitous route through the old part of town. Tonight, I went along the river, stopping a few times to take in the wonderful sight of the Aare as it tumbled northwards from the mountains, swept around the hilly peninsula that formed the heart of the city, and onward eventually to meet the Rhine, then flowed, reluctantly and ominously into Germany. The powerful, rushing water was a natural contrast to the staid, elegant city, and lights from across the way seemed to bob in the churning water.

I saw a taxi moving slowly, maybe looking for a fare, except there were no pedestrians or other vehicles.

I was approaching the spot where I would disappear into a thicket of brush and trees. For a second, I thought I heard a noise. The sound of a footstep? I stopped and listened. But now all was silent.

At long last, was I being followed? Had some of my more loyal colleagues in the embassy and in Berlin begun to wonder about my enthusiasm for these trips and my nighttime disappearances in Bern?

My cover story? I was entranced by Bern's normalcy and couldn't wait for something similar to return to Germany, which, of course, would happen with Final Victory!

I stepped into the thicket of brush and trees next to the sidewalk, following the familiar path. I made my way up the overgrown hill to the gardens behind the houses on the southern side of Herrengasse. Several times I stopped to listen, hearing only the hint of a breeze in the bare trees, a tram in the distance.

I arrived at the back door of the house where Mr. Clark lived. On the last two trips, when I got here, I knocked eagerly, feeling I was passing through a gate to a magical place, where I could breathe freely and think freely and speak freely. I had been stepping back a decade to the way my homeland had been and the way I wanted it to be again.

But tonight, when I raised my fist to the door, I paused.

I heard no sound behind me in the dark brush, but my hesitation wasn't a matter of caution. I realized that something about this place was changing for me. I was unhappy that after all my efforts, little or nothing had been done with the information I'd provided.

But what would I do if I didn't knock? Turn around and take the papers I had with me back to the hotel, then back to Berlin? Send a postcard to them later, saying Auf Wiedersehen*? Try to figure out a different way to end the war and the regime? Spend my spare time in Bern sipping coffee in a café?*

I took a deep breath, then knocked.

From the beginning I had liked Mr. Clark, a man with the best American qualities. Unlike some of his compatriots, who would use first names as if we'd known each other all our lives rather than just for 20 seconds, he gripped my hand firmly, nodding, glancing into my eyes, making me feel he would be straightforward and direct with me.

He shared none of the parochial views of many Americans. Also, he seemed to be a true democrat. From what I saw, he treated everyone on his staff as equals. I imagined he was well-born, at least for the United States, where standards were lower than in Europe. Several times, I remembered that after the British rebuffed our inquiries, I had been reluctant to turn to the Americans. Now I was happy the British had driven me to Mr. Clark.

He was a bit portly, which was an impressive, reassuring sight to a Berliner, since at home severe rationing affected everyone but Reichsmarschall Göring. And because he wasn't hungry, Mr. Clark didn't talk incessantly about food.

His deep, rumbling voice made even the most trite comment sound pleasant, and he remained calm, as though he had all the time in the world. Even at that first meeting, when I'd told him I had only a short-term visa and had to return to Germany within two days, he merely smiled.

His wavy hair swept back in a regal yet casual way. He smiled or laughed at anything that was the slightest bit funny or ironic, which made joking with him more satisfying than I could have imagined. When we both started talking at the same time, he insisted I continue.

And what a listener he was. He settled back, cradling his pipe, seeming to enjoy the rituals of emptying the old tobacco, scraping the bowl with a tool, tapping it upside down into the ashtray, then cleaning the stem, refilling the bowl, gently pressing the tobacco into place. He would hold the unlit pipe a while and finally take out a slim silver lighter and hold it horizontally over the bowl. He would start to light it but then stop, leaning forward and saying something or listening intently and seeming to forget about the lighter, which remained hovering over the bowl. A few minutes would go by, and I guessed he wouldn't light the pipe, when, without acknowledging it in any way, his fingers, as if acting on their own, would move. A small flame would appear, and he would suck on the pipe as the tobacco slowly lit. Only after the tobacco glowed did he put the lighter on the table and settle back into his chair.

He was patient with my poor English and was willing to use his basic and sometimes amusing German when I was tired and couldn't make the effort anymore.

Mr. Clark greeted me with a familiar and firm handshake, calling me Mr. Baumann. I wished I could call him by his real name, too, but he and his colleagues had never divulged that.

As always, his assistant, Mr. Wallace, was with us. He rarely said anything but did take notes on a long pad and sometimes translated key words or phrases between Mr. Clark and me. His German was impeccable.

"I've brought more documents than usual," I said, as we all sat down. "Some are very, very important."

"Excellent!"

"And quite different from what I usually bring."

Mr. Clark said nothing in response as he walked to the credenza with bottles of Scotch and other whiskey on it. He asked if I wanted a drink, but as always, I declined. For these conversations, I wanted to be as alert and energetic as possible. As usual, Mr. Wallace also declined a drink.

Mr. Clark poured himself a bit of whiskey and water and inquired about my trip from Berlin and my day at the embassy. We sat in our usual spots in stuffed chairs with armrests that faced a stone fireplace and a small table between us. Mr. Wallace sat to the side on a straight-back chair.

I told Mr. Clark the train was again delayed for hours, partly because of bombing damage, and the official meetings were perfunctory. *He knew how government bureaucracies worked, no matter the politics of their leaders?*

His quiet snort of amusement encouraged me to continue. My colleagues in Bern, who in a group exuded confidence about Germany and the war, pestered me with questions when we were alone.

How bad were the bombings in Berlin?

Were people being pushed to the brink?

What did everyone think about the steady retreat on the Eastern Front?

Mr. Clark held his glass with both hands just above his lap. His eyes were nearly closed. When I first met him, I thought he was constantly on the verge of sleep but quickly learned this wasn't the case.

His eyes opened, and he said, "I'm as eager as your colleagues to know the answers to those questions."

I told them most Germans knew, whether they admitted it or not, that their Jewish neighbors who had been "resettled" to the East in the past several years were not working on farms or in factories, but were likely dead. That on a deep, unspoken level, most Germans felt guilty and saw the bombings and losses in the East as retribution and punishment for the murderous policy, done by the Royal Air Force and the Red Army somehow on behalf of the Jews. In the early years of the Third Reich, a majority of Germans knew that Jews weren't really the enemy as the Nazis depicted them. But after the killing of so many Jews, how could Jews not hate Germany? In the same way, after our brutal invasion, how could the Soviets not want to destroy Germany?

I continued to explain that even though they had caused the war, the Nazis were almost irrelevant. Germans wanted to defend themselves and their country. It was a matter of national survival. In fact, ordinary citizens sometimes cursed the Nazis, who seemed most concerned about a military putsch or spontaneous uprisings against them. Luckily for the regime, most citizens were so exhausted by day-to-day life that acts of mass rebellion were unimaginable.

Mr. Clark listened quietly while Mr. Wallace wrote furiously on his notepad.

The pair also asked about Germany's allies. What was happening in the rump state of Italy, in Hungary, Romania, Slovakia, and Japan? At the mention of their Pacific enemy, Mr. Clark and Mr. Wallace both sat forward.

On my first two trips, Mr. Clark and Mr. Wallace had pored over each sentence of the many reports and memoranda and studies I had brought, most of which concerned Germany. They had asked me to decipher abbreviations and acronyms, to explain certain language, to give context for what was stated. I answered as best I could; back in Berlin, I sought more information and documents about matters they requested. In return, I asked for very little: a camera and money for expenses, and for gifts to take back to Frau Riegler and other colleagues in Berlin to make it more likely that I'd be sent back to Bern soon.

On my last trip, I had noticed a shift in interest. They seemed especially curious about documents having to do with our ally in the Far East. These included material about the dispositions of Japanese forces, military plans, public morale, Japanese estimates of Allied forces, and more. When I mentioned recent meetings of German and Japanese submarines and the exchange of documents near the Cape of Good Hope, they nearly jumped up out of their chairs.

Of course, I understood that the Pacific was of special interest to the Americans, whose distant two-front war was so different from Germany's suicidal two-front war.

I took off my glasses, looked at them a moment, set the frames on the table, and closed my eyes.

"And the Japanese forces on Okinawa that you mentioned—" Mr. Clark said.

I reminded him that at other meetings, I had listed in detail targets they could bomb in Germany and in eastern Europe. I had told them about armaments factories, armament depots, secret weapon test bases, concentration camps, the Führer's *Wolfsschanze* military headquarters in East Prussia. I gave them the coordinates and the layout of the camp, including the buildings the Führer used and the spots where Himmler's and Göring's trains parked.

I shook my head and said, "I don't understand why you're bombing cities at random when there are essential targets you could be hitting."

Mr. Clark didn't say a word.

"You could level the Chancellery or one of the Führer's headquarters and kill him and his top henchmen," I went on. "You could destroy factories that produce all kinds of key military materiel. You could hit the camps and the railroads and railyards that serve them."

He folded his hands together as he listened. Mr. Wallace stopped taking notes.

"This horrible war and horrible regime could end much sooner," I said. "And then we could begin rebuilding Germany into the progressive, democratic power it once was."

I stopped, and he waited, as though expecting me to continue. But I didn't. Finally, he stirred and said slowly, "You are providing us with the most valuable information."

"But you aren't doing anything with it!"

"As I've said before, it's a slow, laborious process for us to go through all the documents, to check them and compare them with other information we have. Then we have to decide who can have access to this information." He paused. "Ultimately, we have to decide what, if any, actions we take because of the information." He paused again. "The information you supply us likely won't result in an immediate, direct action of the kind you'd like, but it deeply influences our strategy and tactics, which is most significant. Unfortunately, I can't reveal more, but I want to impress on you again how important your work is."

"Taking no direct action is disappointing."

"Yes, this must be difficult and frustrating," Mr. Clark said.

An image of Dr. Traum flashed in my mind.

"Every day you risk your life," he continued. "You work so hard to collect this invaluable information and bring it to us. You're surrounded by people who can't be trusted, who might turn you in."

I nodded.

"You don't know when there might be a pounding on the door or you're seized on the street."

I nodded again.

"And despite all you do, this awful war continues, seemingly unchanged by your heroic effort."

"Correct."

His voice rose and he seemed to slash at the air in front of him with his pipe. "The information you give us and your observations about life in Berlin are the best we have."

"If the information is so good, why don't you do anything with it?" I asked.

"Acting on the material you share with us presents enormous difficulties."

"Difficulties?"

He looked away. It was as if he were speaking with someone beyond me in the corner.

"Imagine if you brought us the name of every German spy working against the Allies," he said.

"I don't see any material about that," I said. "Do you want me to go after it?"

He smiled. "No, thank you. My point is that if you were able to give us their names and we rounded all of them up, the Abwehr would know instantly that we had access to the highest levels of the German government. They would instantly change all operational methods."

"Can't you do at least a few things? In your example, what if you picked up one or two of the most important spies?"

He sighed. "You must know that deciding how we act on these matters is time-consuming and deliberate. It's a process that involves many people, agencies, and organizations. And, of course, a major consideration is not letting the Germans know we know what they're doing, even if it means allowing some things to happen that we abhor."

"Has *anything* been done with my information?"

"We have gotten to know and understand the enemy so much better, which helps the war effort. It helps the Allies make the best decisions possible."

I said nothing.

"I can't promise anything, but plans are underway for taking action in ways that would make you very happy," he said.

"Wonderful," I said. "And I'd like to propose something else."

Mr. Clark glanced at me.

"Everyone knows Germany will lose the war," I said. "Even the Nazis. But they'll never surrender. They'll fight to the death and take down the entire country with them."

He nodded.

"We need to create a new government as soon as possible to keep Germany and all that's valuable about it from being destroyed," I said. "People opposed to the Nazis are waiting for a signal. They need a force to rise and show the way to taking back the country, establishing a peaceful regime, and ending the war with the Allies. An uprising in the Berlin would surprise the Nazis completely."

Lighting his pipe, Mr. Clark asked, "How would that be done?"

"Of course," I continued. "There are challenges. Making contact and coordinating with everyone will be difficult. But people are looking at everything differently because of inevitable defeat."

"The more people involved in plans like that, the more likely the regime will learn about it," he said. "And as you've said, they've become even more brutal as the tide has turned."

"You underestimate the German opposition," I said. "I can tell it's growing."

"How so?"

"Comments. Looks."

He had no reaction.

"This is what we need," I said. "Equipment. Uniforms. Radios. Trucks. Jeeps."

At first, he was quiet. Then he asked, "How do we get them in?"

"By parachute. Drop something besides bombs."

"There are resistance groups ready to seize power?" he asked in a tone of astonishment. "They're organized?"

"It could happen. With the right encouragement and supplies."

He said slowly, "There's a major stumbling block you may or may not be aware of. The Allies have a policy of unconditional surrender as the only option for the Axis powers."

Of course, I knew about it. All Germans knew about it.

"It doesn't matter who's in charge, even if there was a complete change of government," he continued. "And unconditional surrender has to be with all the Allies. The only anti-Nazi group the Soviets would support is the Communist Party."

I shook my head. "That wouldn't work."

"There can't be a separate peace," he went on. "Overthrowing Hitler's a lot harder than it should be."

"The Americans can't do anything to help?" I asked.

He shook his head.

I paused, then said, "This is very disappointing."

"My deepest apologies, Mr. Baumann."

"Okay," I said, pointing at the pile of papers lying on the table in front of me. "As I mentioned earlier, I brought a different kind of document. It's even more important than the usual ones."

"Yes?"

The pages were filled with my handwriting. At first glance, they looked like other documents I had copied by hand and brought with me to Bern. But these were not copies of documents.

As he always did, Mr. Clark grasped the first page of what I gave him with both hands and held it just a few inches from his face. His reading comprehension of German, I had learned, was much better than his speaking ability.

He read what might have been a few sentences before glancing up at me. "What is this? Something from a court case?"

"It could be a court case," I said. "Eventually."

He read aloud, "The policeman heading the trio who comes for me has checked on me several times in the past year. He has always been very proper and deferential, asking questions that I knew he was required to ask. I sensed an apologetic tone. If you overheard us, you might have thought he was filling out paperwork that would benefit me in some way."

"Is this a deposition?"

"It's a kind of testimony."

"From whom?"

"I wrote it."

"A policeman has been checking on you regularly?" He sounded alarmed.

"It's the testimony of someone whose voice has been silenced. A composite person."

He put the papers down and stared at me, saying, "I don't understand."

"I want the voices of the dead and dying and barely surviving to be heard."

"That's quite admirable." He paused. "But why are you giving this to me?"

"To remind you of why I'm here talking to you."

He took his glasses off and sat back. "Mr. Baumann," he said, reminding me again of Dr. Traum. "I can barely imagine what it's like to be at the epicenter of horror and not see much change. I hope it's a consolation for you to know that my government is doing everything we can to crush the Nazis. And your help is invaluable."

"You've said that," I responded. "And I understand. Somewhat."

He smiled.

It was too easy for Mr. Clark and the other Americans to ponder and wait and check and double check while others took incredible risks to try to change the course of the war.

I blurted out: "I have to go."

"Oh?" Mr. Clark glanced at his wristwatch. "It's early. Well, early for us."

He was right. It was almost two in the morning. Usually, we talked until an hour or so before dawn. Still, I left.

The night sky was colder than when I had walked to Mr. Clark's house. The moon had disappeared, and the air felt heavy and damp. I felt moisture on my face, as though I had walked into mist. But it wasn't mist. Small flakes of snow were falling and gently hitting me. I stopped and looked up, letting the flakes fall on my face and turn to water.

I remembered another night long ago, a night when I had left someone I loved and had no idea what would happen, where I would go, if I could continue. That snow had absorbed sound. It had coated the trees and walkways and roads and orderly buildings with a lovely white sheen.

That snow from long ago and this snow were unlike the snow I had become used to in Berlin. In the capital, snow was invisible in the blackouts, and during the day, snow didn't hide the debris and destruction. It quickly became dirty. It didn't quiet the patrols and police vans and flak guns and air raid sirens and the sounds of bombs dropping and exploding. Like so much in Berlin, snow, once beautiful, had become just another nuisance.

Chapter Forty-Four

Winter 1944

Sara slowly cleaned the villa, even rooms we didn't use. She washed the walls, scrubbed the floors. She rescued furniture from the driver's apartment in the garage.

Our part of the villa began to feel cozy, nothing like what it had been a decade earlier, but still a home, a place where Sara and I might wait out the war.

So long as she remained hidden and no bombs hit.

The place began to feel like an island. The nearby villas were wrecked and uninhabited. There was little traffic on the winding roads in the neighborhood. We were so isolated that there was no house warden as in so many Berlin apartment buildings.

Who could imagine that so close to this oasis of peace was the center of a force of death and destruction that radiated outward?

At the same time, from here, my actions also radiated outward, potentially affecting thousands, maybe hundreds of thousands, of people across the continent. I mulled over Mr. Clark's assurance that my work was valuable and slowly convinced myself I was helping the Allies even if I didn't agree with their approach. For one, I hoped that at least the Americans would target the *Wolfsschanze* in East Prussia. I wanted to hear a radio announcement or word in the Ministry of a "dastardly, cowardly" attack on the complex.

I did have one regret. I hoped Max had evaded Hans and his colleagues, who might or might not have chased him and who might or might not have been helped by me. Max was certainly smart enough to elude them without my help. But if they had caught him and if I had been involved, he was a martyr for the wider cause.

I would have warned him if I had known how to contact him, I liked to think.

"I painted the old guest room," Sara said one day when I arrived home in the evening from work. "The paint I found in the cellar survived all these years."

"Wonderful that something is outlasting this regime," I said, glad that she was finding things to do that didn't endanger her.

"You'll be so happy. It's almost impossible to find my cubby hole now."

Her cubby hole was under the eaves, a crawl space that had a door whose outline matched the moulding.

When the Traums lived here, a bed had been in front of the door, nearly blocking it. The door swung inward, so if you knew about the hiding place, it was easy to come around the bed to the narrow strip of space between it and the wall, push against the door, and slip out of sight. Sara did this mainly when winter or rain made it difficult to go to her preferred secret place under the trees at the far end of the garden.

The cubby hole under the eaves was high enough for Sara to sit in if she lowered her head and was long enough for her to lie down in. She had outfitted it with a blanket and several pillows. When she returned with me to the house, the blanket and pillows were just where she had left them a decade earlier. Of the things in the house that remained from her family's time there, they were in the best condition, apparently no one, not even an animal, had been in the cubby hole since Sara last shut the door.

She remembered several times as a child being so comfortable she had fallen asleep in the crawl space, and when her family's frantic calls woke her, she came out, but only when no one was in the room.

Sometimes she had taken a candle or light into the space and read. Several times, she had overheard conversations that were supposed to be private. Sadly, there was no such entertainment for her these days. At best, she might hear me talking to myself.

When she revealed the space to me, she climbed in and showed me how she could sit and lie there, then came back out and had me try it, too. I lay on my back, rolled to my side, sat up slightly, then lay back again, with my knees drawn up. Even though I was slightly taller than she, I was still comfortable. And I was impressed by her ingenuity, especially a latch she had made to lock the door from the inside and a magnet lock that kept the door from swinging open on its own when she wasn't there.

"Nice," I said. "It could come in handy. Just like your outdoor hiding place."

"They aren't hiding places. They're places I go to to be alone, to be myself."

"Okay. Your place to be by yourself could come in handy someday," I said.

She nodded.

"Even for me," I said. "Although, of course, you have first dibs."

"Maybe we can both fit in there. If we need to."

Sara was vague about where her *Bubbe* lived, and I didn't pry, since I'd long ago realized it was better not to know the hiding place of any Jew. If I didn't know such a thing, I couldn't be forced to disclose it.

But it was difficult not knowing much of anything about the person who had drawn Sara back to Berlin. Twice.

One night, Sara was nearly asleep, and I said, "So nice to have a quiet night. No sirens. No rush to the shelter."

"Lovely," she said, half asleep.

"Imagine how hard it is for babies and the very old." I shook my head. "Your grandmother."

"She doesn't have to worry about that." Her dreamy voice tailed off. "About anything."

"She doesn't?" I said.

Sara's answer was a soft snore.

The next day, I asked when her grandmother had died.

Sara glanced at me, then looked down, but said nothing.

I waited.

Eventually, she whispered, "She lives on."

"When did she die?"

Again, there was a long pause, then a whisper. "A few weeks ago."

"Why are you still here?" My voice was louder.

Her hands fluttered as she said, "I can't leave."

"Sara," I murmured. "You should have stayed in Switzerland. Both times. When you went with your family and when I took you."

"I can't leave my home."

"You stayed for this?" I waved my hand at the damaged house that barely sheltered us.

"I can't leave Berlin."

"It's a ruin, too. And you're not exactly welcome."

"I can't leave you."

"I don't understand," I said.

"You protect me," she said. "As you promised."

"I'm a man of my word."

"And I had to help you do the right thing."

Did she know what I was doing on my trips to Bern? Or did she mean supplying papers to people trying to go abroad?

"I always try to do the right thing."

Perhaps she had a vague sense.

A decade earlier, Sara had said we were doomed in this time and place, even though we had both said our love mattered most.

We had many conversations about this. Years later, it felt like a single conversation. She said I needed to find someone who wouldn't cause me problems:

"You don't cause me problems!" I said. "You make me feel so alive."

She said I wanted a wife and children, all of whom should be adorable, pure Germans, just like me.

I shrugged. "A wife and children could be nice, I must admit, but you know I don't believe in that German race crap."

She said she didn't want to get married and didn't want children.

"I know," I said. "I know. And that's fine. What matters most to me is you. As you are. How you feel. How you think. Don't you know that by now?"

She said I wanted a comfortable job and a nice home and a pleasant life.

"Who doesn't want a pleasant life?" I asked. "When it's possible. Same with a comfortable job and nice home. But that's in normal times. These aren't normal times. I want what's best for us, for our love."

She said she did not want to live the German bürgerlich ideal.

"Sara! Do you really think I want that, either?"

She said all that was lovely between us was fated to destroy us.

"Only if we let it," I said. "We can win. We can keep what's lovely and make it thrive. As long as we both want to."

She said I shouldn't be tied down.

"Why do you think you would tie me down?" I asked. "I like you. I love you. I want to be with you. That's not being tied down."

She said she didn't want to be tied down.

"I can't imagine either of us being tied down with each other," I said. "That's one of the beautiful things about you. And about us. We're attracted to each other. We're not bound to each other. Right?"

She said too much. She didn't say enough.

And nothing I said seemed to matter.

“Have I done the right thing?” I asked, one morning as we slowly awoke.

“About what?”

“About everything.”

“You know best.”

“I’m glad to have this time with you.” I laughed. “Who’d have imagined that love could blossom in this devastation?”

I tried to collect myself and found surprising inspiration. I remembered words that Hans had recently spoken. I told Sara she was a reminder of what was good and wonderful about life when I was often exhausted by the nastiness of being in the capital of a fascist state that waged brutal wars and committed murder. I said she helped remind me of what I believed in and how I had been before the world turned evil.

I worried I might sound incoherent, but the longer I spoke, the more she smiled. This made me smile, too, and all kinds of things made more sense.

There was more I didn’t say: that she distracted me from the fears I might have about work with Mr. Clark. That she created a place, a kind of home for me that would be difficult if Magda and the children were with me in Berlin and I would worry too much about them. That she protected the house, where I hid dangerous files and documents, even from her. That just by her existence, she distracted Hans from prying into my activities. And weirdly, that perhaps Hans was letting her live to help me.

Sara loved to read travel books, children’s books, fairy tales—any story that transported her far away, especially because she couldn’t go farther outside than the destroyed garden. Sometimes she made up trips, closing her eyes and taking me with her, narrating an adventure. We sailed in the Caribbean. We climbed in the Andes. We explored glaciers in Antarctica.

We journeyed among Australian aboriginals who lived before any Europeans arrived.

"Time to travel west, to the American West!" Sara said one evening as we lay in bed together, whispering in the dark, me sitting up slightly with an arm around her. "I know you've wanted to go there your entire life."

"Maybe..."

"Of course! Like every German boy, you loved Karl May."

"Yes, but I'm a grown man now." And I didn't like it that some of the Nazis, including the Führer, loved Karl May's tales of the Wild West.

"Every grown man is still a boy." She laughed loudly. "And you boys fantasize about living in a simple, natural state, at one with the land and animals, a place where everyone lives by the same noble rules. You imagine that in the end, you can win all conflicts." She laughed again.

"You're painting a picture that resonates, I have to admit."

"Okay," she said excitedly. "Let's go to America!"

"The dream of so many people."

"To a part of the country that's warm and exotic."

In English, I said, "What is your pleasure, Miss?"

"As far away as possible. California!" She squeezed my hands, murmuring, "Feel the heat. The sun is so large in the sky, as if here it passes especially close to the Earth, baking the ground and rocks and shrubs and trees. The landscape is tan and brown, with a few spots of pale green. As we walk, we kick up dust."

She sighed happily, then continued: "Every little spot in the shade is shelter from the sun's rays. We're walking along a path on a hill and can see far in all directions. There are peaks in the distance. We look at the views. All is quiet, and then a large bird appears."

"A hawk?" I ask. "A falcon? An eagle?"

"A hawk," she murmured. "It drifts on the wind currents, barely moving its wings, looking as though it might be asleep. But it's fully alert. As it sweeps in big looping circles, it gazes down, waiting, waiting, waiting, for a twitch, some movement. Finally it sees something, and in a split second it dives, shooting down like a bolt of lightning, almost faster than we can see. Its talons grab an unsuspecting little creature that merely stuck its head out of a burrow."

"Perhaps other kinds of hawks can hunt the evil creatures we were talking about a minute ago, even if takes a long, long time for the moment to come."

She squeezed my hand again.

"And then we walk to the northern side of a hill, away from the sun, and find a small stream whose waters gurgle as they wash over many small rocks, where a cottonwood shelters the soft, inviting bank. We sit there and take in the brightness beyond, the shade around us, the refreshing smell and the sound of the running water."

We continued to squeeze each other's hands.

"Sun and water," I said. "We always find sun and water."

"There's nothing more beautiful."

Chapter Forty-Five

March 1944

The next time I saw Hans, he was sober. Very sober. If anything, his glare was icier and more intimidating than I'd ever seen.

"About that matter we have discussed several times," he said, not finishing the sentence.

I was glad he hadn't summoned me to his office, but instead to the lobby of the Adlon, which as usual was full of people wearing S.S. and Gestapo uniforms, including the hotel staff, I was the only person not in uniform.

I had hoped in the twilight and smoke and turmoil, he wouldn't have recognized her. She had been visible only for a moment, only from the back, only in silhouette. But I knew if I had seen her that way, I, too, would have recognized her.

I wanted to look away but didn't dare. I thought of the comments he'd made the last time we'd seen each other that could be cause enough for his colleagues to shoot him. I also thought of Sara. Finally, I said, "You're referring to…?" Then I stopped.

There was a long pause, and just as he opened his mouth to begin speaking, I added quickly, "We talked about so much."

"We talked about something in particular."

"Our former mutual friend? The painful memory you and I share?"

I expected him to react to my joke, but he said sharply, "Where is she?"

"I thought you knew everything."

"Tell me now."

I sighed and said, "She's always been elusive. From me. From you."

"True," he said.

"And elusive from the state, apparently."

He smiled, more of a facial tic, but still a semblance of a smile.

"Please don't insult me," he said. "I saw her, and you know I saw her."

He described the moment from five months earlier exactly as I remembered it and said, "It's taken me forever to admit to myself that I did see her and that you were with her. And, of course, I have been even busier than usual with urgent matters."

He sighed, then continued. "And still you have the nerve to tell me you weren't with her? When I saw the two of you."

"I have seen her, but not in a while."

"How long ago is a while?"

"When did you supposedly see me on the street?" I said, flipping my hand in the air. "A couple months ago?"

"You continue to insult me, my friend. You were walking with her."

"No, no, no."

"Have you had contact with her recently?"

"I have no idea where she is," I said.

No idea at this moment. The old living room? The old den? The bedroom? Or perhaps she's gone for a walk even though I've warned her a thousand times not to go outside.

"I probably don't need to point out that you haven't answered my question," he said. He was silent a moment before continuing, "I hope you aren't doing anything stupid. Because we know she causes otherwise intelligent people to do all kinds of stupid things."

"I'm not stupid," I said.

"Only a stupid person would say that."

"You're remarkably focused on someone who's as significant as a grain of sand at the beach."

"She's very important," he insisted. "No Jews are allowed in the Reich, especially in the capital!"

"You've intimated she's not the only one in Berlin."

"That's correct, my friend."

"I could repeat my observation about your unusual focus."

His smile faded, and he said, "Yes, I have a major personal interest. I want things to be settled once and for all. I really do abhor this limbo."

"Come to the house and see for yourself," I said. "I have nothing to hide. Then, at least part of this can be settled."

"It'll be strange to see her family's old house. But not as strange as you living in it."

"A bizarre coincidence," I said. "But, even damaged, it's a very nice house."

"I imagine it's changed."

"I'm living there now. That should answer your question."

We both laughed.

"Come out late some afternoon. There are chairs, however rickety."

"I'll bring the champagne."

I lifted my glass toward him.

"To all the memories."

"To a memorable visit."

We clicked our glasses together.

I tried to warn Sara, but she didn't grasp the danger. "I haven't seen Hans in years," she exclaimed.

I imagined her meeting him at the front door, as if her family still owned what was once a magnificent mansion and it was her choice whether or not to invite a person inside.

"I'm so curious."

"You don't want to know," I said.

"How bad could he be?"

"Dangerously bad. He's high up in the S.S."

"They poisoned him, too." She frowned but then brightened again. "Does he still have an amazing smile that can make you melt no matter what idiocy he spouts?"

"Like everyone, well, most everyone." I waved a hand at her. "The war has changed him."

"How sad," she said. "He was always so amusing. About everything."

Amusing about everything. I mulled that over a moment, then said, "I see flashes of that, but most of the time he's driven. In a way you wouldn't like."

"I understand he's a Nazi. But I saw what you saw in him. In the end, he's more than a uniform."

"I'm not sure how much is left of what either of us have liked about him." I laughed. "You're either remarkably understanding and generous or crazy."

"Everybody's a mix of good and bad and conflicted about things."

"He does have conflicts about you, my dear."

"Really?" She raised her brows.

"You're a threat to him in a variety of ways."

She smiled as though this were a supreme compliment.

"He always seemed so self-assured and true to himself," she said. "He wasn't afraid of anyone or anything."

"That may have changed," I said. "And now I dared him to search the house."

"You accuse me of doing dangerous things?"

"If he comes by, you have to hide and be absolutely silent."

"It'd be fascinating to see him again."

"Fascinating isn't the right word."

"Don't be a worrywart."

Chapter Forty-Six

Fall 1944

In the summer of 1944 a kind of thunderstorm raged for months—bolts of lightning hitting one after the other, the buzz of electricity and acrid smell in the air.

The July attempt to assassinate the Führer had failed. The bomb exploded in a *Wolfsschanze* conference room in a building I had seen but not been in, and had only wounded its target. A fury gripped the capital. There were reports of plots uncovered, arrests, swift executions, more arrests, quick trials, more executions. There hadn't been so many high-level Nazis sacrificed since the leadership of the Brown Shirts was liquidated ten years before. The most shocking involved the Desert Fox, General Rommel, who had appeared in good health. *Could he really have died suddenly from a heart attack?* I had heard he was at least sympathetic and maybe encouraging to a loosely organized group that believed changes had to be made in the country, starting at the top. I had also heard he was given the option of having a hero's death or being hung by piano wire from a ceiling hook in the basement on Prinz-Albrecht-Strasse. He hadn't mulled over the choice very long.

The fury grew because, with the Red Army steadily advancing in the East and their Western allies expanding their beachhead in France, only a child could still believe in final victory. If the leadership had a superbomb, it would have been used by now.

As the end became apparent, true believers embraced what they saw as a pure version of the old German ideal of a heroic death: destruction not just of themselves, but the nation, too. If the National Socialist state were to fall, it would take with it all loyalists and all enemies. In other words, everyone would die for the cause. It was time for accounts to be settled.

In the aftermath of the failed assassination, in conversations over several weeks, I learned that some acquaintances had been arrested and disappeared. They included three of the group I once played chess with, whose leaflets I had distributed one dark night, as well as one friend of the Traums to whom I had given some blank passports and exit visas.

Although I had tended to keep my political views to myself during the past several years, any of these people might give me up. And Sara could be careless. Hans could figure out that I was hiding Sara. And the Abwehr could yet learn that I was giving secrets to my friends in Bern. In any of these ways, I could wind up like the rest, tortured in myriad ways, then hung from a meat hook or garroted.

I began to think about a way to disappear for the rest of the war and avoid being caught and punished for my crimes against the Nazis. So far, there had been no missteps. But how long would my luck run? I liked the idea that Rügen could be a stepping stone to full safety in neutral Sweden.

Although he lived on the most beautiful island I had ever seen, Magda's father seemed to ignore the water—the lagoons and inlets that wound in and out of the island and the wild sea that surrounded it. But he knew I loved to row, and the few times I visited after Magda and the children moved there, he arranged it so that I could borrow a neighbor's rowboat.

On my first outings, I rowed on the quieter inland waters, protected from the Baltic winds and tides by the bluffs along the beaches, by pines, and by the narrow isthmuses and peninsulas. I hadn't rowed on salt water before, and I had wanted to begin modestly. The protected water was calm, and the breezes subdued, much like what I was used to on the rivers and small lakes in Berlin. The tides were gradual. There were few boats or ships in these shallow inlets and no reefs or rocks to be wary of.

Sometimes, I took Magda and the children out in the rowboat during my rare visits. I wanted to see them more. I wanted us to be together. But the war disrupted everything, and we all had to make do. When I saw them, I regretted my other secret—that Sara was living with me. But again, I made do, however disagreeable that was by the standards of normal life.

Most of the time, I rowed alone. I liked not relying on anyone else, just as I liked not relying on any other force to move forward—wind or an engine. By myself, I focused on the currents, the waves, the wind, the other boats and ships, and their wakes. There was no distracting conversation. As I became comfortable with these unfamiliar waters, I focused on the simple but demanding process of rowing.

Holding the oar handles, I extended my arms forward from my body, dipped the blades in the water, pulled the handles toward me, lifted the oars out of the water, feathered them so the blade was parallel to the water and sliced through the air, twisted the oar handles so the blades were perpendicular to the water, put them in the water, and pulled the them toward me again.

The boat went fastest when I did these movements as smoothly and mechanically and forcefully as possible. The art came in balancing these conflicting movements. If I pulled too fast, the slightest catch on the water would throw me off. With a constant speed, the boat moved faster than if there were many shifts in speed. If my hands fluttered, the blades might catch the water and brake the boat or make it turn. If I didn't use enough force, I'd lose momentum.

I didn't always try to go as fast as possible. Every so often, I stopped rowing and made the boat pivot in a slow circle, watching what was around me. If I wanted to feel the sun on my face, I turned the boat so the stern faced sunwards. Sometimes, I stared at the scenery, particularly at the clouds and the light shimmering on the water or at the hills and farms in the distance. Or, I listened to the wind zipping along the water or the sound of a sailboat speeding along, the fabric of its sails humming.

Eventually I rowed out onto the sea. I quickly learned the steady onshore breezes made rowing a challenge. Sometimes, no matter how strongly I rowed, I didn't move forward. I was pushed ever closer to the beaches and would have wound up among swimmers if it were summer.

Every so often, the ocean breeze died down and the tide turned, and the *Ostsee*, the Baltic Sea, resembled a huge, pleasant lake—the water still, the air calm, a place I could row fast and sure.

At these times, I worked my way north up the coast, past the hulking unfinished buildings at Prora—the National Socialist sea resort whose completion had been sacrificed, like so much else, for the war—past chalk cliffs, past piney woods that came down to the sea's edge. I came to Cape Arkona, where centuries earlier pagan Slavs from all over the north had gathered regularly. For me, the shrine on the old temple hill Jaromarsburg wasn't for gods of yore, whose straightforward, simple earthiness contrasted to the pagan gods who ruled the land now. To me, the temple hill was a shrine to something else. It was a lighthouse of sorts, a marker on a route to safety. It was the part of Germany closest to neutral Sweden, one of just a few sanctuaries left in continental Europe. Sweden's southern coast was immediately across the Baltic, about 80 kilometers.

The trip would take many hours, but it could be done. I had never rowed quite so long a distance in one stretch, but I had come close and had rowed nearly that far in several days. I would be motivated, and in the right weather, the Baltic was easy to navigate. The wide Swedish coast made for an easy target. Of course, I would need to avoid German patrol boats, so some mist or low clouds would help. I could time my trip so I left Rügen in the dark and would be in international waters as the sun rose.

I couldn't take Magda and the children. The boat wasn't large enough for four people and our belongings, and the load would make for a slow trip. By myself I could make it—I would be gone only until the war ended in a few years. Magda and the children would continue to be safe on Rügen, and I would be safer in Sweden than AWOL on Rügen or still working amid the death and destruction in Berlin.

The family could easily report the truth. I hadn't returned from a long row along the coast. A search was unlikely to happen at a time every able-bodied man was needed for the war. And I wouldn't tell them my plans so that their report about my sudden and worrying disappearance would be sincere and convincing.

After a reasonable amount of time I would let them know I was safe and eventually be reunited with them. I would send an anonymous postcard in familiar handwriting with a reference to something only we knew about.

But every time I began to row north of Cape Arkona, even when I saw a hint of land on the northern horizon, I didn't go farther. Either a squall came up or what looked like an official boat appeared or I began to tire. Or maybe it was slowly dawning on me that I should stay. At the end of my row, safely back on land, I would hug Magda tightly and spend even more time laughing and playing with the children.

In the end, it was exile enough to be on Rügen for a few days and row a short distance from German soil under my own power, free of encumbrances, in control, theoretically able to go exactly where I wanted.

Puffy white clouds piled high on one another, farther up into the heavens than imaginable, making the wooded hills and the sea below all appear so small. The clouds barely moved across the sky, but if you watched carefully, you could see their progression, as steady and unnoticeable as the pacing of the minute hand on a clock. It was an eternal scene and would continue to endure.

Part IV
1945-1947

Chapter Forty-Seven

March 1945

The sound of vehicles in the neighborhood had become so unusual that one might have thought a plane had crashed or a tank approached. But this was more ominous. A black car slowly came up the drive. I set down the hoe in the garden and went into the house through the back door.

The net had finally reached me. Even if they hadn't discovered exactly what I did in Bern, these days the suspicion of treason was enough for someone to be arrested.

I tiptoed upstairs and was happy to see that Sara had already stopped reading and was opening the door to her secret hiding place.

I wanted to hug her, hug her for a long time. After all, I might never see her again.

She folded her body and moved into the space. After she squeezed into the dark enclosure, she turned and smiled at me. I held her head a moment and kissed her deeply. Then she pulled the door shut.

I walked slowly downstairs and heard the car engine stop and a door close, a clanging metallic sound much louder than the softness of Sara's door. Were the Gestapo so confident I would comply with orders that most of them waited in the car?

By the time I got to the front hall, there was knocking on the piece of wood that protected the doorway. The knock was solid, not insistent, perhaps even polite—the sound of just one hand.

No need to smash the door down and draw attention to what was happening. That had never been their style.

I gripped the handle, took a breath, and just as the second knock sounded—slightly more insistent, implying it did not want to have to knock a third time—I pulled the door open.

There was so much to take in. A man wearing the kind of uniform I expected stood in front of me. But there was only one man.

"Hans!" I exclaimed, partly in greeting, partly in surprise. I had invited him to visit, but that had been months ago, the last time I had seen him.

The ends of his closed mouth twitched upwards, which I took for a smile.

"Rudi," he said. His tone was formal. "We must talk."

"I always enjoy talking with you," I said. "Come in! Come in!"

Looking around the foyer, he said, "This building's in decent shape, all things considered."

"It has four walls and a roof," I said. "That's better than much of Berlin."

He nodded, standing stiffly in the center of the room where I'd often waited for Sara, after a maid notified her I'd arrived. Back then, there were many chairs and settees where one could wait comfortably. Now the room was nearly empty.

"There's a few chairs inside," I said. "Otherwise, I can't offer much. No Scotch or cigars. Just water, which is drinkable."

"No, thank you," he said.

"Do you want to see the place? It's a shadow of its former self," I said. "Despite my best intentions."

I didn't understand why I felt more comfortable than he looked.

"Or do you want to go somewhere?" I asked.

This sounded better to me than *Do you want to take me in?*

He shrugged.

Did I have to take charge?

"Is this official business?" I asked.

We sat at a small table in the old living room.

I tried to think of something else to say, but then he began speaking, but not looking at me, in an odd monotone, as if he were reciting.

"People continue to engage in treason," he said. "Some of it's relatively innocuous." A group, perhaps Communist cells, made innocents spread subversion unwittingly, he told me. A man walking would be stopped in a friendly way by another man. The stranger usually asked for directions. They would have a pleasant conversation for a minute or two, then part, and the appreciative stranger would give the man a warm pat on the back as he left. With the pat, it turned out, the stranger affixed a small sign by tape to his back.

"What do the signs say?" I asked.

"The usual rubbish. 'Workers unite.' We're losing the war.' 'Down with Hitler.' "

I laughed. "I can't believe you of all people said that last one."

His looked startled for a moment. Then his cool demeanor returned, and he said, "You know the context."

Hans continued, "The first guy we picked up for wearing one of these traitorous signs nearly died of fright. But his story checked out. As did the stories of similar cases."

Those included leaflets and cards randomly dropped or posted around the city. The material had the same tone but was more detailed.

"Most people turn in the treasonous material after reading only a few words."

"But perhaps some read them and don't turn them in?"

"You like the idea that some people read treasonous material?" he said, finally looking at me directly.

I laughed. "A few more readers and maybe our lives would be different."

"My friend," he said, frowning. "Sometimes, you are such a fool. But at least you are a likeable fool."

Without protesting, I smiled in what I hoped was a likeable way.

He paused. "Would you have any idea who these people are? People who could work against the nation and the Führer?"

I threw up my hands, remembering a few years earlier having wandered the quiet, dark streets of Berlin, stuffing pieces of paper in mailboxes and doorways and apartment building foyers. Had it made any difference then? Would it make a difference now?

"They plot to overthrow the government and take other traitorous actions. Some have helped Jews, for example."

Was the official part of his visit coming now?

"In Berlin, we estimate at least ten thousand of them are living underground. Most can't survive without the help of Germans who hide them."

"Where?"

"In their houses or apartments. In cellars. In attics. In garden huts. In hollowed-out walls or concealed rooms. Even in pieces of furniture."

"Pieces of furniture?"

He nodded, then gazed at me a moment before saying, "You're trying to act surprised?"

So this was about Sara.

"Why shouldn't they do everything possible to hide?" I said. "Everyone knows on some level what happens to them eventually."

"The strong, the young, are put to work."

"Work is the wrong word. Slave labor is more like it."

"There is much turnover."

"You know what *turnover* means. How can you be so cavalier about it? Last I knew, Jews were still people."

"Cavalier? I'm just telling you facts."

"You don't have a hint of regret? Or sympathy? Sara and her family may be dead for all we know."

"We know they aren't dead." He paused, then said, "Reports have been made about you."

"That I'm Jewish?"

He snorted. "Of course not."

Finally, I thought. *It was happening.*

But still I didn't understand what Hans was doing. If he were convinced I was hiding her, wouldn't he have brought others along? Because we were old friends, was he was being more civilized about it than he would otherwise? Because it involved a woman we both had loved?

I felt calmer than I had in years. *Something would be settled.*

"I like to speak my mind," I said. "You of all people know that."

"You can't help yourself."

"Still, I work hard in my position."

"Maybe working hard on the wrong things."

This was the perfect opening for him to state the obvious.

"I've bought some food on the black market," I said. "But then, who hasn't?"

He shook his head impatiently. "This is much more serious. Against the highest law of the land."

"The law of this land has been thoroughly debased."

He shook his head.

"I maintain the blackout," I said. "I use my ration cards. Usually. I go to the basement during raids."

"It has nothing to do with those things."

He turned away from me and spoke as if he were addressing someone in the next room—Sara?

"I told them I didn't believe it," he went on. "My old friend Rudi from Gymnasium. A high-ranking official in the Foreign Ministry."

I said nothing.

"I had to start an official investigation of my old comrade." He went on. "But I didn't need to investigate. I would recognize her anywhere."

I nodded, as if agreeing with his observation that he could recognize her anywhere.

"The bombings have made it harder to keep track of everyone," he said. "It's not so difficult to hide a lone adult, even if she's not suited to being caged."

I was silent.

He took a few breaths. "I can understand you hiding Jews, but why her? She dumped you."

"You should understand that doesn't make her less attractive."

He breathed in deeply. "Maybe being with her would have made everything more bearable."

"The war? The regime?" I was surprised. "Now you're sounding defeatist."

"I can't argue anymore with reality, the personal or political." He shrugged. "We accomplished so much in the early years. But the price has been total war. No life other than war. No life at all."

He stopped speaking. I partly expected him to arrest me or even shoot me to keep me quiet about what he'd said.

"I know you're surprised to hear me talk like this," he said softly.

I nodded.

"On the other hand, National Socialism has its own logic. And that logic continues to apply."

At that, I feared he would push me aside and then sweep through the house, looking for Sara. But he kept talking, saying, "That's why I'm here. You're battling something bigger than you, and I'm going to set it right."

"I don't understand, Hans." I paused. He was more determined about Sara than I'd ever seen him. This no longer resembled a cat-and-mouse game. "You want to take her in?"

I was surprised at how refreshed I felt. Pretending was exhausting, and I had done it for so long. He and I were both wanting several different things to end.

His smile seemed slightly triumphant.

"This is a matter of state, yes, but also a personal matter. It has to be settled differently, privately. Because of our shared past. That's why I came here alone. I still wish things had been different between her and me, but that was impossible in my position. Much as I don't want it, I have been soft with her and you. Still, the matter must be settled, once and for all. Otherwise, I am not doing my duty, and I am determined to do my duty until the end, whenever that comes."

I realized something. "You want to settle everything with both of us? Her and me?"

"You *are* part of it."

Of course I was. I began to understand that Hans might be doing something merciful. If he shot us both quietly, we would avoid all the horror that entailed if I were taken to Prinz-Albrecht-Strasse and she were transported. Over time, I had become somewhat numb to the specifics of what would happen to me, but I dreaded Sara being raped, beaten, and garroted. Just thinking about that was a form of torture for me.

"It's the end in so many ways," he said. "For all of us." He waved vaguely in the air. "This war. This country. This life."

I noticed, as though for the first time, the pistol in the holster on his belt. It struck me that what threatened me most was not the Abwehr or secret police but someone who had been my best friend in childhood.

After a long pause, he said, "Where is she? Which room?"

"A favor, please," I asked. "Because our friendship and bonds go back decades."

"Yes?"

"I don't care what you do with me, but I do care about her," I said. "She's my responsibility. Let me take the responsibility for whatever needs to be done."

He didn't respond.

"It's a matter of honor," I added. "Please respect that."

We stared into each other's eyes a moment. Then I held out my hand. He grasped it, solemnly saying, "Accepted."

Chapter Forty-Eight

March 1945

There was still a chance that he wouldn't discover her hiding place and that I could pretend she had left the house. In fact, maybe she had slipped away.

But then I heard footsteps on the stairs, which could be only one person.

I coughed. I stood and moved away from the stairs. I did all but shout and clap my hands to try to hide the noise.

When I quieted, all was silent in the house.

I was relieved for a few seconds.

"Hans!" Sara said. "Hello!"

She stood in the doorway, an arm stretched out toward him, palm up.

She looked as if she would invite him to take a seat in the parlor and ask if he wanted something refreshing to drink. Except the servants who would take the order and make the drink weren't here. And, of course, there weren't any drinks in the kitchen or a chair in the parlor. And her family no longer owned the house. And she was considered a subhuman, stateless criminal enemy deserving extinction by the government that this guest represented.

He gazed at her without expression.

"Welcome," she added.

"Sara," he finally said, neither friendly nor coldly official.

"It's been ages," she said. "Too long." Then she laughed. "But understandable."

I wondered if she was the last person in Berlin who laughed in such a carefree way, all the more remarkable because she had done something that might end her life.

Then the situation became even more odd. Hans stood almost at attention, as if a superior officer were in the room. While he stayed in this pose, from just far enough away so he couldn't reach out and touch her, she slowly walked around him, commenting as she looked him up and down.

"You're fit, I'm glad to see," she said. "The good thing about your awful uniform is that it's tailored to the lines of your body." Her eyebrows rose. "I bet you'd look just as good in civilian clothes, which wouldn't have those dreadful symbols on them."

He didn't move or change expression.

"You've aged," she went on. "We all have. You look like you could use more sleep. Then again, we all could. I imagine your job is very demanding. Like Rudi's, but probably more so, whatever your job is." She laughed again. "But I don't think I want to know what you do, do I?"

She peered into his eyes a moment.

"You have quite a commanding presence," she continued. "Even without speaking, without moving. I sense you're used to following orders. Sometimes you prefer following orders, whatever the orders are. Such a pity."

She completed a circle around him and faced him again.

He nodded slightly, then took off his cap and cradled it under one arm at his side.

Excitedly, she said, "Do you have *orders*?"

Still, he didn't speak. Neither did I.

"I can barely imagine what it must be like for you to be working with them." She shook her head.

Then she gestured at me. "Much worse than Rudi."

I frowned. *Did she not know after all?*

She continued, "You're so full of life, but you have to suppress that. And worse, you have to suppress the life in others, in many others. And when I say suppress, I'm being diplomatic." She pointed at some of the insignia on his uniform. "Those death's heads are too appropriate."

He flinched, just a muscle spasm, unnoticeable unless you were watching him carefully.

"You were a beautiful person," she went on. "And no matter what unspeakable crimes and atrocities you've committed or will commit, at your core you'll always be a beautiful person. It may sound terribly naïve, but this I believe."

Now he raised the hand that wasn't holding his hat. "Okay," he said. "Enough."

This was a command, with even more authority than a shout because it was stated so calmly.

Sara laughed. "You know I'm right," she said, smiling broadly.

"I'm here on business," he said.

"Of course you would say that." She might have batted her eyelashes at him. "Even though it's personal. Extremely personal."

I heard a noise that sounded like a groan.

"You deny it?" she laughed.

He looked at me.

I tried not to look away, but I didn't know what to do or say.

"Go ahead and deny it," Sara said. "Deny everything. Whatever the reason, I'm glad to see you. Really."

He shook his head. "I'm not sure why you're glad to see me," he said. "I am the enemy."

"You may feel that way, but I don't."

He might have smiled. "Well, it was decided long ago that you were the enemy."

She seemed to beam as she said, "Yes, but the tide's turned. The killers will be killed, dying miserably and alone, their bodies disposed of in unmarked places." She nearly jumped in excitement now. "The people whose lives have been destroyed will be the ones honored and remembered. They're the ones who will live forever."

Hans had gone still again. I wondered when he would finally explode. He had become angry when I had said things that were much milder.

When he turned to me, I feared what he would say. He whispered, "What do you think?"

Was he asking for my opinion about her last few comments? Or about what we had talked about earlier?

I shrugged, saying, "Of course she's right. As usual."

He stared at me, and I wondered if he would dispose of me first, since in the Nazi view of things, a member of the master race who was a traitor and aided criminals was much more objectionable than a mere subhuman.

And it would be easier to dispose of me than her. He could shoot me at any time and face no repercussions because of my capital crime of having sheltered a Jewess. By odd contrast, the Nazis seemed not to want to kill Jews in Berlin. Instead, they preferred to transport them far away first.

Sara opened her mouth, but Hans raised a hand and again said, "Enough." Then he unbuckled the holster at his side and took out the pistol.

Sara looked at the Luger. I imagined her thinking, *What are you going to do with that?*

Hans surprised Sara by handing me the Luger.

I had held pistols before, but I had fired one only a few times at a shooting range. I had appreciated the power of it, the sensation of sending a sleek, shiny piece of lead at supersonic speed toward a piece of paper with a cross hatch on it, a process that began when I tugged my index finger on a little steel bar and created an explosion. But I had fired the pistol in a safe, antiseptic place and satisfied my curiosity. I understood why some people loved firearms, but I didn't lust to shoot again. I had never held even an empty pistol near a person, let alone a loaded pistol.

I was unlike so many of my compatriots, but then I was lucky not to serve in the armed forces.

"That looks so strange in your hand," Sara said to me. "It makes sense for Hans, but not you."

I felt as though I might as well be holding a grenade that would obliterate us all.

"Yes, it does feel strange," I said.

Why had I asked Hans to do what he planned to do?

"It makes you look a little like Hans, too." She smiled. "Well, except for the uniform and the death's head and a shade of black that looks so evil." She laughed.

"I never thought it would come to this," she said, still beaming, gesturing at both of us. "You two. Together again." Then she gestured at the pistol in my hand. "And with *that*."

We were all silent a moment, then Sara added, "Whatever are you going to do?"

Hans seemed to go pale. He might have begun sweating.

Perhaps he regretted ending all this as much as I did. He might have loved Sara as much as I did.

I glanced at him. He nodded.

"Okay," I said, lifting the Luger.

I was protecting her to the end in a way I'd never imagined. I had to keep her from being taken in and all the torment and horror that would follow. Here maybe I could give her the dignity of a funeral and a proper burial. Hans would allow that before he did whatever he planned to do with me, wouldn't he?

Sara was quiet and still, unlike the way she'd been since she'd appeared in the doorway. She must have realized what was going to happen.

I put an arm around her and felt her shudder as I put the barrel of the pistol to her head.

She gazed at me, her eyes wide open, more in wonder than in fear.

"Really?" she asked.

I thought of all the times she and I made love, our arms and legs entwined, our faces touching, our eyes so close together they were blurs of color, completely visible but unfathomable at the same time, focused and separated, together and apart. We were as close as two people could physically be.

And now, I held her in the same way. I kissed her. I wanted yet again to try to bridge the last things that divided us and make us one. I wanted to ask forgiveness, to let her know I loved her perhaps more than anything or anyone, to let her know I would never let her down, to let her know we would always be together one way or another. I would remember and honor her always. She would live forever in my soul.

I squeezed her even more tightly. I wanted to wait, wait, wait. But I couldn't keep waiting.

I shuddered, then calmed myself. I breathed in deeply, almost shut my eyes, and I pulled the trigger.

Chapter Forty-Nine

March 1945

The smell of gunpowder, more pungent than any explosive residue I'd taken in over the past few years, filled the air.

Mainly because of the bombings, I had seen many dead people—bodies that were intact, bodies that were mangled, bodies that looked at peace, bodies that were dismembered, bodies in such small pieces I couldn't imagine anyone identifying them. I thought I knew death. But this was different. For one, I didn't know so much blood could come out of a person. That alone made my stomach turn. *How did soldiers do what they did?*

I didn't realize bodies could twitch and shake so much in the throes of death. I would have thought they dropped to the floor like a stone.

But more important, I loved the person who was dying, and I had fired the shot that caused this horror.

I bent over, breathing deeply, suddenly drenched in sweat.

The two of us looked at each other silently. What could we say? Even though I had pulled the trigger, we were both complicit. We had made a quick, surprising agreement, but an agreement nonetheless. I'd had no choice, I felt, but it was the best solution.

When I finally spoke, it was as if to no one and as if someone else were uttering the words.

"After everything, I can't believe it came to this," I said. "I had no idea." After a pause that might have lasted a few seconds or a few minutes, I said, "I don't know how I was able to do it. But it had to be done."

I stood over the body, shaking slightly.

I might have heard a grunt in agreement.

After this horrible act, I felt utter blankness. All that remained was a kind of animal drive to continue, to survive. And to survive, I needed to do several things.

"We have to clean this up," I said. "Clean it all up. Do it properly."

I had no idea I would do what I did. It was only at the last moment I realized what I needed to do, and in that instant, I knew it was the right and true thing. It was our destiny, as Sara might have said. Our fate.

It happened so quickly. I felt the kiss that Sara and I shared throughout my body, as if we were back in bed, skin pressing against skin, as alive and connected as any two people can be.

Our special love was as strong as ever, always existing—in the past, in the future, now. When we were apart for long periods, it seemed to fade, but every time we were together, it was there. I couldn't deny it. I couldn't refuse it. And somehow it didn't matter what happened, if we lived or didn't live.

The way she gripped me. How she kissed me. What she whispered to me. How she opened herself to me. Our love will always exist.

She had gazed at me in a way that forgave anything I might do.

Hans stood close to me, as though to help me pull the trigger if I wound up unable to do so. He appeared decided but resigned, not at all the triumphant hunter I expected. Almost jealous?

Sara raised her eyebrows in a way only I could see. *Poor Hans*, she seemed to say.

Perhaps she was trying to save herself. Perhaps it was a simple, innocent observation.

He was the forlorn one, while she was full of life, as she'd always been.

He had made it clear he was asking for death. But I realized he wasn't asking for Sara's death.

If she was gone, I was still in trouble and might vanish, too. If he was gone, she and I both would be safe.

I don't know if Hans had time to comprehend what was happening, but he didn't look surprised. Still holding Sara, I swiveled my hand so the pistol aimed at his head, pulling the trigger as the barrel moved and touched his forehead. The movement of my arm and the firing of the pistol took all of an instant.

He had begun to smile as the pistol swiveled toward him. Even if he hadn't fully realized beforehand this was what he wanted, right then he must have understood. He looked relieved. After all, why had he come alone? Why hadn't he stormed the place and shot her without a word and made others drag her away?

As soon as the pistol flashed, I carefully set the weapon on the floor, feeling as though someone else had shot it. Yet my hand still stung from the recoil.

We had to clean the floor, and his car had to be driven away. His body had to disappear.

I didn't talk about any of this with Sara. She was silent but looked at me, her eyes occasionally opening wide again, in a combination of astonishment and appreciation.

I was glad she said nothing, and if it weren't for the help I needed, I would have asked her to leave me by myself. I wanted to take in the enormity of what I had done and not do anything else for a long time. I wanted to let my mind roam where it wanted to. It was all such a surprise and such a horror.

But I didn't yet have time to do that.

First, I tied several towels around his head to stem the bleeding, all the while moving my hands carefully, arms extended, squatting, shifting to keep from staining my clothes. I wrapped his body in one of the few spare blankets, a blanket that was so thin it wouldn't provide a living creature much warmth. This felt like a slight to Hans. I wished I had a thicker blanket, which besides keeping him warm, would absorb blood better.

I put his body in the basement in case anyone came to search for him. I had imagined carrying him out of the room fireman style, but I discovered he was heavier than I expected and difficult to maneuver. I asked Sara for help.

She nodded, and together we managed. He was still flexible, but in some ways, I wished his body were stiff because it might have made it easier to forget what I was carrying. When we lowered him onto the basement floor, for a moment I wanted to make him comfortable, maybe by putting him into a chair. But this was absurd. Still, I made sure he was on a dry part of the floor.

This resting place was only temporary. Before I figured out something permanent, I had to dispose of the car. It was the most obvious sign of a connection between Hans and us and the villa. Parked in the driveway by the front door, it was visible to anyone passing by.

I told Sara what I planned to do, then changed into my most formal clothes. Using a key I found in Hans's pocket, I drove his car into the center of the city. I worried that someone, maybe someone from his office, might see me in the car and wonder why I, someone not in uniform, was driving this official vehicle. But much of the time, I was thrilled to be driving again, even if I wasn't used to this car's clutch and made the poor gear box shriek and grind too often. Several times when this happened, people walking on the paths around and through rubble glanced over, which caused me to make even more mistakes. After so many years of war, few people were surprised by anything.

Bombing debris made some of the streets difficult to pass through, and several roads were blocked, so I had to take detours. In a few spots, I drove onto a sidewalk or across a park, following a set of tracks that were like something in the woods.

Eventually I arrived in the Mitte, the center of the capital. Near the building where Hans worked, I found a cleared section of street that had enough space to park. Even though I wasn't in uniform, I acted as though I were—scowling, staring at anyone who even glanced at me. I hoped my manner, which I modeled on Hans, would make anyone believe I was so high-ranking that I could wear civilian clothes.

I rolled up the windows and made sure every door was locked. I locked the trunk, too. I felt like saying goodbye, as though I were parting from Hans himself.

After walking a few blocks, I slowed down. For the first time in several hours, my heart stopped racing.

At least the car was gone.

Then I stopped. I was in front of the wreckage of a row of buildings that had been shattered by bombs, one of tens of thousands of blocks like this in the capital.

This was an appropriate spot, one created by Hans and his friends.

I waited until no one was nearby, then tossed the key to Hans's car as far as I could into the center of a pile of rubble.

I walked several blocks before finding a bus line that still was operating and could take me where I wanted to go.

Back at the house, I changed out of my suit and into some of the clothes I gardened in. Then I cleaned, as well as I could, where Hans had fallen. The water mains were working, but this blood took on properties I didn't know blood had. Possibly because there was so much of it, it seemed to congeal faster, becoming almost tar-like. It had a strong stench I also hadn't smelled before. And it saturated the few rags I used for wiping.

I kept pouring the watery crimson mess into the bathtub, continually scrubbing the enamel, trying to keep it from turning red, too. Finally there was no more blood on the floor, only a damp area.

Once more I changed my clothes and sat a few minutes in the cellar next to Hans, then went outside and began digging in the garden near where Sara and I had planted vegetables and the soil was relatively loose. If anyone noticed me, I could easily say I was expanding the garden.

I decided to dig a deep, roomy grave, something else that might honor him. But soon I regretted my ambitious goal. There were more roots and rocks than I had imagined. The digging took several hours, and by the end I wished he were the size of a child and that this property were at a beach.

We waited until dusk for the last task. I took the upper part of his body, and Sara held his legs. Moving him was more difficult than before because his body had begun to stiffen. It was a longer trip outdoors to the hole I'd dug than from the main floor to the cellar, where gravity had been a help. Sara lost her grip several times and let his legs thump to the floor. I wanted to apologize to Hans, as if this might be more insulting than anything else that had occurred today.

Once we got outside, Sara said we ought to put him in the wheelbarrow, take him to the ruins of some house, and dump him there. "The people he's killed have wound up in much worse spots."

I pointed out that among other problems, the starving dogs that ran wild these days could easily find him and drag him into the open while trying to devour him. One way or another, he would likely be discovered.

Once Hans's body was in the hole, fitting easily into the space I'd created, Sara left, without looking at him or me. It was as though she'd never met him. Had it always been just an affair of convenience? Had she gotten over him long ago despite his obsession with her? Was her flirting with him an hour ago an act?

I wished I had a box to put Hans in. But this was wartime, and a blanket, however tattered, was a valuable commodity.

I shoveled the dirt over him. I tamped the soil down to try to make the ground as level as possible. I brought over some branches that had been shorn from the trees during the bombings and scattered them over the freshly dug dirt.

When I finished, I stood several steps back and stared at the ground.

In one way, this was a sad, pathetic ending for Hans. He was wrapped in a blanket in a rudimentary grave without a marker. Sara and I were the only people who knew where he was, and she appeared indifferent.

But as Sara had said, Hans had fared well compared to most people who had died in the last several years. He had died quickly and painlessly, and he seemed to approve of it. He had been buried by someone who not only knew his name but knew him. He was in his own city, not herded into a ghetto or camp far from home. He hadn't been lined up against a wall or shot in a trench or starved to death.

He was very lucky indeed.

I wanted to remember my oldest friend solemnly, but at this moment, what I remembered most about him was his smile in the second or two before the shot rang out. It seemed he was about to give me that broad grin that had always mocked everyone and everything, including maybe his own end.

I took a deep breath and tried to remember Hans from long ago—my amusing school comrade, the man who had sought me out again and again when he could have said good riddance to a troublemaker or, in more recent years, could have locked me up, or worse. Maybe he kept up our friendship because I was the last possible connection to Sara. But after all that had happened today, the only thing that came to mind, I said aloud:

"Sorry, my friend." After a long pause, I added, "Goodbye."

I went back to the house, barely finding my way in the pitch-black night.

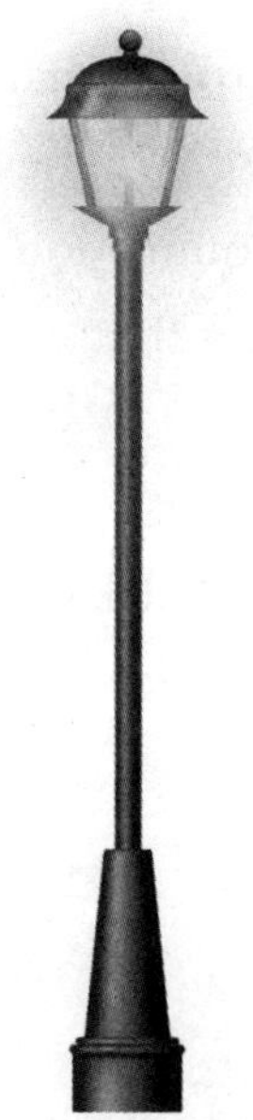

Chapter Fifty

April 1945

At first, I went to Hans's grave every day because I wanted to make sure that branches continued to cover it, that no animals had dug him up, that breezes and rains hadn't uncovered raw earth. Day after day, however, the spot remained undisturbed, and it struck me that I didn't need to check so frequently. At the same time, I realized I looked forward to standing near him, remembering things about him, and in my mind, speaking with him.

"You won't like the news, my friend," I would say, trying to remain silent but sometimes moving my lips and uttering words. "The war keeps getting worse and worse. The Reds are on German soil. Nothing stops them."

"Secret weapons, Rudi," I heard. The voice was Hans's. And it was so accurate and casual that the implausibility of him speaking didn't register right away.

"Too little too late," I said. "If there really are any." Again, I thought this, but I might have muttered it aloud.

"Dr. Goebbels says they exist."

Hans again, pitch perfect.

"The club foot says a lot," I answered. "I wonder what he says among friends."

"Nothing compared to what we say with each other."

"Yes, my friend!"

Another time, I mentioned a mutual acquaintance from school days, "I saw Felix yesterday. Remember him? First time in years. Other than what you'd expect, he hasn't changed much: leaner, a bit sallow, got that haunted look."

"My haunted look is worse. I can guarantee it."

I laughed out loud and said, "Felix asked after you. I told him I hadn't seen or heard of you in a while, which is true. I just talk with you and hear you."

He had no reaction as far as I could tell.

After a pause, I added, "Belated thanks for apparently not telling anyone where you were going when you came here. No one's stopped by. The first few days, I jumped whenever I heard a car or truck on the road."

"When I left that morning, I said only that I needed to check on a situation in Charlottenburg, which was true," I heard. "I didn't tell anyone I might stop here, too. I *knew* she was here. It was finally time to do something about it, even if I didn't know what."

"She has a way of being at the center of big decisions."

"I wanted to do it right," he said. "But everything shifted at the last moment."

"I was as surprised as you."

"You played your part. You asked for the pistol."

"I didn't know I was asking for the pistol."

"And yet you did. I wanted somehow to go back to simpler, better times, when we were in school, before there were wars, before wars changed everything."

"Going back is impossible."

"You think?" Hans laughed that deep, wild, laugh that swept away all doubts and worries and unhappiness.

"I'm so sorry, Hans."

All was quiet.

"I miss you," I said.

There was still no response, so I stood silently, looking down at the earth that covered him.

IIIIIIIII

One night I brought two shot glasses and a bottle of whiskey. I put one of the glasses on the mound. I told him we were sharing something I knew he liked and probably missed, then filled each shot glass.

I lifted my glass and toasted him and our friendship. Then I drained the glass. As I neared the bottom, I took the other shot glass and turned it upside down over the ground that covered his head.

Another time, I brought a copy of Heinrich Heine's poetry I had kept hidden all these years. I read slowly, pausing between works and stanzas and reminding him we had both read Heine in school. "Deep down," I said. "I know he still speaks to you."

He remained silent. But this made some sense. After all, he and his colleagues had burned Heine's works. They hated the man who predicted that people who burned books would eventually burn people, too.

"Too hot to handle," I said. "I understand."

A moment later, I heard Hans's voice, "Yes, he did speak to me. But I'm not sure if he speaks to me now." He paused. "Nowadays, you're the only one who speaks to me."

I apologized for not being able to tell others he was buried here.

"No one's suspected you?" I couldn't tell if he was incredulous or happy for me.

"Not at all!" I said.

"You are quite good at these games," he said. "I suspected you for a long time, of course, because I knew you so well, and I knew her."

But you missed the other, bigger thing.

"You may well make it through the end of the war. But only if she keeps herself under control. I still can't believe she revealed herself to me. Does she have a death wish?"

"A death wish. But also a life wish," I said.

"I thought a lot about death beforehand."

"Really?"

"Unlike many of my colleagues and the leadership, I didn't see the point in waiting." He paused. "The war ended a while ago."

"For Sara and me and so many others, the war's end can't come soon enough. Then there'll be a new beginning."

I went on a bit, but he stopped responding. Maybe he didn't want to be reminded that there would be a new beginning he wouldn't be a part of. Maybe he thought belief in a new beginning was naïve.

After a few gentle rains, Hans's grave fit in well with the uncut lawn and shrubbery. No one would know a body lay here. But at the same time, I wished something could signify his grave.

Nothing obvious could identify the site. No cross. No plaque. No sign. Any marker would have to appear to be a natural part of the landscape.

Among the scattered pieces of broken brick, chunks of concrete, and dead branches, I found part of a toppled bird feeder, a shallow, stone water bowl that had rested atop a pillar. The bowl wasn't light, but I was able to cradle it in my arms like a baby and move it to Hans's grave.

Near his head, I dug a round area an inch or so into the dirt and placed the bowl there. Then I smoothed the dirt around the bowl. It looked as though the bowl had been there for years.

That night, I crouched and put a few rolled-up pages of a newspaper in the bowl, piled a few twigs and sticks on top of it, lit a match and held it to the paper. After a smoky moment or two, the material ignited.

I stared at the red and yellow flames. Hans would like the warm, flickering light that illuminated so nicely what was around him.

I wished it weren't so meager, but this was as much of a ceremony as I could manage. No one played the national anthem. No one discussed the accomplishments of his life. No one even said his name aloud. But he was being honored. I was honoring him. At least, honoring the Hans I remembered from long ago.

He said nothing, which somehow seemed appropriate. I believed his silence meant that with this sendoff, he was finally at peace.

Then, as swiftly as they had shot up, the flames died down. There were only a few embers left from little branches, embers that quickly turned dark.

Chapter Fifty-One

April 1945

As the Nazi dictatorship neared its end, Waffen S.S. units roamed the city, hunting down anyone they deemed defeatist, whether for suggesting that the war was lost, or for preparing to travel to the western part of the country to surrender to the Anglophones rather than the Red Army, or for ridding their homes of Nazi symbols, portraits, and other material. Able-bodied men in civilian clothing without documents exempting them from military service, or people buying and selling food on the black market, or soldiers separated from their units all faced the same brutal end. Within minutes they were shot and sometimes hung from a tree or lamppost, often with signs on their bodies branding them "traitor" or "coward." Prisoners who had rotted in jail cells for years, some since as far back as the *Machtergreifung*, were being executed, not allowed to survive if their tormentors wouldn't either.

For the secret police, things had gotten so bad that they spent little time torturing prisoners, now simply killing them.

Teenagers, invalids, men who earlier were deemed unfit for service, even the elderly, were forced into the *Volkssturm*, the People's Storm, the pathetic militia that in combat was usually mowed down within minutes by the Red Army.

The British and Americans stopped bombing the city, which at first seemed a wonderful miracle. But then we realized they did this because the Red Army was so close that they might bomb their allies by mistake. This was confirmed when, in the east, there were different kinds of explosions. Instead of bombs dropping from the sky, shells came from field artillery. Then came another, more frightening sound—Katyusha rockets or, as we called them, Stalin Organs. Like wolves deep in the woods, their wild howling and whining was frightening and mesmerizing. When I heard them, I seemed unable to think of or do anything else, and I pitied the poor German soldiers who stood in the path of the hundreds of little rockets screaming through the air toward them.

After a few days, the steady roar began to sound familiar—a dull, distant hum, as much a part of daily life as the sun that was rising earlier every day or the brave birds who were returning to the area.

The city had been battered enough by several years of bombing, but now things became worse. Much of the time, electricity stopped functioning. Trains rarely ran. Throughout the city, *Volkssturm* units created barriers on streets that included the wrecks of trams, trucks, and cars; trees and light posts; and paving blocks, making the streets more difficult to navigate.

Herr Becker had told us the department would remain open officially, but that he understood "circumstances" made coming to work difficult. He did not mention that soon there would be other hurdles—the area would be behind enemy lines. And there was little work to do.

The last day we were all together, we gathered in Frau Riegler's office, where a table held many glasses and several bottles of schnaps. I sipped from a glass as the others gulped. The only sound besides our conversation was the dull roar of distant rockets and shells.

"What are you planning to do?" Frau Riegler asked me. "Is it too late to get out?"

"The noose hasn't been fully pulled yet," I said. "Some routes to the west are still open. The Americans aren't far. They're charging up through Bavaria and Bohemia."

"At least the bombings have ended," someone said.

"Unless the Soviets and their allies turn against each other," someone else said.

"It'd be nice if that battle took place somewhere other than in Berlin," yet another person said.

"I'm looking forward to simple things. No more food rationing, regular electricity and running water, lit streets, shops with things I want to buy," Frau Riegler said.

"Don't hold your breath."

"I'm looking forward to when people can say anything they want again," I said.

"Our glorious future is being able to complain freely about the lack of those simple things instead of just putting up with them silently."

"For now, we still have to be careful." Several in the group turned their heads to the side, perhaps out of habit, perhaps as a joke.

"Except when you're among friends."

"We hope!" We all laughed, and a few raised their glasses in a toast.

If they knew everything about me, they'd be shocked.

At that, I downed a healthy dose of schnaps.

As we began to leave, there were many vigorous handshakes, but then Frau Riegler began dabbing her eyes with a handkerchief, whispering, "Wait. Wait a moment. Let me keep looking at you all a little longer, so you'll be in my memory forever."

Herr Becker stood up straight, which must have taken some effort after all he had imbibed in the last hour. He breathed in deeply, then intoned, "It was an honor and a privilege to work with such a wonderful group of people."

I joined in the hugs and sighs and might have dabbed away some moisture in my eyes.

I was having to say goodbye to too many people I loved.

Chapter Fifty-Two

July 1945

Many people thought the end of Nazi rule meant the end of all that was vile. But now food was even harder to find, all infrastructure and services had collapsed, and the propaganda about the Red Army proved in some ways to be accurate: the war continued in a primitive, age-old form, via rape.

The Soviet soldiers behaved during the day, when officers were present, but many became violent and vicious at night—after much drinking. The first nights were the worst. It was an awful surprise to hear the commands ("Komm, Frau!") and the cries and shouts of their victims.

For years, the heroic women of Berlin had done so much to fill in for the many men who had left to fight in distant places. They had taken on all tasks that formerly only men were deemed worthy of doing, from running the subways and trams to rebuilding roads and rail yards, from operating stores and services to delivering mail. Suddenly they were the targets of a kind of violence that, in many ways, was more personal, brutal, and debilitating than what their fathers and husbands and sons had experienced. Almost all females were targets, from girls to grandmothers.

Now they had to hide from the Red Army, staying inside, especially at night, not coming out until well after dawn. And if caught, they had to use their wits to avoid drunken, aggressive soldiers.

I hid, too, obviously for different reasons. While the Red Army held sway in Berlin, I was affected in a personal way, too. Some Germans who had had roles in the old government, even as lowly as an air raid warden in the neighborhood, had disappeared, and rumors said this was the work of the Soviets. Someone high enough in the Foreign Ministry to travel to the *Wolfsschanze* and to Switzerland would awaken their interest.

So, for the first two months after the unconditional surrender, I stayed in a small room at the back of the garage that a decade earlier had been used to store supplies for the Traums' cars. I had cleaned out the place, covered the windows with blackout paper, brought in a few pieces of furniture. I was constantly alert to the sound of cars and trucks and Russian voices, but no one ventured into the garage. The villa had been damaged enough that from the outside it looked as though the building were uninhabitable. And most of the garage was caved in, appearing even less useful than the house.

In early July, I nearly saluted the Union Jack when I saw it waving from a small truck as the first units of the Royal Army arrived in the Villa Colony Grunewald. The Tommies seemed like cousins. They looked like us, they acted like us. In small groups, they treated us as equals, and many of them even spoke German, although with atrocious accents.

We should have been most angry at the British, since their six years of bombings had inflicted more damage on us, more than American bombers in the last couple of years or the Red Army in the weeks of fierce fighting at the very end of the war. Yet we heard the British treated German POWs much better than the other allies did, especially the Soviets, who forced many of them to work as slave laborers, just as we had done with their POWs.

With the British in charge of our part of Berlin, life became slightly more normal. After weeks of avoiding Red Army soldiers by living in the garage, being in the house felt like a wild luxury. Who cared that breezes swept through the openings here and there? Who cared that there was no heat or running water or electricity?

For the first time in six years, I could use lamps and flashlights without worrying about being fined or imprisoned, or worse, if some light escaped into the night. Best of all, there was no need to worry about roaming animals, particularly humans.

I waited for my American friends to make contact. I hadn't seen them in nearly a year and hadn't heard a word since the winter, when the postal system began to fall apart. I wanted to know how they had fared in the last stages of the war. I wanted to congratulate them on the destruction of the Nazi state. I wanted to help them do whatever needed to be done to reconstitute a democratic republic in Germany

I was patient. When the first American soldiers arrived in Berlin, I knew it would take longer for the more secretive, elaborate parts of the American war effort to settle in the capital. Logistics aside, they would be surrounded by the Red Army. This would be as much an opportunity for them as a danger. Mr. Clark and his assistants had to be shifting much of their work to learning about their official ally in the East.

In my time working with the Americans, I had made a couple of requests: a little money to help defray expenses and a camera to make copying documents easier, with which they had eventually helped me. In addition, I had asked that after the war they consider having me help them in any way I could.

With the arrival of the Americans, the British, and the French, I hoped to be able to talk publicly about my efforts to subvert the Nazis, especially now that others were telling stories about how they had bravely resisted a government they had in truth supported for so long.

And I wanted to see Magda and the children and live with them again.

But there was no regular transportation between Rügen and Berlin. Mail continued to be almost nonexistent, and telephone service was unreliable. Besides, Magda's parents had no phone in their house, where I was sure Magda and the children were thriving despite all that had happened in the country in the past two years. I didn't want them in Berlin until life here had improved dramatically.

It wasn't until almost two weeks after the British had officially taken possession of our part of Berlin that a U.S. Army Jeep, which we'd heard so much about, came up the driveway late one day. The Jeep, with no top and its windshield down, was dirty and dinged, much like the driver, who had a worn, plain uniform and dull helmet. This made the passenger, who gripped handles around him, stand out all the more. He had a neat, crisp uniform with silver insignia on the shoulders and a shiny helmet.

When the Jeep came to a stop, the passenger jumped out, after which the driver turned off the engine and leaned back in his seat. He gazed up at the sky, lit a cigarette, and showed absolutely no interest in his passenger or the villa.

The officer walked briskly toward the house. I stepped out the front door as I had in early spring when Hans had arrived for the last time. This, I hoped, would be a more pleasant visit.

"Mr. Baumann, I presume," he said.

Like Mr. Clark, he had an easy, self-assured manner. But unlike Mr. Clark, he had a lean frame, tanned skin, thick brown hair, and a new uniform that made him look as though he had spent the earlier part of the day playing tennis or sailing. He was in his late 20s or early 30s, and I imagined he was one of Mr. Clark's men in the field.

"I am he," I said.

He spoke very good German, much better than Mr. Clark's and better than my English, with only a slight American accent.

"I bring greetings from a friend," he said.

For a split second, I felt a knot I hadn't known existed loosen in my chest. I could have grinned with joy—if I weren't a man, an adult, a

German, and both eager and worried about how this conversation would unfold.

As if the sentiment had just occurred to me, I said, "Is his mother feeling better?"

"She's recovering in the mountains."

"What good news," I said, happy that we both had passed the identifying quiz.

He introduced himself by his family name, without military rank, which I assumed was because he was not officially in the military. He might have worn the uniform for show. I wondered, too, if his last name was the usual group fabrication. It was as common in the U.S. as its German equivalent, Schmidt. In fact, I would have been surprised if he had told me his real name.

But I wished it were a more imaginative name.

I asked Mr. Smith to come inside, and we sat in the former dining room in what were a pair of the few intact chairs on the property.

"How were the last few months?" he asked. "We were concerned about you."

"I don't know what was worse—the Red Army approaching or the Red Army here."

He nodded.

"But obviously, I made it through."

"And your family?"

I told him my wife and children were in the country in the Soviet zone, with her family, in an isolated place with plenty of places to hide, if needed. But, I continued, I hoped to be reunited with them soon in Berlin, depending on my situation.

"And your work?"

"The Red Army effectively ended my employment."

"But you're coping? You seem in good shape and spirits."

"Berliners are nothing if not resourceful."

I asked about Mr. Clark. Of course, Mr. Smith didn't offer concrete information except to say that Mr. Clark was well and that, as always, he appreciated and valued all that I had done for him.

I said I was only too happy to have helped and happy that the war had ended.

Mr. Smith nodded and thanked me again. Then, without me having to ask, he began to outline the work they hoped I would do for them. Much of it would take advantage of knowledge I had gained in the Foreign Ministry. They had learned that German fascists did nothing if not create documents, most of which were incriminatory. They wanted help deciphering and understanding these, in part to help specific legal actions and to understand generally what had happened in Germany in the last dozen years. Someone who could read bureaucratic German, which was tedious enough, and understand Nazi language, which was worse, would be invaluable.

They also wanted help in identifying organizations and personnel as well as assistance in monitoring Germans who might assist the Soviets, former Communists and far-left Social Democrats.

The organization that Mr. Clark represented had offices in the American sector, Mr. Smith continued, which would be relatively easy for me to travel to since there was only one zone border to cross, and it was between true allies.

They would pay me a salary that was likely minimal for them but tremendous by German civilian standards. They would also provide me with food and incidentals like cigarettes, which already were a kind of currency, more desired than Reichsmarks. This meant I would live better than just about any other German in Berlin, and I could consider bringing my wife and children to live with me.

I asked if Mr. Clark was in Berlin.

"Mr. Clark is here—and there. Everywhere."

"Will I be able to see him sometime soon?"

"I can't say for sure. Although the war against Japan is our first priority, Berlin continues to be important for us."

"Of course, because of your ally in the East." I paused. "For years, Dr. Goebbels predicted you would be at each other's throats. Only his timing was off."

Mr. Smith didn't react, which made me want to smile.

"As for Japan, we're lacking the same invaluable source of information that we had in Berlin." He nodded slightly.

I was about to explain I did my work for the Americans because I believed in the same democratic ideals as the country they were lucky enough to be citizens of, but Mr. Smith said they wanted me to start as soon as possible. I suggested the following day, which he agreed to.

I wanted to chat more, but as soon as we settled on my starting day, Mr. Smith rose.

"Good to find you safe and sound and have you back on board," he said in a rather mechanical way. Then he turned and left.

As he approached the Jeep, the driver sat up abruptly and started the engine, revving it a little more than seemed necessary. Mr. Smith said a few words to him, and in a moment they were speeding back down the driveway, Mr. Smith hanging on precariously to the dashboard as the Jeep bounded through potholes and over debris.

Chapter Fifty-Three

July 1945

Sara surprised me yet again. When Mr. Clark's emissary left and I came back inside, she said, "That sounded very business-like and cheerful at the same time."

I considered not answering fully or changing the subject, but then I thought I should finally be able to tell someone the truth, particularly her.

"He is the friend of a friend I used to see regularly in Bern."

"You had American friends in Bern from before the war?"

"From *during* the war."

She gazed at me with both brows raised, what I liked to think of as a new appreciation.

"Not friends at a bar?"

I nodded.

"You helped the Americans?"

"I told them what was happening in the Reich," I said. "I gave them top-secret material I saw at the Ministry. Sorry not to tell you, but it would have been too dangerous for anyone to know, even you."

"I knew."

"You knew?" I thought a minute. "Did your father tell you?"

"He wrote that he'd seen you again, but he didn't tell me." She laughed. "I knew, and I didn't know."

"You knew, but you didn't know?" I shook my head. "You could say that about anything."

"I could—" she paused. "And I couldn't."

We both laughed, and she said, "Seriously, you wanted me to know, and I can sense when you want to tell me something."

"I knew, and I didn't know."

"You're a fast learner," she said. "I knew you hated the Nazis and would do whatever you could against them, not just hide me. So I tried to make things easier for you in general. In our whole time here, I didn't do anything dangerous." She paused. "And I tried to give you a kind of home. A refuge. A place of playfulness. A place of love."

I smiled. "You did that very well, my dearest."

"That I know."

After I stopped laughing, I asked, "If you're so clairvoyant, what did I just hear from that man?"

She smiled, more to herself than me, as she said, "I know, and I don't."

"So I don't need to tell you."

"I don't know the details."

"But you know generally?"

"It's good news."

"Why do you say that?" I asked.

"This is easy. You came back beaming."

"You know and don't know me so well," I said. Then I told her about my new plans.

She gave me a quick hug. "I'm so happy you're moving forward," she said. "And I'm glad you told me. So I could know. Even though I already knew."

"I know."

"I'll be moving forward, too," she said.

I felt as though I couldn't breathe for a moment. "Where will you go?" I asked.

"I'm not sure. Down the street? To my family in Switzerland? To Palestine? To America?" She shook her head. "Now that I can do anything, I'm not sure what I want to do."

"I know."

"And you don't know."

I nodded, and once more we laughed.

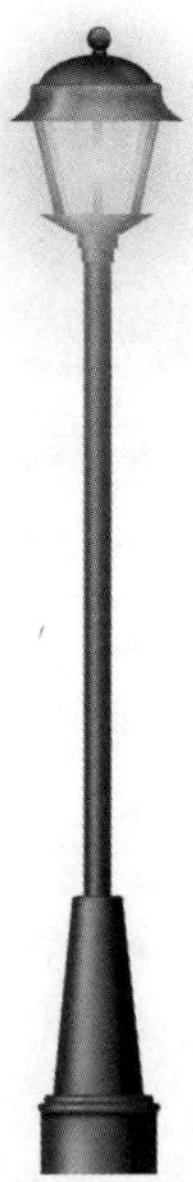

Chapter Fifty-Four

1946

For a time, I was probably the happiest German in Berlin.

Paid in dollars, the equivalent of bars of bullion, I was able to send money to Magda and her parents. I was able to help several friends and former colleagues with money. I found an apartment that would be big enough for Magda, me, and the children, and I found a smaller apartment for Sara, where for now Sara and I stayed.

The work, which felt both like an honor and a gesture of gratitude for my help during the war, kept me busy. It was work that supported a ruined country as it tried to feed itself, come to terms with the crimes and horrors it had committed, and move in a new direction.

I kept in touch with former colleagues from the Ministry, including a group that was creating a kind of Foreign Ministry-in-waiting for the day a new republic would be founded. Some of them had retained records from the old days so they could resume work as quickly as possible. They had even found a temporary office. All were ready to do the work of the Ministry more like what they had done before 1933.

Whenever my position with the Americans wound down and ended, I hoped to have the option of joining my former colleagues, especially after the people who had joined during the Nazi period were excluded.

"You're working for the Amis?"

"Aren't we all?" I said.

"We're cooperating, but not working for them."

"What's the difference?"

"It's a big difference."

Frau Riegler and I sat at a café near U.S. Army headquarters. She had returned to Berlin after the British, French, and Americans arrived, surviving with help from me and others.

"Some say you're badmouthing people you don't like to the Amis, settling old scores."

"No, no," I said. "Denazification is so important. For them and us. The Amis need all kinds of guidance, from reading German documents and questioning in German to understanding German organizations to learning what people's posts entailed during the war."

She nodded but was silent as she inhaled a cigarette from the American pack I had given her. Then she said, "Speaking of the war, quite a few of our friends wonder why you're so close with the Amis, as though you knew them before they ever arrived in Berlin."

If I were a smoker, I might have asked for several of her cigarettes and smoked them one after the other before I spoke. I wanted to make a leap, but I hesitated. I realized that sooner or later I would be pushed if I didn't leap of my own accord. And if I leapt now, I could leap in a way I might want.

"Those trips to Switzerland," I said. "I didn't visit relatives in my free time."

"You visited friends?"

"I made friends. Friends who are here now. And I helped them. In all kinds of ways. Sharing talk, documents, gossip, anything I thought would help."

She stared at me a long moment, then said, "Oh my."

"You must've known," I said, feeling as relieved as I had when I let

Hans know his feeling about Sara being in the house was correct. "On some level."

"I knew you needed fresh air and a taste of normalcy, however briefly." She stared at me again, then said, "You broke all kinds of oaths and rules. It was treason."

"The government was a criminal enterprise," I answered. "I did what I did to try to subvert it and end the war sooner. I had my own oaths and rules."

"We worked for the state, not the Nazis," she said.

"But the Nazis had taken over the state."

Frau Riegler folded her arms in front of her chest, which made me want to reach across the table and unfold them. This was an era when people should open themselves to new, refreshing ideas, not slide back into the narrow visions that had led to disaster.

"Your help likely killed Germans."

"Possibly. But they used the information I gave them only generally. Even though I wished that weren't so. And if a few people died as a result of my help, many, many more lives were saved—German lives, the lives of innocent foreigners, and the lives of the ones the regime was trying to destroy."

As the U.S. and British alliance with the Soviets collapsed, I became less important to the Amis, who decided they needed the support of people whom at first they wanted to investigate and punish. Industrial leaders who had built the German war machine, intelligence agents who had worked against the British and Americans, and scientists like the rocket men of Peenemünde whose work was advanced enough for them to be moved en masse to the U.S., were "cleared" by the Western allies. I found this increasingly depressing.

My friends from Bern remembered and helped me after the American government cut back on my services. Mr. Clark and Mr. Smith regularly checked in with me by mail, and once Mr. Clark himself met me for coffee while on a visit to Berlin.

In the café near the U.S. military headquarters, the waiters had picked up key American slang and hung a framed photo of President Truman. The picture was the centerpiece of the main wall, likely the very spot where not long ago, as in just about every German business, a large photo of the Führer had hung. The new portrait might even rest on the same hook that had held the old photo.

I imagined that cafés in the Soviet Zone, only a kilometer or so east, might have waiters picking up Russian in the same way, and feature photos of the General Secretary, who also tended to gaze luminously, but not so far into the distance as his vanquished foe.

We all adapt in our own ways.

Mr. Clark had shaken my hand vigorously, and his smile seemed warm and sincere. He looked much as I remembered, although he was a little slimmer than in Bern, as though he was eating less fondue.

"How striking to meet you here of all places," he said. "Only a few years ago, this city was a distant, dark fortress. The most we knew about it we knew from you. But now, you and I are sitting here in the open, talking about anything we want, more relaxed than we ever were in Bern, even behind closed doors."

I waved toward the deep blue sky on this sunny, warm day. "The famous Berlin air is fresh and light, and ultimately prevails over every ill wind."

"Now there's one from the East."

"Time will tell. Look at what we overcame already."

"Yes, you provided the most astounding information. You were our only person in Berlin. Otherwise, we just heard stories second hand and never saw documents like yours before you arrived."

I bowed slightly. "I was glad to help."

"A striking thing about it," he continued, "is that even though what you did was so risky, you were never found out. No one involved died or was even injured."

"For the most part."

He looked at me alertly for the first time during this conversation. "For the most part?" he asked.

"There was a little trouble," I said. "But all was settled quickly and in my favor."

He waited, giving me the opportunity to explain. But I was silent, too. What happened during the war, some of the choices I had to make, were things I didn't want to remember, much less tell anyone about.

He nodded and asked, "These days I hope you're faring as well, my friend."

In a warm tone, I said, "The war's over. What more could anyone ask for? Beyond that, my wife and children are moving to Berlin soon. We'll be reunited with a roof over our heads. Our health is good. There's a semblance of normalcy."

"And work?"

"You were very generous. I liked my assignments. Thank you so much."

"I'm sorry it ended."

"It's understandable."

"Have you found work with the future German government?"

I shrugged.

He puffed a moment on his pipe, then said, "Mr. Baumann, I hope you're not finding the help you gave us has put you at a disadvantage." The smoke he exhaled drifted slowly upwards and lingered between us.

For a moment, his face across the table was barely visible. I felt like batting aside the tiny cloud. Instead, I waited as the smoke dissipated, and I saw for sure that he was staring at me, waiting for an answer.

Softly I said, "Apparently, even after the horrors we've been through, many Germans still think one is supposed to serve and obey no matter what the orders are, no matter the nature of the authorities."

Mr. Clark helped me interview for several jobs with American companies interested in building or rebuilding operations in Central Europe. These companies needed a German speaker, someone who knew Germany, someone who got along with and understood Americans, someone who wasn't a war criminal, someone who was well-organized, someone who was adept at paperwork. The positions were not as prestigious as a job at the Foreign Ministry or as inspiring and thrilling as my work with the Americans in Bern, but after the past decade and a half, I appreciated the idea of doing work that wasn't so nerve-wracking and risky.

I did well enough to get by and provide for my family, but I was restless.

Back in Berlin with the children, Magda had changed. Was it because she had been caring for the children with only her parents' help for several years? Had living again at her childhood home somehow given her new confidence? Did the largely ruined capital city no longer intimidate her?

Not long after the family returned, she and I sat at the kitchen table late in the evening.

"I'm not sure how you survived," she said. "You took some risks again." She paused. "You helped the Traum woman, right?"

I gazed at her a moment, then said, "Yes, I gave her shelter. You could say I saved her."

"Protecting a Jew was so dangerous." She paused. "I hope she made it worth your while."

Surprised by this comment, I sighed in a way I regretted. I said, "I was so busy with work. And then there was something else that occupied me, something I need to tell you about. More dangerous than anything else."

Her face tightened, as if to defend herself from whatever I was about to divulge.

After all, to protect her and the children, I had told her nothing about these dangerous things before.

Now I told her about helping the Americans in Bern. I spoke matter of factly. Once I had been proud of this work and bordered on boasting; now I was wary of people's reactions, even the reaction of my wife. After I outlined it all, I stopped, and for a moment there was silence.

"You spied for the Americans?" she said finally.

I nodded.

"Wow. If you had been caught—" She put a hand over her mouth.

"I was very, very careful."

"You took some risks long ago, like when you handed out leaflets, but that wasn't as risky as this." She paused again. "The children could have lost you. I could have lost you."

I nodded once more and felt a sadness that had come over me several times recently.

She shook herself and said, "I hope all of that is over with."

"Yes, it's ended."

Chapter Fifty-Five

1946

At first, Sara dreamed of punishing the people who had destroyed her world. Not violently or dramatically. There would be no bombs, no shots fired, no demonstrations. Instead, she could punish Germans by staying in Germany. Her existence would be their punishment. *No, they hadn't exterminated every Jew,* she wanted them to know. Berlin was not *Judenfrei* and never had been. She considered showing them by taking a symbol of Nazi hatred, the 1941 edict that all Jews had to wear a Star of David patch, and giving it a twist. She would wear a necklace with a large Star. Her choice, her look.

As we talked, she was wearing nothing, not even a Star of David necklace. As we often did, we were snuggled in bed together, skin against skin. This is where we talked about all kinds of things, from the trivial to the existential, where we read to each other, where we kissed and hugged and made love. It had been the center of our little world, a place where the most tender, decent feelings survived. Now that this time was drawing to a close, I realized I would miss it and her more than I had imagined.

"I don't want seeking justice or revenge to be the focus of my life," she said. "I want to live for myself, to find peace and happiness, wherever that is, whatever it is." She sighed. "And Germany isn't going to be the place. The Nazis ruined the German language for me. Whenever I hear it, I wonder what that person did—or didn't do."

This also meant she couldn't live with her family, who had stayed in Zürich and were as comfortable as any Swiss family who had been there for centuries. "Being with them will remind me too much of Berlin," she said. And she didn't want to go anywhere else in Europe. Some countries were more antisemitic than Germany, although blessedly they weren't organized and efficient enough to go to the same murderous extremes.

"Forget Palestine, too," she continued. "What about the people who already live there. I don't want to do unto others what was done unto us. I need to go somewhere I can be Jewish and forget I'm Jewish at the same time."

I laughed. "You're always so easy to please."

She jabbed me with her elbow.

"How about somewhere far, far away?" I said. "America? Australia? South Africa?"

"Ha. Why not the moon then?" She ran her fingers over my face. "I do like the idea of America. But not New York. It's full of Jews. Maybe Los Angeles, where it's sunny in more ways than one."

"Yes," I said. "Some of the Amis are naïve and overly optimistic, but that's better than what we're used to. And America's far from the troubled places in the world. There are too many racial groups for a single one to dominate the others."

"I wish it was better for blacks," she said. "And all the people from the Spanish-speaking world. Not to mention Native Americans. But it's better than anywhere else. And it'll get better."

"That kind of optimism makes America the perfect place for you."

She smiled. "I'd like a nice spot with a view of the Pacific. So well-named. I'm hoping paradise can be created twice in one lifetime."

"Of all people, you can do that. And of all places, in California."

Chapter Fifty-Six

1947

I went to see Sara off on the train that would take her to LeHavre, where she would sail to New York and then cross North America by rail.

I knew I would miss her, even though I was now with my family and saw Sara only occasionally, always at cafés or for walks in parks. A few times, she took my arm in hers, but otherwise we behaved properly. I didn't understand how much I would miss her until I saw her at the railroad station.

This could be the last time I see her.

We hugged, longer than usual. Then she pressed her right hand flat against my chest and said, "Rudi. I wish you were coming along."

She looked at me with as much surprise as I felt, as if she hadn't thought this until she uttered it.

Her words and her hand made me shudder.

She waited a moment, as if reconsidering what she'd said, then nodded, saying, "Yes, I do wish you were coming, too." She looked at me in a familiar way that mixed longing and teasing.

"Coming to LeHavre to see you off?" I knew what she really meant, but I couldn't quite believe it.

"No, silly," she said. "To Los Angeles."

The idea felt familiar, as if on some level I had been considering such a thing for a long time.

My hopes for the reestablishment of a democratic Germany were overshadowed by the battles between the occupation powers, played out daily in Berlin, which remained encircled by the Red Army. Likely I would not be included on the staff of the reconstituted Foreign Ministry. Many of my friends and acquaintances continued to be negative about my work during the war for the Amis. Treason was a word I heard too often. A few people were uncomfortable that I had sheltered a Jew. Magda continued to seem on edge, not at all comfortable back in Berlin and possibly back with me. The children often acted as though I were a stranger.

What kept me here?

"Really?" I said. "Los Angeles? With you? Los Angeles! With you!"

"Oh my." She was laughing. "You *would* come along? That's so sweet, Rudi."

I wanted to say, "I can't come along," but I couldn't seem to put the words together. Instead, I remembered when she had impulsively climbed aboard a train that I was on, changing her life and mine. It would be just as simple for me to do so now as it was for her in Basel in 1943.

By climbing a few steps up onto the train, I would jettison one part of my life and return yet again to the wonderful relationship we had that ultimately had survived the horrible time under the Nazis.

At the same time, my mind coldly considered facts that seemed simultaneously insurmountable and ridiculously trivial. I had no ticket for the train trip let alone for the cruise to the North America. I had no passport and no visa for France or the U.S. I had only 20 or 30 nearly worthless marks, and no dollars, with me. I had no job lined up. Mr. Clark or any of the other Americans I knew or worked with, who could help me in America, didn't know I might be there in a week.

Above all, there was Magda and the children.

"Wow, Rudi," Sara said, laughing again. "You're seriously thinking about it." She leaned over and kissed me on the cheek. "I love that. I love you."

I closed my eyes, wanting to stop feeling dizzy.

Then she kissed me again, which, of course, didn't help drive away the dizziness.

"We would flourish in Los Angeles," I said.

"Yes." She smiled yet again.

I stood there silently, unable to turn around and go back into the main part of the station but also unable to take her hand and step aboard the train.

Whistles sounded. A conductor yelled, "All aboard!"

Couldn't they wait?

"My darling," she said, reaching for my face, holding it in her hands, staring into my eyes.

I felt so shaky I might fall, possibly fall up into the train and make a decision that way. More likely, I would land on my back on the platform.

"You're so full of emotion, Rudi," she said approvingly. "A lot of conflicting emotions." She kept holding onto my head and moved even closer, so that our noses almost touched. "You're so beautiful right now," she whispered.

She lowered her hands, and the last two words she said stood out: right now.

Was this the first time I'd ever felt she was wooing me, that I had some kind of advantage she usually had?

Right now. I knew what this meant. In as much time as it would take for me to climb into the car and settle into a compartment with her, I might not look so beautiful. As she had happily pointed out many times, feelings changed. Constantly.

Her loving feelings could dissipate like morning dew in sunlight, and she wouldn't care how that made me feel.

I smiled, and her eyes opened wide. "Yes, Rudi?"

"Sara, Sara, Sara," I said, taking her face in my hands. "You are the most wonderful person. I can't imagine living without you." My eyes filled with moisture. I kissed her on the cheeks.

She was nodding and shaking her head at the same time as she said, "We share so much. We'll always share so much."

In Los Angeles, we could meander along a wide beach, where waves from the Pacific steadily pounded on the sand. The salt water would lap at our feet, the water much warmer than what we were used to in the lakes and rivers around Berlin. Likewise, the sun would hover large and benevolent, so different from the reluctant northern European sun. We would absorb the heat, the spray of the waves, the sand on our feet, the wind on our bare skin.

Yet, in a flash, the tide could recede, the sun could set, the breeze could turn into a howling wind, and Sara could let go of my hand.

Perhaps I could accept the ebb and flow of her feelings, the ebb and flow of life, as cyclical as the tide we would watch from the beach. Wasn't it best to experience utter bliss and excitement even if the feelings might not last long and the rest of the time might be difficult and painful?

Conductors' whistles blew again. Steam billowed from the locomotive.

I remembered the night several years earlier in Basel, when she boarded the train at the last minute. She wanted to go back to Berlin. She needed to be in Berlin.

I realized I felt the same way. Berlin was my home and my family was here. I needed to stay.

"I love you," I said.

"Oh, dear Rudi." Tears fell down her cheeks. "I love you, too."

She hugged me, and I hugged her back. Over her shoulder, I noticed a conductor gesturing for us either to climb aboard or move away from the train.

As she began to climb up into the train car, she turned and looked at me inquisitively.

Was I coming along?

I took a step forward.

She smiled.

"I'm sorry," I said. "I can't live without you. But I can't live with you."

Her eyes opened wide, but she kept smiling, saying, "I understand. I understand everything."

"I know you do." I stepped back. "You always do."

Once inside the train, she gazed at me. A whistle blew, and the doors began to shut.

"We'll always be together," she called to me. "Especially if we never see each other again."

I was stunned for a moment as the door closed. Then, as the whistle blew again, I shouted, "*Auf Wiedersehen!*" Until we meet again. Then I added, "Always!"

Through a grimy window, I saw she was mouthing something. *Had she heard me? Did she agree or disagree? Did it matter?* The train lurched and began to move. I kissed my right hand and put it against the window. I stepped with the train as it slowly headed away. Sara smiled, then kissed her hand and put it against the glass where mine was. Our hands pressed together, separated by the pane of glass. I took several more steps as the train gathered speed, then pulled my hand back and blew her a kiss.

She blew me a kiss, then tilted her head and gazed at me. She looked as though she were about to burst into tears.

I had to walk quickly to keep up with the train, which was moving faster. I began to run, but soon I couldn't keep up with the car.

Car after car rolled by me, until the end of the train swept by. I stopped and watched the train as it moved down the tracks and around the curve. It became smaller and quieter, just a few flashes of light moving in the darkness. Then it disappeared from view, heading west, away from me and away from everything and everyone she had ever known.

The train had been out of sight for a minute or two and the platform was nearly empty before I lowered my gaze, turned, and headed back to the main part of the terminal. Back to Berlin, back to my country, back to my life, back to my wife and children, back to all I served and loved and honored, even if they didn't greet me with open arms.

Except.

Except that once or twice I turned around, looking at where the train had been, as if it might reappear and wait for me to sprint after it.

"Always," I whispered after one last view, then turned and left.

FINIS

About the Author

John Mutter is a journalist who covers the book world and is the editor-in-chief and co-founder of SHELF AWARENESS, the online company with publications for booksellers, librarians, and book lovers. He earlier was an editor for more than 20 years at PUBLISHERS WEEKLY. He graduated from Sarah Lawrence College and studied for a year in Germany. He has long been interested in history, literature, language, and politics. A resident of various points in the Northeast, including New York City, he now lives in the mountains of New Hampshire with his family.

Acknowledgements

I would like to thank the readers of the manuscript of this book who offered all kinds of valuable advice and comments, including, early on, Marina Antropow Cramer and Rosa Soy, and more recently Davida G. Breier, Kimberly Olson Fakih, Jeff Hart, Julie Morris, Cynthia Clark, Kristen Gilligan, and Len Vlahos.

And special thanks go to my family for their support and for putting up with me during the sometimes hectic writing and editing process: Cynthia Clark, Tobias Mutter, and Alex Mutter.

Signature Drinks

The Quiet Repeat

With Alcohol

VIBE: Elegant, slightly dangerous, layered.
Like secrets under the surface.

INGREDIENTS:

- 2 oz bourbon
- ½ oz cherry liqueur (or muddled dark cherries)
- ¼ oz fresh lemon juice
- ½ oz simple syrup (or honey syrup for depth)
- Dash of Angostura bitters

PRESENTATION:

Serve over a large cracked ice cube.
Garnish: orange peel over the top + tiny sprig of thyme.

Berlin, Through Glass

Non Alcoholic

VIBE: Clean, reflective, slightly haunting.
Beauty with restraint.

INGREDIENTS:

- 3 oz high-quality apple cider (or pressed apple juice)
- 1 oz white grape juice or pear nectar
- Splash of fresh lemon
- Top with sparkling water
- Tiny drizzle of honey

PRESENTATION:

Serve in a clear glass.
Garnish: thin apple slice + thyme sprig.

Discussion Questions

1. Which character did you feel most drawn to, and did that change at any point?
2. What meaning does the title FORTUNE AND GLASS take on by the end of the novel?
3. Do you think the characters are in control of their lives or reacting to forces around them? Why?
4. What does the story suggest about the trade-offs people make to get what they want?
5. Throughout the novel, characters are often navigating incomplete or distorted information. How does it shape the choices they make?
6. Did any particular scene or image stay with you after finishing? Why that one?
7. Several characters make decisions they believe are justified in the moment. In those situations, which choices do you think you would have made?
8. The novel touches on how quickly situations can escalate when systems break down or communication fails. Where do you see parallels to real-world situations today?
9. In what ways does FORTUNE AND GLASS mirror current events or dynamics in today's world, whether in business, politics, power structures, trust, or information?
10. Do you think the kinds of decisions made in the book are more common or more visible in today's world? Why or why not?

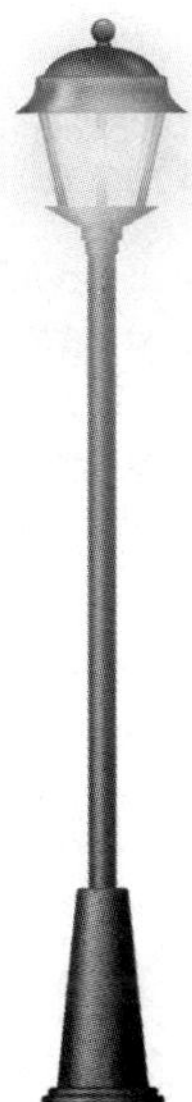

About the Publisher

LEFT FIELD PUBLISHING–where creativity meets collaboration. We're a forward-thinking publishing company created to combine the best attributes of traditional publishing with the best attributes of independent publishing. We exist to help authors bring their work to market in a cost-effective way while allowing them to retain control over their writing projects.

Our vision is to reimagine what publishing can be—bold, collaborative, and purpose-driven—by amplifying genre-defying voices across fiction, non-fiction, YA and kids books. Because great books aren't defined by a category.

Visit us at www.Left-Field-Publishing.com.

Connect with us!

Facebook: /leftfieldpublishing
Instagram: @leftfieldpublishing
TikTok: leftfieldpublishing
YouTube: @LeftFieldPublishing-m4g
LinkedIn: Left Field Publishing